Wayside Edition

———

THE COMPLETE WORKS

OF

NATHANIEL HAWTHORNE

IN THIRTEEN VOLUMES

VOLUME XI

THE DOLLIVE

FANSHAWE, A

FELT

WITH AN APPE

THE ANCEST

NATHANIE

JAMES R. OSGOOD & CO.

IGHTON, MIFFLIN & CO.

RNE LATHROP

CONTENTS.

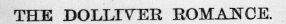

THE DOLLIVER ROMANCE.

INTRODUCTORY NOTE.

THE DOLLIVER ROMANCE.

IN " The Dolliver Romance," only three chapters of which the author lived to complete, we get an intimation as to what would have been the ultimate form given to that romance founded on the Elixir of Life, for which " Septimius Felton" was the preliminary study. Having abandoned this study, and apparently forsaken the whole scheme in 1862, Hawthorne was moved to renew his meditation upon it in the following year; and as the plan of the romance had now seemingly developed to his satisfaction, he listened to the publisher's proposal that it should begin its course as a serial story in the " Atlantic Monthly" for January, 1864 — the first instance in which he had attempted such a mode of publication.

But the change from England to Massachusetts had been marked by, and had perhaps in part caused, a decline in his health. Illness in his family, the depressing and harrowing effect of the Civil War upon his sensibilities, and anxiety with regard to pecuniary affairs, all combined to make still further inroads upon his vitality; and so early as the autumn of 1862 Mrs. Hawthorne noted in her private diary that her husband was looking " miserably ill." At no time since boyhood had he suffered any serious sickness, and his strong constitution enabled him to rally from this first attack ; but the gradual decline continued. After sending forth " Our Old Home," he had little strength for any employment more arduous than reading, or than walking his accustomed path among the pines and sweetfern on the hill behind The Wayside, known to his family as the Mount of Vision. The projected work, therefore, advanced but slowly. He wrote to Mr. Fields : —

" I don't see much probability of my having the first chapter of the Romance ready so soon as you want it. There are two or three chapters ready to be written, but I am not yet robust enough to begin, and I feel as if I should never carry it through."

The presentiment proved to be only too well founded. He had previously written : —

" There is something preternatural in my reluctance to begin. I linger at the threshold, and have a perception of very disagreeable phantasms to be encountered if I enter. I wish God had given me the faculty of writing a sunshiny book."

And again, in November, he says : " I foresee that there is little probability of my getting the first chapter ready by the 15th, although I have a resolute purpose to write it by the end of the month." He did indeed send it by that time, but it began to be apparent in January that he could not go on.

" Seriously," he says, in one letter, " my mind has, for the present, lost its temper and its fine edge, and I have an instinct that I had better keep quiet. Perhaps I shall have a new spirit of vigor if I wait quietly for it; perhaps not." In another: " I hardly know what to say to the public about this abortive Romance, though I know pretty well what the case

will be. I shall never finish it. . . . I cannot finish
it unless a great change comes over me ; and if I make
too great an effort to do so, it will be my death."

Finally, work had to be given over indefinitely. In
April he went southward with Mr. Ticknor, the senior
partner of his publishing house ; but Mr. Ticknor died
suddenly in Philadelphia, and Hawthorne returned to
The Wayside more feeble than ever. He lingered
there a little while. Then, early in May, came the
last effort to recover tone, by means of a carriage-jour-
ney, with his friend Ex-President Pierce, through the
southern part of New Hampshire. A week passed, and
all was ended : at the hotel in Plymouth, New Hampshire, where he and his companion had stopped to rest,
he died in the night, between the 18th and the 19th
of May, 1864. Like Thackeray and Dickens, he was
touched by death's " petrific mace " before he had had
time to do more than lay the groundwork and begin
the main structure of the fiction he had in hand ; and,
as in the case of Thackeray, the suddenness of his de-
cease has never been clearly accounted for. The precise nature of his malady was not known, since with
quiet hopelessness he had refused to take medical advice. His friend Dr. Oliver Wendell Holmes was the
only physician who had an opportunity to take even
a cursory view of his case, which he did in the course
of a brief walk and conversation in Boston before
Hawthorne started with Mr. Pierce ; but he was unable, with that slight opportunity, to reach any definite conclusion. Dr. Holmes prescribed and had put
up for him a remedy to palliate some of the poignant
symptoms, and this Hawthorne carried with him ; but
" I feared," Dr. Holmes writes to the editor, " that
there was some internal organic — perhaps malignant

— disease; for he looked wasted and as if stricken with a mortal illness."

The manuscript of the unfinished " Dolliver Romance " lay upon his coffin during the funeral services at Concord, but, contrary to the impression sometimes entertained on this point, was not buried with him. It is preserved in the Concord Public Library. The first chapter was published in the " Atlantic " as an isolated portion, soon after his death; and subsequently the second chapter, which he had been unable to revise, appeared in the same periodical. Between this and the third fragment there is a gap, for bridging which no material was found among his papers; but, after hesitating for several years, Mrs. Hawthorne copied and placed in the publishers' hands that final portion, which, with the two parts previously printed, constitutes the whole of what Hawthorne had put into tangible form.

Hawthorne had purposed prefixing a sketch of Thoreau, " because, from a tradition which he told me about this house of mine, I got the idea of a deathless man, which is now taking a shape very different from the original one." This refers to the tradition mentioned in the editor's note to " Septimius Felton," and forms a link in the interesting chain of evidence connecting that romance with the " Dolliver Romance." With the plan respecting Thoreau he combined the idea of writing an autobiographical preface, wherein The Wayside was to be described, after the manner of his Introduction to the "Mosses from an Old Manse "; but, so far as is known, nothing of this was ever actually committed to paper.

Beginning with the idea of producing an English romance, fragments of which remain to us in " The

Ancestral Footstep," and the incomplete work known as " Doctor Grimshawe's Secret," he replaced these by another design, of which " Septimius Felton " represents the partial execution. But that elaborate study yielded, in its turn, to "The Dolliver Romance." The last-named work, had the author lived to carry it out, would doubtless have become the vehicle of a profound and pathetic drama, based on the instinctive yearning of man for an immortal existence, the attempted gratification of which would have been set forth in a variety of ways : First, through the selfish old sensualist, Colonel Dabney, who greedily seized the mysterious elixir and took such a draught of it that he perished on the spot ; then, through the simple old Grandsir, anxious to live for Pansie's sake ; and, perhaps, through Pansie herself, who, coming into the enjoyment of some ennobling love, would wish to defeat death, so that she might always keep the perfection of her mundane happiness, — all these forms of striving to be made the adumbration of a higher one, the shadow-play that should direct our minds to the true immortality beyond this world.

G. P. L.

THE DOLLIVER ROMANCE.

A SCENE FROM THE DOLLIVER ROMANCE.

Dr. Dolliver, a worthy personage of extreme antiquity, was aroused rather prematurely, one summer
morning, by the shouts of the child Pansie, in an adjoining chamber, summoning old Martha (who performed the duties of nurse, housekeeper, and kitchen-
maid, in the Doctor's establishment) to take up her
little ladyship and dress her. The old gentleman
woke with more than his customary alacrity, and, after taking a moment to gather his wits about him,
pulled aside the faded moreen curtains of his ancient
bed, and thrust his head into a beam of sunshine that
caused him to wink and withdraw it again. This transitory glimpse of good Dr. Dolliver showed a flannel
night-cap, fringed round with stray locks of silvery
white hair, and surmounting a meagre and duskily yellow visage, which was crossed and criss-crossed with a
record of his long life in wrinkles, faithfully written,
no doubt, but with such cramped chirography of Father
Time that the purport was illegible. It seemed hardly
worth while for the patriarch to get out of bed any
more, and bring his forlorn shadow into the summer
day that was made for younger folks. The Doctor,
however, was by no means of that opinion, being considerably encouraged towards the toil of living twenty

four hours longer by the comparative ease with which he found himself going through the usually painful process of bestirring his rusty joints (stiffened by the very rest and sleep that should have made them pliable) and putting them in a condition to bear his weight upon the floor. Nor was he absolutely disheartened by the idea of those tonsorial, ablutionary, and personally decorative labors which are apt to become so intolerably irksome to an old gentleman, after performing them daily and daily for fifty, sixty, or seventy years, and finding them still as immitigably recurrent as at first. Dr. Dolliver could nowise account for this happy condition of his spirits and physical energies, until he remembered taking an experimental sip of a certain cordial which was long ago prepared by his grandson, and carefully sealed up in a bottle, and had been reposited in a dark closet, among a parcel of effete medicines, ever since that gifted young man's death.

"It may have wrought effect upon me," thought the doctor, shaking his head as he lifted it again from the pillow. "It may be so; for poor Edward oftentimes instilled a strange efficacy into his perilous drugs. But I will rather believe it to be the operation of God's mercy, which may have temporarily invigorated my feeble age for little Pansie's sake."

A twinge of his familiar rheumatism, as he put his foot out of bed, taught him that he must not reckon too confidently upon even a day's respite from the intrusive family of aches and infirmities, which, with their proverbial fidelity to attachments once formed, had long been the closest acquaintances that the poor old gentleman had in the world. Nevertheless, he fancied the twinge a little less poignant than those of yester-

day; and, moreover, after stinging him pretty smartly,
it passed gradually off with a thrill, which, in its latter stages, grew to be almost agreeable. Pain is but
pleasure too strongly emphasized. With cautious movements, and only a groan or two, the good Doctor trans-
ferred himself from the bed to the floor, where he stood
awhile, gazing from one piece of quaint furniture to
another (such as stiff-backed Mayflower chairs, an
oaken chest-of-drawers carved cunningly with shapes
of animals and wreaths of foliage, a table with multi-
tudinous legs, a family record in faded embroidery, a
shelf of black-bound books, a dirty heap of gallipots
and phials in a dim corner), — gazing at these things,
and steadying himself by the bedpost, while his inert
brain, still partially benumbed with sleep, came slowly
into accordance with the realities about him. The object which most helped to bring Dr. Dolliver completely to his waking perceptions was one that common observers might suppose to have been snatched
bodily out of his dreams. The same sunbeam that had
dazzled the doctor between the bed-curtains gleamed
on the weather-beaten gilding which had once adorned
this mysterious symbol, and showed it to be an enormous serpent, twining round a wooden post, and reaching quite from the floor of the chamber to its ceiling.

It was evidently a thing that could boast of considerable antiquity, the dry-rot having eaten out its eyes
and gnawed away the tip of its tail; and it must have
stood long exposed to the atmosphere, for a kind of
gray moss had partially overspread its tarnished gilt
surface, and a swallow, or other familiar little bird in
some by-gone summer, seemed to have built its nest in
the yawning and exaggerated mouth. It looked like a
kind of Manichean idol, which might have been ele-

vated on a pedestal for a century or so, enjoying the
worship of its votaries in the open air, until the impious
sect perished from among men, — all save old Dr.
Dolliver, who had set up the monster in his bedchamber for the convenience of private devotion. But we
are unpardonable in suggesting such a fantasy to the
prejudice of our venerable friend, knowing him to have
been as pious and upright a Christian, and with as little of the serpent in his character, as ever came of Puritan lineage. Not to make a further mystery about
a very simple matter, this bedimmed and rotten reptile
was once the medical emblem or apothecary's sign of
the famous Dr. Swinnerton, who practised physic in the
earlier days of New England, when a head of Æscula-
pius or Hippocrates would have vexed the souls of the
righteous as savoring of heathendom. The ancient
dispenser of drugs had therefore set up an image of
the Brazen Serpent, and followed his business for many
years with great credit, under this Scriptural device;
and Dr. Dolliver, being the apprentice, pupil, and
humble friend of the learned Swinnerton's old age,
had inherited the symbolic snake, and much other valuable property by his bequest.

While the patriarch was putting on his small-clothes,
he took care to stand in the parallelogram of bright
sunshine that fell upon the uncarpeted floor. The
summer warmth was very genial to his system, and
yet made him shiver; his wintry veins rejoiced at it,
though the reviving blood tingled through them with
a half - painful and only half - pleasurable titillation.
For the first few moments after creeping out of bed,
he kept his back to the sunny window, and seemed
mysteriously shy of glancing thitherward; but, as the
June fervor pervaded him more and more thoroughly,

he turned bravely about, and looked forth at a burial-ground on the corner of which he dwelt. There lay many an old acquaintance, who had gone to sleep with the flavor of Dr. Dolliver's tinctures and powders upon his tongue; it was the patient's final bitter taste of this world, and perhaps doomed to be a recol-lected nauseousness in the next. Yesterday, in the chill of his forlorn old age, the Doctor expected soon to stretch out his weary bones among that quiet com-munity, and might scarcely have shrunk from the prospect on his own account, except, indeed, that he dreamily mixed up the infirmities of his present con-dition with the repose of the approaching one, being haunted by a notion that the damp earth, under the grass and dandelions, must needs be pernicious for his cough and his rheumatism. But, this morning, the cheerful sunbeams, or the mere taste of his grandson's cordial that he had taken at bedtime, or the fitful vigor that often sports irreverently with aged people, had caused an unfrozen drop of youthfulness, some-where within him, to expand.

"Hem! ahem!" quoth the Doctor, hoping with one effort to clear his throat of the dregs of a ten-years' cough. "Matters are not so far gone with me as I thought. I have known mighty sensible men, when only a little age-stricken or otherwise out of sorts, to die of mere faint-heartedness, a great deal sooner than they need."

He shook his silvery head at his own image in the looking-glass, as if to impress the apothegm on that shadowy representative of himself; and, for his part, he determined to pluck up a spirit and live as long as he possibly could, if it were only for the sake of little Pansie, who stood as close to one extremity of human

life as her great-grandfather to the other. This child
of three years old occupied all the unfossilized portion
of Dr. Dolliver's heart. Every other interest that he
formerly had, and the entire confraternity of persons
whom he once loved, had long ago departed; and the
poor Doctor could not follow them, because the grasp
of Pansie's baby-fingers held him back.

So he crammed a great silver watch into his fob,
and drew on a patchwork morning-gown of an ancient
fashion. Its original material was said to have been
the embroidered front of his own wedding-waistcoat
and the silken skirt of his wife's bridal attire, which
his eldest granddaughter had taken from the carved
chest-of-drawers, after poor Bessie, the beloved of his
youth, had been half a century in the grave. Throughout many of the intervening years, as the garment got
ragged, the spinsters of the old man's family had
quilted their duty and affection into it in the shape of
patches upon patches, rose-color, crimson, blue, violet,
and green, and then (as their hopes faded, and their
life kept growing shadier, and their attire took a sombre hue) sober gray and great fragments of funereal
black, until the Doctor could revive the memory of
most things that had befallen him by looking at his
patchwork-gown, as it hung upon a chair. And now
it was ragged again, and all the fingers that should
have mended it were cold. It had an Eastern fragrance, too, a smell of drugs, strong-scented herbs, and
spicy gums, gathered from the many potent infusions
that had from time to time been spilt over it; so that,
snuffing him afar off, you might have taken Dr. Dolliver for a mummy, and could hardly have been unde-
ceived by his shrunken and torpid aspect, as he crept
nearer.

Wrapt in his odorous and many-colored robe, he took staff in hand, and moved pretty vigorously to the head of the staircase. As it was somewhat steep, and but dimly lighted, he began cautiously to descend, putting his left hand on the banister, and poking down his long stick to assist him in making sure of the successive steps ; and thus he became a living illustration of the accuracy of Scripture, where it describes the aged as being " afraid of that which is high," — a truth that is often found to have a sadder purport than its external one. Half-way to the bottom, however, the Doctor heard the impatient and authoritative tones of little Pansie, — Queen Pansie, as she might fairly have been styled, in reference to her position in the household, — calling amain for grandpapa and breakfast. He was startled into such perilous activity by the summons, that his heels slid on the stairs, the slippers were shuffled off his feet, and he saved himself from a tumble only by quickening his pace, and coming down at almost a run.

" Mercy on my poor old bones ! " mentally exclaimed the Doctor, fancying himself fractured in fifty places. " Some of them are broken, surely, and, methinks, my heart has leaped out of my mouth ! What ! all right ? Well, well ! but Providence is kinder to me than I deserve, prancing down this steep staircase like a kid of three months old ! "

He bent stiffly to gather up his slippers and fallen staff ; and meanwhile Pansie had heard the tumult of her great-grandfather's descent, and was pounding against the door of the breakfast-room in her haste to come at him. The Doctor opened it, and there she stood, a rather pale and large-eyed little thing, quaint in her aspect, as might well be the case with a mother-

less child, dwelling in an uncheerful house, with no
other playmates than a decrepit old man and a kitten,
and no better atmosphere within-doors than the odor
of decayed apothecary's stuff, nor gayer neighborhood
than that of the adjacent burial-ground, where all her
relatives, from her great-grandmother downward, lay
calling to her, " Pansie, Pansie, it is bedtime ! " even
in the prime of the summer morning. For those dead
women-folk, especially her mother and the whole row
of maiden aunts and grand-aunts, could not but be
anxious about the child, knowing that little Pansie
would be far safer under a tuft of dandelions than
if left alone, as she soon must be, in this difficult and
deceitful world.

Yet, in spite of the lack of damask roses in her
cheeks, she seemed a healthy child, and certainly
showed great capacity of energetic movement in the
impulsive capers with which she welcomed her venerable progenitor. She shouted out her satisfaction, moreover (as her custom was, having never had any over-
sensitive auditors about her to tame down her voice),
till even the Doctor's dull ears were full of the clamor.

" Pansie, darling," said Dr. Dolliver, cheerily, patting her brown hair with his tremulous fingers, " thou
hast put some of thine own friskiness into poor old
grandfather, this fine morning ! Dost know, child,
that he came near breaking his neck down-stairs at
the sound of thy voice ? What wouldst thou have
done then, little Pansie ? "

" Kiss poor grandpapa and make him well ! " answered the child, remembering the Doctor's own mode
of cure in similar mishaps to herself. " It shall do
poor grandpapa good ! " she added, putting up her
mouth to apply the remedy.

"Ah, little one, thou hast greater faith in thy medicines than ever I had in my drugs," replied the patriarch, with a giggle, surprised and delighted at his own
readiness of response. "But the kiss is good for my
feeble old heart, Pansie, though it might do little to
mend a broken neck; so give grandpapa another dose,
and let us to breakfast."

In this merry humor they sat down to the table,
great-grandpapa and Pansie side by side, and the
kitten, as soon appeared, making a third in the party.
First, she showed her mottled head out of Pansie's lap,
delicately sipping milk from the child's basin without
rebuke; then she took post on the old gentleman's
shoulder, purring like a spinning-wheel, trying her
claws in the wadding of his dressing-gown, and still
more impressively reminding him of her presence by
putting out a paw to intercept a warmed-over morsel of
yesterday's chicken on its way to the Doctor's mouth.
After skilfully achieving this feat, she scrambled down
upon the breakfast-table and began to wash her face
and hands. Evidently, these companions were all three
on intimate terms, as was natural enough, since a great
many childish impulses were softly creeping back on
the simple-minded old man; insomuch that, if no
worldly necessities nor painful infirmity had disturbed
him, his remnant of life might have been as cheaply
and cheerily enjoyed as the early playtime of the kitten
and the child. Old Dr. Dolliver and his great-grand-
daughter (a ponderous title, which seemed quite to
overwhelm the tiny figure of Pansie) had met one another at the two extremities of the life-circle: her sunrise served him for a sunset, illuminating his locks of
silver and hers of golden brown with a homogeneous
shimmer of twinkling light.

Little Pansie was the one earthly creature that inherited a drop of the Dolliver blood. The Doctor's only child, poor Bessie's offspring, had died the better part of a hundred years before, and his grandchildren, a numerous and dimly remembered brood, had vanished along his weary track in their youth, maturity, or incipient age, till, hardly knowing how it had all happened, he found himself tottering onward with an infant's small fingers in his nerveless grasp. So mistily did his dead progeny come and go in the patriarch's decayed recollection, that this solitary child represented for him the successive babyhoods of the many that had gone before. The emotions of his early paternity came back to him. She seemed the baby of a past age oftener than she seemed Pansie. A whole family of grand-aunts (one of whom had perished in her cradle, never so mature as Pansie now, another in her virgin bloom, another in autumnal maidenhood, yellow and shrivelled, with vinegar in her blood, and still another, a forlorn widow, whose grief outlasted even its vitality, and grew to be merely a torpid habit, and was saddest then), — all their hitherto forgotten features peeped through the face of the great-grand-child, and their long-inaudible voices sobbed, shouted, or laughed, in her familiar tones. But it often happened to Dr. Dolliver, while frolicking amid this throng of ghosts, where the one reality looked no more vivid than its shadowy sisters, — it often happened that his eyes filled with tears at a sudden perception of what a sad and poverty-stricken old man he was, already remote from his own generation, and bound to stray further onward as the sole playmate and protector of a child !

As Dr. Dolliver, in spite of his advanced epoch of

life, is likely to remain a considerable time longer upon our hands, we deem it expedient to give a brief sketch of his position, in order that the story may get onward with the greater freedom when he rises from the breakfast-table. Deeming it a matter of courtesy, we have allowed him the honorary title of Doctor, as did all his towns-people and contemporaries, except, perhaps, one or two formal old physicians, stingy of civil phrases and over-jealous of their own professional dignity. Nevertheless, these crusty graduates were technically right in excluding Dr. Dolliver from their fraternity. He had never received the degree of any medical school, nor (save it might be for the cure of a toothache, or a child's rash, or a whitlow on a seamstress's finger, or some such trifling malady) had he ever been even a practitioner of the awful science with which his popular designation connected him. Our old friend, in short, even at his highest social elevation, claimed to be nothing more than an apothecary, and, in these later and far less prosperous days, scarcely so much. Since the death of his last surviving grandson (Pansie's father, whom he had instructed in all the mysteries of his science, and who, being distinguished by an experimental and inventive tendency, was generally believed to have poisoned himself with an infallible panacea of his own distillation), — since that final bereavement, Dr. Dolliver's once pretty flourishing business had lamentably declined. After a few months of unavailing struggle, he found it expedient to take down the Brazen Serpent from the position to which Dr. Swinnerton had originally elevated it, in front of his shop in the main street, and to retire to his private dwelling, situated in a by-lane and on the edge of a burial-ground.

This house, as well as the Brazen Serpent, some old medical books, and a drawer full of manuscripts, had come to him by the legacy of Dr. Swinnerton. The dreariness of the locality had been of small importance to our friend in his young manhood, when he first led his fair wife over the threshold, and so long as neither of them had any kinship with the human dust that rose into little hillocks, and still kept accumulating beneath their window. But, too soon afterwards, when poor Bessie herself had gone early to rest there, it is probable that an influence from her grave may have prematurely calmed and depressed her widowed husband, taking away much of the energy from what should have been the most active portion of his life. Thus he never grew rich. His thrifty townsmen used to tell him, that, in any other man's hands, Dr. Swinnerton's Brazen Serpent (meaning, I presume, the inherited credit and good-will of that old worthy's trade) would need but ten years' time to transmute its brass into gold. In Dr. Dolliver's keeping, as we have seen, the inauspicious symbol lost the greater part of what superficial gilding it originally had. Matters had not mended with him in more advanced life, after he had deposited a further and further portion of his heart and its affections in each successive one of a long row of kindred graves; and as he stood over the last of them, holding Pansie by the hand and looking down upon the coffin of his grandson, it is no wonder that the old man wept, partly for those gone before, but not so bitterly as for the little one that stayed behind. Why had not God taken her with the rest? And then, so hopeless as he was, so destitute of possibilities of good, his weary frame, his decrepit bones, his dried-up heart, might have crumbled into dust at once, and

have been scattered by the next wind over all the
heaps of earth that were akin to him.

This intensity of desolation, however, was of too
positive a character to be long sustained by a person
of Dr. Dolliver's original gentleness and simplicity,
and now so completely tamed by age and misfortune.
Even before he turned away from the grave, he grew
conscious of a slightly cheering and invigorating effect
from the tight grasp of the child's warm little hand.
Feeble as he was, she seemed to adopt him willingly
for her protector. And the Doctor never afterwards
shrank from his duty nor quailed beneath it, but bore
himself like a man, striving, amid the sloth of age and
the breaking-up of intellect, to earn the competency
which he had failed to accumulate even in his most
vigorous days.

To the extent of securing a present subsistence for
Pansie and himself, he was successful. After his son's
death, when the Brazen Serpent fell into popular disrepute, a small share of tenacious patronage followed
the old man into his retirement. In his prime, he had
been allowed to possess more skill than usually fell to
the share of a Colonial apothecary, having been regularly apprenticed to Dr. Swinnerton, who, throughout
his long practice, was accustomed personally to concoct
the medicines which he prescribed and dispensed. It
was believed, indeed, that the ancient physician had
learned the art at the world-famous drug-manufactory
of Apothecary's Hall, in London, and, as some people
half-malignly whispered, had perfected himself under
masters more subtle than were to be found even there.
Unquestionably, in many critical cases he was known
to have employed remedies of mysterious composition
and dangerous potency, which, in less skilful hands,

would have been more likely to kill than cure. He would willingly, it is said, have taught his apprentice the secrets of these prescriptions, but the latter, being of a timid character and delicate conscience, had shrunk from acquaintance with them. It was probably as the result of the same scrupulosity that Dr. Dolliver had always declined to enter the medical profession, in which his old instructor had set him such heroic examples of adventurous dealing with matters of life and death. Nevertheless, the aromatic fragrance, so to speak, of the learned Swinnerton's reputation, had clung to our friend through life; and there were elaborate preparations in the pharmacopœia of that day, requiring such minute skill and conscientious fidelity in the concocter that the physicians were still glad to confide them to one in whom these qualities were so evident.

Moreover, the grandmothers of the community were kind to him, and mindful of his perfumes, his rose-water, his cosmetics, tooth-powders, pomanders, and pomades, the scented memory of which lingered about their toilet-tables, or came faintly back from the days when they were beautiful. Among this class of customers there was still a demand for certain comfortable little nostrums (delicately sweet and pungent to the taste, cheering to the spirits, and fragrant in the breath), the proper distillation of which was the airiest secret that the mystic Swinnerton had left behind him. And, besides, these old ladies had always liked the manners of Dr. Dolliver, and used to speak of his gentle courtesy behind the counter as having positively been something to admire; though of later years, an unrefined, and almost rustic simplicity, such as belonged to his humble ancestors, appeared to have taken possession of him, as it often does of prettily mannered men in their late decay.

But it resulted from all these favorable circum stances that the Doctor's marble mortar, though worn with long service and considerably damaged by a crack that pervaded it, continued to keep up an occasional intimacy with the pestle ; and he still weighed drachms and scruples in his delicate scales, though it seemed impossible, dealing with such minute quantities, that his tremulous fingers should not put in too little or too much, leaving out life with the deficiency, or spilling in death with the surplus. To say the truth, his stanchest friends were beginning to think that Dr. Dolliver's fits of absence (when his mind appeared absolutely to depart from him, while his frail old body worked on mechanically) rendered him not quite trustworthy without a close supervision of his proceedings. It was impossible, however, to convince the aged apothecary of the necessity for such vigilance ; and if anything could stir up his gentle temper to wrath, or, as oftener happened, to tears, it was the attempt (which he was marvellously quick to detect) thus to interfere with his long-familiar business.

The public, meanwhile, ceasing to regard Dr. Dolliver in his professional aspect, had begun to take an interest in him as perhaps their oldest fellow-citizen. It was he that remembered the Great Fire and the Great Snow, and that had been a grown-up stripling at the terrible epoch of Witch-Times, and a child just breeched at the breaking out of King Philip's Indian War. He, too, in his school-boy days, had received a benediction from the patriarchal Governor Bradstreet, and thus could boast (somewhat as Bishops do of their unbroken succession from the Apostles) of

a transmitted blessing from the whole company of
sainted Pilgrims, among whom the venerable magis-
trate had been an honored companion. Viewing their
townsman in this aspect, the people revoked the courteous Doctorate with which they had heretofore decorated him, and now knew him most familiarly as
Grandsir Dolliver. His white head, his Puritan band,
his threadbare garb (the fashion of which he had
ceased to change, half a century ago), his gold-headed
staff, that had been Dr. Swinnerton's, his shrunken,
frosty figure, and its feeble movement, — all these
characteristics had a wholeness and permanence in
the public recognition, like the meeting-house steeple
or the town-pump. All the younger portion of the
inhabitants unconsciously ascribed a sort of aged immortality to Grandsir Dolliver's infirm and reverend
presence. They fancied that he had been born old
(at least, I remember entertaining some such notions
about age-stricken people, when I myself was young),
and that he could the better tolerate his aches and in-
commodities, his dull ears and dim eyes, his remoteness from human intercourse within the crust of in-
durated years, the cold temperature that kept him
always shivering and sad, the heavy burden that in-
visibly bent down his shoulders, — that all these intolerable things might bring a kind of enjoyment to
Grandsir Dolliver, as the lifelong conditions of his
peculiar existence.

But, alas! it was a terrible mistake. This weight
of years had a perennial novelty for the poor sufferer.
He never grew accustomed to it, but, long as he had
now borne the fretful torpor of his waning life, and
patient as he seemed, he still retained an inward consciousness that these stiffened shoulders, these quailing

knees, this cloudiness of sight and brain, this confused forgetfulness of men and affairs, were troublesome accidents that did not really belong to him. He possibly cherished a half-recognized idea that they might pass away. Youth, however eclipsed for a season, is undoubtedly the proper, permanent, and genuine condition of man; and if we look closely into this dreary delusion of growing old, we shall find that it never absolutely succeeds in laying hold of our innermost convictions. A sombre garment, woven of life's unrealities, has muffled us from our true self, but within it smiles the young man whom we knew; the ashes of many perishable things have fallen upon our youthful fire, but beneath them lurk the seeds of inextinguishable flame. So powerful is this instinctive faith, that men of simple modes of character are prone to antedate its consummation. And thus it happened with poor Grandsir Dolliver, who often awoke from an old man's fitful sleep with a sense that his senile predicament was but a dream of the past night; and hobbling hastily across the cold floor to the looking-glass, he would be grievously disappointed at beholding the white hair, the wrinkles and furrows, the ashen visage and bent form, the melancholy mask of Age, in which, as he now remembered, some strange and sad enchantment had involved him for years gone by!

To other eyes than his own, however, the shrivelled old gentleman looked as if there were little hope of his throwing off this too artfully wrought disguise, until, at no distant day, his stooping figure should be straightened out, his hoary locks be smoothed over his brows, and his much-enduring bones be laid safely away, with a green coverlet spread over them, beside his Bessie, who doubtless would recognize her youthful

companion in spite of his ugly garniture of decay.
He longed to be gazed at by the loving eyes now
closed ; he shrank from the hard stare of them that
loved him not. Walking the streets seldom and reluctantly, he felt a dreary impulse to elude the people's observation, as if with a sense that he had gone
irrevocably out of fashion, and broken his connecting
links with the net-work of human life ; or else it was
that nightmare-feeling which we sometimes have in
dreams, when we seem to find ourselves wandering
through a crowded avenue, with the noonday sun upon
us, in some wild extravagance of dress or nudity. He
was conscious of estrangement from his towns-people,
but did not always know how nor wherefore, nor why
he should be thus groping through the twilight mist
in solitude. If they spoke loudly to him, with cheery
voices, the greeting translated itself faintly and
mournfully to his ears ; if they shook him by the
hand, it was as if a thick, insensible glove absorbed
the kindly pressure and the warmth. When little
Pansie was the companion of his walk, her childish
gayety and freedom did not avail to bring him into
closer relationship with men, but seemed to follow him
into that region of indefinable remoteness, that dismal
Fairy-Land of aged fancy, into which old Grandsir
Dolliver had so strangely crept away.

Yet there were moments, as many persons had noticed, when the great-grandpapa would suddenly take
stronger hues of life. It was as if his faded figure
had been colored over anew, or at least, as he and
Pansie moved along the street, as if a sunbeam had
fallen across him, instead of the gray gloom of an instant before. His chilled sensibilities had probably
been touched and quickened by the warm contiguity

of his little companion through the medium of her
hand, as it stirred within his own, or some inflection
of her voice that set his memory ringing and chiming
with forgotten sounds. While that music lasted, the
old man was alive and happy. And there were seasons, it might be, happier than even these, when Pansie had been kissed and put to bed, and Grandsir Dolliver sat by his fireside gazing in among the massive
coals, and absorbing their glow into those cavernous
abysses with which all men communicate. Hence
come angels or fiends into our twilight musings, according as we may have peopled them in by-gone years.
Over our friend's face, in the rosy flicker of the fire-
gleam, stole an expression of repose and perfect trust
that made him as beautiful to look at, in his high-
backed chair, as the child Pansie on her pillow; and
sometimes the spirits that were watching him beheld
a calm surprise draw slowly over his features and
brighten into joy, yet not so vividly as to break his
evening quietude. The gate of heaven had been
kindly left ajar, that this forlorn old creature might
catch a glimpse within. All the night afterwards, he
would be semi-conscious of an intangible bliss diffused
through the fitful lapses of an old man's slumber, and
would awake, at early dawn, with a faint thrilling of
the heart-strings, as if there had been music just now
wandering over them.

ANOTHER SCENE FROM THE DOLLIVER RO MANCE.[1]

WE may now suppose Grandsir Dolliver to have finished his breakfast, with a better appetite and sharper
perception of the qualities of his food than he has generally felt of late years, whether it were due to old
Martha's cookery or to the cordial of the night before.
Little Pansie had also made an end of her bread and
milk with entire satisfaction, and afterwards nibbled
a crust, greatly enjoying its resistance to her little
white teeth.

How this child came by the odd name of Pansie,
and whether it was really her baptismal name, I have
not ascertained. More probably it was one of those
pet appellations that grow out of a child's character,
or out of some keen thrill of affection in the parents,
an unsought-for and unconscious felicity, a kind of
revelation, teaching them the true name by which the
child's guardian angel would know it, — a name with
playfulness and love in it, that we often observe to
supersede, in the practice of those who love the child
best, the name that they carefully selected, and caused
the clergyman to plaster indelibly on the poor little
forehead at the font, — the love-name, whereby, if the
child lives, the parents know it in their hearts, or by
which, if it dies, God seems to have called it away,
leaving the sound lingering faintly and sweetly through

[1] This scene was not revised by the author, but is printed from his
first draught.

the house. In Pansie's case, it may have been a certain pensiveness which was sometimes seen under her childish frolic, and so translated itself into French (*pensée*), her mother having been of Acadian kin; or, quite as probably, it alluded merely to the color of her eyes, which, in some lights, were very like the dark petals of a tuft of pansies in the Doctor's garden. It might well be, indeed, on account of the suggested pensiveness; for the child's gayety had no example to sustain it, no sympathy of other children or grown people, — and her melancholy, had it been so dark a feeling, was but the shadow of the house, and of the old man. If brighter sunshine came, she would brighten with it. This morning, surely, as the three companions, Pansie, puss, and Grandsir Dolliver, emerged from the shadow of the house into the small adjoining enclosure, they seemed all frolicsome alike.

The Doctor, however, was intent over something that had reference to his lifelong business of drugs. This little spot was the place where he was wont to cultivate a variety of herbs supposed to be endowed with medicinal virtue. Some of them had been long known in the pharmacopœia of the Old World; and others, in the early days of the country, had been adopted by the first settlers from the Indian medicine-men, though with fear and even contrition, because these wild doctors were supposed to draw their pharmaceutic knowledge from no gracious source, the Black Man himself being the principal professor in their medical school. From his own experience, however, Dr. Dolliver had long since doubted, though he was not bold enough quite to come to the conclusion, that Indian shrubs, and the remedies prepared from them, were much less perilous than those so freely used in

European practice, and singularly apt to be followed
by results quite as propitious. Into such heterodoxy
our friend was the more liable to fall, because it had
been taught him early in life by his old master, Dr.
Swinnerton, who, at those not infrequent times when
he indulged a certain unhappy predilection for strong
waters, had been accustomed to inveigh in terms of
the most cynical contempt and coarsest ridicule against
the practice by which he lived, and, as he affirmed,
inflicted death on his fellow-men. Our old apothecary, though too loyal to the learned profession with
which he was connected fully to believe this bitter
judgment, even when pronounced by his revered master, was still so far influenced that his conscience was
possibly a little easier when making a preparation
from forest herbs and roots than in the concoction of
half a score of nauseous poisons into a single elaborate
drug, as the fashion of that day was.

But there were shrubs in the garden of which he
had never ventured to make a medical use, nor, indeed,
did he know their virtue, although from year to year
he had tended and fertilized, weeded and pruned them,
with something like religious care. They were of the
rarest character, and had been planted by the learned
and famous Dr. Swinnerton, who, on his death-bed,
when he left his dwelling and all his abstruse manuscripts to his favorite pupil, had particularly directed
his attention to this row of shrubs. They had been
collected by himself from remote countries, and had
the poignancy of torrid climes in them; and he told
him, that, properly used, they would be worth all the
rest of the legacy a hundred-fold. As the apothecary,
however, found the manuscripts, in which he conjec-
tured there was a treatise on the subject of these

shrubs, mostly illegible, and quite beyond his comprehension in such passages as he succeeded in puzzling out (partly, perhaps, owing to his very imperfect knowledge of Latin, in which language they were written), he had never derived from them any of the promised benefit. And, to say the truth, remembering that Dr. Swinnerton himself never appeared to triturate or decoct or do anything else with the mysterious herbs, our old friend was inclined to imagine the weighty commendation of their virtues to have been the idly solemn utterance of mental aberration at the hour of death. So, with the integrity that belonged to his character, he had nurtured them as tenderly as was possible in the ungenial climate and soil of New England, putting some of them into pots for the winter; but they had rather dwindled than flourished, and he had reaped no harvests from them, nor observed them with any degree of scientific interest.

His grandson, however, while yet a school-boy, had listened to the old man's legend of the miraculous virtues of these plants ; and it took so firm a hold of his mind, that the row of outlandish vegetables seemed rooted in it, and certainly flourished there with richer luxuriance than in the soil where they actually grew. The story, acting thus early upon his imagination, may be said to have influenced his brief career in life, and, perchance, brought about its early close. The young man, in the opinion of competent judges, was endowed with remarkable abilities, and according to the rumor of the people had wonderful gifts, which were proved by the cures he had wrought with remedies of his own invention. His talents lay in the direction of scientific analysis and inventive combination of chemical powers. While under the pupilage of his grandfather, his

progress had rapidly gone quite beyond his instructor's
hope, — leaving him even to tremble at the audacity
with which he overturned and invented theories, and to
wonder at the depth at which he wrought beneath the
superficialness and mock-mystery of the medical science of those days, like a miner sinking his shaft and
running a hideous peril of the earth caving in above
him. Especially did he devote himself to these plants;
and under his care they had thriven beyond all former
precedent, bursting into luxuriance of bloom, and most
of them bearing beautiful flowers, which, however, in
two or three instances, had the sort of natural repulsiveness that the serpent has in its beauty, compelled
against its will, as it were, to warn the beholder of an
unrevealed danger. The young man had long ago, it
must be added, demanded of his grandfather the documents included in the legacy of Professor Swinnerton, and had spent days and nights upon them, growing pale over their mystic lore, which seemed the fruit
not merely of the Professor's own labors, but of those
of more ancient sages than he ; and often a whole volume seemed to be compressed within the limits of a
few lines of crabbed manuscript, judging from the
time which it cost even the quick-minded student to
decipher them.

Meantime these abstruse investigations had not
wrought such disastrous effects as might have been
feared, in causing Edward Dolliver to neglect the
humble trade, the conduct of which his grandfather
had now relinquished almost entirely into his hands.
On the contrary, with the mere side results of his
study, or what may be called the chips and shavings
of his real work, he created a prosperity quite beyond
anything that his simple-minded predecessor had ever

hoped for, even at the most sanguine epoch of his life.
The young man's adventurous endowments were mirac-
ulously alive, and connecting themselves with his remarkable ability for solid research, and perhaps his
conscience being as yet imperfectly developed (as it
sometimes lies dormant in the young), he spared not
to produce compounds which, if the names were anywise to be trusted, would supersede all other remedies,
and speedily render any medicine a needless thing,
making the trade of apothecary an untenable one, and
the title of Doctor obsolete. Whether there was real
efficacy in these nostrums, and whether their author
himself had faith in them, is more than can safely be
said; but, at all events, the public believed in them,
and thronged to the old and dim sign of the Brazen
Serpent, which, though hitherto familiar to them and
their forefathers, now seemed to shine with auspicious
lustre, as if its old Scriptural virtues were renewed.
If any faith was to be put in human testimony, many
marvellous cures were really performed, the fame of
which spread far and wide, and caused demands for
these medicines to come in from places far beyond the
precincts of the little town. Our old apothecary, now
degraded by the overshadowing influence of his grandson's character to a position not much above that of a
shop-boy, stood behind the counter with a face sad and
distrustful, and yet with an odd kind of fitful excitement in it, as if he would have liked to enjoy this new
prosperity, had he dared. Then his venerable figure
was to be seen dispensing these questionable compounds by the single bottle and by the dozen, wrong-
ing his simple conscience as he dealt out what he
feared was trash or worse, shrinking from the reproach-
ful eyes of every ancient physician who might chance

to be passing by, but withal examining closely the silver, or the New England coarsely printed bills, which he took in payment, as if apprehensive that the delusive character of the commodity which he sold might be balanced by equal counterfeiting in the money received, or as if his faith in all things were shaken.

Is it not possible that this gifted young man had indeed found out those remedies which Nature has provided and laid away for the cure of every ill?

The disastrous termination of the most brilliant epoch that ever came to the Brazen Serpent must be told in a few words. One night, Edward Dolliver's young wife awoke, and, seeing the gray dawn creeping into the chamber, while her husband, it should seem, was still engaged in his laboratory, arose in her nightdress, and went to the door of the room to put in her gentle remonstrance against such labor. There she found him dead, — sunk down out of his chair upon the hearth, where were some ashes, apparently of burnt manuscripts, which appeared to comprise most of those included in Dr. Swinnerton's legacy, though one or two had fallen near the heap, and lay merely scorched beside it. It seemed as if he had thrown them into the fire, under a sudden impulse, in a great hurry and passion. It may be that he had come to the perception of something fatally false and deceptive in the successes which he had appeared to win, and was too proud and too conscientious to survive it. Doctors were called in, but had no power to revive him. An inquest was held, at which the jury, under the instruction, perhaps, of those same revengeful doctors, expressed the opinion that the poor young man, being given to strange contrivances with poisonous drugs, had died by incautiously tasting them himself. This

verdict, and the terrible event itself, at once deprived
the medicines of all their popularity; and the poor old
apothecary was no longer under any necessity of disturbing his conscience by selling them. They at once
lost their repute, and ceased to be in any demand. In
the few instances in which they were tried the experiment was followed by no good results; and even those
individuals who had fancied themselves cured, and had
been loudest in spreading the praises of these benefi-
cent compounds, now, as if for the utter demolition
of the poor youth's credit, suffered under a recurrence
of the worst symptoms, and, in more than one case,
perished miserably: insomuch (for the days of witchcraft were still within the memory of living men and
women) it was the general opinion that Satan had
been personally concerned in this affliction, and that
the Brazen Serpent, so long honored among them, was
really the type of his subtle malevolence and perfect
iniquity. It was rumored even that all preparations
that came from the shop were harmful: that teeth
decayed that had been made pearly white by the use
of the young chemist's dentifrice; that cheeks were
freckled that had been changed to damask roses by
his cosmetics; that hair turned gray or fell off that
had become black, glossy, and luxuriant from the application of his mixtures; that breath which his drugs
had sweetened had now a sulphurous smell. Moreover,
all the money heretofore amassed by the sale of them
had been exhausted by Edward Dolliver in his lavish
expenditure for the processes of his study; and nothing
was left for Pansie, except a few valueless and unsal-
able bottles of medicine, and one or two others, perhaps more recondite than their inventor had seen fit
to offer to the public. Little Pansie's mother lived

but a short time after the shock of the terrible catastrophe; and, as we began our story with saying, she
was left with no better guardianship or support than
might be found in the efforts of a long superannuated
man.

Nothing short of the simplicity, integrity, and piety
of Grandsir Dolliver's character, known and acknowledged as far back as the oldest inhabitants remembered anything, and inevitably discoverable by the
dullest and most prejudiced observers, in all its natural manifestations, could have protected him in still
creeping about the streets. So far as he was personally concerned, however, all bitterness and suspicion
had speedily passed away; and there remained still
the careless and neglectful good-will, and the prescrip-
tive reverence, not altogether reverential, which the
world heedlessly awards to the unfortunate individual
who outlives his generation.

And now that we have shown the reader sufficiently,
or at least to the best of our knowledge, and perhaps
at tedious length, what was the present position of
Grandsir Dolliver, we may let our story pass onward,
though at such a pace as suits the feeble gait of an
old man.

The peculiarly brisk sensation of this morning, to
which we have more than once alluded, enabled the
Doctor to toil pretty vigorously at his medicinal herbs,
— his catnip, his vervain, and the like; but he did
not turn his attention to the row of mystic plants,
with which so much of trouble and sorrow either was,
or appeared to be, connected. In truth, his old soul
was sick of them, and their very fragrance, which the
warm sunshine made strongly perceptible, was odious
to his nostrils. But the spicy, homelike scent of his

other herbs, the English simples, was grateful to him, and so was the earth-smell, as he turned up the soil about their roots, and eagerly snuffed it in. Little Pansie, on the other hand, perhaps scandalized at great-grandpapa's neglect of the prettiest plants in his garden, resolved to do her small utmost towards balancing his injustice; so with an old shingle, fallen from the roof, which she had appropriated as her agricultural tool, she began to dig about them, pulling up the weeds, as she saw grandpapa doing. The kitten, too, with a look of elfish sagacity, lent her assistance, plying her paws with vast haste and efficiency at the roots of one of the shrubs. This particular one was much smaller than the rest, perhaps because it was a native of the torrid zone, and required greater care than the others to make it flourish; so that, shrivelled, cankered, and scarcely showing a green leaf, both Pansie and the kitten probably mistook it for a weed. After their joint efforts had made a pretty big trench about it, the little girl seized the shrub with both hands, bestriding it with her plump little legs, and giving so vigorous a pull, that, long accustomed to be transplanted annually, it came up by the roots, and little Pansie came down in a sitting posture, making a broad impress on the soft earth. " See, see, Doctor ! " cries Pansie, comically enough giving him his title of courtesy, — "look, grandpapa, the big, naughty weed ! "

Now the Doctor had at once a peculiar dread and a peculiar value for this identical shrub, both because his grandson's investigations had been applied more ardently to it than to all the rest, and because it was associated in his mind with an ancient and sad recollection. For he had never forgotten that his wife, the early lost, had once taken a fancy to wear its flowers, day after day, through the whole season of their bloom, in her bosom, where they glowed like a gem, and deepened her somewhat pallid beauty with a richness never before seen in it. At least such was the effect which this tropical flower imparted to the beloved form in his memory, and thus it somehow both brightened and wronged her. This had happened not long before her death; and whenever, in the subsequent years, this plant had brought its annual flower, it had proved a kind of talisman to bring up the image of Bessie, radiant with this glow that did not really belong to her naturally passive beauty, quickly interchanging with another image of her form, with the snow of death on cheek and forehead. This reminiscence had remained among the things of which the Doctor was always conscious, but had never breathed a word, through the whole of his long life, — a sprig of sensibility that perhaps helped to keep him tenderer and purer than other men, who entertain no such follies. And the sight of the shrub often brought back the faint, golden gleam of her hair, as if her spirit were in the sunlights of the garden, quivering into view and out of it. And therefore, when he saw what Pansie had done, he sent forth a strange, inarticulate, hoarse, tremulous exclamation, a sort of aged and decrepit cry of mingled emotion. "Naughty Pansie, to pull up grandpapa's flower!" said he, as soon as he could speak. "Poison, Pansie, poison! Fling it away, child!"

And dropping his spade, the old gentleman scrambled towards the little girl as quickly as his rusty joints would let him, — while Pansie, as apprehensive and quick of motion as a fawn, started up with a shriek of mirth and fear to escape him. It so happened that the garden-gate was ajar ; and a puff of wind blowing it wide open, she escaped through this fortuitous avenue, followed by great - grandpapa and the kitten.

"Stop, naughty Pansie, stop ! " shouted our old friend. " You will tumble into the grave ! " The kitten, with the singular sensitiveness that seems to affect it at every kind of excitement, was now on her back.

And, indeed, this portentous warning was better grounded and had a more literal meaning than might be supposed ; for the swinging gate communicated with the burial-ground, and almost directly in little Pansie's track there was a newly dug grave, ready to receive its tenant that afternoon. Pansie, however, fled onward with outstretched arms, half in fear, half in fun, plying her round little legs with wonderful promptitude, as if to escape Time. or Death, in the person of Grandsir Dolliver, and happily avoiding the ominous pitfall that lies in every person's path, till, hearing a groan from her pursuer, she looked over her shoulder, and saw that poor grandpapa had stumbled over one of the many hillocks. She then suddenly wrinkled up her little visage, and sent forth a full-breathed roar of sympathy and alarm.

" Grandpapa has broken his neck now! " cried little Pansie, amid her sobs.

" Kiss grandpapa, and make it well, then," said the old gentleman, recollecting her remedy, and scrambling up more readily than could be expected. " Well," he murmured to himself, " a hair's-breadth more, and I should have been tumbled into yonder grave. Poor little Pansie ! what wouldst thou have done then ? "

"Make the grass grow over grandpapa," answered
Pansie, laughing up in his face.

"Poh, poh, child, that is not a pretty thing to say,"
said grandpapa, pettishly and disappointed, as people
are apt to be when they try to calculate on the fitful
sympathies of childhood. "Come, you must go in to
old Martha now."

The poor old gentleman was in the more haste to
leave the spot because he found himself standing right
in front of his own peculiar row of gravestones, consisting of eight or nine slabs of slate, adorned with
carved borders rather rudely cut, and the earliest one,
that of his Bessie, bending aslant, because the frost of
so many winters had slowly undermined it. Over one
grave of the row, that of his gifted grandson, there
was no memorial. He felt a strange repugnance,
stronger than he had ever felt before, to linger by
these graves, and had none of the tender sorrow, mingled with high and tender hopes, that had sometimes
made it seem good to him to be there. Such moods,
perhaps, often come to the aged, when the hardened
earth-crust over their souls shuts them out from spiritual influences.

Taking the child by the hand, — her little efferves-
cence of infantile fun having passed into a downcast
humor, though not well knowing as yet what a dusky
cloud of disheartening fancies arose from these green
hillocks, — he went heavily toward the garden-gate.
Close to its threshold, so that one who was issuing
forth or entering must needs step upon it or over it,
lay a small flat stone, deeply imbedded in the ground,
and partly covered with grass, inscribed with the name
of "Dr. John Swinnerton, Physician."

"Ay," said the old man, as the well-remembered

figure of his ancient instructor seemed to rise before him in his grave-apparel, with beard and gold-headed cane, black velvet doublet and cloak, " here lies a man who, as people have thought, had it in his power to avoid the grave! He had no little grandchild to tease him. He had the choice to die, and chose it."

So the old gentleman led Pansie over the stone, and carefully closed the gate ; and, as it happened, he forgot the uprooted shrub, which Pansie, as she ran, had flung away, and which had fallen into the open grave ; and when the funeral came that afternoon, the coffin was let down upon it, so that its bright, inauspicious flower never bloomed again.

ANOTHER FRAGMENT OF THE DOLLIVER ROMANCE.

"BE secret!" and he kept his stern eye fixed upon him, as the coach began to move.

"Be secret!" repeated the apothecary. "I know not any secret that he has confided to me thus far, and as for his nonsense (as I will be bold to style it now he is gone) about a medicine of long life, it is a thing I forget in spite of myself, so very empty and trashy it is. I wonder, by the by, that it never came into my head to give the Colonel a dose of the cordial whereof I partook last night. I have no faith that it is a valuable medicine — little or none — and yet there has been an unwonted briskness in me all the morning."

Then a simple joy broke over his face — a flickering sunbeam among his wrinkles — as he heard the laughter of the little girl, who was running rampant with a kitten in the kitchen.

"Pansie! Pansie!" cackled he, "grandpapa has sent away the ugly man now. Come, let us have a frolic in the garden."

And he whispered to himself again, "That is a cordial yonder, and I will take it according to the prescription, knowing all the ingredients." Then, after a moment's thought, he added, "All, save one."

So, as he had declared to himself his intention, that night, when little Pansie had long been asleep, and his small household was in bed, and most of the quiet, old-fashioned townsfolk likewise, this good apothecary went into his laboratory, and took out of a cupboard in the wall a certain ancient-looking bottle, which was cased over with a net-work of what seemed to be woven silver, like the wicker-woven bottles of our days. He had previously provided a goblet of pure water. Before opening the bottle, however, he seemed to hesitate, and pondered and babbled to himself; having long since come to that period of life when the bodily frame, having lost much of its value, is more tenderly cared for than when it was a perfect and inestimable machine.

"I triturated, I infused, I distilled it myself in these very rooms, and know it — know it all — all the ingredients, save one. They are common things enough — comfortable things — some of them a little queer — one or two that folks have a prejudice against — and then there is that one thing that I don't know. It is foolish in me to be dallying with such a mess, which I thought was a piece of quackery, while that strange visitor bade me do it, — and yet, what a strength has come from it! He said it was a rare cordial, and, methinks, it has brightened up my weary life all day, so that Pansie has found me the fitter playmate. And then the dose — it is so absurdly small! I will try it again."

He took the silver stopple from the bottle, and with a practised hand, tremulous as it was with age, so that one would have thought it must have shaken the liquor into a perfect shower of misapplied drops, he dropped — I have heard it said — only one single drop into the goblet of water. It fell into it with a dazzling brightness, like a spark of ruby flame, and

subtly diffusing itself through the whole body of water,
turned it to a rosy hue of great brilliancy. He held it
up between his eyes and the light, and seemed to admire and wonder at it.

"It is very odd," said he, "that such a pure, bright
liquor should have come out of a parcel of weeds that
mingled their juices here. The thing is a folly, — it is
one of those compositions in which the chemists — the
cabalists, perhaps — used to combine what they thought
the virtues of many plants, thinking that something
would result in the whole, which was not in either of
them, and a new efficacy be created. Whereas, it has
been the teaching of my experience that one virtue
counteracts another, and is the enemy of it. I never
believed the former theory, even when that strange
madman bade me do it. And what a thick, turbid
matter it was, until that last ingredient, — that powder
which he put in with his own hand! Had he let me
see it, I would first have analyzed it, and discovered
its component parts. The man was mad, undoubtedly,
and this may have been poison. But its effect is good.
Poh! I will taste again, because of this weak, agued,
miserable state of mine; though it is a shame in me, a
man of decent skill in my way, to believe in a quack's
nostrum. But it is a comfortable kind of thing."

Meantime, that single drop (for good Dr. Dolliver
had immediately put a stopper into the bottle) diffused
a sweet odor through the chamber, so that the ordinary
fragrances and scents of apothecaries' stuff seemed to
be controlled and influenced by it, and its bright potency also dispelled a certain dimness of the antiquated room.

The Doctor, at the pressure of a great need, had
given incredible pains to the manufacture of this med-

icine ; so that, reckoning the pains rather than the ingredients (all except one, of which he was not able to estimate the cost nor value), it was really worth its weight in gold. And, as it happened, he had bestowed upon it the hard labor of his poor life, and the time that was necessary for the support of his family, without return ; for the customers, after playing off this cruel joke upon the old man, had never come back ; and now, for seven years, the bottle had stood in a corner of the cupboard. To be sure, the silver-cased bottle was worth a trifle for its silver, and still more, perhaps, as an antiquarian knick-knack. But, all things considered, the honest and simple apothecary thought that he might make free with the liquid to such small extent as was necessary for himself. And there had been something in the concoction that had struck him ; and he had been fast breaking lately ; and so, in the dreary fantasy and lonely recklessness of his old age, he had suddenly bethought himself of this medicine (cordial, — as the strange man called it, which had come to him by long inheritance in his family) and he had determined to try it. And again, as the night before, he took out the receipt — a roll of antique parchment, out of which, provokingly, one fold had been lost — and put on his spectacles to puzzle out the passage.

Guttam unicam in aquam puram, two gills. "If the Colonel should hear of this," said Dr. Dolliver, "he might fancy it his nostrum of long life, and insist on having the bottle for his own use. The foolish, fierce old gentleman ! He has grown very earthly, of late, else he would not desire such a thing. And a strong desire it must be to make him feel it desirable. For my part, I only wish for something that, for a

short time, may clear my eyes, so that I may see little Pansie's beauty, and quicken my ears, that I may
hear her sweet voice, and give me nerve, while God
keeps me here, that I may live longer to earn bread
for dear Pansie. She provided for, I would gladly lie
down yonder with Bessie and our children. Ah! the
vanity of desiring lengthened days! — There! — I
have drunk it, and methinks its final, subtle flavor
hath strange potency in it."

The old man shivered a little, as those shiver who
have just swallowed good liquor, while it is permeat-
ing their vitals. Yet he seemed to be in a pleasant
state of feeling, and, as was frequently the case with
this simple soul, in a devout frame of mind. He read
a chapter in the Bible, and said his prayers for Pansie
and himself, before he went to bed, and had much better sleep than usually comes to people of his advanced
age; for, at that period, sleep is diffused through their
wakefulness, and a dim and tiresome half-perception
through their sleep, so that the only result is weariness.

Nothing very extraordinary happened to Dr. Dolliver or his small household for some time afterwards.
He was favored with a comfortable winter, and thanked
Heaven for it, and put it to a good use (at least he intended it so) by concocting drugs; which perhaps did
a little towards peopling the graveyard, into which his
windows looked; but that was neither his purpose nor
his fault. None of the sleepers, at all events, interrupted their slumbers to upbraid him. He had done
according to his own artless conscience and the recipes
of licensed physicians, and he looked no further, but
pounded, triturated, infused, made electuaries, boluses,
juleps, or whatever he termed his productions, with

skill and diligence, thanking Heaven that he was spared to do so, when his contemporaries generally were getting incapable of similar efforts. It struck him with some surprise, but much gratitude to Providence, that his sight seemed to be growing rather better than worse. He certainly could read the crabbed handwriting and hieroglyphics of the physicians with more readiness than he could a year earlier. But he had been originally near-sighted, with large, projecting eyes ; and near-sighted eyes always seem to get a new lease of light as the years go on. One thing was perceptible about the Doctor's eyes, not only to himself in the glass, but to everybody else ; namely, that they had an unaccustomed gleaming brightness in them ; not so very bright either, but yet so much so, that little Pansie noticed it, and sometimes, in her playful, roguish way, climbed up into his lap, and put both her small palms over them ; telling Grandpapa that he had stolen somebody else's eyes, and given away his own, and that she liked his old ones better. The poor old Doctor did his best to smile through his eyes, and so to reconcile Pansie to their brightness : but still she continually made the same silly remonstrance, so that he was fain to put on a pair of green spectacles when he was going to play with Pansie, or took her on his knee. Nay, if he looked at her, as had always been his custom, after she was asleep, in order to see that all was well with her, the little child would put up her hands, as if he held a light that was flashing on her eyeballs ; and unless he turned away his gaze quickly, she would wake up in a fit of crying.

On the whole, the apothecary had as comfortable a time as a man of his years could expect. The air of the house and of the old graveyard seemed to suit

him. What so seldom happens in man's advancing
age, his night's rest did him good, whereas, generally,
an old man wakes up ten times as nervous and dispirited as he went to bed, just as if, during his sleep
he had been working harder than ever he did in the
daytime. It had been so with the Doctor himself till
within a few months. To be sure, he had latterly begun to practise various rules of diet and exercise,
which commended themselves to his approbation. He
sawed some of his own fire-wood, and fancied that, as
was reasonable, it fatigued him less day by day. He
took walks with Pansie, and though, of course, her
little footsteps, treading on the elastic air of childhood,
far outstripped his own, still the old man knew that
he was not beyond the recuperative period of life, and
that exercise out of doors and proper food can do
somewhat towards retarding the approach of age. He
was inclined, also, to impute much good effect to a
daily dose of Santa Cruz rum (a liquor much in vogue
in that day), which he was now in the habit of quaff-
ing at the meridian hour. All through the Doctor's
life he had eschewed strong spirits: "But after seventy," quoth old Dr. Dolliver, "a man is all the better in head and stomach for a little stimulus"; and
it certainly seemed so in his case. Likewise, I know
not precisely how often, but complying punctiliously
with the recipe, as an apothecary naturally would, he
took his drop of the mysterious cordial.

He was inclined, however, to impute little or no efficacy to this, and to laugh at himself for having ever
thought otherwise. The dose was so very minute !
and he had never been sensible of any remarkable
effect on taking it, after all. A genial warmth, he
sometimes fancied, diffused itself throughout him, and

perhaps continued during the next day. A quiet and refreshing night's rest followed, and alacritous waking in the morning; but all this was far more probably owing, as has been already hinted, to excellent and well-considered habits of diet and exercise. Nevertheless he still continued the cordial with tolerable regularity, — the more, because on one or two occasions, happening to omit it, it so chanced that he slept wretchedly, and awoke in strange aches and pains, torpors, nervousness, shaking of the hands, blearedness of sight, lowness of spirits and other ills, as is the misfortune of some old men, — who are often threatened by a thousand evil symptoms that come to nothing, foreboding no particular disorder, and passing away as unsatisfactorily as they come. At another time, he took two or three drops at once, and was alarmingly feverish in consequence. Yet it was very true, that the feverish symptoms were pretty sure to disappear on his renewal of the medicine. "Still it could not be that," thought the old man, a hater of empiricism (in which, however, is contained all hope for man), and disinclined to believe in anything that was not according to rule and art. And then, as aforesaid, the dose was so ridiculously small!

Sometimes, however, he took, half laughingly, another view of it, and felt disposed to think that chance might really have thrown in his way a very remarkable mixture, by which, if it had happened to him earlier in life, he might have amassed a larger fortune, and might even have raked together such a competency as would have prevented his feeling much uneasiness about the future of little Pansie. Feeling as strong as he did nowadays, he might reasonably count upon ten years more of life, and in that time the

precious liquor might be exchanged for much gold.
" Let us see ! " quoth he, " by what attractive name
shall it be advertised ? ' The old man's cordial ?
That promises too little. Poh, poh ! I would stain
my honesty, my fair reputation, the accumulation of a
lifetime, and befool my neighbor and the public, by
any name that would make them imagine I had
found that ridiculous talisman that the alchemists have
sought. The old man's cordial, — that is best. And
five shillings sterling the bottle. That surely were
not too costly, and would give the medicine a better
reputation and higher vogue (so foolish is the world)
than if I were to put it lower. I will think further
of this. But pshaw, pshaw ! "

" What is the matter, Grandpapa," said little Pansie, who had stood by him, wishing to speak to him at
least a minute, but had been deterred by his absorption ; " why do you say ' Pshaw ' ? "

" Pshaw ! " repeated Grandpapa, " there is one ingredient that I don't know."

So this very hopeful design was necessarily given
up, but that it had occurred to Dr. Dolliver was perhaps a token that his mind was in a very vigorous
state ; for it had been noted of him through life, that
he had little enterprise, little activity, and that, for
the want of these things, his very considerable skill in
his art had been almost thrown away, as regarded his
private affairs, when it might easily have led him to
fortune. Whereas, here in his extreme age, he had
first bethought himself of a way to grow rich. Sometimes this latter spring causes — as blossoms come on
the autumnal tree — a spurt of vigor, or untimely
greenness, when Nature laughs at her old child, half
in kindness and half in scorn. It is observable, how-

ever, I fancy, that after such a spurt, age comes on with redoubled speed, and that the old man has only run forward with a show of force, in order to fall into his grave the sooner.

Sometimes, as he was walking briskly along the street, with little Pansie clasping his hand, and perhaps frisking rather more than became a person of his venerable years, he had met the grim old wreck of Colonel Dabney, moving goutily, and gathering wrath anew with every touch of his painful foot to the ground; or driving by in his carriage, showing an ashen, angry, wrinkled face at the window, and frowning at him — the apothecary thought — with a peculiar fury, as if he took umbrage at his audacity in being less broken by age than a gentleman like himself. The apothecary could not help feeling as if there were some unsettled quarrel or dispute between himself and the Colonel, he could not tell what or why. The Colonel always gave him a haughty nod of half-recognition; and the people in the street, to whom he was a familiar object, would say, "The worshipful Colonel begins to find himself mortal like the rest of us. He feels his years." "He'd be glad, I warrant," said one, "to change with you, Doctor. It shows what difference a good life makes in men, to look at him and you. You are half a score of years his elder, methinks, and yet look what temperance can do for a man. By my credit, neighbor, seeing how brisk you have been lately, I told my wife you seemed to be growing younger. It does me good to see it. We are about of an age, I think, and I like to notice how we old men keep young and keep one another in heart. I myself — ahem — ahem — feel younger this season than for these five years past."

"It rejoices me that you feel so," quoth the apothecary, who had just been thinking that this neighbor
of his had lost a great deal, both in mind and body,
within a short period, and rather scorned him for it.
"Indeed, I find old age less uncomfortable than I
supposed. Little Pansie and I make excellent companions for one another."

And then, dragged along by Pansie's little hand,
and also impelled by a certain alacrity that rose with
him in the morning, and lasted till his healthy rest at
night, he bade farewell to his contemporary, and
hastened on ; while the latter, left behind, was somewhat irritated as he looked at the vigorous movement
of the apothecary's legs.

"He need not make such a show of briskness
neither," muttered he to himself. "This touch of
rheumatism troubles me a bit just now, but try it on
a good day, and I'd walk with him for a shilling.
Pshaw! I'll walk to his funeral yet."

One day, while the Doctor, with the activity that
bestirred itself in him nowadays, was mixing and man-
ufacturing certain medicaments that came in frequent
demand, a carriage stopped at his door, and he recognized the voice of Colonel Dabney, talking in his customary stern tone to the woman who served him.
And, a moment afterwards, the coach drove away,
and he actually heard the old dignitary lumbering up
stairs, and bestowing a curse upon each particular
step, as if that were the method to make them soften
and become easier when he should come down again.
"Pray, your worship," said the Doctor from above,
"let me attend you below stairs."

"No," growled the Colonel, "I'll meet you on your

own ground. I can climb a stair yet, and be hanged to you."

So saying, he painfully finished the ascent, and came into the laboratory, where he let himself fall into the Doctor's easy-chair, with an anathema on the chair, the Doctor, and himself ; and, staring round through the dusk, he met the wide-open, startled eyes of little Pansie, who had been reading a gilt picture-book in the corner.

" Send away that child, Dolliver," cried the Colonel, angrily. " Confound her, she makes my bones ache. I hate everything young."

" Lord, Colonel," the poor apothecary ventured to say, " there must be young people in the world as well as old ones. 'T is my mind, a man's grandchildren keep him warm round about him."

" I have none, and want none," sharply responded the Colonel ; " and as for young people, let me be one of them, and they may exist, otherwise not. It is a cursed bad arrangement of the world, that there are young and old here together."

When Pansie had gone away, which she did with anything but reluctance, having a natural antipathy to this monster of a Colonel, the latter personage tapped with his crutch-handled cane on a chair that stood near, and nodded in an authoritative way to the apothecary to sit down in it. Dr. Dolliver complied submissively, and the Colonel, with dull, unkindly eyes, looked at him sternly, and with a kind of intelligence amid the aged stolidity of his aspect, that somewhat puzzled the Doctor. In this way he surveyed him all over, like a judge, when he means to hang a man, and for some reason or none, the apothecary felt his nerves shake, beneath this steadfast look.

" Aha! Doctor!" said the Colonel at last, with a doltish sneer, " you bear your years well."

" Decently well, Colonel; I thank Providence for it," answered the meek apothecary.

" I should say," quoth the Colonel, " you are younger at this moment than when we spoke together two or three years ago. I noted then that your eyebrows were a handsome snow-white, such as befits a man who has passed beyond his threescore years and ten, and five years more. Why, they are getting dark again, Mr. Apothecary."

" Nay, your worship must needs be mistaken there," said the Doctor, with a timorous chuckle. " It is many a year since I have taken a deliberate note of my wretched old visage in a glass, but I remember they were white when I looked last."

" Come, Doctor, I know a thing or two," said the Colonel, with a bitter scoff; " and what 's this, you old rogue? Why, you 've rubbed away a wrinkle since we met. Take off those infernal spectacles, and look me in the face. Ha! I see the devil in your eye. How dare you let it shine upon me so?"

" On my conscience, Colonel," said the apothecary, strangely struck with the coincidence of this accusation with little Pansie's complaint, " I know not what you mean. My sight is pretty well for a man of my age. We near-sighted people begin to know our best eyesight, when other people have lost theirs."

" Ah! ah! old rogue," repeated the insufferable Colonel, gnashing his ruined teeth at him, as if, for some incomprehensible reason, he wished to tear him to pieces and devour him. " I know you. You are taking the life away from me, villain! and I told you it was my inheritance. And I told you there was a

Bloody Footstep, bearing its track down through my race."

"I remember nothing of it," said the Doctor, in a quake, sure that the Colonel was in one of his mad fits. "And on the word of an honest man, I never wronged you in my life, Colonel."

"We shall see," said the Colonel, whose wrinkled visage grew absolutely terrible with its hardness; and his dull eyes, without losing their dulness, seemed to look through him.

"Listen to me, sir. Some ten years ago, there came to you a man on a secret business. He had an old musty bit of parchment, on which were written some words, hardly legible, in an antique hand, — an old deed, it might have been, — some family document, and here and there the letters were faded away. But this man had spent his life over it, and he had made out the meaning, and he interpreted it to you, and left it with you, only there was one gap, — one torn or obliterated place. Well, sir, — and he bade you, with your poor little skill at the mortar, and for a certain sum, — ample repayment for such a service, — to manufacture this medicine, — this cordial. It was an affair of months. And just when you thought it finished, the man came again, and stood over your cursed beverage, and shook a powder, or dropped a lump into it, or put in some ingredient, in which was all the hidden virtue, — or, at least, it drew out all the hidden virtue of the mean and common herbs, and married them into a wondrous efficacy. This done, the man bade you do certain other things with the potation, and went away " — the Colonel hesitated a moment — " and never came back again."

"Surely, Colonel, you are correct," said the apothe

cary ; much startled, however, at the Colonel's showing himself so well acquainted with an incident which
he had supposed a secret with himself alone. Yet he
had a little reluctance in owning it, although he did
not exactly understand why, since the Colonel had, apparently, no rightful claim to it, at all events.

"That medicine, that receipt," continued his visitor,
"is my hereditary property, and I challenge you, on
your peril, to give it up."

"But what if the original owner should call upon
me for it," objected Dr. Dolliver.

"I'll warrant you against that," said the Colonel ; and the apothecary thought there was something
ghastly in his look and tone. "Why, 't is ten year,
you old fool ; and do you think a man with a treasure like that in his possession would have waited so
long?"

"Seven years it was ago," said the apothecary.
"Septem annis passatis : so says the Latin."

"Curse your Latin," answers the Colonel. "Produce the stuff. You have been violating the first rule
of your trade, — taking your own drugs, — your own,
in one sense ; mine by the right of three hundred
years. Bring it forth, I say!"

"Pray excuse me, worthy Colonel," pleaded the
apothecary ; for though convinced that the old gentleman was only in one of his insane fits, when he talked
of the value of this concoction, yet he really did not
like to give up the cordial, which perhaps had wrought
him some benefit. Besides, he had at least a claim
upon it for much trouble and skill expended in its
composition. This he suggested to the Colonel, who
scornfully took out of his pocket a net-work purse,
with more golden guineas in it than the apothecary

had seen in the whole seven years, and was rude enough to fling it in his face. "Take that," thundered he, "and give up the thing, or I will have you in prison before you are an hour older. Nay," he continued, growing pale, which was his mode of showing terrible wrath; since all through life, till extreme age quenched it, his ordinary face had been a blazing red, "I 'll put you to death, you villain, as I 've a right!" And thrusting his hand into his waistcoat-pocket, lo! the madman took a small pistol from it, which he cocked, and presented at the poor apothecary. The old fellow quaked and cowered in his chair, and would indeed have given his whole shopful of better concocted medicines than this, to be out of this danger. Besides, there were the guineas; the Colonel had paid him a princely sum for what was probably worth nothing.

"Hold! hold!" cried he as the Colonel, with stern eye pointed the pistol at his head. "You shall have it."

So he rose all trembling, and crept to that secret cupboard, where the precious bottle — since precious it seemed to be — was reposited. In all his life, long as it had been, the apothecary had never before been threatened by a deadly weapon; though many as deadly a thing had he seen poured into a glass, without winking. And so it seemed to take his heart and life away, and he brought the cordial forth feebly, and stood tremulously before the Colonel, ashy pale, and looking ten years older than his real age, instead of five years younger, as he had seemed just before this disastrous interview with the Colonel.

"You look as if you needed a drop of it yourself," said Colonel Dabney, with great scorn. "But not a drop shall you have. Already have you stolen too much," said he, lifting up the bottle, and marking the space to which the liquor had subsided in it in consequence of the minute doses with which the apothecary had made free. "Fool, had you taken your glass like a man, you might have been young again. Now, creep on, the few months you have left, poor, torpid knave, and die! Come — a goblet! quick!"

He clutched the bottle meanwhile voraciously, miserly, eagerly, furiously, as if it were his life that he held in his grasp; angry, impatient, as if something long sought were within his reach, and not yet secure, — with longing thirst and desire; suspicious of the world and of fate; feeling as if an iron hand were over him, and a crowd of violent robbers round about him, struggling for it. At last, unable to wait longer, just as the apothecary was tottering away in quest of a drinking-glass, the Colonel took out the stopple, and lifted the flask itself to his lips.

"For Heaven's sake, no!" cried the Doctor. "The dose is one single drop! — one drop, Colonel, one drop!"

"Not a drop to save your wretched old soul," responded the Colonel; probably thinking that the apothecary was pleading for a small share of the precious liquor. He put it to his lips, and, as if quenching a lifelong thirst, swallowed deep draughts, sucking it in with desperation, till, void of breath, he set it down upon the table. The rich, poignant perfume spread itself through the air.

The apothecary, with an instinctive carefulness that was rather ludicrous under the circumstances, caught up the stopper, which the Colonel had let fall, and forced it into the bottle to prevent any farther escape of virtue. He then fearfully watched the result of the madman's potation.

The Colonel sat a moment in his chair, panting for breath; then started to his feet with a prompt vigor that contrasted widely with the infirm and rheumatic movements that had heretofore characterized him. He struck his forehead violently with one hand, and smote his chest with the other: he stamped his foot thunderously on the ground; then he leaped up to the ceiling, and came down with an elastic bound. Then he laughed, a wild, exulting ha! ha! with a strange triumphant roar that filled the house and reëchoed through it; a sound full of fierce, animal rapture, — enjoyment of sensual life mixed up with a sort of horror. After all, real as it was, it was like the sounds a man makes in a dream. And this, while the potent draught seemed still to be making its way through his system; and the frightened apothecary thought that he intended a revengeful onslaught upon himself. Finally, he uttered a loud unearthly screech, in the midst of which his voice broke, as if some unseen hand were throttling him, and, starting forward, he fought frantically, as if he would clutch the life that was being rent away, — and fell forward with a dead thump upon the floor.

" Colonel! Colonel! " cried the terrified Doctor.

The feeble old man, with difficulty, turned over the heavy frame, and saw at once, with practised eye, that he was dead. He set him up, and the corpse looked at him with angry reproach. He was so startled, that his subsequent recollections of the moment were neither distinct nor steadfast; but he fancied, though he told the strange impression to no one, that on his first glimpse of the face, wi'h a dark flush of what looked like rage still upon it, it was a young man's face that he saw, — a face with all the passionate energy of early manhood, — the capacity for furious anger which the man had lost half a century ago, crammed to the brim with vigor till it became agony. But the next moment, if it were so (which it could not have been), the face grew ashen, withered, shrunken, more aged than in life, though still the murderous fierceness remained, and seemed to be petrified forever upon it.

After a moment's bewilderment, Dolliver ran to the window looking to the street, threw it open, and called loudly for assistance. He opened also another window, for the air to blow through, for he was almost stifled with the rich odor of the cordial which filled the room, and was now exuded from the corpse.

He heard the voice of Pansie, crying at the door, which was locked, and, turning the key, he caught her in his arms, and hastened with her below stairs, to give her into the charge of Martha, who seemed half stupefied with a sense of something awful that had occurred.

Meanwhile there was a rattling and a banging at the street portal, to which several people had been attracted both by the Doctor's outcry from the window, and by the awful screech in which the Colonel's spirit (if, indeed, he had that divine part) had just previously taken its flight.

He let them in, and, pale and shivering, ushered them up to the death-chamber, where one or two, with a more delicate sense of smelling than the rest, snuffed the atmosphere, as if sensible of an unknown fragrance, yet appeared afraid to breathe, when they saw the terrific countenance leaning back against the chair. and eying them so truculently.

I would fain quit the scene and have done with the Colonel, who, I am glad, has happened to die at so early a period of the narrative. I therefore hasten to say that a coroner's inquest was held on the spot, though everybody felt that it was merely ceremonial, and that the testimony of their good and ancient townsman, Dr. Dolliver, was amply sufficient to settle the matter. The verdict was, " Death by the visitation of God."

The apothecary gave evidence that the Colonel, without asking leave, and positively against his advice, had drunk a quantity of distilled spirits; and one or two servants, or members of the Colonel's family, testified that he had been in a very uncomfortable state of mind for some days past, so that they fancied he was insane. Therefore nobody thought of blaming Dr. Dolliver for what had happened; and, if the plain truth must be told, everybody who saw the wretch was too well content to be rid of him, to trouble themselves more than was quite necessary about the way in which the incumbrance had been removed.

The corpse was taken to the mansion in order to receive a magnificent funeral; and Dr. Dolliver was left outwardly in quiet, but much disturbed, and indeed almost overwhelmed inwardly, by what had happened. Yet it is to be observed, that he had accounted for the death with a singular dexterity of expression, when he attributed it to a dose of distilled spirits. What kind of distilled spirits were those, Doctor? and will you venture to take any more of them?

FANSHAWE.

INTRODUCTORY NOTE.

FANSHAWE.

In 1828, three years after graduating from Bowdoin College, Hawthorne published his first romance, "Fanshawe." It was issued at Boston by Marsh & Capen, but made little or no impression on the public. The motto on the title-page of the original was from Southey: "Wilt thou go on with me?"

Afterwards, when he had struck into the vein of fiction that came to be known as distinctively his own, he attempted to suppress this youthful work, and was so successful that he obtained and destroyed all but a few of the copies then extant.

Some twelve years after his death it was resolved, in view of the interest manifested in tracing the growth of his genius from the beginning of his activity as an author, to revive this youthful romance; and the reissue of "Fanshawe" was then made.

Little biographical interest attaches to it, beyond the fact that Mr. Longfellow found in the descriptions and general atmosphere of the book a decided suggestion of the situation of Bowdoin College, at Brunswick, Maine, and the life there at the time when he and Hawthorne were both undergraduates of that institution.

Professor Packard, of Bowdoin College, who was

then in charge of the study of English literature, and has survived both of his illustrious pupils, recalls Hawthorne's exceptional excellence in the composition of English, even at that date (1821–1825) ; and it is not impossible that Hawthorne intended, through the character of Fanshawe, to present some faint projection of what he then thought might be his own obscure history. Even while he was in college, however, and meditating perhaps the slender elements of this first romance, his fellow-student Horatio Bridge, whose " Journal of an African Cruiser " he afterwards edited, recognized in him the possibilities of a writer of fiction — a fact to which Hawthorne alludes in the dedicatory Preface to " The Snow-Image."

G. P. L.

FANSHAWE.

CHAPTER I.

"Our court shall be a little Academe." — SHAKESPEARE.

IN an ancient though not very populous settlement, in a retired corner of one of the New England States, arise the walls of a seminary of learning, which, for the convenience of a name, shall be entitled "Harley College." This institution, though the number of its years is inconsiderable compared with the hoar antiquity of its European sisters, is not without some claims to reverence on the score of age; for an almost countless multitude of rivals, by many of which its reputation has been eclipsed, have sprung up since its foundation. At no time, indeed, during an existence of nearly a century, has it acquired a very extensive fame; and circumstances, which need not be particularized, have, of late years, involved it in a deeper obscurity. There are now few candidates for the degrees that the college is authorized to bestow. On two of its annual "Commencement Days," there has been a total deficiency of baccalaureates; and the lawyers and divines, on whom doctorates in their respective professions are gratuitously inflicted, are not accustomed to consider the distinction as an honor. Yet the sons of this seminary have always maintained their full share of reputation, in whatever paths of life they

trod. Few of them, perhaps, have been deep and
finished scholars; but the college has supplied — what
the emergencies of the country demanded — a set of
men more useful in its present state, and whose deficiency in theoretical knowledge has not been found
to imply a want of practical ability.

The local situation of the college, so far secluded
from the sight and sound of the busy world, is peculiarly favorable to the moral, if not to the literary,
habits of its students; and this advantage probably
caused the founders to overlook the inconveniences
that were inseparably connected with it. The humble edifices rear themselves almost at the farthest extremity of a narrow vale, which, winding through a
long extent of hill-country, is wellnigh as inaccessible,
except at one point, as the Happy Valley of Abyssinia.
A stream, that farther on becomes a considerable river,
takes its rise at a short distance above the college, and
affords, along its wood-fringed banks, many shady re-
treats, where even study is pleasant, and idleness delicious. The neighborhood of the institution is not
quite a solitude, though the few habitations scarcely
constitute a village. These consist principally of
farm-houses, of rather an ancient date (for the settlement is much older than the college), and of a little
inn, which even in that secluded spot does not fail of
a moderate support. Other dwellings are scattered
up and down the valley; but the difficulties of the soil
will long avert the evils of a too dense population.
The character of the inhabitants does not seem — as
there was, perhaps, room to anticipate — to be in any
degree influenced by the atmosphere of Harley College. They are a set of rough and hardy yeomen,
much inferior, as respects refinement, to the corre-

sponding classes in most other parts of our country. This is the more remarkable, as there is scarcely a family in the vicinity that has not provided, for at least one of its sons, the advantages of a " liberal education."

Having thus described the present state of Harley College, we must proceed to speak of it as it existed about eighty years since, when its foundation was recent, and its prospects flattering. At the head of the institution, at this period, was a learned and Orthodox divine, whose fame was in all the churches. He was the author of several works which evinced much erudition and depth of research; and the public, perhaps, thought the more highly of his abilities from a singularity in the purposes to which he applied them, that added much to the curiosity of his labors, though little to their usefulness. But, however fanciful might be his private pursuits, Dr. Melmoth, it was universally allowed, was diligent and successful in the arts of instruction. The young men of his charge prospered beneath his eye, and regarded him with an affection that was strengthened by the little foibles which occasionally excited their ridicule. The president was assisted in the discharge of his duties by two inferior officers, chosen from the alumni of the college, who, while they imparted to others the knowledge they had already imbibed, pursued the study of divinity under the direction of their principal. Under such auspices the institution grew and flourished. Having at that time but two rivals in the country (neither of them within a considerable distance), it became the general resort of the youth of the Province in which it was situated. For several years in succession, its students amounted to nearly fifty, — a number which, relatively to the circumstances of the country, was very considerable.

From the exterior of the collegians, an accurate observer might pretty safely judge how long they had been inmates of those classic walls. The brown cheeks and the rustic dress of some would inform him that they had but recently left the plough to labor in a not less toilsome field; the grave look, and the intermingling of garments of a more classic cut, would distinguish those who had begun to acquire the polish of their new residence; and the air of superiority, the paler cheek, the less robust form, the spectacles of green, and the dress, in general of threadbare black, would designate the highest class, who were understood to have acquired nearly all the science their Alma Mater could bestow, and to be on the point of assuming their stations in the world. There were, it is true, exceptions to this general description. A few young men had found their way hither from the distant seaports; and these were the models of fashion to their rustic companions, over whom they asserted a superiority in exterior accomplishments, which the fresh though unpolished intellect of the sons of the forest denied them in their literary competitions. A third class, differing widely from both the former, consisted of a few young descendants of the aborigines, to whom an impracticable philanthropy was endeavoring to impart the benefits of civilization.

If this institution did not offer all the advantages of elder and prouder seminaries, its deficiencies were compensated to its students by the inculcation of regular habits, and of a deep and awful sense of religion, which seldom deserted them in their course through life. The mild and gentle rule of Dr. Melmoth, like that of a father over his children, was more destructive to vice than a sterner sway; and though youth is never without its follies, they have seldom been more harmless than they were here. The students, indeed, ignorant of their own bliss, sometimes wished to hasten the time of their entrance on the business of life; but they found, in after-years, that many of their happiest remembrances, many of the scenes which they would with least reluctance live over again, referred to the seat of their early studies. The exceptions to this remark were chiefly those whose vices had drawn down, even from that paternal government, a weighty retribution.

Dr. Melmoth, at the time when he is to be introduced to the reader, had borne the matrimonial yoke (and in his case it was no light burden) nearly twenty years. The blessing of children, however, had been denied him, — a circumstance which he was accustomed to consider as one of the sorest trials that checkered his pathway; for he was a man of a kind and affectionate heart, that was continually seeking objects to rest itself upon. He was inclined to believe, also, that a common offspring would have exerted a meliorating influence on the temper of Mrs. Melmoth, the character of whose domestic government often compelled him to call to mind such portions of the wisdom of antiquity as relate to the proper endurance of the shrewishness of woman. But domestic comforts, as well as comforts of every other kind, have their drawbacks; and, so long as the balance is on the side of happiness, a wise man will not murmur. Such was the opinion of Dr. Melmoth; and with a little aid from philosophy, and more from religion, he journeyed on contentedly through life. When the storm was loud by the parlor hearth, he had always a sure and quiet retreat in his study; and there, in his deep though not always useful labors, he soon forgot whatever of disagreeable nature pertained to his situation. This small and dark apartment was the only portion of the house to which, since one firmly repelled invasion, Mrs. Melmoth's omnipotence did not extend. Here (to reverse the words of Queen Elizabeth) there was "but one master and no mistress"; and that man has little right to complain who possesses so much as one corner in the world where he may be happy or miserable, as best suits him. In his study, then, the doctor was accustomed to spend most of the hours that were unoccupied by the duties of his station. The flight of time was here as swift as the wind, and noiseless as the snow-flake; and it was a sure proof of real happiness that night often came upon the student before he knew it was midday.

Dr. Melmoth was wearing towards age (having lived nearly sixty years), when he was called upon to assume a character to which he had as yet been a stranger. He had possessed in his youth a very dear friend, with whom his education had associated him, and who in his early manhood had been his chief intimate. Circumstances, however, had separated them for nearly thirty years, half of which had been spent by his friend, who was engaged in mercantile pursuits, in a foreign country. The doctor had, nevertheless, retained a warm interest in the welfare of his old associate, though the different nature of their thoughts and occupations had prevented them from corresponding. After a silence of so long continuance, therefore, he was surprised by the receipt of a letter from his friend, containing a request of a most unexpected nature.

Mr. Langton had married rather late in life; and his wedded bliss had been but of short continuance. Certain misfortunes in trade, when he was a Benedict of three years' standing, had deprived him of a large portion of his property, and compelled him, in order to save the remainder, to leave his own country for what he hoped would be but a brief residence in another. But, though he was successful in the immediate objects of his voyage, circumstances occurred to lengthen his stay far beyond the period which he had assigned to it. It was difficult so to arrange his extensive concerns that they could be safely trusted to the management of others; and, when this was effected, there was another not less powerful obstacle to his return. His affairs, under his own inspection, were so prosperous, and his gains so considerable, that, in the words of the old ballad, "He set his heart to gather gold"; and to this absorbing passion he sacrificed his domestic happiness. The death of his wife, about four years after his departure, undoubtedly contributed to give him a sort of dread of returning, which it required a strong effort to overcome. The welfare of his only child he knew would be little affected by this event; for she was under the protection of his sister, of whose tenderness he was well assured. But, after a few more years, this sister, also, was taken away by death; and then the father felt that duty imperatively called upon him to return. He realized, on a sudden, how much of life he had thrown away in the acquisition of what is only valuable as it contributes to the happiness of life, and how short a time was left him for life's true enjoyments. Still, however, his mercantile habits were too deeply seated to allow him to hazard his present prosperity by any hasty measures; nor was Mr. Langton, though capable of strong affections, naturally liable to manifest them violently. It was probable, therefore, that many months might yet elapse before he would again tread the shores of his native country.

But the distant relative, in whose family, since the death of her aunt, Ellen Langton had remained, had been long at variance with her father, and had unwillingly assumed the office of her protector. Mr. Langton's request, therefore, to Dr. Melmoth, was, that his ancient friend (one of the few friends that time had left him) would be as a father to his daughter till he could himself relieve him of the charge.

The doctor, after perusing the epistle of his friend, lost no time in laying it before Mrs. Melmoth, though this was, in truth, one of the very few occasions on which he had determined that his will should be absolute law. The lady was quick to perceive the firmness of his purpose, and would not (even had she been particularly averse to the proposed measure) hazard her usual authority by a fruitless opposition. But, by long disuse, she had lost the power of consenting graciously to any wish of her husband's.

"I see your heart is set upon this matter," she observed; "and, in truth, I fear we cannot decently refuse Mr. Langton's request. I see little good of such a friend, doctor, who never lets one know he is alive till he has a favor to ask."

"Nay; but I have received much good at his hand," replied Dr. Melmoth; "and, if he asked more of me, it should be done with a willing heart. I remember in my youth, when my worldly goods were few and ill managed (I was a bachelor, then, dearest Sarah, with none to look after my household), how many times I

have been beholden to him. And see — in his letter
he speaks of presents, of the produce of the country,
which he has sent both to you and me."

" If the girl were country-bred," continued the lady,
" we might give her house-room, and no harm done.
Nay, she might even be a help to me ; for Esther, our
maid-servant, leaves us at the month's end. But I
warrant she knows as little of household matters as
you do yourself, doctor."

" My friend's sister was well grounded in the *re
familiari*," answered her husband ; " and doubtless
she hath imparted somewhat of her skill to this damsel. Besides, the child is of tender years, and will
profit much by your instruction and mine."

"The child is eighteen years of age, doctor," observed Mrs. Melmoth, " and she has cause to be thankful that she will have better instruction than yours."

This was a proposition that Dr. Melmoth did not
choose to dispute ; though he perhaps thought that his
long and successful experience in the education of the
other sex might make him an able coadjutor to his wife
in the care of Ellen Langton. He determined to journey in person to the seaport where his young charge
resided, leaving the concerns of Harley College to the
direction of the two tutors. Mrs. Melmoth, who, indeed, anticipated with pleasure the arrival of a new
subject to her authority, threw no difficulties in the
way of his intention. To do her justice, her preparations for his journey, and the minute instructions with
which she favored him, were such as only a woman's
true affection could have suggested. The traveller
met with no incidents important to this tale ; and,
after an absence of about a fortnight, he and Ellen
Langton alighted from their steeds (for on horseback

had the journey been performed) in safety at his own door.

If pen could give an adequate idea of Ellen Langton's loveliness, it would achieve what pencil (the pencils, at least, of the colonial artists who attempted it) never could; for, though the dark eyes might be painted, the pure and pleasant thoughts that peeped through them could only be seen and felt. But descriptions of beauty are never satisfactory. It must, therefore, be left to the imagination of the reader to conceive of something not more than mortal, nor, indeed, quite the perfection of mortality, but charming men the more, because they felt, that, lovely as she was, she was of like nature to themselves.

From the time that Ellen entered Dr. Melmoth's habitation, the sunny days seemed brighter and the cloudy ones less gloomy, than he had ever before known them. He naturally delighted in children; and Ellen, though her years approached to womanhood, had yet much of the gayety and simple happiness, because the innocence, of a child. She consequently became the very blessing of his life, — the rich recreation that he promised himself for hours of literary toil. On one occasion, indeed, he even made her his companion in the sacred retreat of his study, with the purpose of entering upon a course of instruction in the learned languages. This measure, however, he found inexpedient to repeat; for Ellen, having discovered an old romance among his heavy folios, contrived, by the charm of her sweet voice, to engage his attention therein till all more important concerns were forgotten.

With Mrs. Melmoth, Ellen was not, of course, so great a favorite as with her husband; for women cannot, so readily as men, bestow upon the offspring of others those affections that nature intended for their own ; and the doctor's extraordinary partiality was anything rather than a pledge of his wife's. But Ellen differed so far from the idea she had previously formed of her, as a daughter of one of the principal merchants, who were then, as now, like nobles in the land, that the stock of dislike which Mrs. Melmoth had provided was found to be totally inapplicable. The young stranger strove so hard, too (and undoubtedly it was a pleasant labor), to win her love, that she was successful to a degree of which the lady herself was not, perhaps, aware. It was soon seen that her education had not been neglected in those points which Mrs. Melmoth deemed most important. The nicer departments of cookery, after sufficient proof of her skill, were committed to her care ; and the doctor's table was now covered with delicacies, simple indeed, but as tempting on account of their intrinsic excellence as of the small white hands that made them. By such arts as these, — which in her were no arts, but the dictates of an affectionate disposition, — by making herself useful where it was possible, and agreeable on all occasions, Ellen gained the love of everyone within the sphere of her influence.

But the maiden's conquests were not confined to the members of Dr. Melmoth's family. She had numerous admirers among those whose situation compelled them to stand afar off, and gaze upon her loveliness, as if she were a star, whose brightness they saw, but whose warmth they could not feel. These were the young men of Harley College, whose chief opportunities of beholding Ellen were upon the Sabbaths, when she worshipped with them in the little chapel, which ȷerved the purposes of a church to all the families of the vicinity. There was, about this period (and the fact was undoubtedly attributable to Ellen's influence,) a general and very evident decline in the scholarship of the college, especially in regard to the severer studies. The intellectual powers of the young men seemed to be directed chiefly to the construction of Latin and Greek verse, many copies of which, with a characteristic and classic gallantry, were strewn in the path where Ellen Langton was accustomed to walk. They, however, produced no perceptible effect; nor were the aspirations of another ambitious youth, who celebrated her perfections in Hebrew, attended with their merited success.

But there was one young man, to whom circumstances, independent of his personal advantages, afforded a superior opportunity of gaining Ellen's favor. He was nearly related to Dr. Melmoth, on which account he received his education at Harley College, rather than at one of the English universities, to the expenses of which his fortune would have been adequate. This connection entitled him to a frequent and familiar access to the domestic hearth of the dignitary, — an advantage of which, since Ellen Langton became a member of the family, he very constantly availed himself.

Edward Walcott was certainly much superior, in most of the particulars of which a lady takes cognizance, to those of his fellow-students who had come under Ellen's notice. He was tall; and the natural grace of his manners had been improved (an advantage which few of his associates could boast) by early intercourse with polished society. His features, also, were handsome, and promised to be manly and dignified when they should cease to be youthful. His character as a scholar was more than respectable, though many youthful follies, sometimes, perhaps, approaching near to vices, were laid to his charge. But his occasional derelictions from discipline were not such as to create any very serious apprehensions respecting his future welfare; nor were they greater than, perhaps, might be expected from a young man who possessed a considerable command of money, and who was, besides, the fine gentleman of the little community of which he was a member, — a character which generally leads its possessor into follies that he would otherwise have avoided.

With this youth Ellen Langton became familiar, and even intimate; for he was her only companion, of an age suited to her own, and the difference of sex did not occur to her as an objection. He was her constant companion on all necessary and allowable occasions, and drew upon himself, in consequence, the envy of the college.

CHAPTER II.

"Why, all delights are vain, but that most vain,
  Which, with pain purchased, doth inherit pain:
  As painfully to pore upon a book
    To seek the light of truth, while truth, the while,
    Doth falsely blind the eyesight of his look."

SHAKESPEARE.

ON one of the afternoons which afforded to the students a relaxation from their usual labors, Ellen was attended by her cavalier in a little excursion over the rough bridle-roads that led from her new residence. She was an experienced equestrian, — a necessary accomplishment at that period, when vehicles of every kind were rare. It was now the latter end of spring; but the season had hitherto been backward, with only a few warm and pleasant days. The present afternoon, however, was a delicious mingling of spring and summer, forming in their union an atmosphere so mild and pure, that to breathe was almost a positive happiness. There was a little alternation of cloud across the brow of heaven, but only so much as to render the sunshine more delightful.

The path of the young travellers lay sometimes among tall and thick standing trees, and sometimes over naked and desolate hills, whence man had taken the natural vegetation, and then left the soil to its barrenness. Indeed, there is little inducement to a cultivator to labor among the huge stones which there peep forth from the earth, seeming to form a continued ledge for several miles. A singular contrast to this unfavored tract of country is seen in the narrow but luxuriant, though sometimes swampy, strip of interval, on both sides of the stream, that, as has been noticed, flows down the valley. The light and buoyant spirits of Edward Walcott and Ellen rose higher as they rode on; and their way was enlivened, wherever its roughness did not forbid, by their conversation and pleasant laughter. But at length Ellen drew her bridle, as they emerged from a thick portion of the forest, just at the foot of a steep hill.

"We must have ridden far," she observed, — "farther than I thought. It will be near sunset before we can reach home."

"There are still several hours of daylight," replied Edward Walcott; "and we will not turn back without ascending this hill. The prospect from the summit is beautiful, and will be particularly so now, in this rich sunlight. Come, Ellen, — one light touch of the whip, — your pony is as fresh as when we started."

On reaching the summit of the hill, and looking back in the direction in which they had come, they could see the little stream, peeping forth many times to the daylight, and then shrinking back into the shade. Farther on, it became broad and deep, though rendered incapable of navigation, in this part of its course, by the occasional interruption of rapids.

"There are hidden wonders of rock and precipice and cave, in that dark forest," said Edward, pointing to the space between them and the river. "If it were earlier in the day, I should love to lead you there. Shall we try the adventure now, Ellen?"

"Oh no!" she replied. "Let us delay no longer. I fear I must even now abide a rebuke from Mrs. Melmoth, which I have surely deserved. But who is this, who rides on so slowly before us?"

She pointed to a horseman, whom they had not before observed. He was descending the hill; but, as his steed seemed to have chosen his own pace, he made a very inconsiderable progress.

"Oh, do you not know him? But it is scarcely possible you should," exclaimed her companion. "We must do him the good office, Ellen, of stopping his progress, or he will find himself at the village, a dozen miles farther on, before he resumes his consciousness."

"Has he then lost his senses?" inquired Miss Langton.

"Not so, Ellen, — if much learning has not made him mad," replied Edward Walcott. "He is a deep scholar and a noble fellow; but I fear we shall follow him to his grave erelong. Dr. Melmoth has sent him to ride in pursuit of his health. He will never overtake it, however, at this pace."

As he spoke, they had approached close to the subject of their conversation; and Ellen had a moment's space for observation before he started from the abstraction in which he was plunged. The result of her scrutiny was favorable, yet very painful.

The stranger could scarcely have attained his twentieth year, and was possessed of a face and form such as Nature bestows on none but her favorites. There was a nobleness on his high forehead, which time would have deepened into majesty; and all his features were formed with a strength and boldness, of which the paleness, produced by study and confinement, could not deprive them. The expression of his countenance was not a melancholy one: on the contrary, it was proud and high, perhaps triumphant, like one who was a ruler in a world of his own, and independent of the beings that surrounded him. But a blight, of which his thin pale cheek, and the brightness of his eye, were alike proofs, seemed to have come over him ere his maturity.

The scholar's attention was now aroused by the hoof-tramps at his side; and, starting, he fixed his eyes on Ellen, whose young and lovely countenance was full of the interest he had excited. A deep blush immediately suffused his cheek, proving how well the glow of health would have become it. There was nothing awkward, however, in his manner; and, soon recovering his self-possession, he bowed to her, and would have ridden on.

"Your ride is unusually long to-day, Fanshawe," observed Edward Walcott. "When may we look for your return?"

The young man again blushed, but answered, with a smile that had a beautiful effect upon his countenance, "I was not, at the moment, aware in which direction my horse's head was turned. I have to thank you for arresting me in a journey which was likely to prove much longer than I intended."

The party had now turned their horses, and were about to resume their ride in a homeward direction; but Edward perceived that Fanshawe, having lost the excitement of intense thought, now looked weary and dispirited.

"Here is a cottage close at hand," he observed. "We have ridden far, and stand in need of refreshment. Ellen, shall we alight?"

She saw the benevolent motive of his proposal, and did not hesitate to comply with it. But, as they paused at the cottage door, she could not but observe that its exterior promised few of the comforts which they required. Time and neglect seemed to have conspired for its ruin ; and, but for a thin curl of smoke from its clay chimney, they could not have believed it to be inhabited. A considerable tract of land in the vicinity of the cottage had evidently been, at some former period, under cultivation, but was now overrun by bushes and dwarf pines, among which many huge gray rocks, ineradicable by human art, endeavored to conceal themselves. About half an acre of ground was occupied by the young blades of Indian-corn, at which a half-starved cow gazed wistfully over the mouldering log-fence. These were the only agricultural tokens. Edward Walcott, nevertheless, drew the latch of the cottage door, after knocking loudly but in vain.

The apartment which was thus opened to their view was quite as wretched as its exterior had given them reason to anticipate. Poverty was there, with all its necessary and unnecessary concomitants. The intruders would have retired had not the hope of affording relief detained them.

The occupants of the small and squalid apartment were two women, both of them elderly, and, from the resemblance of their features, appearing to be sisters. The expression of their countenances, however, was very different. One, evidently the younger, was seated on the farther side of the large hearth, opposite to the door at which the party stood. She had the sallow look of long and wasting illness; and there was an unsteadiness of expression about her eyes, that immediately struck the observer. Yet her face was mild and gentle, therein contrasting widely with that of her companion.

The other woman was bending over a small fire of decayed branches, the flame of which was very disproportionate to the smoke, scarcely producing heat sufficient for the preparation of a scanty portion of food. Her profile only was visible to the strangers, though, from a slight motion of her eye, they perceived that she was aware of their presence. Her features were pinched and spare, and wore a look of sullen discontent, for which the evident wretchedness of her situation afforded a sufficient reason. This female, not-withstanding her years, and the habitual fretfulness (that is more wearing than time), was apparently healthy and robust, with a dry, leathery complexion. A short space elapsed before she thought proper to turn her face towards her visitors; and she then regarded them with a lowering eye, without speaking, or rising from her chair.

"We entered," Edward Walcott began to say, "in the hope"— But he paused, on perceiving that the sick woman had risen from her seat, and with slow and tottering footsteps was drawing near to him. She took his hand in both her own; and, though he shud-dered at the touch of age and disease, he did not attempt to withdraw it. She then perused all his features, with an expression, at first of eager and hopeful anxiety, which faded by degrees into disappointment. Then, turning from him, she gazed into Fanshawe's countenance with the like eagerness, but with the same result. Lastly, tottering back to her chair, she hid her face and wept bitterly. The strangers, though they knew not the cause of her grief, were deeply affected; and Ellen approached the mourner with words of comfort, which, more from their tone than their meaning, produced a transient effect.

"Do you bring news of him?" she inquired, raising her head. "Will he return to me? Shall I see him before I die?" Ellen knew not what to answer; and,

ere she could attempt it, the other female prevented
her.

" Sister Butler is wandering in her mind," she said,
" and speaks of one she will never behold again. The
sight of strangers disturbs her, and you see we have
nothing here to offer you."

The manner of the woman was ungracious; but her
words were true. They saw that their presence could
do nothing towards the alleviation of the misery they
witnessed; and they felt that mere curiosity would not
authorize a longer intrusion. So soon, therefore, as
they had relieved, according to their power, the poverty that seemed to be the least evil of this cottage,
they emerged into the open air.

The breath of heaven felt sweet to them, and removed a part of the weight from their young hearts,
which were saddened by the sight of so much wretchedness. Perceiving a pure and bright little fountain
at a short distance from the cottage, they approached
it, and, using the bark of a birch-tree as a cup, partook of its cool waters. They then pursued their
homeward ride with such diligence, that, just as the
sun was setting, they came in sight of the humble
wooden edifice which was dignified with the name of
Harley College. A golden ray rested upon the spire
of the little chapel, the bell of which sent its tinkling
murmur down the valley to summon the wanderers to
evening prayers.

Fanshawe returned to his chamber that night, and
lighted his lamp as he had been wont to do. The
books were around him which had hitherto been to
him like those fabled volumes of Magic, from which
the reader could not turn away his eye till death were
the consequence of his studies. But there were unac-

customed thoughts in his bosom now; and to these, leaning his head on one of the unopened volumes, he resigned himself.

He called up in review the years, that, even at his early age, he had spent in solitary study, in conversation with the dead, while he had scorned to mingle with the living world, or to be actuated by any of its motives. He asked himself to what purpose was all this destructive labor, and where was the happiness of superior knowledge. He had climbed but a few steps of a ladder that reached to infinity: he had thrown away his life in discovering, that, after a thousand such lives, he should still know comparatively nothing. He even looked forward with dread — though once the thought had been dear to him — to the eternity of improvement that lay before him. It seemed now a weary way, without a resting-place and without a termination; and at that moment he would have preferred the dreamless sleep of the brutes that perish to man's proudest attribute, — of immortality.

Fanshawe had hitherto deemed himself unconnected with the world, unconcerned in its feelings, and uninfluenced by it in any of his pursuits. In this respect he probably deceived himself. If his inmost heart could have been laid open, there would have been discovered that dream of undying fame, which, dream as it is, is more powerful than a thousand realities. But, at any rate, he had seemed, to others and to himself, a solitary being, upon whom the hopes and fears of ordinary men were ineffectual.

But now he felt the first thrilling of one of the many ties, that, so long as we breathe the common air, (and who shall say how much longer?) unite us to our kind. The sound of a soft, sweet voice, the glance of

a gentle eye, had wrought a change upon him ; and in
his ardent mind a few hours had done the work of
many.   Almost in spite of himself, the new sensation
was inexpressibly delightful.   The recollection of his
ruined health, of his habits (so much at variance with
those of the world), — all the difficulties that reason
suggested, were inadequate to check the exulting tide
of hope and joy.

CHAPTER III.

' And let the aspiring youth beware of love, —
Of the smooth glance beware ; for 't is too late
When on his heart the torrent softness pours ;
Then wisdom prostrate lies, and fading fame
Dissolves in air away."   THOMSON.

A FEW months passed over the heads of Ellen
Langton and her admirers, unproductive of events,
that, separately, were of sufficient importance to be
related. The summer was now drawing to a close ;
and Dr. Melmoth had received information that his
friend's arrangements were nearly completed, and that
by the next home-bound ship he hoped to return to his
native country. The arrival of that ship was daily
expected.

During the time that had elapsed since his first
meeting with Ellen, there had been a change, yet not
a very remarkable one, in Fanshawe's habits. He
was still the same solitary being, so far as regarded
his own sex ; and he still confined himself as sedulously to his chamber, except for one hour — the sunset hour — of every day. At that period, unless prevented by the inclemency of the weather, he was accustomed to tread a path that wound along the banks
of the stream. He had discovered that this was the
most frequent scene of Ellen's walks ; and this it was
that drew him thither.

Their intercourse was at first extremely slight, — a
bow on the one side, a smile on the other, and a passing word from both ; and then the student hurried

back to his solitude. But, in course of time, opportunities occurred for more extended conversation; so
that, at the period with which this chapter is con
cerned, Fanshawe was, almost as constantly as Edward
Walcott himself, the companion of Ellen's walks.

His passion had strengthened more than proportionably to the time that had elapsed since it was conceived; but the first glow and excitement which attended it had now vanished. He had reasoned calmly
with himself, and rendered evident to his own mind
the almost utter hopelessness of success. He had also
made his resolution strong, that he would not even en-
deavor to win Ellen's love, the result of which, for a
thousand reasons, could not be happiness. Firm in
this determination, and confident of his power to adhere to it; feeling, also, that time and absence could
not cure his own passion, and having no desire for
such a cure, — he saw no reason for breaking off the
intercourse that was established between Ellen and
himself. It was remarkable, that, notwithstanding
the desperate nature of his love, that, or something
connected with it, seemed to have a beneficial effect
upon his health. There was now a slight tinge of
color in his cheek, and a less consuming brightness in
his eye. Could it be that hope, unknown to himself,
was yet alive in his breast; that a sense of the possibility of earthly happiness was redeeming him from
the grave?

Had the character of Ellen Langton's mind been
different, there might, perhaps, have been danger to
her from an intercourse of this nature with such a being as Fanshawe; for he was distinguished by many
of those asperities around which a woman's affection
will often cling. But she was formed to walk in the

calm and quiet paths of life, and to pluck the flowers of happiness from the wayside where they grow. Singularity of character, therefore, was not calculated to win her love. She undoubtedly felt an interest in the solitary student, and perceiving, with no great exercise of vanity, that her society drew him from the destructive intensity of his studies, she perhaps felt it a duty to exert her influence. But it did not occur to her that her influence had been sufficiently strong to change the whole current of his thoughts and feelings.

Ellen and her two lovers (for both, though perhaps not equally, deserved that epithet) had met, as usual, at the close of a sweet summer day, and were standing by the side of the stream, just where it swept into a deep pool. The current, undermining the bank, had formed a recess, which, according to Edward Walcott, afforded at that moment a hiding-place to a trout of noble size.

"Now would I give the world," he exclaimed with great interest, "for a hook and line, a fish-spear, or any piscatorial instrument of death! Look, Ellen, you can see the waving of his tail from beneath the bank!"

"If you had the means of taking him, I should save him from your cruelty, thus," said Ellen, dropping a pebble into the water, just over the fish. "There! he has darted down the stream. How many pleasant caves and recesses there must be under these banks, where he may be happy! May there not be happiness in the life of a fish?" she added, turning with a smile to Fanshawe.

"There may," he replied, "so long as he lives quietly in the caves and recesses of which you speak,

Yes, there may be happiness, though such as few would envy; but, then, the hook and line "—

" Which, there is reason to apprehend, will shortly destroy the happiness of our friend the trout," interrupted Edward, pointing down the stream. " There is an angler on his way toward us, who will intercept him."

" He seems to care little for the sport, to judge by the pace at which he walks," said Ellen.

" But he sees, now, that we are observing him, and is willing to prove that he knows something of the art," replied Edward Walcott. " I should think him well acquainted with the stream; for, hastily as he walks, he has tried every pool and ripple where a fish usually hides. But that point will be decided when he reaches yonder old bare oak-tree."

" And how is the old tree to decide the question?" inquired Fanshawe. " It is a species of evidence of which I have never before heard."

" The stream has worn a hollow under its roots," answered Edward, — " a most delicate retreat for a trout. Now, a stranger would not discover the spot; or, if he did, the probable result of a cast would be the loss of hook and line, — an accident that has occurred to me more than once. If, therefore, this angler takes a fish from thence, it follows that he knows the stream."

They observed the fisher, accordingly, as he kept his way up the bank. He did not pause when he reached the old leafless oak, that formed with its roots an obstruction very common in American streams; but, throwing his line with involuntary skill as he passed, he not only escaped the various entanglements. but drew forth a fine large fish.

"There, Ellen, he has captivated your *protégé*, the trout, or, at least, one very like him in size," observed Edward. "It is singular," he added, gazing earnestly at the man.

"Why is it singular?" inquired Ellen Langton. "This person, perhaps, resides in the neighborhood, and may have fished often in the stream."

"Do but look at him, Ellen, and judge whether his life can have been spent in this lonely valley," he replied. "The glow of many a hotter sun than ours has darkened his brow; and his step and air have something foreign in them, like what we see in sailors who have lived more in other countries than in their own. Is it not so, Ellen? for your education in a seaport must have given you skill in these matters. But come, let us approach nearer."

They walked towards the angler, accordingly, who still remained under the oak, apparently engaged in arranging his fishing-tackle. As the party drew nigh, he raised his head, and threw one quick, scrutinizing glance towards them, disclosing, on his part, a set of bold and rather coarse features, weather-beaten, but indicating the age of the owner to be not above thirty. In person he surpassed the middle size, was well set, and evidently strong and active.

"Do you meet with much success, sir?" inquired Edward Walcott, when within a convenient distance for conversation.

"I have taken but one fish," replied the angler, in an accent which his hearers could scarcely determine to be foreign, or the contrary. "I am a stranger to the stream, and have doubtless passed over many a likely place for sport."

"You have an angler's eye, sir," rejoined Edward.

"I observed that you made your casts as if you had often trod these banks, and I could scarcely have guided you better myself."

"Yes, I have learned the art, and I love to practise it," replied the man. "But will not the young lady try her skill?" he continued, casting a bold eye on Ellen. "The fish will love to be drawn out by such white hands as those."

Ellen shrank back, though almost imperceptibly, from the free bearing of the man. It seemed meant for courtesy; but its effect was excessively disagreeable. Edward Walcott, who perceived and coincided in Ellen's feelings, replied to the stranger's proposal.

"The young lady will not put the gallantry of the fish to the proof, sir," he said, "and she will therefore have no occasion for your own."

"I shall take leave to hear my answer from the young lady's own mouth," answered the stranger, haughtily. "If you will step this way, Miss Langton" (here he interrupted himself), — "if you will cast the line by yonder sunken log, I think you will meet with success."

Thus saying, the angler offered his rod and line to Ellen. She at first drew back, then hesitated, but finally held out her hand to receive them. In thus complying with the stranger's request, she was actuated by a desire to keep the peace, which, as her notice of Edward Walcott's crimsoned cheek and flashing eye assured her, was considerably endangered. The angler led the way to the spot which he had pointed out, which, though not at such a distance from Ellen's companions but that words in a common tone could be distinguished, was out of the range of a lowered voice.

Edward Walcott and the student remained by the oak : the former biting his lip with vexation ; the latter, whose abstraction always vanished where Ellen was concerned, regarding her and the stranger with fixed and silent attention. The young men could at first hear the words that the angler addressed to Ellen. They related to the mode of managing the rod ; and she made one or two casts under his direction. At length, however, as if to offer his assistance, the man advanced close to her side, and seemed to speak, but in so low a tone, that the sense of what he uttered was lost before it reached the oak. But its effect upon Ellen was immediate and very obvious. Her eyes flashed ; and an indignant blush rose high on her cheek, giving to her beauty a haughty brightness, of which the gentleness of her disposition in general deprived it. The next moment, however, she seemed to recollect herself, and, restoring the angling-rod to its owner, she turned away calmly, and approached her companions.

" The evening breeze grows chill ; and mine is a dress for a summer day," she observed. " Let us walk homeward."

" Miss Langton, is it the evening breeze alone that sends you homeward ? " inquired Edward.

At this moment the angler, who had resumed, and seemed to be intent upon his occupation, drew a fish from the pool, which he had pointed out to Ellen.

" I told the young lady," he exclaimed, " that, if she would listen to me a moment longer, she would be repaid for her trouble; and here is the proof of my words."

" Come, let us hasten towards home," cried Ellen, eagerly ; and she took Edward Walcott's arm, with a freedom that, at another time, would have enchanted him. He at first seemed inclined to resist her wishes, but complied, after exchanging, unperceived by Ellen, a glance with the stranger, the meaning of which the latter appeared perfectly to understand. Fanshawe also attended her. Their walk towards Dr. Melmoth's dwelling was almost a silent one; and the few words that passed between them did not relate to the adventure which occupied the thoughts of each. On arriving at the house, Ellen's attendants took leave of her, and retired.

Edward Walcott, eluding Fanshawe's observation with little difficulty, hastened back to the old oak-tree. From the intelligence with which the stranger had received his meaning glance, the young man had supposed that he would here await his return. But the banks of the stream, upward and downward, so far as his eye could reach, were solitary. He could see only his own image in the water, where it swept into a silent depth; and could hear only its ripple, where stones and sunken trees impeded its course. The object of his search might, indeed, have found concealment among the tufts of alders, or in the forest that was near at hand; but thither it was in vain to pursue him. The angler had apparently set little store by the fruits of his assumed occupation; for the last fish that he had taken lay, yet alive, on the bank, gasping for the element to which Edward was sufficiently compassionate to restore him. After watching him as he glided down the stream, making feeble efforts to resist its current, the youth turned away, and sauntered slowly towards the college.

Ellen Langton, on her return from her walk, found Dr. Melmoth's little parlor unoccupied; that gentleman being deeply engaged in his study, and his lady busied in her domestic affairs. The evening, notwithstanding Ellen's remark concerning the chillness of the breeze, was almost sultry ; and the windows of the apartment were thrown open. At one of these, which looked into the garden, she seated herself, listening, almost unconsciously, to the monotonous music of a thousand insects, varied occasionally by the voice of a whippoorwill, who, as the day departed, was just commencing his song. A dusky tint, as yet almost imperceptible, was beginning to settle on the surrounding objects, except where they were opposed to the purple and golden clouds, which the vanished sun had made the brief inheritors of a portion of his brightness. In these gorgeous vapors, Ellen's fancy, in the interval of other thoughts, pictured a fairy-land, and longed for wings to visit it.

But as the clouds lost their brilliancy, and assumed first a dull purple, and then a sullen gray tint, Ellen's thoughts recurred to the adventure of the angler, which her imagination was inclined to invest with an undue singularity. It was, however, sufficiently unaccountable that an entire stranger should venture to demand of her a private audience ; and she assigned, in turn, a thousand motives for such a request, none of which were in any degree satisfactory. Her most prevailing thought, though she could not justify it to her reason, inclined her to believe that the angler was a messenger from her father. But wherefore he should deem it necessary to communicate any intelligence that he might possess only by means of a private interview, and without the knowledge of her friends, was a mystery she could not solve. In this view of the matter, however, she half regretted that her instinctive delicacy had impelled her so suddenly to break off their conference, admitting, in the secrecy of her own mind, that, if an opportunity were again to occur, it might not again be shunned. As if that unuttered thought had power to conjure up its object, she now became aware of a form standing in the garden, at a short distance from the window where she sat. The dusk had deepened, during Ellen's abstraction, to such a degree, that the man's features were not perfectly distinguishable; but the maiden was not long in doubt of his identity, for he approached, and spoke in the same low tone in which he had addressed her when they stood by the stream.

"Do you still refuse my request, when its object is but your own good, and that of one who should be most dear to you?" he asked.

Ellen's first impulse had been to cry out for assistance; her second was to fly: but, rejecting both these measures, she determined to remain, endeavoring to persuade herself that she was safe. The quivering of her voice, however, when she attempted to reply, betrayed her apprehensions.

"I cannot listen to such a request from a stranger," she said. "If you bring news from — from my father, why is it not told to Dr. Melmoth?"

"Because what I have to say is for your ear alone," was the reply; "and if you would avoid misfortune now, and sorrow hereafter, you will not refuse to hear me."

"And does it concern my father?" asked Ellen, eagerly.

"It does — most deeply," answered the stranger.

She meditated a moment, and then replied, "I will not refuse, I will hear — but speak quickly."

"We are in danger of interruption in this place, and that would be fatal to my errand," said the stranger. "I will await you in the garden."

With these words, and giving her no opportunity for reply, he drew back ; and his form faded from her eyes. This precipitate retreat from argument was the most probable method that he could have adopted of gaining his end. He had awakened the strongest interest in Ellen's mind ; and he calculated justly in supposing that she would consent to an interview upon his own terms.

Dr. Melmoth had followed his own fancies in the mode of laying out his garden ; and, in consequence, the plan that had undoubtedly existed in his mind was utterly incomprehensible to every one but himself. It was an intermixture of kitchen and flower garden, a labyrinth of winding paths, bordered by hedges, and impeded by shrubbery. Many of the original trees of the forest were still flourishing among the exotics which the doctor had transplanted thither. It was not without a sensation of fear, stronger than she had ever before experienced, that Ellen Langton found herself in this artificial wilderness, and in the presence of the mysterious stranger. The dusky light deepened the lines of his dark, strong features ; and Ellen fancied that his countenance wore a wilder and a fiercer look than when she had met him by the stream. He perceived her agitation, and addressed her in the softest tones of which his voice was capable.

"Compose yourself," he said ; "you have nothing to fear from me. But we are in open view from the house, where we now stand ; and discovery would not be without danger to both of us."

"No eye can see us here," said Ellen, trembling at

the truth of her own observation, when they stood beneath a gnarled, low-branched pine, which Dr. Melmoth's ideas of beauty had caused him to retain in his garden. "Speak quickly; for I dare follow you no farther."

The spot was indeed sufficiently solitary; and the stranger delayed no longer to explain his errand.

"Your father," he began, — "do you not love him? Would you do aught for his welfare?"

"Everything that a father could ask I would do," exclaimed Ellen, eagerly. "Where is my father? and when shall I meet him?"

"It must depend upon yourself, whether you shall meet him in a few days or never."

"Never!" repeated Ellen. "Is he ill? Is he in danger?"

"He is in danger," replied the man, "but not from illness. Your father is a ruined man. Of all his friends, but one remains to him. That friend has travelled far to prove if his daughter has a daughter's affection."

"And what is to be the proof?" asked Ellen, with more calmness than the stranger had anticipated; for she possessed a large fund of plain sense, which revolted against the mystery of these proceedings. Such a course, too, seemed discordant with her father's character, whose strong mind and almost cold heart were little likely to demand, or even to pardon, the romance of affection.

"This letter will explain," was the reply to Ellen's question. "You will see that it is in your father's hand; and that may gain your confidence, though I am doubted."

She received the letter; and many of her suspicions

of the stranger's truth were vanquished by the apparent openness of his manner. He was preparing to speak further, but paused, for a footstep was now heard, approaching from the lower part of the garden. From their situation, — at some distance from the path, and in the shade of the tree, — they had a fair chance of eluding discovery from any unsuspecting passenger ; and, when Ellen saw that the intruder was Fanshawe, she hoped that his usual abstraction would assist their concealment.

But, as the student advanced along the path, his air was not that of one whose deep inward thoughts withdrew his attention from all outward objects. He rather resembled the hunter, on the watch for his game ; and, while he was yet at a distance from Ellen, a wandering gust of wind waved her white garment, and betrayed her.

"It is as I feared," said Fanshawe to himself. He then drew nigh, and addressed Ellen with a calm authority that became him well, notwithstanding that his years scarcely exceeded her own. "Miss Langton," he inquired, "what do you here at such an hour, and with such a companion ? "

Ellen was sufficiently displeased at what she deemed the unauthorized intrusion of Fanshawe in her affairs ; but his imposing manner and her own confusion prevented her from replying.

"Permit me to lead you to the house," he continued, in the words of a request, but in the tone of a command. "The dew hangs dank and heavy on these branches ; and a longer stay would be more dangerous than you are aware."

Ellen would fain have resisted ; but though the tears hung as heavy on her eyelashes, between shame and anger, as the dew upon the leaves, she felt compelled to accept the arm that he offered her. But the stranger, who, since Fanshawe's approach, had remained a little apart, now advanced.

"You speak as one in authority, young man," he said. "Have you the means of compelling obedience? Does your power extend to men? Or do you rule only over simple girls? Miss Langton is under my protection, and, till you can bend me to your will, she shall remain so."

Fanshawe turned calmly, and fixed his eyes on the stranger. "Retire, sir," was all he said.

Ellen almost shuddered, as if there were a mysterious and unearthly power in Fanshawe's voice; for she saw that the stranger endeavored in vain, borne down by the influence of a superior mind, to maintain the boldness of look and bearing that seemed natural to him. He at first made a step forward, then muttered a few half-audible words; but, quailing at length beneath the young man's bright and steady eye, he turned and slowly withdrew.

Fanshawe remained silent a moment after his opponent had departed; and, when he next spoke, it was in a tone of depression. Ellen observed, also, that his countenance had lost its look of pride and authority; and he seemed faint and exhausted. The occasion that called forth his energies had passed; and they had left him.

"Forgive me, Miss Langton," he said almost humbly, "if my eagerness to serve you has led me too far. There is evil in this stranger, more than your pure mind can conceive. I know not what has been his errand; but let me entreat you to put confidence in those to whose care your father has intrusted you.

Or if I — or — or Edward Walcott — But I have no right to advise you ; and your own calm thoughts will guide you best."

He said no more ; and, as Ellen did not reply, they reached the house, and parted in silence.

CHAPTER IV.

"The seeds by nature planted
Take a deep root in the soil, and though for a time
The trenchant share and tearing harrow may
Sweep all appearance of them from the surface,
Yet with the first warm rains of spring they 'll shoot,
And with their rankness smother the good grain.
Heaven grant, it may n't be so with him."

RICHES.

THE scene of this tale must now be changed to the little inn, which at that period, as at the present, was situated in the vicinity of Harley College. The site of the modern establishment is the same with that of the ancient; but everything of the latter that had been built by hands has gone to decay and been removed, and only the earth beneath and around it remains the same. The modern building, a house of two stories, after a lapse of twenty years, is yet unfinished. On this account, it has retained the appellation of the "New Inn," though, like many who have frequented it, it has grown old ere its maturity. Its dingy whiteness, and its apparent superfluity of windows (many of them being closed with rough boards), give it somewhat of a dreary look, especially in a wet day.

The ancient inn was a house, of which the eaves approached within about seven feet of the ground; while the roof, sloping gradually upward, formed an angle at several times that height. It was a comfortable and pleasant abode to the weary traveller, both in summer and winter; for the frost never ventured

within the sphere of its huge hearths; and it was protected from the heat of the sultry season by three large
elms that swept the roof with their long branches, and
seemed to create a breeze where there was not one.
The device upon the sign, suspended from one of these
trees, was a hand holding a long-necked bottle, and
was much more appropriate than the present unmean-
ing representation of a black eagle. But it is necessary to speak rather more at length of the landlord
than of the house over which he presided.

Hugh Crombie was one for whom most of the wise
men, who considered the course of his early years, had
predicted the gallows as an end before he should arrive
at middle age. That these prophets of ill had been
deceived was evident from the fact that the doomed
man had now passed the fortieth year, and was in
more prosperous circumstances than most of those who
had wagged their tongues against him. Yet the failure of their forebodings was more remarkable than
their fulfilment would have been.

He had been distinguished, almost from his earliest
infancy, by those precocious accomplishments, which,
because they consist in an imitation of the vices and
follies of maturity, render a boy the favorite plaything
of men. He seemed to have received from nature the
convivial talents, which, whether natural or acquired,
are a most dangerous possession; and, before his twelfth
year, he was the welcome associate of all the idle and
dissipated of his neighborhood, and especially of those
who haunted the tavern of which he had now become
the landlord. Under this course of education, Hugh
Crombie grew to youth and manhood; and the lovers
of good words could only say in his favor, that he was
a greater enemy to himself than to any one else, and

that, if he should reform, few would have a better
chance of prosperity than he.

The former clause of this modicum of praise (if
praise it may be termed) was indisputable; but it may
be doubted, whether, under any circumstances where
his success depended on his own exertions, Hugh would
have made his way well through the world. He was
one of those unfortunate persons, who, instead of being perfect in any single art or occupation, are superficial in many, and who are supposed to possess a
larger share of talent than other men, because it consists of numerous scraps, instead of a single mass.
He was partially acquainted with most of the manual
arts that gave bread to others; but not one of them,
nor all of them, would give bread to him. By some
fatality, the only two of his multifarious accomplishments in which his excellence was generally conceded
were both calculated to keep him poor rather than to
make him rich. He was a musician and a poet.

There are yet remaining in that portion of the country many ballads and songs, — set to their own peculiar tunes, — the authorship of which is attributed
to him. In general, his productions were upon subjects of local and temporary interest, and would consequently require a bulk of explanatory notes to render them interesting or intelligible to the world at
large. A considerable proportion of the remainder are
Anacreontics; though, in their construction, Hugh
Crombie imitated neither the Teian nor any other
bard. These latter have generally a coarseness and
sensuality intolerable to minds even of no very fastidi-
ous delicacy. But there are two or three simple little
songs, into which a feeling and a natural pathos have
found their way, that still retain their influence over

the heart. These, after two or three centuries, may perhaps be precious to the collectors of our early poetry. At any rate, Hugh Crombie's effusions, tavern-haunter and vagrant though he was, have gained a continuance of fame (confined, indeed, to a narrow section of the country), which many who called themselves poets then, and would have scorned such a brother, have failed to equal.

During the long winter evenings, when the farmers were idle round their hearths, Hugh was a courted guest; for none could while away the hours more skilfully than he. The winter, therefore, was his season of prosperity; in which respect he differed from the butterflies and useless insects, to which he otherwise bore a resemblance. During the cold months, a very desirable alteration for the better appeared in his outward man. His cheeks were plump and sanguine; his eyes bright and cheerful; and the tip of his nose glowed with a Bardolphian fire, — a flame, indeed, which Hugh was so far a vestal as to supply with its necessary fuel at all seasons of the year. But, as the spring advanced, he assumed a lean and sallow look, wilting and fading in the sunshine that brought life and joy to every animal and vegetable except himself. His winter patrons eyed him with an austere regard; and some even practised upon him the modern and fashionable courtesy of the " cut direct."

Yet, after all, there was good, or something that Nature intended to be so, in the poor outcast, — some lovely flowers, the sweeter even for the weeds that choked them. An instance of this was his affection for an aged father, whose whole support was the broken reed, — his son. Notwithstanding his own necessities, Hugh contrived to provide food and raiment for the old man : how, it would be difficult to say, and perhaps as well not to inquire. He also exhibited traits of sensitiveness to neglect and insult, and of gratitude for favors ; both of which feelings a course of life like his is usually quick to eradicate.

At length the restraint — for such his father had ever been — upon Hugh Crombie's conduct was removed by death ; and then the wise men and the old began to shake their heads ; and they who took pleasure in the follies, vices, and misfortunes of their fellow-creatures, looked for a speedy gratification. They were disappointed, however ; for Hugh had apparently determined, that, whatever might be his catastrophe, he would meet it among strangers, rather than at home. Shortly after his father's death, he disappeared altogether from the vicinity ; and his name became, in the course of years, an unusual sound, where once the lack of other topics of interest had given it a considerable degree of notoriety. Sometimes, however, when the winter blast was loud round the lonely farm-house, its inmates remembered him who had so often chased away the gloom of such an hour, and, though with little expectation of its fulfilment, expressed a wish to behold him again.

Yet that wish, formed, perhaps, because it appeared so desperate, was finally destined to be gratified. One summer evening, about two years previous to the period of this tale, a man of sober and staid deportment, mounted upon a white horse, arrived at the Hand and Bottle, to which some civil or military meeting had chanced, that day, to draw most of the inhabitants of the vicinity. The stranger was well though plainly dressed, and anywhere but in a retired country town would have attracted no particular attention :

but here, where a traveller was not of every-day occurrence, he was soon surrounded by a little crowd, who, when his eye was averted, seized the opportunity diligently to peruse his person. He was rather a thick-set man, but with no superfluous flesh ; his hair was of iron-gray ; he had a few wrinkles ; his face was so deeply sunburnt, that, excepting a half-smothered glow on the tip of his nose, a dusky yellow was the only apparent hue. As the people gazed, it was observed that the elderly men, and the men of substance, gat themselves silently to their steeds, and hied homeward with an unusual degree of haste ; till at length the inn was deserted, except by a few wretched objects to whom it was a constant resort. These, instead of re-treating, drew closer to the traveller, peeping anxiously into his face, and asking, ever and anon, a question, in order to discover the tone of his voice. At length, with one consent, and as if the recognition had at once burst upon them, they hailed their old boon-companion, Hugh Crombie, and, leading him into the inn, did him the honor to partake of a cup of welcome at his expense.

But, though Hugh readily acknowledged the not very reputable acquaintances who alone acknowledged him, they speedily discovered that he was an altered man. He partook with great moderation of the liquor for which he was to pay ; he declined all their flattering entreaties for one of his old songs ; and finally, being urged to engage in a game at all-fours, he calmly observed, almost in the words of an old clergyman on a like occasion, that his principles forbade a profane appeal to the decision by lot.

On the next Sabbath Hugh Crombie made his appearance at public worship in the chapel of Harley

College; and here his outward demeanor was unexceptionably serious and devout,—a praise which, on that particular occasion, could be bestowed on few besides. From these favorable symptoms, the old established prejudices against him began to waver; and as he seemed not to need, and to have no intention to ask, the assistance of any one, he was soon generally acknowledged by the rich as well as by the poor. His account of his past life, and of his intentions for the future, was brief, but not unsatisfactory. He said that, since his departure, he had been a seafaring man, and that, having acquired sufficient property to render him easy in the decline of his days, he had returned to live and die in the town of his nativity.

There was one person, and the one whom Hugh was most interested to please, who seemed perfectly satisfied of the verity of his reformation. This was the landlady of the inn, whom, at his departure, he had left a gay, and, even at thirty-five, a rather pretty wife, and whom, on his return, he found a widow of fifty, fat, yellow, wrinkled, and a zealous member of the church. She, like others, had, at first, cast a cold eye on the wanderer; but it shortly became evident to close observers, that a change was at work in the pious matron's sentiments respecting her old acquaintance. She was now careful to give him his morning dram from her own peculiar bottle, to fill his pipe from her private box of Virginia, and to mix for him the sleeping-cup in which her late husband had delighted. Of all these courtesies Hugh Crombie did partake with a wise and cautious moderation, that, while it proved them to be welcome, expressed his fear of trespassing on her kindness. For the sake of brevity, it shall suffice to say, that, about six weeks after Hugh's return, a writing appeared on one of the elm-trees in front of the tavern (where, as the place of greatest resort, such notices were usually displayed) setting forth that marriage was intended between Hugh Crombie and the Widow Sarah Hutchins. And the ceremony, which made Hugh a landholder, a householder, and a substantial man, in due time took place.

As a landlord, his general conduct was very praiseworthy. He was moderate in his charges, and attentive to his guests; he allowed no gross and evident disorders in his house, and practised none himself; he was kind and charitable to such as needed food and lodging, and had not wherewithal to pay, — for with these his experience had doubtless given him a fellow-feeling. He was also sufficiently attentive to his wife; though it must be acknowledged that the religious zeal which had had a considerable influence in gaining her affections grew, by no moderate degrees, less fervent. It was whispered, too, that the new landlord could, when time, place, and company were to his mind, upraise a song as merrily, and drink a glass as jollily, as in the days of yore. These were the weightiest charges that could now be brought against him; and wise men thought, that, whatever might have been the evil of his past life, he had returned with a desire (which years of vice, if they do not sometimes produce, do not always destroy) of being honest, if opportunity should offer; and Hugh had certainly a fair one.

On the afternoon previous to the events related in the last chapter, the personage whose introduction to the reader has occupied so large a space was seated under one of the elms in front of his dwelling. The bench which now sustained him, and on which were carved the names of many former occupants, was

Hugh Crombie's favorite lounging-place, unless when his attentions were required by his guests. No demand had that day been made upon the hospitality of the Hand and Bottle; and the landlord was just then murmuring at the unfrequency of employment. The slenderness of his profits, indeed, were no part of his concern; for the Widow Hutchins's chief income was drawn from her farm, nor was Hugh ever miserly inclined. But his education and habits had made him delight in the atmosphere of the inn, and in the society of those who frequented it; and of this species of enjoyment his present situation certainly did not afford an overplus.

Yet had Hugh Crombie an enviable appearance of indolence and ease, as he sat under the old tree, polluting the sweet air with his pipe, and taking occasional draughts from a brown jug that stood near at hand. The basis of the potation contained in this vessel was harsh old cider, from the widow's own orchard; but its coldness and acidity were rendered innocuous by a due proportion of yet older brandy. The result of this mixture was extremely felicitous, pleasant to the taste, and producing a tingling sensation on the coats of the stomach, uncommonly delectable to so old a toper as Hugh.

The landlord cast his eye, ever and anon, along the road that led down the valley in the direction of the village; and at last, when the sun was wearing westward, he discovered the approach of a horseman. He immediately replenished his pipe, took a long draught from the brown jug, summoned the ragged youth who officiated in most of the subordinate departments of the inn, and who was now to act as hostler, and then prepared himself for confabulation with his guest.

"He comes from the sea-coast," said Hugh to him-self, as the traveller emerged into open view on the level road. "He is two days in advance of the post, with its news of a fortnight old. Pray Heaven he prove communicative!" Then, as the stranger drew nigher, "One would judge that his dark face had seen as hot a sun as mine. He has felt the burning breeze of the Indies, East and West, I warrant him. Ah, I see we shall send away the evening merrily! Not a penny shall come out of his purse, — that is, if his tongue runs glibly. Just the man I was praying for — Now may the Devil take me if he is!" inter-rupted Hugh, in accents of alarm, and starting from his seat. He composed his countenance, however, with the power that long habit and necessity had given him over his emotions, and again settled himself quietly on the bench.

The traveller, coming on at a moderate pace, alighted, and gave his horse to the ragged hostler. He then advanced towards the door near which Hugh was seated, whose agitation was manifested by no per-ceptible sign, except by the shorter and more frequent puffs with which he plied his pipe. Their eyes did not meet till just as the stranger was about to enter, when he started apparently with a surprise and alarm similar to those of Hugh Crombie. He recovered himself, however, sufficiently to return the nod of rec-ognition with which he was favored, and immediately entered the house, the landlord following.

"This way, if you please, sir," said Hugh. "You will find this apartment cool and retired."

He ushered his guest into a small room the windows of which were darkened by the creeping plants that clustered round them. Entering, and closing the

door, the two gazed at each other a little space without speaking.   The traveller first broke silence.

"Then this is your living self, Hugh Crombie?" he
said.   The landlord extended his hand as a practical
reply to the question.   The stranger took it, though
with no especial appearance of cordiality.

"Ay, this seems to be flesh and blood," he said, in
the tone of one who would willingly have found it
otherwise.   "And how happens this, friend Hugh?
I little thought to meet you again in this life.   When
I last heard from you, your prayers were said, and
you were bound for a better world."

"There would have been small danger of your meeting me there," observed the landlord, dryly.

"It is an unquestionable truth, Hugh," replied the
traveller.   "For which reason I regret that your voyage was delayed."

"Nay, that is a hard word to bestow on your old
comrade," said Hugh Crombie.   "The world is wide
enough for both of us; and why should you wish me
out of it?"

"Wide as it is," rejoined the stranger, "we have
stumbled against each other, — to the pleasure of
neither of us, if I may judge from your countenance.
Methinks I am not a welcome guest at Hugh Crombie's inn."

"Your welcome must depend on the cause of your
coming, and the length of your stay," replied the landlord.

"And what if I come to settle down among these
quiet hills where I was born?" inquired the other.
"What if I, too, am weary of the life we have led, —
or afraid, perhaps, that it will come to too speedy an
end?   Shall I have your good word, Hugh, to set me

up in an honest way of life? Or will you make me a partner in your trade, since you know my qualifications? A pretty pair of publicans should we be; and the quart pot would have little rest between us."

"It may be as well to replenish it now," observed Hugh, stepping to the door of the room, and giving orders accordingly. "A meeting between old friends should never be dry. But for the partnership, it is a matter in which you must excuse me. Heaven knows I find it hard enough to be honest, with no tempter but the Devil and my own thoughts; and, if I have you also to contend with, there is little hope of me."

"Nay, that is true. Your good resolutions were always like cobwebs, and your evil habits like five-inch cables," replied the traveller. "I am to understand, then, that you refuse my offer?"

"Not only that; but, if you have chosen this valley as your place of rest, Dame Crombie and I must look through the world for another. But hush! here comes the wine."

The hostler, in the performance of another part of his duty, now appeared, bearing a measure of the liquor that Hugh had ordered. The wine of that period, owing to the comparative lowness of the duties, was of more moderate price than in the mother-country, and of purer and better quality than at the present day.

"The stuff is well chosen, Hugh," observed the guest, after a draught large enough to authorize an opinion. "You have most of the requisites for your present station; and I should be sorry to draw you from it. I trust there will be no need."

"Yet you have a purpose in your journey hither," observed his comrade.

"Yes; and you would fain be informed of it," replied the traveller. He arose, and walked once or twice across the room; then, seeming to have taken his resolution, he paused, and fixed his eye steadfastly on Hugh Crombie. "I could wish, my old acquaintance," he said, "that your lot had been cast anywhere rather than here. Yet, if you choose it, you may do me a good office, and one that shall meet with a good reward. Can I trust you?"

"My secrecy, you can," answered the host, "but nothing further. I know the nature of your plans, and whither they would lead me, too well to engage in them. To say the truth, since it concerns not me, I have little desire to hear your secret."

"And I as little to tell it, I do assure you," rejoined the guest. "I have always loved to manage my affairs myself, and to keep them to myself. It is a good rule; but it must sometimes be broken. And now, Hugh, how is it that you have become possessed of this comfortable dwelling and of these pleasant fields?"

"By my marriage with the Widow Sarah Hutchins," replied Hugh Crombie, staring at a question which seemed to have little reference to the present topic of conversation.

"It is a most excellent method of becoming a man of substance," continued the traveller; "attended with little trouble, and honest withal."

"Why, as to the trouble," said the landlord, "it follows such a bargain, instead of going before it. And for honesty, — I do not recollect that I have gained a penny more honestly these twenty years."

"I can swear to that," observed his comrade. "Well, mine host, I entirely approve of your doings, and, moreover, have resolved to prosper after the same fashion myself."

" If that be the commodity you seek," replied Hugh Crombie, " you will find none here to your mind. We have widows in plenty, it is true ; but most of them have children, and few have houses and lands. But now to be serious, — and there has been something serious in your eye all this while, — what is your purpose in coming hither ? You are not safe here. Your name has had a wider spread than mine, and, if discovered, it will go hard with you."

" But who would know me now ? " asked the guest.

" Few, few indeed ! " replied the landlord, gazing at the dark features of his companion, where hardship, peril, and dissipation had each left their traces. " No, you are not like the slender boy of fifteen, who stood on the hill by moonlight to take a last look at his father's cottage. There were tears in your eyes then ; and, as often as I remember them, I repent that I did not turn you back, instead of leading you on."

" Tears, were there ? Well, there have been few enough since," said his comrade, pressing his eyelids firmly together, as if even then tempted to give way to the weakness that he scorned. " And, for turning me back, Hugh, it was beyond your power. I had taken my resolution, and you did but show me the way to execute it."

" You have not inquired after those you left behind," observed Hugh Crombie.

" No — no ; nor will I have aught of them," exclaimed the traveller, starting from his seat, and pacing rapidly across the room. " My father, I know, is dead, and I have forgiven him. My mother — what could I hear of her but misery ? I will hear nothing."

" You must have passed the cottage as you rode hitherward," said Hugh. " How could you forbear to enter ? "

"I did not see it," he replied.   "I closed my eyes, and turned away my head."

"Oh, if I had had a mother, a loving mother! if there had been one being in the world that loved me, or cared for me, I should not have become an utter castaway," exclaimed Hugh Crombie.

The landlord's pathos, like all pathos that flows from the winecup, was sufficiently ridiculous; and his companion, who had already overcome his own brief feelings of sorrow and remorse, now laughed aloud.

"Come, come, mine host of the Hand and Bottle," he cried in his usual hard, sarcastic tone; "be a man as much as in you lies.   You had always a foolish trick of repentance; but, as I remember, it was commonly of a morning, before you had swallowed your first dram.   And now, Hugh, fill the quart pot again, and we will to business."

When the landlord had complied with the wishes of his guest, the latter resumed in a lower tone than that of his ordinary conversation, —

"There is a young lady lately become a resident hereabouts.   Perhaps you can guess her name; for you have a quick apprehension in these matters."

"A young lady?" repeated Hugh Crombie.   "And what is your concern with her?   Do you mean Ellen Langton, daughter of the old merchant Langton, whom you have some cause to remember?"

"I do remember him; but he is where he will speedily be forgotten," answered the traveller.   "And this girl, — I know your eye has been upon her, Hugh, — describe her to me."

"Describe her!" exclaimed Hugh with much animation.   "It is impossible in prose; but you shall have her very picture in a verse of one of my own songs."

"Nay, mine host, I beseech you to spare me. This is no time for quavering," said the guest. "However, I am proud of your approbation, my old friend; for this young lady do I intend to take to wife. What think you of the plan?"

Hugh Crombie gazed into his companion's face for the space of a moment, in silence. There was nothing in its expression that looked like a jest. It still retained the same hard, cold look, that, except when Hugh had alluded to his home and family, it had worn through their whole conversation.

"On my word, comrade!" he at length replied, "my advice is, that you give over your application to the quart pot, and refresh your brain by a short nap. And yet your eye is cool and steady. What is the meaning of this?"

"Listen, and you shall know," said the guest. "The old man, her father, is in his grave."

"Not a bloody grave, I trust," interrupted the landlord, starting, and looking fearfully into his comrade's face.

"No, a watery one," he replied calmly. "You see, Hugh, I am a better man than you took me for. The old man's blood is not on my head, though my wrongs are on his. Now listen: he had no heir but this only daughter; and to her, and to the man she marries, all his wealth will belong. She shall marry me. Think you her father will rest easy in the ocean, Hugh Crombie, when I am his son-in-law?"

"No, he will rise up to prevent it, if need be," answered the landlord. "But the dead need not interpose to frustrate so wild a scheme."

"I understand you," said his comrade. "You are of opinion that the young lady's consent may not be

so soon won as asked. Fear not for that, mine host.
I have a winning way with me, when opportunity
serves; and it shall serve with Ellen Langton. I will
have no rivals in my wooing."

"Your intention, if I take it rightly, is to get this
poor girl into your power, and then to force her into a
marriage," said Hugh Crombie.

"It is; and I think I possess the means of doing
it," replied his comrade. "But methinks, friend
Hugh, my enterprise has not your good wishes."

"No; and I pray you to give it over," said Hugh
Crombie, very earnestly. "The girl is young, lovely,
and as good as she is fair. I cannot aid in her ruin.
Nay, more: I must prevent it."

"Prevent it!" exclaimed the traveller, with a darkening countenance. "Think twice before you stir in
this matter, I advise you. Ruin, do you say? Does a
girl call it ruin to be made an honest wedded wife?
No, no, mine host! nor does a widow either, else have
you much to answer for."

"I gave the Widow Hutchins fair play, at least,
which is more than poor Ellen is like to get," observed
the landlord. "My old comrade, will you not give up
this scheme?"

"My old comrade, I will not give up this scheme,"
returned the other, composedly. "Why, Hugh, what
has come over you since we last met? Have we not
done twenty worse deeds of a morning, and laughed
over them at night?"

"He is right there," said Hugh Crombie, in a meditative tone. "Of a certainty, my conscience has grown
unreasonably tender within the last two years. This
one small sin, if I were to aid in it, would add but a
trifle to the sum of mine. But then the poor girl!"

His companion overheard him thus communing with himself, and having had much former experience of his infirmity of purpose, doubted not that he should bend him to his will. In fact, his arguments were so effectual, that Hugh at length, though reluctantly, promised his coöperation. It was necessary that their motions should be speedy; for on the second day thereafter, the arrival of the post would bring intelligence of the shipwreck by which Mr. Langton had perished.

"And after the deed is done," said the landlord, "I beseech you never to cross my path again. There have been more wicked thoughts in my head within the last hour than for the whole two years that I have been an honest man."

"What a saint art thou become, Hugh!" said his comrade. "But fear not that we shall meet again. When I leave this valley, it will be to enter it no more."

"And there is little danger that any other who has known me will chance upon me here," observed Hugh Crombie. "Our trade was unfavorable to length of days, and I suppose most of our old comrades have arrived at the end of theirs."

"One whom you knew well is nearer to you than you think," answered the traveller; "for I did not travel hitherward entirely alone."

CHAPTER V.

"A naughty night to swim in." — SHAKESPEARE.

THE evening of the day succeeding the adventure of the angler was dark and tempestuous. The rain descended almost in a continuous sheet; and occasional powerful gusts of wind drove it hard against the northeastern windows of Hugh Crombie's inn. But at least one apartment of the interior presented a scene of comfort and of apparent enjoyment, the more delightful from its contrast with the elemental fury that raged without. A fire, which the chillness of the evening, though a summer one, made necessary, was burning brightly on the hearth; and in front was placed a small round table, sustaining wine and glasses. One of the guests for whom these preparations had been made was Edward Walcott; the other was a shy, awkward young man, distinguished, by the union of classic and rural dress, as having but lately become a student of Harley College. He seemed little at his ease, probably from a consciousness that he was on forbidden ground, and that the wine, of which he nevertheless swallowed a larger share than his companion, was an unlawful draught.

In the catalogue of crimes provided against by the laws of Harley College, that of tavern-haunting was one of the principal. The secluded situation of the seminary, indeed, gave its scholars but a very limited choice of vices; and this was, therefore, the usual channel by which the wildness of youth discharged itself. Edward Walcott, though naturally temperate, had been not an unfrequent offender in this respect, for which a superfluity both of time and money might plead some excuse. But, since his acquaintance with Ellen Langton, he had rarely entered Hugh Crombie's doors; and an interruption in that acquaintance was the cause of his present appearance there.

Edward's jealous pride had been considerably touched on Ellen's compliance with the request of the angler. He had, by degrees, imperceptible perhaps to himself, assumed the right of feeling displeased with her conduct; and she had, as imperceptibly, accustomed herself to consider what would be his wishes, and to act accordingly. He would, indeed, in no contingency have ventured an open remonstrance; and such a proceeding would have been attended by a result the reverse of what he desired. But there existed between them a silent compact (acknowledged perhaps by neither, but felt by both), according to which they had regulated the latter part of their intercourse. Their lips had yet spoken no word of love; but some of love's rights and privileges had been assumed on the one side, and at least not disallowed on the other.

Edward's penetration had been sufficiently quick to discover that there was a mystery about the angler, that there must have been a cause for the blush that rose so proudly on Ellen's cheek; and his Quixotism had been not a little mortified, because she did not immediately appeal to his protection. He had, however, paid his usual visit the next day at Dr. Melmoth's, expecting that, by a smile of more than common brightness, she would make amends to his wounded feelings; such having been her usual mode of reparation in the few instances of disagreement that had occurred between them. But he was disappointed. He found her cold, silent, and abstracted, inattentive when he spoke, and indisposed to speak herself. Her eye was sedulously averted from his; and the casual meeting of their glances only proved that there were feelings in her bosom which he did not share. He was unable to account for this change in her deportment; and, added to his previous conceptions of his wrongs, it produced an effect upon his rather hasty temper, that might have manifested itself violently, but for the presence of Mrs. Melmoth. He took his leave in very evident displeasure; but, just as he closed the door, he noticed an expression in Ellen's countenance, that, had they been alone, and had not he been quite so proud, would have drawn him down to her feet. Their eyes met, when, suddenly, there was a gush of tears into those of Ellen; and a deep sadness, almost despair, spread itself over her features. He paused a moment, and then went his way, equally unable to account for her coldness, or for her grief. He was well aware, however, that his situation in respect to her was unaccountably changed, — a conviction so disagreeable, that, but for a hope that is latent even in the despair of youthful hearts, he would have been sorely tempted to shoot himself.

The gloom of his thoughts — a mood of mind the more intolerable to him, because so unusual — had driven him to Hugh Crombie's inn in search of artificial excitement. But even the wine had no attractions; and his first glass stood now almost untouched before him, while he gazed in heavy thought into the glowing embers of the fire. His companion perceived his melancholy, and essayed to dispel it by a choice of such topics of conversation as he conceived would be most agreeable.

" There is a lady in the house," he observed. " I caught a glimpse of her in the passage as we came in. Did you see her, Edward ? "

" A lady ! " repeated Edward, carelessly. " What know you of ladies ? No, I did not see her ; but I will venture to say that it was Dame Crombie's self, and no other."

" Well, perhaps it might," said the other, doubtingly. " Her head was turned from me, and she was gone like a shadow."

" Dame Crombie is no shadow, and never vanishes like one," resumed Edward. " You have mistaken the slipshod servant-girl for a lady."

" Ay ; but she had a white hand, a small white hand," said the student, piqued at Edward's contemptuous opinion of his powers of observation ; "as white as Ellen Langton's." He paused ; for the lover was offended by the profanity of the comparison, as was made evident by the blood that rushed to his brow.

" We will appeal to the landlord," said Edward, recovering his equanimity, and turning to Hugh, who just then entered the room. " Who is this angel, mine host, that has taken up her abode in the Hand and Bottle ? "

Hugh cast a quick glance from one to another before he answered, " I keep no angels here, gentlemen. Dame Crombie would make the house anything but heaven for them and me."

" And yet Glover has seen a vision in the passageway, — a lady with a small white hand."

" Ah, I understand ! A slight mistake of the young gentleman's," said Hugh. with the air of one who

could perfectly account for the mystery. "Our passageway is dark; or perhaps the light had dazzled his
eyes. It was the Widow Fowler's daughter, that came
to borrow a pipe of tobacco for her mother. By the
same token, she put it into her own sweet mouth, and
puffed as she went along."

"But the white hand," said Glover, only half convinced.

"Nay, I know not," answered Hugh. "But her
hand was at least as white as her face: that I can
swear. Well, gentlemen, I trust you find everything
in my house to your satisfaction. When the fire needs
renewing, or the wine runs low, be pleased to tap on
the table. I shall appear with the speed of a sunbeam."

After the departure of the landlord, the conversation of the young men amounted to little more than
monosyllables. Edward Walcott was wrapped in his
own contemplations; and his companion was in a half-
slumberous state, from which he started every quarter
of an hour, at the chiming of the clock that stood in a
corner. The fire died gradually away; the lamps began to burn dim; and Glover, rousing himself from
one of his periodical slumbers, was about to propose
a return to their chambers. He was prevented, however, by the approach of footsteps along the passageway; and Hugh Crombie, opening the door, ushered a
person into the room, and retired.

The new-comer was Fanshawe. The water that
poured plentifully from his cloak evinced that he had
but just arrived at the inn; but, whatever was his
object, he seemed not to have attained it in meeting
with the young men. He paused near the door, as if
meditating whether to retire.

"My intrusion is altogether owing to a mistake,

either of the landlord's or mine," he said. " I came hither to seek another person ; but, as I could not mention his name, my inquiries were rather vague."

"I thank Heaven for the chance that sent you to us," replied Edward, rousing himself. " Glover is wretched company ; and a duller evening have I never spent. We will renew our fire and our wine, and you must sit down with us. And for the man you seek," he continued in a whisper, " he left the inn within a half - hour after we encountered him. I inquired of Hugh Crombie last night."

Fanshawe did not express his doubts of the correctness of the information on which Edward seemed to rely. Laying aside his cloak, he accepted his invitation to make one of the party, and sat down by the fireside.

The aspect of the evening now gradually changed. A strange wild glee spread from one to another of the party, which, much to the surprise of his companions, began with and was communicated from, Fanshawe. He seemed to overflow with conceptions inimitably ludicrous, but so singular, that, till his hearers had imbibed a portion of his own spirit, they could only wonder at, instead of enjoying them. His applications to the wine were very unfrequent ; yet his conversation was such as one might expect from a bottle of champagne endowed by a fairy with the gift of speech. The secret of this strange mirth lay in the troubled state of his spirits, which, like the vexed ocean at midnight (if the simile be not too magnificent), tossed forth a mysterious brightness. The undefined apprehensions that had drawn him to the inn still distracted his mind ; but, mixed with them, there was a sort of joy not easily to be described. By degrees, and by the

assistance of the wine, the inspiration spread, each one
contributing such a quantity, and such quality of wit
and whim, as was proportioned to his genius ; but each
one, and all, displaying a greater share of both than
they had ever been suspected of possessing.

At length, however, there was a pause, — the deep
pause of flagging spirits, that always follows mirth
and wine. No one would have believed, on beholding
the pensive faces, and hearing the involuntary sighs of
the party, that from these, but a moment before, had
arisen so loud and wild a laugh. During this interval
Edward Walcott (who was the poet of his class) vol-
unteered the following song, which, from its want of
polish, and from its application to his present feelings,
might charitably be taken for an extemporaneous production : —

> The wine is bright, the wine is bright ;
>   And gay the drinkers be :
> Of all that drain the bowl to-night,
>   Most jollily drain we.
> Oh, could one search the weary earth, —
>   The earth from sea to sea, —
> He 'd turn and mingle in our mirth ;
>   For we 're the merriest three.
>
> Yet there are cares, oh, heavy cares !
>   We know that they are nigh :
> When forth each lonely drinker fares,
>   Mark then his altered eye.
> Care comes upon us when the jest
>   And frantic laughter die ;
> And care will watch the parting guest —
>   Oh late, then let us fly !

Hugh Crombie, whose early love of song and min-
strelsy was still alive, had entered the room at the
sound of Edward's voice, in sufficient time to accompany the second stanza on the violin. He now, with

the air of one who was entitled to judge in these matters, expressed his opinion of the performance.

" Really, Master Walcott, I was not prepared for this," he said in the tone of condescending praise that a great man uses to his inferior when he chooses to overwhelm him with excess of joy. " Very well, indeed, young gentleman ! Some of the lines, it is true, seem to have been dragged in by the head and shoulders ; but I could scarcely have done much better myself at your age. With practice, and with such instruction as I might afford you, I should have little doubt of your becoming a distinguished poet. A great defect in your seminary, gentlemen, — the want of due cultivation in this heavenly art."

"Perhaps, sir," said Edward, with much gravity, "you might yourself be prevailed upon to accept the professorship of poetry ? "

"Why, such an offer would require consideration," replied the landlord. "Professor Hugh Crombie of Harley College : it has a good sound, assuredly. But I am a public man, Master Walcott ; and the public would be loath to spare me from my present office."

"Will Professor Crombie favor us with a specimen of his productions ? " inquired Edward.

"Ahem, I shall be happy to gratify you, young gentleman," answered Hugh. " It is seldom, in this rude country, Master Walcott, that we meet with kindred genius ; and the opportunity should never be thrown away."

Thus saying, he took a heavy draught of the liquor by which he was usually inspired, and the praises of which were the prevailing subject of his song ; then, after much hemming, thrumming, and prelusion, and with many queer gestures and gesticulations, he began to effuse a lyric in the following fashion : —

> I 've been a jolly drinker this five-and-twenty year,
> And still a jolly drinker, my friends, you see me here:
> I sing the joys of drinking; bear a chorus, every man,
> With pint pot and quart pot and clattering of can.

The sense of the professor's first stanza was not in exact proportion to the sound; but, being executed with great spirit, it attracted universal applause. This Hugh appropriated with a condescending bow and smile; and, making a signal for silence, he went on,—

> King Solomon of old, boys (a jolly king was he), —

But here he was interrupted by a clapping of hands, that seemed a continuance of the applause bestowed on his former stanza. Hugh Crombie, who, as is the custom of many great performers, usually sang with his eyes shut, now opened them, intending gently to rebuke his auditors for their unseasonable expression of delight. He immediately perceived, however, that the fault was to be attributed to neither of the three young men; and, following the direction of their eyes, he saw near the door, in the dim background of the apartment, a figure in a cloak. The hat was flapped forward, the cloak muffled round the lower part of the face; and only the eyes were visible.

The party gazed a moment in silence, and then rushed *en masse* upon the intruder, the landlord bringing up the rear, and sounding a charge upon his fiddle. But, as they drew nigh, the black cloak began to assume a familiar look; the hat, also, was an old acquaintance; and, these being removed, from beneath them shone forth the reverend face and form of Dr. Melmoth.

The president, in his quality of clergyman, had, late in the preceding afternoon, been called to visit an aged female who was supposed to be at the point of death. Her habitation was at the distance of several miles from Harley College; so that it was nightfall before Dr. Melmoth stood at her bedside. His stay had been lengthened beyond his anticipation, on account of the frame of mind in which he found the dying woman; and, after essaying to impart the comforts of religion to her disturbed intellect, he had waited for the abatement of the storm that had arisen while he was thus engaged. As the evening advanced, however, the rain poured down in undiminished cataracts; and the doctor, trusting to the prudence and sure-footedness of his steed, had at length set forth on his return. The darkness of the night, and the roughness of the road, might have appalled him, even had his horsemanship and his courage been more considerable than they were; but by the special protection of Providence, as he reasonably supposed (for he was a good man, and on a good errand), he arrived safely as far as Hugh Crombie's inn. Dr. Melmoth had no intention of making a stay there; but, as the road passed within a very short distance, he saw lights in the windows, and heard the sound of song and revelry. It immediately occurred to him, that these midnight rioters were, probably, some of the young men of his charge; and he was impelled, by a sense of duty, to enter and disperse them. Directed by the voices, he found his way, with some difficulty, to the apartment, just as Hugh concluded his first stanza; and, amidst the subsequent applause, his entrance had been unperceived.

There was a silence of a moment's continuance after the discovery of Dr. Melmoth, during which he attempted to clothe his round, good-natured face in a look of awful dignity. But, in spite of himself, there was a little twisting of the corners of his mouth, and a smothered gleam in his eye.

"This has, apparently, been a very merry meeting, young gentlemen," he at length said; "but I fear my presence has cast a damp upon it."

"Oh yes! your reverence's cloak is wet enough to cast a damp upon anything," exclaimed Hugh Crombie, assuming a look of tender anxiety. "The young gentlemen are affrighted for your valuable life. Fear deprives them of utterance: permit me to relieve you of these dangerous garments."

"Trouble not yourself, honest man," replied the doctor, who was one of the most gullible of mortals. "I trust I am in no danger; my dwelling being near at hand. But for these young men" —

"Would your reverence but honor my Sunday suit, — the gray broadcloth coat, and the black velvet smallclothes, that have covered my unworthy legs but once? Dame Crombie shall have them ready in a moment," continued Hugh, beginning to divest the doctor of his garments.

"I pray you to appease your anxiety," cried Dr. Melmoth, retaining a firm hold on such parts of his dress as yet remained to him. "Fear not for my health. I will but speak a word to those misguided youth, and be gone."

"Misguided youth, did your reverence say?" echoed Hugh, in a tone of utter astonishment. "Never were they better guided than when they entered my poor house. Oh, had your reverence but seen them, when I heard their cries, and rushed forth to their assistance. Dripping with wet were they, like three drowned men at the resurrec — Ahem!" interrupted Hugh, recollecting that the comparison he meditated might not suit the doctor's ideas of propriety.

" But why were they abroad on such a night ? " inquired the president.

" Ah ! doctor, you little know the love these good young gentlemen bear for you," replied the landlord. " Your absence, your long absence, had alarmed them ; and they rushed forth through the rain and darkness to seek you."

" And was this indeed so ? " asked the doctor, in a softened tone, and casting a tender and grateful look upon the three students. They, it is but justice to mention, had simultaneously made a step forward in order to contradict the egregious falsehoods of which Hugh's fancy was so fertile ; but he assumed an expression of such ludicrous entreaty, that it was irresistible.

" But methinks their anxiety was not of long continuance," observed Dr. Melmoth, looking at the wine, and remembering the song that his entrance had interrupted.

" Ah ! your reverence disapproves of the wine, I see," answered Hugh Crombie. " I did but offer them a drop to keep the life in their poor young hearts. My dame advised strong waters ; ' But, Dame Crombie,' says I, ' would ye corrupt their youth ? ' And in my zeal for their good, doctor, I was delighting them, just at your entrance, with a pious little melody of my own against the sin of drunkenness."

" Truly, I remember something of the kind," observed Dr. Melmoth. " And, as I think, it seemed to meet with good acceptance."

" Ay, that it did ! " said the landlord. " Will it please your reverence to hear it ? —

King Solomon of old, boys (a wise man I 'm thinking),
Has warned you to beware of the horrid vice of drinking — .

But why talk I of drinking, foolish man that I am! And all this time, doctor, you have not sipped a drop of my wine. Now I entreat your reverence, as you value your health and the peace and quiet of these youth."

Dr. Melmoth drank a glass of wine, with the benevolent intention of allaying the anxiety of Hugh Crombie and the students. He then prepared to depart; for a strong wind had partially dispersed the clouds, and occasioned an interval in the cataract of rain. There was, perhaps, a little suspicion yet remaining in the good man's mind respecting the truth of the landlord's story: at least, it was his evident intention to see the students fairly out of the inn before he quitted it himself. They therefore proceeded along the passageway in a body. The lamp that Hugh Crombie held but dimly enlightened them; and the number and contiguity of the doors caused Dr. Melmoth to lay his hand upon the wrong one.

"Not there, not there, doctor! It is Dame Crombie's bedchamber," shouted Hugh, most energetically. "Now Beelzebub defend me!" he muttered to himself, perceiving that his exclamation had been a moment too late.

"Heavens! what do I see?" ejaculated Dr. Melmoth, lifting his hands, and starting back from the entrance of the room. The three students pressed forward; Mrs. Crombie and the servant-girl had been drawn to the spot by the sound of Hugh's voice; and all their wondering eyes were fixed on poor Ellen Langton.

The apartment in the midst of which she stood was dimly lighted by a solitary candle at the farther extremity; but Ellen was exposed to the glare of the three lamps, held by Hugh, his wife, and the servant-girl. Their combined rays seemed to form a focus exactly at the point where they reached her; and the beholders, had any been sufficiently calm, might have watched her features in their agitated workings and frequent change of expression, as perfectly as by the broad light of day. Terror had at first blanched her as white as a lily, or as a marble statue, which for a moment she resembled, as she stood motionless in the centre of the room. Shame next bore sway; and her blushing countenance, covered by her slender white fingers, might fantastically be compared to a variegated rose with its alternate stripes of white and red. The next instant, a sense of her pure and innocent intentions gave her strength and courage; and her attitude and look had now something of pride and dignity. These, however, in their turn, gave way; for Edward Walcott pressed forward, and attempted to address her.

"Ellen, Ellen!" he said, in an agitated and quivering whisper; but what was to follow cannot be known; for his emotion checked his utterance. His tone and look, however, again overcame Ellen Langton, and she burst into tears. Fanshawe advanced, and took Edward's arm. "She has been deceived," he whispered. "She is innocent: you are unworthy of her if you doubt it."

"Why do you interfere, sir?" demanded Edward, whose passions, thoroughly excited, would willingly have wreaked themselves on any one. "What right have you to speak of her innocence? Perhaps," he continued, an undefined and ridiculous suspicion arising in his mind, — "perhaps you are acquainted with her intentions. Perhaps you are the deceiver."

Fanshawe's temper was not naturally of the meekest character; and having had a thousand bitter feelings of his own to overcome, before he could attempt to console Edward, this rude repulse had almost aroused him to fierceness. But his pride, of which a more moderate degree would have had a less peaceable effect, came to his assistance; and he turned calmly and contemptuously away.

Ellen, in the mean time, had been restored to some degree of composure. To this effect, a feeling of pique against Edward Walcott had contributed. She had distinguished his voice in the neighboring apartment, had heard his mirth and wild laughter, without being aware of the state of feeling that produced them. She had supposed that the terms on which they parted in the morning (which had been very grievous to herself) would have produced a corresponding sadness in him. But while she sat in loneliness and in tears, her bosom distracted by a thousand anxieties and sorrows, of many of which Edward was the object, his reckless gayety had seemed to prove the slight regard in which he held her. After the first outbreak of emotion, therefore, she called up her pride (of which, on proper occasions, she had a reasonable share), and sustained his upbraiding glance with a passive composure, which women have more readily at command than men.

Dr. Melmoth's surprise had during this time kept him silent and inactive. He gazed alternately from one to another of those who stood around him, as if to seek some explanation of so strange an event. But the faces of all were as perplexed as his own; even Hugh Crombie had assumed a look of speechless wonder, — speechless, because his imagination, prolific as it was, could not supply a plausible falsehood.

"Ellen, dearest child," at length said the doctor, "what is the meaning of this?"

Ellen endeavored to reply; but, as her composure was merely external, she was unable to render her words audible. Fanshawe spoke in a low voice to Dr. Melmoth, who appeared grateful for his advice.

"True, it will be the better way," he replied. "My wits are utterly confounded, or I should not have remained thus long. Come, my dear child," he continued, advancing to Ellen, and taking her hand, "let us return home, and defer the explanation till the morrow. There, there: only dry your eyes, and we will say no more about it."

"And that will be your wisest way, old gentleman," muttered Hugh Crombie.

Ellen at first exhibited but little desire, or, rather, an evident reluctance, to accompany her guardian. She hung back, while her glance passed almost imperceptibly over the faces that gazed so eagerly at her; but the one she sought was not visible among them. She had no alternative, and suffered herself to be led from the inn.

Edward Walcott alone remained behind, the most wretched being (at least such was his own opinion) that breathed the vital air. He felt a sinking and sickness of the heart, and alternately a feverish frenzy, neither of which his short and cloudless existence had heretofore occasioned him to experience. He was jealous of, he knew not whom, and he knew not what. He was ungenerous enough to believe that Ellen — his pure and lovely Ellen — had degraded herself; though from what motive, or by whose agency, he could not conjecture. When Dr. Melmoth had taken her in charge, Edward returned to the apartment where he had spent the evening. The wine was still upon the table ; and, in the desperate hope of stupefying his faculties, he unwisely swallowed huge successive draughts. The effect of his imprudence was not long in manifesting itself ; though insensibility, which at another time would have been the result, did not now follow. Acting upon his previous agitation, the wine seemed to set his blood in a flame ; and, for the time being, he was a perfect madman.

A phrenologist would probably have found the organ of destructiveness in strong development, just then, upon Edward's cranium ; for he certainly manifested an impulse to break and destroy whatever chanced to be within his reach. He commenced his operations by upsetting the table, and breaking the bottles and glasses. Then, seizing a tall heavy chair in each hand, he hurled them with prodigious force, — one through the window, and the other against a large looking-glass, the most valuable article of furniture in Hugh Crombie's inn. The crash and clatter of these outrageous proceedings soon brought the master, mistress, and maid-servant to the scene of action ; but the two latter, at the first sight of Edward's wild demeanor and gleaming eyes, retreated with all imaginable expedition. Hugh chose a position behind the door, from whence, protruding his head, he endeavored to mollify his inebriated guest. His interference, however, had nearly been productive of most unfortunate consequences ; for a massive andiron, with round brazen head, whizzed past him, within a hair's - breadth of his ear.

" I might as safely take my chance in a battle," exclaimed Hugh, withdrawing his head, and speaking to a man who stood in the passageway. " A little twist of his hand to the left would have served my turn as well as if I stood in the path of a forty-two pound ball. And here comes another broadside," he added, as some other article of furniture rattled against the door.

"Let us return his fire, Hugh," said the person whom he addressed, composedly lifting the andiron. "He is in want of ammunition : let us send him back his own."

The sound of this man's voice produced a most singular effect upon Edward. The moment before, his actions had been those of a raving maniac ; but, when the words struck his ear, he paused, put his hand to his forehead, seemed to recollect himself, and finally advanced with a firm and steady step. His countenance was dark and angry, but no longer wild.

"I have found you, villain !" he said to the angler. "It is you who have done this."

"And, having done it, the wrath of a boy — his drunken wrath — will not induce me to deny it," replied the other, scornfully.

"The boy will require a man's satisfaction," returned Edward, "and that speedily."

"Will you take it now ?" inquired the angler, with a cool, derisive smile, and almost in a whisper. At the same time he produced a brace of pistols, and held them towards the young man.

"Willingly," answered Edward, taking one of the weapons. "Choose your distance."

The angler stepped back a pace ; but before their deadly intentions, so suddenly conceived, could be executed, Hugh Crombie interposed himself between them.

"Do you take my best parlor for the cabin of the

Black Andrew, where a pistol-shot was a nightly pastime?" he inquired of his comrade. "And you, Master Edward, with what sort of a face will you walk into the chapel to morning prayers, after putting a ball through this man's head, or receiving one through your own? Though, in this last case, you will be past praying for, or praying either."

"Stand aside: I will take the risk. Make way, or I will put the ball through your own head," exclaimed Edward, fiercely: for the interval of rationality that circumstances had produced was again giving way to intoxication.

"You see how it is," said Hugh to his companion, unheard by Edward. "You shall take a shot at me, sooner than at the poor lad in his present state. You have done him harm enough already, and intend him more. I propose," he continued aloud, and with a peculiar glance towards the angler, "that this affair be decided to-morrow, at nine o'clock, under the old oak, on the bank of the stream. In the mean time, I will take charge of these popguns, for fear of accidents."

"Well, mine host, be it as you wish," said his comrade. "A shot more or less is of little consequence to me." He accordingly delivered his weapon to Hugh Crombie and walked carelessly away.

"Come, Master Walcott, the enemy has retreated. Victoria! And now, I see, the sooner I get you to your chamber, the better," added he aside; for the wine was at last beginning to produce its legitimate effect, in stupefying the young man's mental and bodily faculties.

Hugh Crombie's assistance, though not, perhaps, quite indispensable, was certainly very convenient to our unfortunate hero, in the course of the short walk that brought him to his chamber. When arrived there, and in bed, he was soon locked in a sleep scarcely less deep than that of death.

The weather, during the last hour, had appeared to be on the point of changing: indeed, there were, every few minutes, most rapid changes. A strong breeze sometimes drove the clouds from the brow of heaven, so as to disclose a few of the stars; but, immediately after, the darkness would again become Egyptian, and the rain rush like a torrent from the sky.

CHAPTER VI.

"About her neck a packet-mail
Fraught with advice, some fresh, some stale,
Of men that walked when they were dead."

HUDIBRAS.

SCARCELY a word had passed between Dr. Melmoth
and Ellen Langton, on their way home; for, though
the former was aware that his duty towards his ward
would compel him to inquire into the motives of her
conduct, the tenderness of his heart prompted him to
defer the scrutiny to the latest moment. The same
tenderness induced him to connive at Ellen's stealing
secretly up to her chamber, unseen by Mrs. Melmoth;
to render which measure practicable, he opened the
house-door very softly, and stood before his half-sleep-
ing spouse (who waited his arrival in the parlor) without any previous notice. This act of the doctor's be-
nevolence was not destitute of heroism; for he was
well assured that, should the affair come to the lady's
knowledge through any other channel, her vengeance
would descend not less heavily on him for concealing,
than on Ellen for perpetrating, the elopement. That
she had, thus far, no suspicion of the fact, was evident
from her composure, as well as from the reply to a
question, which, with more than his usual art, her husband put to her respecting the non-appearance of his
ward. Mrs. Melmoth answered, that Ellen had complained of indisposition, and after drinking, by her
prescription, a large cup of herb-tea, had retired to

her chamber early in the evening. Thankful that all was yet safe, the doctor laid his head upon his pillow; but, late as was the hour, his many anxious thoughts long drove sleep from his eyelids.

The diminution in the quantity of his natural rest did not, however, prevent Dr. Melmoth from rising at his usual hour, which at all seasons of the year was an early one. He found, on descending to the parlor, that breakfast was nearly in readiness; for the lady of the house (and, as a corollary, her servant-girl) was not accustomed to await the rising of the sun in order to commence her domestic labors. Ellen Langton, however, who had heretofore assimilated her habits to those of the family, was this morning invisible, — a circumstance imputed by Mrs. Melmoth to her indisposition of the preceding evening, and by the doctor, to mortification on account of her elopement and its discovery.

" I think I will step into Ellen's bedchamber," said Mrs. Melmoth, "and inquire how she feels herself. The morning is delightful after the storm, and the air will do her good."

" Had we not better proceed with our breakfast? If the poor child is sleeping, it were a pity to disturb her," observed the doctor; for, besides his sympathy with Ellen's feelings, he was reluctant, as if he were the guilty one, to meet her face.

" Well, be it so. And now sit down, doctor; for the hot cakes are cooling fast. I suppose you will say they are not so good as those Ellen made yesterday morning. I know not how you will bear to part with her, though the thing must soon be."

" It will be a sore trial, doubtless," replied Dr. Melmoth, — " like tearing away a branch that is grafted

on an old tree.   And yet there will be a satisfaction
in delivering her safe into her father's hands.''

" A satisfaction for which you may thank me, doctor," observed the lady.   " If there had been none but
you to look after the poor thing's doings, she would
have been enticed away long ere this, for the sake of
her money."

Dr. Melmoth's prudence could scarcely restrain a
smile at the thought that an elopement, as he had
reason to believe, had been plotted, and partly carried
into execution, while Ellen was under the sole care of
his lady, and had been frustrated only by his own despised agency.   He was not accustomed, however, —
nor was this an eligible occasion, — to dispute any of
Mrs. Melmoth's claims to superior wisdom.

The breakfast proceeded in silence, or, at least, without any conversation material to the tale.   At its conclusion, Mrs. Melmoth was again meditating on the
propriety of entering Ellen's chamber ; but she was
now prevented by an incident that always excited
much interest both in herself and her husband.

This was the entrance of the servant, bearing the
letters and newspaper, with which, once a fortnight, the
mail-carrier journeyed up the valley.   Dr. Melmoth's
situation at the head of a respectable seminary, and
his character as a scholar, had procured him an extensive correspondence among the learned men of his own
country ; and he had even exchanged epistles with one
or two of the most distinguished dissenting clergymen
of Great Britain.   But, unless when some fond mother
enclosed a one-pound note to defray the private expenses of her son at college, it was frequently the case
that the packets addressed to the doctor were the sole
contents of the mail-bag.   In the present instance, his

letters were very numerous, and, to judge from the one he chanced first to open, of an unconscionable length. While he was engaged in their perusal, Mrs. Melmoth amused herself with the newspaper, — a little sheet of about twelve inches square, which had but one rival in the country. Commencing with the title, she labored on through advertisements old and new, through poetry lamentably deficient in rhythm and rhymes, through essays, the ideas of which had been trite since the first week of the creation, till she finally arrived at the department that, a fortnight before, had contained the latest news from all quarters. Making such remarks upon these items as to her seemed good, the dame's notice was at length attracted by an article which her sudden exclamation proved to possess uncommon interest. Casting her eye hastily over it, she immediately began to read aloud to her husband; but he, deeply engaged in a long and learned letter, instead of listening to what she wished to communicate, exerted his own lungs in opposition to hers, as is the custom of abstracted men when disturbed. The result was as follows : —

"A brig just arrived in the outer harbor," began Mrs. Melmoth, "reports, that on the morning of the 25th ult." — Here the doctor broke in, " Wherefore I am compelled to differ from your exposition of the said passage, for those reasons, of the which I have given you a taste; provided " — The lady's voice was now almost audible, " ship bottom upward, discovered by the name on her stern to be the Ellen of " — " and in the same opinion are Hooker, Cotton, and divers learned divines of a later date."

The doctor's lungs were deep and strong, and victory seemed to incline toward him; but Mrs. Mel-

moth now made use of a tone whose peculiar shrill-
ness, as long experience had taught her husband, au-
gured a mood of mind not to be trifled with.

"On my word, doctor," she exclaimed, "this is most
unfeeling and unchristian conduct! Here am I endeavoring to inform you of the death of an old friend,
and you continue as deaf as a post."

Dr. Melmoth, who had heard the sound, without receiving the sense, of these words, now laid aside the
letter in despair, and submissively requested to be informed of her pleasure.

"There, read for yourself," she replied, handing
him the paper, and pointing to the passage containing
the important intelligence, — "read, and then finish
your letter, if you have a mind."

He took the paper, unable to conjecture how the
dame could be so much interested in any part of its
contents; but, before he had read many words, he
grew pale as death. "Good Heavens! what is this?"
he exclaimed. He then read on, "being the vessel
wherein that eminent son of New England, John
Langton, Esq., had taken passage for his native country, after an absence of many years."

"Our poor Ellen, his orphan child!" said Dr. Melmoth, dropping the paper. "How shall we break the
intelligence to her? Alas! her share of the affliction
causes me to forget my own."

"It is a heavy misfortune, doubtless; and Ellen
will grieve as a daughter should," replied Mrs. Melmoth, speaking with the good sense of which she had
a competent share. "But she has never known her
father; and her sorrow must arise from a sense of
duty, more than from strong affection. I will go and
inform her of her loss. It is late, and I wonder if she
be still asleep."

"Be cautious, dearest wife," said the doctor. "Ellen has strong feelings, and a sudden shock might be dangerous."

"I think I may be trusted, Dr. Melmoth," replied the lady, who had a high opinion of her own abilities as a comforter, and was not averse to exercise them.

Her husband, after her departure, sat listlessly turning over the letters that yet remained unopened, feeling little curiosity, after such melancholy intelligence, respecting their contents. But, by the handwriting of the direction on one of them, his attention was gradually arrested, till he found himself gazing earnestly on those strong, firm, regular characters. They were perfectly familiar to his eye; but from what hand they came, he could not conjecture. Suddenly, however, the truth burst upon him; and after noticing the date, and reading a few lines, he rushed hastily in pursuit of his wife.

He had arrived at the top of his speed and at the middle of the staircase, when his course was arrested by the lady whom he sought, who came, with a velocity equal to his own, in an opposite direction. The consequence was a concussion between the two meeting masses, by which Mrs. Melmoth was seated securely on the stairs; while the doctor was only preserved from precipitation to the bottom by clinging desperately to the balustrade. As soon as the pair discovered that they had sustained no material injury by their contact, they began eagerly to explain the cause of their mutual haste, without those reproaches, which, on the lady's part, would at another time have followed such an accident.

"You have not told her the bad news, I trust?" cried Dr. Melmoth, after each had communicated his and her intelligence, without obtaining audience of the other.

"Would you have me tell it to the bare walls?" inquired the lady in her shrillest tone. "Have I not just informed you that she has gone, fled, eloped? Her chamber is empty; and her bed has not been occupied."

"Gone!" repeated the doctor. "And, when her father comes to demand his daughter of me, what answer shall I make?"

"Now, Heaven defend us from the visits of the dead and drowned!" cried Mrs. Melmoth. "This is a serious affair, doctor, but not, I trust, sufficient to raise a ghost."

"Mr. Langton is yet no ghost," answered he; "though this event will go near to make him one. He was fortunately prevented, after he had made every preparation, from taking passage in the vessel that was lost."

"And where is he now?" she inquired.

"He is in New England. Perhaps he is at this moment on his way to us," replied her husband. "His letter is dated nearly a fortnight back; and he expresses an intention of being with us in a few days."

"Well, I thank Heaven for his safety," said Mrs. Melmoth. "But truly the poor gentleman could not have chosen a better time to be drowned, nor a worse one to come to life, than this. What we shall do, doctor, I know not; but had you locked the doors, and fastened the windows, as I advised, the misfortune could not have happened."

"Why, the whole country would have flouted us!" answered the doctor. "Is there a door in all the Province that is barred or bolted, night or day? Never theless, it might have been advisable last night, had it occurred to me."

"And why at that time more than at all times?" she inquired. "We had surely no reason to fear this event."

Dr. Melmoth was silent; for his worldly wisdom was sufficient to deter him from giving his lady the opportunity, which she would not fail to use to the utmost, of laying the blame of the elopement at his door. He now proceeded, with a heavy heart, to Ellen's chamber, to satisfy himself with his own eyes of the state of affairs. It was deserted too truly; and the wild-flowers with which it was the maiden's custom daily to decorate her premises were drooping, as if in sorrow for her who had placed them there. Mrs. Melmoth, on this second visit, discovered on the table a note addressed to her husband, and containing a few words of gratitude from Ellen, but no explanation of her mysterious flight. The doctor gazed long on the tiny letters, which had evidently been traced with a trembling hand, and blotted with many tears.

"There is a mystery in this, — a mystery that I cannot fathom," he said. "And now I would I knew what measures it would be proper to take."

"Get you on horseback, Dr. Melmoth, and proceed as speedily as may be down the valley to the town," said the dame, the influence of whose firmer mind was sometimes, as in the present case, most beneficially exerted over his own. "You must not spare for trouble, no, nor for danger. Now — Oh, if I were a man!"—

"Oh, that you were!" murmured the doctor, in a perfectly inaudible voice. "Well — and when I reach the town, what then?"

"As I am a Christian woman, my patience cannot

endure you!" exclaimed Mrs. Melmoth. "Oh, I love to see a man with the spirit of a man! but you"—— And she turned away in utter scorn.

"But, dearest wife," remonstrated the husband, who was really at a loss how to proceed, and anxious for her advice, "your worldly experience is greater than mine, and I desire to profit by it. What should be my next measure after arriving at the town?"

Mrs. Melmoth was appeased by the submission with which the doctor asked her counsel; though, if the truth must be told, she heartily despised him for needing it. She condescended, however, to instruct him in the proper method of pursuing the runaway maiden, and directed him, before his departure, to put strict inquiries to Hugh Crombie respecting any stranger who might lately have visited his inn. That there would be wisdom in this, Dr. Melmoth had his own reasons for believing; and still, without imparting them to his lady, he proceeded to do as he had been bid.

The veracious landlord acknowledged that a stranger had spent a night and day at his inn, and was missing that morning; but he utterly denied all acquaintance with his character, or privity to his purposes. Had Mrs. Melmoth, instead of her husband, conducted the examination, the result might have been different. As the case was, the doctor returned to his dwelling but little wiser than he went forth; and, ordering his steed to be saddled, he began a journey of which he knew not what would be the end.

In the mean time, the intelligence of Ellen's disappearance circulated rapidly, and soon sent forth hunters more fit to follow the chase than Dr. Melmoth.

CHAPTER VII.

"There was racing and chasing o'er Cannobie Lee."
                                    WALTER SCOTT.

WHEN Edward Walcott awoke the next morning from his deep slumber, his first consciousness was of a heavy weight upon his mind, the cause of which he was unable immediately to recollect. One by one, however, by means of the association of ideas, the events of the preceding night came back to his memory; though those of latest occurrence were dim as dreams. But one circumstance was only too well remembered, — the discovery of Ellen Langton. By a strong effort he next attained to an uncertain recollection of a scene of madness and violence, followed, as he at first thought, by a duel. A little further reflection, however, informed him that this event was yet among the things of futurity; but he could by no means recall the appointed time or place. As he had not the slightest intention (praiseworthy and prudent as it would unquestionably have been) to give up the chance of avenging Ellen's wrongs and his own, he immediately arose, and began to dress, meaning to learn from Hugh Crombie those particulars which his own memory had not retained. His chief apprehension was, that the appointed time had already elapsed; for the early sunbeams of a glorious morning were now peeping into his chamber.

More than once, during the progress of dressing, he was inclined to believe that the duel had actually

taken place, and been fatal to him, and that he was
now in those regions to which, his conscience told him,
such an event would be likely to send him. This idea
resulted from his bodily sensations, which were in the
highest degree uncomfortable. He was tormented by
a raging thirst, that seemed to have absorbed all the
moisture of his throat and stomach ; and, in his present agitation, a cup of icy water would have been his
first wish, had all the treasures of earth and sea been
at his command. His head, too, throbbed almost to
bursting ; and the whirl of his brain at every movement promised little accuracy in the aim of his pistol,
when he should meet the angler. These feelings, together with the deep degradation of his mind, made
him resolve that no circumstances should again draw
him into an excess of wine. In the mean time, his
head was, perhaps, still too much confused to allow
him fully to realize his unpleasant situation.

Before Edward was prepared to leave his chamber,
the door was opened by one of the college bed-makers,
who, perceiving that he was nearly dressed, entered,
and began to set the apartment in order. There were
two of these officials pertaining to Harley College ;
each of them being (and, for obvious reasons, this was
an indispensable qualification) a model of perfect ugliness in her own way. One was a tall, raw-boned, huge-
jointed, double-fisted giantess, admirably fitted to sustain the part of Glumdalia, in the tragedy of "Tom
Thumb." Her features were as excellent as her form,
appearing to have been rough-hewn with a broadaxe,
and left unpolished. The other was a short, squat
figure, about two thirds the height, and three times
the circumference, of ordinary females. Her hair
was gray, her complexion of a deep yellow ; and her

most remarkable feature was a short snub nose, just discernible amid the broad immensity of her face. This latter lady was she who now entered Edward's chamber. Notwithstanding her deficiency in personal attractions, she was rather a favorite of the students, being good-natured, anxious for their comfort, and, when duly encouraged, very communicative. Edward perceived, as soon as she appeared, that she only waited his assistance in order to disburden herself of some extraordinary information; and, more from compassion than curiosity, he began to question her.

"Well, Dolly, what news this morning?"

"Why, let me see, — oh, yes! It had almost slipped my memory," replied the bed-maker. "Poor Widow Butler died last night, after her long sickness. Poor woman! I remember her forty years ago, or so, — as rosy a lass as you could set eyes on."

"Ah! has she gone?" said Edward, recollecting the sick woman of the cottage which he had entered with Ellen and Fanshawe. "Was she not out of her right mind, Dolly?"

"Yes, this seven years," she answered. "They say she came to her senses a bit, when Dr. Melmoth visited her yesterday, but was raving mad when she died. Ah, that son of hers! — if he is yet alive. Well, well!"

"She had a son, then?" inquired Edward.

"Yes, such as he was. The Lord preserve me from such a one!" said Dolly. "It was thought he went off with Hugh Crombie, that keeps the tavern now. That was fifteen years ago."

"And have they heard nothing of him since?" asked Edward.

"Nothing good, — nothing good," said the bed

maker. "Stories did travel up the valley now and then; but for five years there has been no word of him. They say Merchant Langton, Ellen's father, met him in foreign parts, and would have made a man of him; but there was too much of the wicked one in him for that. Well, poor woman! I wonder who 'll preach her funeral sermon."

"Dr. Melmoth, probably," observed the student.

"No, no! The doctor will never finish his journey in time. And who knows but his own funeral will be the end of it," said Dolly, with a sagacious shake of her head.

"Dr. Melmoth gone a journey!" repeated Edward. "What do you mean? For what purpose?"

"For a good purpose enough, I may say," replied she. "To search out Miss Ellen, that was run away with last night."

"In the Devil's name, woman, of what are you speaking?" shouted Edward, seizing the affrighted bed-maker forcibly by the arm.

Poor Dolly had chosen this circuitous method of communicating her intelligence, because she was well aware that, if she first told of Ellen's flight, she should find no ear for her account of the Widow Butler's death. She had not calculated, however, that the news would produce so violent an effect upon her auditor; and her voice faltered as she recounted what she knew of the affair. She had hardly concluded, before Edward — who, as she proceeded, had been making hasty preparations — rushed from his chamber, and took the way towards Hugh Crombie's inn. He had no difficulty in finding the landlord, who had already occupied his accustomed seat, and was smoking his accustomed pipe, under the elm-tree.

"Well, Master Walcott, you have come to take a stomach-reliever this morning, I suppose," said Hugh, taking the pipe from his mouth. "What shall it be? — a bumper of wine with an egg? or a glass of smooth, old, oily brandy, such as Dame Crombie and I keep for our own drinking? Come, that will do it, I know."

"No, no! neither," replied Edward, shuddering involuntarily at the bare mention of wine and strong drink. "You know well, Hugh Crombie, the errand on which I come."

"Well, perhaps I do," said the landlord. "You come to order me to saddle my best horse. You are for a ride, this fine morning."

"True; and I must learn of you in what direction to turn my horse's head," replied Edward Walcott.

"I understand you," said Hugh, nodding and smiling. "And now, Master Edward, I really have taken a strong liking to you; and, if you please to hearken to it, you shall have some of my best advice."

"Speak," said the young man, expecting to be told in what direction to pursue the chase.

"I advise you, then," continued Hugh Crombie, in a tone in which some real feeling mingled with assumed carelessness, — "I advise you to forget that you have ever known this girl, that she has ever existed; for she is as much lost to you as if she never had been born, or as if the grave had covered her. Come, come, man, toss off a quart of my old wine, and keep up a merry heart. This has been my way in many a heavier sorrow than ever you have felt; and you see I am alive and merry yet." But Hugh's merriment had failed him just as he was making his boast of it; for Edward saw a tear in the corner of his eye.

"Forget her? Never, never!" said the student, while his heart sank within him at the hopelessness of pursuit which Hugh's words implied. "I will follow her to the ends of the earth."

"Then so much the worse for you and for my poor nag, on whose back you shall be in three minutes," rejoined the landlord. "I have spoken to you as I would to my own son, if I had such an incumbrance. — Here, you ragamuffin; saddle the gray, and lead him round to the door."

"The gray? I will ride the black," said Edward. "I know your best horse as well as you do yourself, Hugh."

"There is no black horse in my stable. I have parted with him to an old comrade of mine," answered the landlord, with a wink of acknowledgment to what he saw were Edward's suspicions. "The gray is a stout nag, and will carry you a round pace, though not so fast as to bring you up with them you seek. I reserved him for you, and put Mr. Fanshawe off with the old white, on which I travelled hitherward a year or two since."

"Fanshawe! Has he, then, the start of me?" asked Edward.

"He rode off about twenty minutes ago," replied Hugh; "but you will overtake him within ten miles, at farthest. But, if mortal man could recover the girl, that fellow would do it, even if he had no better nag than a broomstick, like the witches of old times."

"Did he obtain any information from you as to the course?" inquired the student.

"I could give him only this much," said Hugh,

pointing down the road in the direction of the town. " My old comrade trusts no man further than is need- ful, and I ask no unnecessary questions."

The hostler now led up to the door the horse which Edward was to ride. The young man mounted with all expedition; but, as he was about to apply the spurs, his thirst, which the bed - maker's intelligence had caused, him to forget, returned most powerfully upon him.

" For Heaven's sake, Hugh, a mug of your sharp- est cider; and let it be a large one ! " he exclaimed. " My tongue rattles in my mouth like "—

" Like the bones in a dice-box," said the landlord, finishing the comparison, and hastening to obey Ed- ward's directions. Indeed, he rather exceeded them, by mingling with the juice of the apple a gill of his old brandy, which his own experience told him would at that time have a most desirable effect upon the young man's internal system.

" It is powerful stuff, mine host; and I feel like a new man already," observed Edward, after draining the mug to the bottom.

" He is a fine lad, and sits his horse most gal- lantly," said Hugh Crombie to himself as the student rode off. " I heartily wish him success. I wish to Heaven my conscience had suffered me to betray the plot before it was too late. Well, well, a man must keep his mite of honesty."

The morning was now one of the most bright and glorious that ever shone for mortals ; and, under other circumstances, Edward's bosom would have been as light, and his spirit would have sung as cheerfully, as one of the many birds that warbled around him. The raindrops of the preceding night hung like glittering diamonds on every leaf of every tree, shaken, and rendered more brilliant, by occasional sighs of wind, that removed from the traveller the superfluous heat of an unclouded sun. In spite of the adventure, so mysterious and vexatious, in which he was engaged, Edward's elastic spirit (assisted, perhaps, by the brandy he had unwittingly swallowed) rose higher as he rode on; and he soon found himself endeavoring to accommodate the tune of one of Hugh Crombie's ballads to the motion of the horse. Nor did this reviving cheerfulness argue anything against his unwavering faith, and pure and fervent love for Ellen Langton. A sorrowful and repining disposition is not the necessary accompaniment of a "leal and loving heart"; and Edward's spirits were cheered, not by forgetfulness, but by hope, which would not permit him to doubt of the ultimate success of his pursuit. The uncertainty itself, and the probable danger of the expedition, were not without their charm to a youthful and adventurous spirit. In fact, Edward would not have been altogether satisfied to recover the errant damsel, without first doing battle in her behalf.

He had proceeded but a few miles before he came in sight of Fanshawe, who had been accommodated by the landlord with a horse much inferior to his own. The speed to which he had been put had almost exhausted the poor animal, whose best pace was now but little beyond a walk. Edward drew his bridle as he came up with Fanshawe.

"I have been anxious to apologize," he said to him, "for the hasty and unjust expressions of which I made use last evening. May I hope that, in consideration of my mental distraction and the causes of it, you will forget what has passed?"

"I had already forgotten it," replied Fanshawe, freely offering his hand. "I saw your disturbed state of feeling, and it would have been unjust both to you and to myself to remember the errors it occasioned."

"A wild expedition this," observed Edward, after shaking warmly the offered hand. "Unless we obtain some further information at the town, we shall hardly know which way to continue the pursuit."

"We can scarcely fail, I think, of lighting upon some trace of them," said Fanshawe. "Their flight must have commenced after the storm subsided, which would give them but a few hours the start of us. May I beg," he continued, noticing the superior condition of his rival's horse, "that you will not attempt to accommodate your pace to mine?"

Edward bowed, and rode on, wondering at the change which a few months had wrought in Fanshawe's character. On this occasion, especially, the energy of his mind had communicated itself to his frame. The color was strong and high in his cheek; and his whole appearance was that of a gallant and manly youth, whom a lady might love, or a foe might fear. Edward had not been so slow as his mistress in discovering the student's affection; and he could not but acknowledge in his heart that he was a rival not to be despised, and might yet be a successful one, if, by his means, Ellen Langton were restored to her friends. This consideration caused him to spur forward with increased ardor; but all his speed could not divest him of the idea that Fanshawe would finally overtake him, and attain the object of their mutual pursuit. There was certainly no apparent ground for this imagination: for every step of his horse increased the advantage which Edward had gained, and he soon lost sight of his rival.

Shortly after overtaking Fanshawe, the young man passed the lonely cottage formerly the residence of the Widow Butler, who now lay dead within. He was at first inclined to alight, and make inquiries respecting the fugitives; for he observed through the windows the faces of several persons, whom curiosity, or some better feeling, had led to the house of mourning. Recollecting, however, that this portion of the road must have been passed by the angler and Ellen at too early an hour to attract notice, he forbore to waste time by a fruitless delay.

Edward proceeded on his journey, meeting with no other noticeable event, till, arriving at the summit of a hill, he beheld, a few hundred yards before him, the Rev. Dr. Melmoth. The worthy president was toiling onward at a rate unexampled in the history either of himself or his steed; the excellence of the latter consisting in sure-footedness rather than rapidity. The rider looked round, seemingly in some apprehension at the sound of hoof-tramps behind him, but was unable to conceal his satisfaction on recognizing Edward Walcott.

In the whole course of his life, Dr. Melmoth had never been placed in circumstances so embarrassing as the present. He was altogether a child in the ways of the world, having spent his youth and early manhood in abstracted study, and his maturity in the solitude of these hills. The expedition, therefore, on which fate had now thrust him, was an entire deviation from the quiet pathway of all his former years; and he felt like one who sets forth over the broad ocean without chart or compass. The affair would undoubtedly have been perplexing to a man of far more experience than he; but the doctor pictured to himself a thousand difficulties and dangers, which, except in his imagination, had no existence. The perturbation of his spirit had compelled him, more than once since his departure, to regret that he had not invited Mrs. Melmoth to a share in the adventure; this being an occasion where her firmness, decision, and confident sagacity — which made her a sort of domestic hedgehog — would have been peculiarly appropriate. In the absence of such a counsellor, even Edward Walcott — young as he was, and indiscreet as the doctor thought him — was a substitute not to be despised; and it was singular and rather ludicrous to observe how the gray-haired man unconsciously became as a child to the beardless youth. He addressed Edward with an assumption of dignity, through which his pleasure at the meeting was very obvious.

"Young gentleman, this is not well," he said. "By what authority have you absented yourself from the walls of Alma Mater during term-time?"

"I conceived that it was unnecessary to ask leave at such a conjuncture, and when the head of the institution was himself in the saddle," replied Edward.

"It was a fault, it was a fault," said Dr. Melmoth, shaking his head; "but, in consideration of the motive, I may pass it over. And now, my dear Edward, I advise that we continue our journey together, as your youth and inexperience will stand in need of the wisdom of my gray head. Nay, I pray you lay not the lash to your steed. You have ridden fast and far; and a slower pace is requisite for a season."

And, in order to keep up with his young companion, the doctor smote his own gray nag; which unhappy beast, wondering what strange concatenation of events had procured him such treatment, endeavored to obey his master's wishes. Edward had sufficient compassion for Dr. Melmoth (especially as his own horse now exhibited signs of weariness) to moderate his pace to one attainable by the former.

"Alas, youth! these are strange times," observed the president, "when a doctor of divinity and an under-graduate set forth, like a knight-errant and his squire, in search of a stray damsel. Methinks I am an epitome of the church militant, or a new species of polemical divinity. Pray Heaven, however, there be no encounter in store for us; for I utterly forgot to provide myself with weapons."

"I took some thought for that matter, reverend knight," replied Edward, whose imagination was highly tickled by Dr. Melmoth's chivalrous comparison.

"Ay, I see that you have girded on a sword," said the divine. "But wherewith shall I defend myself, my hand being empty, except of this golden headed staff, the gift of Mr. Langton?"

"One of these, if you will accept it," answered Edward, exhibiting a brace of pistols, "will serve to begin the conflict, before you join the battle hand to hand."

"Nay, I shall find little safety in meddling with that deadly instrument, since I know not accurately from which end proceeds the bullet," said Dr. Melmoth. "But were it not better, seeing we are so well provided with artillery, to betake ourselves, in the event of an encounter, to some stone-wall or other place of strength?"

"If I may presume to advise," said the squire, "you, as being most valiant and experienced, should ride forward, lance in hand (your long staff serving for a lance), while I annoy the enemy from afar."

"Like Teucer behind the shield of Ajax," interrupted Dr. Melmoth, "or David with his stone and sling. No, no, young man! I have left unfinished in my study a learned treatise, important not only to the present age, but to posterity, for whose sakes I must take heed to my safety. — But, lo! who ride yonder?" he exclaimed, in manifest alarm, pointing to some horsemen upon the brow of a hill at a short distance before them.

"Fear not, gallant leader," said Edward Walcott, who had already discovered the objects of the doctor's terror. "They are men of peace, as we shall shortly see. The foremost is somewhere near your own years, and rides like a grave, substantial citizen, — though what he does here, I know not. Behind come two servants, men likewise of sober age and pacific appearance."

"Truly your eyes are better than mine own. Of a verity, you are in the right," acquiesced Dr. Melmoth, recovering his usual quantum of intrepidity. "We will ride forward courageously, as those who, in a just cause, fear neither death nor bonds."

The reverend knight-errant and his squire, at the time of discovering the three horsemen, were within a very short distance of the town, which was, however, concealed from their view by the hill that the strangers were descending. The road from Harley College, through almost its whole extent, had been rough and wild, and the country thin of population; but now, standing frequent, amid fertile fields on each side of the way, were neat little cottages, from which groups of white-headed children rushed forth to gaze upon the travellers. The three strangers, as well as the doctor and Edward, were surrounded, as they ap-

proached each other, by a crowd of this kind, plying
their little bare legs most pertinaciously in order to
keep pace with the horses.

As Edward gained a nearer view of the foremost
rider, his grave aspect and stately demeanor struck
him with involuntary respect. There were deep lines
of thought across his brow; and his calm yet bright
gray eye betokened a steadfast soul. There was also
an air of conscious importance, even in the manner in
which the stranger sat his horse, which a man's good
opinion of himself, unassisted by the concurrence of
the world in general, seldom bestows. The two servants rode at a respectable distance in the rear; and
the heavy portmanteaus at their backs intimated that
the party had journeyed from afar. Dr. Melmoth endeavored to assume the dignity that became him as
the head of Harley College; and with a gentle stroke
of his staff upon his wearied steed and a grave nod
to the principal stranger, was about to commence the
ascent of the hill at the foot of which they were. The
gentleman, however, made a halt.

"Dr. Melmoth, am I so fortunate as to meet you?"
he exclaimed in accents expressive of as much surprise
and pleasure as were consistent with his staid demeanor. "Have you, then, forgotten your old friend?"

"Mr. Langton! Can it be?" said the doctor, after
looking him in the face a moment. "Yes, it is my
old friend indeed: welcome, welcome! though you
come at an unfortunate time."

"What say you? How is my child? Ellen, I trust,
is well?" cried Mr. Langton, a father's anxiety over-
coming the coldness and reserve that were natural to
him, or that long habit had made a second nature.

"She is well in health. She was so, at least, last

night," replied Dr. Melmoth unable to meet the eye of his friend. "But — but I have been a careless shepherd; and the lamb has strayed from the fold while I slept."

Edward Walcott, who was a deeply interested observer of this scene, had anticipated that a burst of passionate grief would follow the disclosure. He was, however, altogether mistaken. There was a momentary convulsion of Mr. Langton's strong features, as quick to come and go as a flash of lightning; and then his countenance was as composed — though, perhaps, a little sterner — as before. He seemed about to inquire into the particulars of what so nearly concerned him, but changed his purpose on observing the crowd of children, who, with one or two of their parents, were endeavoring to catch the words that passed between the doctor and himself.

"I will turn back with you to the village," he said in a steady voice; "and at your leisure I shall desire to hear the particulars of this unfortunate affair."

He wheeled his horse accordingly, and, side by side with Dr. Melmoth, began to ascend the hill. On reaching the summit, the little country town lay before them, presenting a cheerful and busy spectacle. It consisted of one long, regular street, extending parallel to, and at a short distance from, the river; which here, enlarged by a junction with another stream, became navigable, not indeed for vessels of burden, but for rafts of lumber and boats of considerable size. The houses, with peaked roofs and jutting stories, stood at wide intervals along the street; and the commercial character of the place was manifested by the shop door and windows that occupied the front of almost every dwelling. One or two mansions, however, surrounded by

trees, and standing back at a haughty distance from
the road, were evidently the abodes of the aristocracy
of the village. It was not difficult to distinguish the
owners of these — self-important personages, with canes
and well - powdered periwigs — among the crowd of
meaner men who bestowed their attention upon Dr.
Melmoth and his friend as they rode by. The town
being the nearest mart of a large extent of back country, there were many rough farmers and woodsmen, to
whom the cavalcade was an object of curiosity and
admiration. The former feeling, indeed, was general
throughout the village. The shop-keepers left their
customers, and looked forth from the doors; the female portion of the community thrust their heads from
the windows; and the people in the street formed a
lane through which, with all eyes concentrated upon
them, the party rode onward to the tavern. The general aptitude that pervades the populace of a small
country town to meddle with affairs not legitimately
concerning them was increased, on this occasion, by the
sudden return of Mr. Langton after passing through
the village. Many conjectures were afloat respecting
the cause of this retrograde movement; and, by degrees, something like the truth, though much distorted,
spread generally among the crowd, communicated, probably, from Mr. Langton's servants. Edward Walcott,
incensed at the uncourteous curiosity of which he, as
well as his companions, was the object, felt a frequent
impulse (though, fortunately for himself, resisted) to
make use of his riding-switch in clearing a passage.

On arriving at the tavern, Dr. Melmoth recounted
to his friend the little he knew beyond the bare fact
of Ellen's disappearance. Had Edward Walcott been
called to their conference, he might, by disclosing the

adventure of the angler, have thrown a portion of light upon the affair; but, since his first introduction, the cold and stately merchant had honored him with no sort of notice.

Edward, on his part, was not well pleased at the sudden appearance of Ellen's father, and was little inclined to coöperate in any measures that he might adopt for her recovery. It was his wish to pursue the chase on his own responsibility, and as his own wisdom dictated: he chose to be an independent ally, rather than a subordinate assistant. But, as a step preliminary to his proceedings of every other kind, he found it absolutely necessary, having journeyed far, and fasting, to call upon the landlord for a supply of food. The viands that were set before him were homely but abundant; nor were Edward's griefs and perplexities so absorbing as to overcome the appetite of youth and health.

Dr. Melmoth and Mr. Langton, after a short private conversation, had summoned the landlord, in the hope of obtaining some clew to the development of the mystery. But no young lady, nor any stranger answering to the description the doctor had received from Hugh Crombie (which was indeed a false one), had been seen to pass through the village since daybreak. Here, therefore, the friends were entirely at a loss in what direction to continue the pursuit. The village was the focus of several roads, diverging to widely distant portions of the country; and which of these the fugitives had taken, it was impossible to determine. One point, however, might be considered certain, — that the village was the first stage of their flight; for it commanded the only outlet from the valley, except a rugged path among the hills, utterly impassable by horse. In this dilemma, expresses were sent by each of the different roads; and poor Ellen's imprudence — the tale nowise decreasing as it rolled along — became known to a wide extent of country. Having thus done everything in his power to recover his daughter, the merchant exhibited a composure which Dr. Melmoth admired, but could not equal. His own mind, however, was in a far more comfortable state than when the responsibility of the pursuit had rested upon himself.

Edward Walcott, in the mean time, had employed but a very few moments in satisfying his hunger; after which his active intellect alternately formed and relinquished a thousand plans for the recovery of Ellen. Fanshawe's observation, that her flight must have commenced after the subsiding of the storm, recurred to him. On inquiry, he was informed that the violence of the rain had continued, with a few momentary intermissions, till near daylight. The fugitives must, therefore, have passed through the village long after its inhabitants were abroad; and how, without the gift of invisibility, they had contrived to elude notice, Edward could not conceive.

"Fifty years ago," thought Edward, "my sweet Ellen would have been deemed a witch for this trackless journey. Truly, I could wish I were a wizard, that I might bestride a broomstick, and follow her."

While the young man, involved in these perplexing thoughts, looked forth from the open window of the apartment, his attention was drawn to an individual, evidently of a different, though not of a higher, class than the countrymen among whom he stood. Edward now recollected that he had noticed his rough dark face among the most earnest of those who had watched the arrival of the party. He had then taken him for one of the boatmen, of whom there were many in the village, and who had much of a sailor-like dress and appearance. A second and more attentive observation, however, convinced Edward that this man's life had not been spent upon fresh water; and, had any stronger evidence than the nameless marks which the ocean impresses upon its sons been necessary, it would have been found in his mode of locomotion. While Edward was observing him, he beat slowly up to one of Mr. Langton's servants who was standing near the door of the inn. He seemed to question the man with affected carelessness; but his countenance was dark and perplexed when he turned to mingle again with the crowd. Edward lost no time in ascertaining from the servant the nature of his inquiries. They had related to the elopement of Mr. Langton's daughter, which was, indeed, the prevailing, if not the sole, subject of conversation in the village.

The grounds for supposing that this man was in any way connected with the angler were, perhaps, very slight; yet, in the perplexity of the whole affair, they induced Edward to resolve to get at the heart of his mystery. To attain this end, he took the most direct method, — by applying to the man himself.

He had now retired apart from the throng and bustle of the village, and was seated upon a condemned boat, that was drawn up to rot upon the banks of the river. His arms were folded, and his hat drawn over his brows. The lower part of his face, which alone was visible, evinced gloom and depression, as did also the deep sighs, which, because he thought no one was near him, he did not attempt to restrain.

"Friend, I must speak with you," said Edward

Walcott, laying his hand upon his shoulder, after con templating the man a moment, himself unseen.

He started at once from his abstraction and his seat, apparently expecting violence, and prepared to resist it; but, perceiving the youthful and solitary intruder upon his privacy, he composed his features with much quickness.

"What would you with me?" he asked.

"They tarry long, — or you have kept a careless watch," said Edward, speaking at a venture.

For a moment, there seemed a probability of obtaining such a reply to this observation as the youth had intended to elicit. If any trust could be put in the language of the stranger's countenance, a set of words different from those to which he subsequently gave utterance had risen to his lips. But he seemed naturally slow of speech; and this defect was now, as is frequently the case, advantageous in giving him space for reflection.

"Look you, youngster: crack no jokes on me," he at length said, contemptuously. "Away! back whence you came, or "— And he slightly waved a small rattan that he held in his right hand.

Edward's eyes sparkled, and his color rose. "You must change this tone, fellow, and that speedily," he observed. "I order you to lower your hand, and answer the questions that I shall put to you."

The man gazed dubiously at him, but finally adopted a more conciliatory mode of speech.

"Well, master; and what is your business with me?" he inquired. "I am a boatman out of employ. Any commands in my line?"

"Pshaw! I know you, my good friend, and you cannot deceive me," replied Edward Walcott. "We are private here," he continued, looking around. "I have no desire or intention to do you harm; and, if you act according to my directions, you shall have no cause to repent it."

"And what if I refuse to put myself under your orders?" inquired the man. "You are but a young captain for such an old hulk as mine."

"The ill consequences of a refusal would all be on your own side," replied Edward. "I shall, in that case, deliver you up to justice: if I have not the means of capturing you myself," he continued, observing the seaman's eye to wander rather scornfully over his youthful and slender figure, "there are hundreds within call whom it will be in vain to resist. Besides, it requires little strength to use this," he added, laying his hand on a pistol.

"If that were all, I could suit you there, my lad," muttered the stranger. He continued aloud, "Well, what is your will with me? D——d ungenteel treatment this! But put your questions; and, to oblige you, I may answer them, — if so be that I know anything of the matter."

"You will do wisely," observed the young man. "And now to business. What reason have you to suppose that the persons for whom you watch are not already beyond the village?"

The seaman paused long before he answered, and gazed earnestly at Edward, apparently endeavoring to ascertain from his countenance the amount of his knowledge. This he probably overrated, but, nevertheless, hazarded a falsehood.

"I doubt not they passed before midnight," he said. "I warrant you they are many a league towards the sea-coast ere this."

"You have kept watch, then, since midnight?" asked Edward.

"Ay, that have I! And a dark and rough one it was," answered the stranger.

"And you are certain that, if they passed at all, it must have been before that hour?"

"I kept my walk across the road till the village was all astir," said the seaman. "They could not have missed me. So, you see, your best way is to give chase; for they have a long start of you, and you have no time to lose."

"Your information is sufficient, my good friend," said Edward, with a smile. "I have reason to know that they did not commence their flight before midnight. You have made it evident that they have not passed since: ergo, they have not passed at all, — an indisputable syllogism. And now will I retrace my footsteps."

"Stay, young man," said the stranger, placing himself full in Edward's way as he was about to hasten to the inn. "You have drawn me in to betray my comrade; but, before you leave this place, you must answer a question or two of mine. Do you mean to take the law with you? or will you right your wrongs, if you have any, with your own right hand?"

"It is my intention to take the latter method. But, if I choose the former, what then?" demanded Edward.

"Nay, nothing: only you or I might not have gone hence alive," replied the stranger. "But as you say he shall have fair play" —

"On my word, friend," interrupted the young man, "I fear your intelligence has come too late to do either good or harm. Look towards the inn: my companions are getting to horse, and, my life on it, they know whither to ride."

So saying, he hastened away, followed by the stranger. It was indeed evident that news of some kind or other had reached the village. The people were gathered in groups, conversing eagerly ; and the pale cheeks, uplifted eyebrows, and outspread hands of some of the female sex filled Edward's mind with undefined but intolerable apprehensions. He forced his way to Dr. Melmoth, who had just mounted, and, seizing his bridle, peremptorily demanded if he knew aught of Ellen Langton.

CHAPTER VIII.

"Full many a miserable year hath passed:
  She knows him as one dead, or worse than dead:
  And many a change her varied life hath known;
  But her heart none."   MATURIN.

SINCE her interview with the angler, which was
interrupted by the appearance of Fanshawe, Ellen
Langton's hitherto calm and peaceful mind had been
in a state of insufferable doubt and dismay. She
was imperatively called upon — at least, she so conceived — to break through the rules which nature and
education impose upon her sex, to quit the protection of those whose desire for her welfare was true
and strong, and to trust herself, for what purpose
she scarcely knew, to a stranger, from whom the instinctive purity of her mind would involuntarily have
shrunk, under whatever circumstances she had met
him. The letter which she had received from the
hands of the angler had seemed to her inexperience to
prove beyond a doubt that the bearer was the friend
of her father, and authorized by him, if her duty and
affection were stronger than her fears, to guide her to
his retreat. The letter spoke vaguely of losses and
misfortunes, and of a necessity for concealment on her
father's part, and secrecy on hers; and, to the credit
of Ellen's not very romantic understanding, it must be
acknowledged that the mystery of the plot had nearly
prevented its success. She did not, indeed, doubt
that the letter was from her father's hand; for every
line and stroke, and even many of its phrases, were

familiar to her. Her apprehension was, that his misfortunes, of what nature soever they were, had affected his intellect, and that, under such an influence, he had commanded her to take a step which nothing less than such a command could justify. Ellen did not, however, remain long in this opinion; for when she reperused the letter, and considered the firm, regular characters, and the style, — calm and cold, even in requesting such a sacrifice, — she felt that there was nothing like insanity here. In fine, she came gradually to the belief that there were strong reasons, though incomprehensible by her, for the secrecy that her father had enjoined.

Having arrived at this conviction, her decision lay plain before her. Her affection for Mr. Langton was not, indeed, — nor was it possible, — so strong as that she would have felt for a parent who had watched over her from her infancy. Neither was the conception she had unavoidably formed of his character such as to promise that in him she would find an equivalent for all she must sacrifice. On the contrary, her gentle nature and loving heart, which otherwise would have rejoiced in a new object of affection, now shrank with something like dread from the idea of meeting her father, — stately, cold, and stern as she could not but imagine him. A sense of duty was therefore Ellen's only support in resolving to tread the dark path that lay before her.

Had there been any person of her own sex in whom Ellen felt confidence, there is little doubt that she would so far have disobeyed her father's letter as to communicate its contents, and take counsel as to her proceedings. But Mrs. Melmoth was the only female — excepting, indeed, the maid-servant — to whom it was possible to make the communication; and, though Ellen at first thought of such a step, her timidity, and her knowledge of the lady's character, did not permit her to venture upon it. She next reviewed her acquaintances of the other sex; and Dr. Melmoth first presented himself, as in every respect but one, an unexceptionable confidant. But the single exception was equivalent to many. The maiden, with the highest opinion of the doctor's learning and talents, had sufficient penetration to know, that, in the ways of the world, she was herself the better skilled of the two. For a moment she thought of Edward Walcott; but he was light and wild, and, which her delicacy made an insurmountable objection, there was an untold love between them. Her thoughts finally centred on Fanshawe. In his judgment, young and inexperienced though he was, she would have placed a firm trust; and his zeal, from whatever cause it arose, she could not doubt.

If, in the short time allowed her for reflection, an opportunity had occurred for consulting him, she would, in all probability, have taken advantage of it. But the terms on which they had parted the preceding evening had afforded him no reason to hope for her confidence; and he felt that there were others who had a better right to it than himself. He did not, therefore, throw himself in her way; and poor Ellen was consequently left without an adviser.

The determination that resulted from her own unassisted wisdom has been seen. When discovered by Dr. Melmoth at Hugh Crombie's inn, she was wholly prepared for flight, and, but for the intervention of the storm, would, ere then, have been far away.

The firmness of resolve that had impelled a timid

maiden upon such a step was not likely to be broken by one defeat; and Ellen, accordingly, confident that the stranger would make a second attempt, determined that no effort on her part should be wanting to its success. On reaching her chamber, therefore, instead of retiring to rest (of which, from her sleepless thoughts of the preceding night, she stood greatly in need), she sat watching for the abatement of the storm. Her meditations were now calmer than at any time since her first meeting with the angler. She felt as if her fate was decided. The stain had fallen upon her reputation: she was no longer the same pure being in the opinion of those whose approbation she most valued.

One obstacle to her flight — and, to a woman's mind, a most powerful one — had thus been removed. Dark and intricate as was the way, it was easier now to proceed than to pause; and her desperate and forlorn situation gave her a strength which hitherto she had not felt.

At every cessation in the torrent of rain that beat against the house, Ellen flew to the window, expecting to see the stranger form beneath it. But the clouds would again thicken, and the storm recommence with its former violence; and she began to fear that the approach of morning would compel her to meet the now dreaded face of Dr. Melmoth. At length, however, a strong and steady wind, supplying the place of the fitful gusts of the preceding part of the night, broke and scattered the clouds from the broad expanse of the sky. The moon, commencing her late voyage not long before the sun, was now visible, setting forth like a lonely ship from the dark line of the horizon, and touching at many a little silver cloud the

islands of that aerial deep. Ellen felt that now the
time was come; and, with a calmness wonderful to
herself, she prepared for her final departure.

She had not long to wait ere she saw, between the
vacancies of the trees, the angler advancing along the
shady avenue that led to the principal entrance of Dr.
Melmoth's dwelling. He had no need to summon her
either by word or signal; for she had descended,
emerged from the door, and stood before him, while
he was yet at some distance from the house.

"You have watched well," he observed in a low,
strange tone. "As saith the Scripture, 'Many daughters have done virtuously; but thou excellest them
all.'"

He took her arm; and they hastened down the avenue. Then, leaving Hugh Crombie's inn on their
right, they found its master in a spot so shaded that
the moonbeams could not enlighten it. He held by
the bridle two horses, one of which the angler assisted
Ellen to mount. Then, turning to the landlord he
pressed a purse into his hand; but Hugh drew back,
and it fell to the ground.

"No! this would not have tempted me; nor will it
reward me," he said. "If you have gold to spare,
there are some that need it more than I."

"I understand you, mine host. I shall take thought
for them; and enough will remain for you and me,"
replied his comrade. "I have seen the day when such
a purse would not have slipped between your fingers.
Well, be it so. And now, Hugh, my old friend, a
shake of your hand; for we are seeing our last of
each other."

"Pray Heaven it be so! though I wish you no ill,"
said the landlord, giving his hand.

He then seemed about to approach Ellen, who had been unable to distinguish the words of this brief conversation; but his comrade prevented him. "There is no time to lose," he observed. "The moon is growing pale already, and we should have been many a mile beyond the valley ere this." He mounted as he spoke; and, guiding Ellen's rein till they reached the road, they dashed away.

It was now that she felt herself completely in his power; and with that consciousness there came a sudden change of feeling, and an altered view of her conduct. A thousand reasons forced themselves upon her mind, seeming to prove that she had been deceived; while the motives, so powerful with her but a moment before, had either vanished from her memory or lost all their efficacy. Her companion, who gazed searchingly into her face, where the moonlight, coming down between the pines, allowed him to read its expression, probably discerned somewhat of the state of her thoughts.

"Do you repent so soon?" he inquired. "We have a weary way before us. Faint not ere we have well entered upon it."

"I have left dear friends behind me, and am going I know not whither," replied Ellen, tremblingly.

"You have a faithful guide," he observed, turning away his head, and speaking in the tone of one who endeavors to smother a laugh.

Ellen had no heart to continue the conversation; and they rode on in silence, and through a wild and gloomy scene. The wind roared heavily through the forest, and the trees shed their raindrops upon the travellers. The road, at all times rough, was now broken into deep gullies, through which streams went murmuring down to mingle with the river. The pale moonlight combined with the gray of the morning to give a ghastly and unsubstantial appearance to every object.

The difficulties of the road had been so much increased by the storm, that the purple eastern clouds gave notice of the near approach of the sun just as the travellers reached the little lonesome cottage which Ellen remembered to have visited several months before. On arriving opposite to it, her companion checked his horse, and gazed with a wild earnestness at the wretched habitation. Then, stifling a groan that would not altogether be repressed, he was about to pass on ; but at that moment the cottage-door opened, and a woman, whose sour, unpleasant countenance Ellen recognized, came hastily forth. She seemed not to heed the travellers ; but the angler, his voice thrilling and quivering with indescribable emotion, addressed her.

"Woman, whither do you go?" he inquired.

She started, but, after a momentary pause, replied, "There is one within at the point of death. She struggles fearfully; and I cannot endure to watch alone by her bedside. If you are Christians, come in with me."

Ellen's companion leaped hastily from his horse, assisted her also to dismount, and followed the woman into the cottage, having first thrown the bridles of the horses carelessly over the branch of a tree. Ellen trembled at the awful scene she would be compelled to witness ; but, when death was so near at hand, it was more terrible to stand alone in the dim morning light than even to watch the parting of soul and body. She therefore entered the cottage.

Her guide, his face muffled in his cloak, had taken his stand at a distance from the death-bed, in a part of the room which neither the increasing daylight nor the dim rays of a solitary lamp had yet enlightened. At Ellen's entrance, the dying woman lay still, and apparently calm, except that a plaintive, half-articulate sound occasionally wandered through her lips.

"Hush! For mercy's sake, silence!" whispered the other woman to the strangers. "There is good hope now that she will die a peaceable death; but, if she is disturbed, the boldest of us will not dare to stand by her bedside."

The whisper by which her sister endeavored to preserve quiet perhaps reached the ears of the dying female; for she now raised herself in bed, slowly, but with a strength superior to what her situation promised. Her face was ghastly and wild, from long illness, approaching death, and disturbed intellect; and a disembodied spirit could scarcely be a more fearful object than one whose soul was just struggling forth. Her sister, approaching with the soft and stealing step appropriate to the chamber of sickness and death, attempted to replace the covering around her, and to compose her again upon the pillow. "Lie down and sleep, sister," she said; "and, when the day breaks, I will waken you. Methinks your breath comes freer already. A little more slumber, and to-morrow you will be well."

"My illness is gone: I am well," said the dying woman, gasping for breath. "I wander where the fresh breeze comes sweetly over my face; but a close and stifled air has choked my lungs."

"Yet a little while, and you will no longer draw your breath in pain," observed her sister, again replacing the bedclothes. which she continued to throw off.

"My husband is with me," murmured the widow. "He walks by my side, and speaks to me as in old times; but his words come faintly on my ear. Cheer me and comfort me, my husband; for there is a terror in those dim, motionless eyes, and in that shadowy voice."

As she spoke thus, she seemed to gaze upon some object that stood by her bedside; and the eyes of those who witnessed this scene could not but follow the direction of hers. They observed that the dying woman's own shadow was marked upon the wall, receiving a tremulous motion from the fitful rays of the lamp, and from her own convulsive efforts. "My husband stands gazing on me," she said again; "but my son, — where is he? And, as I ask, the father turns away his face. Where is our son? For his sake, I have longed to come to this land of rest. For him I have sorrowed many years. Will he not comfort me now?"

At these words the stranger made a few hasty steps towards the bed; but, ere he reached it, he conquered the impulse that drew him thither, and, shrouding his face more deeply in his cloak, returned to his former position. The dying woman, in the mean time, had thrown herself back upon the bed; and her sobbing and wailing, imaginary as was their cause, were inexpressibly affecting.

"Take me back to earth," she said; "for its griefs have followed me hither."

The stranger advanced, and, seizing the lamp, knelt down by the bedside, throwing the light full upon his pale and convulsed features.

"Mother, here is your son!" he exclaimed.

At that unforgotten voice, the darkness burst away

at once from her soul. She arose in bed, her eyes and her whole countenance beaming with joy, and threw her arms about his neck. A multitude of words seemed struggling for utterance ; but they gave place to a low moaning sound, and then to the silence of death. The one moment of happiness, that recompensed years of sorrow, had been her last. Her son laid the lifeless form upon the pillow, and gazed with fixed eyes on his mother's face.

As he looked, the expression of enthusiastic joy that parting life had left upon the features faded gradually away ; and the countenance, though no longer wild, assumed the sadness which it had worn through a long course of grief and pain. On beholding this natural consequence of death, the thought, perhaps, occurred to him, that her soul, no longer dependent on the imperfect means of intercourse possessed by mortals, had communed with his own, and become acquainted with all its guilt and misery. He started from the bedside, and covered his face with his hands, as if to hide it from those dead eyes.

Such a scene as has been described could not but have a powerful effect upon any one who retained aught of humanity ; and the grief of the son, whose natural feelings had been blunted, but not destroyed, by an evil life, was much more violent than his outward demeanor would have expressed. But his deep repentance for the misery he had brought upon his parent did not produce in him a resolution to do wrong no more. The sudden consciousness of accumulated guilt made him desperate. He felt as if no one had thenceforth a claim to justice or compassion at his hands, when his neglect and cruelty had poisoned his mother's life, and hastened her death

Thus it was that the Devil wrought with him to his own destruction, reversing the salutary effect which his mother would have died exultingly to produce upon his mind. He now turned to Ellen Langton with a demeanor singularly calm and composed.

"We must resume our journey," he said, in his usual tone of voice. "The sun is on the point of rising, though but little light finds its way into this hovel."

Ellen's previous suspicions as to the character of her companion had now become certainty so far as to convince her that she was in the power of a lawless and guilty man; though what fate he intended for her she was unable to conjecture. An open opposition to his will, however, could not be ventured upon; especially as she discovered, on looking round the apartment, that, with the exception of the corpse, they were alone.

"Will you not attend your mother's funeral?" she asked, trembling, and conscious that he would discover her fears.

"The dead must bury their dead," he replied. "I have brought my mother to her grave, — and what can a son do more? This purse, however, will serve to lay her in the earth, and leave something for the old hag. Whither is she gone?" interrupted he, casting a glance round the room in search of the old woman. "Nay, then, we must speedily to horse. I know her of old."

Thus saying, he threw the purse upon the table, and, without trusting himself to look again towards the dead, conducted Ellen out of the cottage. The first rays of the sun at that moment gilded the tallest trees of the forest.

On looking towards the spot were the horses had stood, Ellen thought that Providence, in answer to her prayers, had taken care for her deliverance. They were no longer there, — a circumstance easily accounted for by the haste with which the bridles had been thrown over the branch of the tree. Her companion, however, imputed it to another cause.

"The hag! She would sell her own flesh and blood by weight and measure," he muttered to himself. "This is some plot of hers, I know well."

He put his hand to his forehead for a moment's space, seeming to reflect on the course most advisable to be pursued. Ellen, perhaps unwisely, interposed.

"Would it not be well to return?" she asked, timidly. "There is now no hope of escaping; but I might yet reach home undiscovered."

"Return!" repeated her guide, with a look and smile from which she turned away her face. "Have you forgotten your father and his misfortunes? No, no, sweet Ellen: it is too late for such thoughts as these."

He took her hand, and led her towards the forest, in the rear of the cottage. She would fain have resisted; but they were all alone, and the attempt must have been both fruitless and dangerous. She therefore trod with him a path so devious, so faintly traced, and so overgrown with bushes and young trees, that only a most accurate acquaintance in his early days could have enabled her guide to retain it. To him, however, it seemed so perfectly familiar, that he was not once compelled to pause, though the numerous windings soon deprived Ellen of all knowledge of the situation of the cottage. They descended a steep hill, and, proceeding parallel to the river, — as Ellen

judged by its rushing sound, — at length found themselves at what proved to be the termination of their
walk.

Ellen now recollected a remark of Edward Walcott's respecting the wild and rude scenery through
which the river here kept its way; and, in less agitat-
ing circumstances, her pleasure and admiration would
have been great. They stood beneath a precipice, so
high that the loftiest pine-tops (and many of them
seemed to soar to heaven) scarcely surmounted it.
This line of rock has a considerable extent, at unequal
heights, and with many interruptions, along the course
of the river; and it seems probable that, at some
former period, it was the boundary of the waters,
though they are now confined within far less ambitious limits. The inferior portion of the crag, beneath
which Ellen and her guide were standing, varies so
far from the perpendicular as not to be inaccessible
by a careful footstep. But only one person has been
known to attempt the ascent of the superior half, and
only one the descent; yet, steep as is the height, trees
and bushes of various kinds have clung to the rock,
wherever their roots could gain the slightest hold;
thus seeming to prefer the scanty and difficult nourish-
ment of the cliff to a more luxurious life in the rich
interval that extends from its base to the river. But,
whether or no these hardy vegetables have voluntarily
chosen their rude resting-place, the cliff is indebted to
them for much of the beauty that tempers its sublimity. When the eye is pained and wearied by the bold
nakedness of the rock, it rests with pleasure on the
cheerful foliage of the birch, or upon the darker green
of the funereal pine. Just at the termination of the accessible portion of the crag, these trees are so numer-

ous, and their foliage so dense, that they completely shroud from view a considerable excavation, formed, probably, hundreds of years since, by the fall of a portion of the rock. The detached fragment still lies at a little distance from the base, gray and moss-grown, but corresponding, in its general outline, to the cavity from which it was rent.

But the most singular and beautiful object in all this scene is a tiny fount of crystal water, that gushes forth from the high, smooth forehead of the cliff. Its perpendicular descent is of many feet; after which it finds its way, with a sweet diminutive murmur, to the level ground.

It is not easy to conceive whence the barren rock procures even the small supply of water that is necessary to the existence of this stream; it is as unaccountable as the gush of gentle feeling which sometimes proceeds from the hardest heart: but there it continues to flow and fall, undiminished and unincreased. The stream is so slender, that the gentlest breeze suffices to disturb its descent, and to scatter its pure sweet waters over the face of the cliff. But in that deep forest there is seldom a breath of wind; so that, plashing continually upon one spot, the fount has worn its own little channel of white sand, by which it finds its way to the river. Alas that the Naiades have lost their old authority! for what a deity of tiny loveliness must once have presided here!

Ellen's companion paused not to gaze either upon the loveliness or the sublimity of this scene, but, assisting her where it was requisite, began the steep and difficult ascent of the lower part of the cliff. The maiden's ingenuity in vain endeavored to assign reasons for this movement; but when they reached the tuft of trees, which, as has been noticed, grew at the ultimate point where mortal footstep might safely tread, she perceived through their thick branches the recess in the rock. Here they entered; and her guide pointed to a mossy seat, in the formation of which, to judge from its regularity, art had probably a share.

"Here you may remain in safety," he observed, "till I obtain the means of proceeding. In this spot you need fear no intruder; but it will be dangerous to venture beyond its bounds."

The meaning glance that accompanied these words intimated to poor Ellen, that, in warning her against danger, he alluded to the vengeance with which he would visit any attempt to escape. To leave her thus alone, trusting to the influence of such a threat, was a bold, yet a necessary and by no means a hopeless measure. On Ellen it produced the desired effect; and she sat in the cave as motionless, for a time, as if she had herself been a part of the rock. In other circumstances this shady recess would have been a delightful retreat during the sultry warmth of a summer's day. The dewy coolness of the rock kept the air always fresh and the sunbeams never thrust themselves so as to dissipate the mellow twilight through the green trees with which the chamber was curtained. Ellen's sleeplessness and agitation for many preceding hours had perhaps deadened her feelings; for she now felt a sort of indifference creeping upon her, an inability to realize the evils of her situation, at the same time that she was perfectly aware of them all. This torpor of mind increased, till her eyelids began to grow heavy and the cave and trees to swim before her sight. In a few moments more she would probably have been in dreamless slumber; but, rousing herself by a strong effort, she looked round the narrow limits of the cave in search of objects to excite her worn-out mind.

She now perceived, wherever the smooth rock afforded place for them, the initials, or the full-length names of former visitants of the cave. What wanderer on mountain-tops or in deep solitudes has not felt the influence of these records of humanity, telling him, when such a conviction is soothing to his heart, that he is not alone in the world? It was singular, that, when her own mysterious situation had almost lost its power to engage her thoughts, Ellen perused these barren memorials with a certain degree of interest. She went on repeating them aloud, and starting at the sound of her own voice, till at length, as one name passed through her lips, she paused, and then, leaning her forehead against the letters, burst into tears. It was the name of Edward Walcott; and it struck upon her heart, arousing her to a full sense of her present misfortunes and dangers, and, more painful still, of her past happiness. Her tears had, however, a soothing, and at the same time a strengthening effect upon her mind ; for, when their gush was over, she raised her head, and began to meditate on the means of escape. She wondered at the species of fascination that had kept her, as if chained to the rock, so long, when there was, in reality, nothing to bar her pathway. She determined, late as it was, to attempt her own deliverance, and for that purpose began slowly and cautiously to emerge from the cave.

Peeping out from among the trees, she looked and listened with most painful anxiety to discover if any living thing were in that seeming solitude, or if any sound disturbed the heavy stillness. But she saw only Nature in her wildest forms, and heard only the plash and murmur (almost inaudible, because continual) of the little waterfall, and the quick, short throbbing of her own heart, against which she pressed her hand as if to hush it. Gathering courage, therefore, she began to descend; and, starting often at the loose stones that even her light footstep displaced and sent rattling down, she at length reached the base of the crag in safety. She then made a few steps in the direction, as nearly as she could judge, by which she arrived at the spot, but paused, with a sudden revulsion of the blood to her heart, as her guide emerged from behind a projecting part of the rock. He approached her deliberately, an ironical smile writhing his features into a most disagreeable expression; while in his eyes there was something that seemed a wild, fierce joy. By a species of sophistry, of which oppressors often make use, he had brought himself to believe that he was now the injured one, and that Ellen, by her distrust of him, had fairly subjected herself to whatever evil it consisted with his will and power to inflict upon her. Her only restraining influence over him, the consciousness, in his own mind, that he possessed her confidence, was now done away. Ellen, as well as her enemy, felt that this was the case. She knew not what to dread; but she was well aware that danger was at hand, and that, in the deep wilderness, there was none to help her, except that Being with whose inscrutable purposes it might consist to allow the wicked to triumph for a season, and the innocent to be brought low.

"Are you so soon weary of this quiet retreat?" demanded her guide, continuing to wear the same sneering smile. "Or has your anxiety for your father induced you to set forth alone in quest of the afflicted old man?"

"Oh, if I were but with him!" exclaimed Ellen. "But this place is lonely and fearful; and I cannot endure to remain here."

"Lonely, is it, sweet Ellen?" he rejoined; "am I not with you? Yes, it is lonely, — lonely as guilt could wish. Cry aloud, Ellen, and spare not. Shriek, and see if there be any among these rocks and woods to hearken to you!"

"There is, there is One," exclaimed Ellen, shuddering, and affrighted at the fearful meaning of his countenance. "He is here! He is there!" And she pointed to heaven.

"It may be so, dearest," he replied. "But if there be an Ear that hears, and an Eye that sees all the evil of the earth, yet the Arm is slow to avenge. Else why do I stand before you a living man?"

"His vengeance may be delayed for a time, but not forever," she answered, gathering a desperate courage from the extremity of her fear.

"You say true, lovely Ellen; and I have done enough, erenow, to insure its heaviest weight. There is a pass, when evil deeds can add nothing to guilt, nor good ones take anything from it."

"Think of your mother, — of her sorrow through life, and perhaps even after death," Ellen began to say. But, as she spoke these words, the expression of his face was changed, becoming suddenly so dark and fiend-like, that she clasped her hands, and fell on her knees before him.

"I have thought of my mother," he replied, speaking very low, and putting his face close to hers. "I remember the neglect, the wrong, the lingering and miserable death, that she received at my hands. By what claim can either man or woman henceforth expect mercy from me? If God will help you, be it so; but by those words you have turned my heart to stone."

At this period of their conversation, when Ellen's peril seemed most imminent, the attention of both was attracted by a fragment of rock, which, falling from the summit of the crag, struck very near them. Ellen started from her knees, and, with her false guide, gazed eagerly upward, — he in the fear of interruption, she in the hope of deliverance.

CHAPTER IX.

"At length, he cries, behold the fated spring!
Yon rugged cliff conceals the fountain blest,
Dark rocks its crystal source o'ershadowing."

PSYCHE.

THE tale now returns to Fanshawe, who, as will be recollected, after being overtaken by Edward Walcott, was left with little apparent prospect of aiding in the deliverance of Ellen Langton.

It would be difficult to analyze the feelings with which the student pursued the chase, or to decide whether he was influenced and animated by the same hopes of successful love that cheered his rival. That he was conscious of such hopes, there is little reason to suppose; for the most powerful minds are not always the best acquainted with their own feelings. Had Fanshawe, moreover, acknowledged to himself the possibility of gaining Ellen's affections, his generosity would have induced him to refrain from her society before it was too late. He had read her character with accuracy, and had seen how fit she was to love, and to be loved, by a man who could find his happiness in the common occupations of the world; and Fanshawe never deceived himself so far as to suppose that this would be the case with him. Indeed, he often wondered at the passion with which Ellen's simple loveliness of mind and person had inspired him, and which seemed to be founded on the principle of contrariety, rather than of sympathy. It was the yearning of a soul, formed by Nature in a peculiar

mould, for communion with those to whom it bore a
resemblance, yet of whom it was not. But there was
no reason to suppose that Ellen, who differed from
the multitude only as being purer and better, would
cast away her affections on the one, of all who surrounded her, least fitted to make her happy. Thus
Fanshawe reasoned with himself, and of this he believed that he was convinced. Yet ever and anon he
found himself involved in a dream of bliss, of which
Ellen was to be the giver and the sharer. Then would
he rouse himself, and press upon his mind the chilling
consciousness that it was and could be but a dream.
There was also another feeling, apparently discordant
with those which have been enumerated. It was a
longing for rest, for his old retirement, that came at
intervals so powerfully upon him, as he rode on, that
his heart sickened of the active exertion on which fate
had thrust him.

After being overtaken by Edward Walcott, Fanshawe continued his journey with as much speed as
was attainable by his wearied horse, but at a pace infinitely too slow for his earnest thoughts. These had
carried him far away, leaving him only such a consciousness of his present situation as to make diligent
use of the spur, when a horse's tread at no great distance struck upon his ear. He looked forward and
behind ; but, though a considerable extent of the narrow, rocky, and grass-grown road was visible, he was
the only traveller there. Yet again he heard the
sound, which, he now discovered, proceeded from
among the trees that lined the roadside. Alighting,
he entered the forest, with the intention, if the steed
proved to be disengaged, and superior to his own, of
appropriating him to his own use. He soon gained a

view of the object he sought ; but the animal rendered a closer acquaintance unattainable, by immediately taking to his heels. Fanshawe had, however, made a most interesting discovery ; for the horse was accoutred with a side-saddle ; and who but Ellen Langton could have been his rider? At this conclusion, though his perplexity was thereby in no degree diminished, the student immediately arrived. Returning to the road, and perceiving on the summit of the hill a cottage, which he recognized as the one he had entered with Ellen and Edward Walcott, he determined there to make inquiry respecting the objects of his pursuit.

On reaching the door of the poverty-stricken dwelling, he saw that it was not now so desolate of inmates as on his previous visit. In the single inhabitable apartment were several elderly women, clad evidently in their well-worn and well-saved Sunday clothes, and all wearing a deep grievous expression of countenance. Fanshawe was not long in deciding that death was within the cottage, and that these aged females were of the class who love the house of mourning, because to them it is a house of feasting. It is a fact, disgusting and lamentable, that the disposition which Heaven, for the best of purposes, has implanted in the female breast — to watch by the sick and comfort the afflicted — frequently becomes depraved into an odious love of scenes of pain and death and sorrow. Such women are like the Ghouls of the Arabian Tales, whose feasting was among tombstones and upon dead carcasses.

(It is sometimes, though less frequently, the case, that this disposition to make a " joy of grief " extends to individuals of the other sex. But in us it is even less excusable and more disgusting, because it is our nature to shun the sick and afflicted ; and, unless restrained by principles other than we bring into the world with us, men might follow the example of many animals in destroying the infirm of their own species. Indeed, instances of this nature might be adduced among savage nations.) Sometimes, however, from an original *lusus naturæ*, or from the influence of circumstances, a man becomes a haunter of death-beds, a tormentor of afflicted hearts, and a follower of funerals. Such an abomination now appeared before Fanshawe, and beckoned him into the cottage. He was considerably beyond the middle age, rather corpulent, with a broad, fat, tallow-complexioned countenance. The student obeyed his silent call, and entered the room, through the open door of which he had been gazing.

He now beheld, stretched out upon the bed where she had so lately lain in life, though dying, the yet uncoffined corpse of the aged woman, whose death has been described. How frightful it seemed! — that fixed countenance of ashy paleness, amid its decorations of muslin and fine linen, as if a bride were decked for the marriage-chamber, as if death were a bridegroom, and the coffin a bridal bed. Alas that the vanity of dress should extend even to the grave!

The female who, as being the near and only relative of the deceased, was supposed to stand in need of comfort, was surrounded by five or six of her own sex. These continually poured into her ear the stale, trite maxims which, where consolation is actually required, add torture insupportable to the wounded heart. Their present object, however, conducted herself with all due decorum, holding her handkerchief to her tearless eyes, and answering with very grievous groans to the words of her comforters. Who could have imagined that there was joy in her heart, because, since her sister's death, there was but one remaining obstacle between herself and the sole property of that wretched cottage?

While Fanshawe stood silently observing this scene, a low, monotonous voice was uttering some words in his ear, of the meaning of which his mind did not immediately take note. He turned, and saw that the speaker was the person who had invited him to enter.

"What is your pleasure with me, sir?" demanded the student.

"I make bold to ask," replied the man, "whether you would choose to partake of some creature comfort, before joining in prayer with the family and friends of our deceased sister?" As he spoke, he pointed to a table, on which was a moderate-sized stone jug and two or three broken glasses; for then, as now, there were few occasions of joy or grief on which ardent spirits were not considered indispensable, to heighten the one or to alleviate the other.

"I stand in no need of refreshment," answered Fanshawe; "and it is not my intention to pray at present."

"I pray your pardon, reverend sir," rejoined the other; "but your face is pale, and you look wearied. A drop from yonder vessel is needful to recruit the outward man. And for the prayer, the sisters will expect it; and their souls are longing for the outpouring of the Spirit. I was intending to open my own mouth with such words as are given to my poor ignorance, but"—

Fanshawe was here about to interrupt this address, which proceeded on the supposition, arising from his black dress and thoughtful countenance, that he was a

clergyman. But one of the females now approached
him, and intimated that the sister of the deceased was
desirous of the benefit of his conversation. He would
have returned a negative to this request, but, looking
towards the afflicted woman, he saw her withdraw her
handkerchief from her eyes, and cast a brief but pene-
trating and most intelligent glance upon him. He immediately expressed his readiness to offer such consolation as might be in his power.

"And in the mean time," observed the lay-preacher,
"I will give the sisters to expect a word of prayer and
exhortation, either from you or from myself."

These words were lost upon the supposed clergyman,
who was already at the side of the mourner. The females withdrew out of ear-shot to give place to a more
legitimate comforter than themselves.

"What know you respecting my purpose?" inquired
Fanshawe, bending towards her.

The woman gave a groan — the usual result of all
efforts at consolation — for the edification of the company, and then replied in a whisper, which reached
only the ear for which it was intended. "I know
whom you come to seek: I can direct you to them.
Speak low, for God's sake!" she continued, observing
that Fanshawe was about to utter an exclamation.
She then resumed her groans with greater zeal than
before.

"Where — where are they?" asked the student, in
a whisper which all his efforts could scarcely keep below his breath. "I adjure you to tell me."

"And, if I should, how am I like to be bettered by
it?" inquired the old woman, her speech still preceded
and followed by a groan.

"O God! The *auri sacra fames!*" thought Fan

shawe with a sickening heart, looking at the motionless corpse upon the bed, and then at the wretched being, whom the course of nature, in comparatively a moment of time, would reduce to the same condition.

He whispered again, however, putting his purse into the hag's hand. "Take this. Make your own terms when they are discovered. Only tell me where I must seek them — and speedily, or it may be too late."

"I am a poor woman, and am afflicted," said she, taking the purse, unseen by any who were in the room. "It is little that worldly goods can do for me, and not long can I enjoy them." And here she was delivered of a louder and a more heartfelt groan than ever. She then continued : "Follow the path behind the cottage, that leads to the river-side. Walk along the foot of the rock, and search for them near the water-spout. Keep a slow pace till you are out of sight," she added, as the student started to his feet.

The guests of the cottage did not attempt to oppose Fanshawe's progress, when they saw him take the path towards the forest, imagining, probably, that he was retiring for the purpose of secret prayer. But the old woman laughed behind the handkerchief with which she veiled her face.

"Take heed to your steps, boy," she muttered ; "for they are leading you whence you will not return. Death, too, for the slayer. Be it so."

Fanshawe, in the mean while, contrived to discover, and for a while to retain, the narrow and winding path that led to the river-side. But it was originally no more than a track, by which the cattle belonging to the cottage went down to their watering-place, and by these four-footed passengers it had long been deserted. The fern-bushes, therefore, had grown over it; and in several places trees of considerable size had shot up in the midst. These difficulties could scarcely have been surmounted by the utmost caution; and as Fanshawe's thoughts were too deeply fixed upon the end to pay a due regard to the means, he soon became desperately bewildered both as to the locality of the river and of the cottage. Had he known, however, in which direction to seek the latter, he would not, probably, have turned back; not that he was infected by any chivalrous desire to finish the adventure alone, but because he would expect little assistance from those he had left there. Yet he could not but wonder — though he had not in his first eagerness taken notice of it — at the anxiety of the old woman that he should proceed singly, and without the knowledge of her guests, on the search. He nevertheless continued to wander on, — pausing often to listen for the rush of the river, and then starting forward with fresh rapidity, to rid himself of the sting of his own thoughts, which became painfully intense when undisturbed by bodily motion. His way was now frequently interrupted by rocks, that thrust their huge gray heads from the ground, compelling him to turn aside, and thus depriving him, fortunately, perhaps, of all remaining idea of the direction he had intended to pursue.

Thus he went on, his head turned back, and taking little heed to his footsteps, when, perceiving that he trod upon a smooth, level rock, he looked forward, and found himself almost on the utmost verge of a precipice.

After the throbbing of the heart that followed this narrow escape had subsided, he stood gazing down where the sunbeams slept so pleasantly at the roots of the tall old trees, with whose highest tops he was upon a level. Suddenly he seemed to hear voices — one well-remembered voice — ascending from beneath; and, approaching to the edge of the cliff, he saw at its base the two whom he sought.

He saw and interpreted Ellen's look and attitude of entreaty, though the words with which she sought to soften the ruthless heart of her guide became inaudible ere they reached the height where Fanshawe stood. He felt that Heaven had sent him thither, at the moment of her utmost need, to be the preserver of all that was dear to him; and he paused only to consider the mode in which her deliverance was to be effected. Life he would have laid down willingly, exultingly: his only care was, that the sacrifice should not be in vain.

At length, when Ellen fell upon her knees, he lifted a small fragment of rock, and threw it down the cliff. It struck so near the pair, that it immediately drew the attention of both.

When the betrayer, at the instant in which he had almost defied the power of the Omnipotent to bring help to Ellen, became aware of Fanshawe's presence, his hardihood failed him for a time, and his knees actually tottered beneath him. There was something awful, to his apprehension, in the slight form that stood so far above him, like a being from another sphere, looking down upon his wickedness. But his half-superstitious dread endured only a moment's space; and then, mustering the courage that in a thousand dangers had not deserted him, he prepared to revenge the intrusion by which Fanshawe had a second time interrupted his designs.

"By Heaven, I will cast him down at her feet!" he muttered through his closed teeth. "There shall be no form nor likeness of man left in him. Then let him rise up, if he is able, and defend her."

Thus resolving, and overlooking all hazard in his eager hatred and desire for vengeance, he began a desperate attempt to ascend the cliff. The space which only had hitherto been deemed accessible was quickly passed; and in a moment more he was half-way up the precipice, clinging to trees, shrubs, and projecting portions of the rock, and escaping through hazards which seemed to menace inevitable destruction.

Fanshawe, as he watched his upward progress, deemed that every step would be his last; but when he perceived that more than half, and apparently the most difficult part, of the ascent was surmounted, his opinion changed. His courage, however, did not fail him as the moment of need drew nigh. His spirits rose buoyantly; his limbs seemed to grow firm and strong; and he stood on the edge of the precipice, prepared for the death-struggle which would follow the success of his enemy's attempt.

But that attempt was not successful. When within a few feet of the summit, the adventurer grasped at a twig too slenderly rooted to sustain his weight. It gave way in his hand, and he fell backward down the precipice. His head struck against the less perpendicular part of the rock, whence the body rolled heavily down to the detached fragment, of which mention has heretofore been made. There was no life left in him. With all the passions of hell alive in his heart, he had met the fate that he intended for Fanshawe.

The student paused not then to shudder at the sudden and awful overthrow of his enemy; for he saw that Ellen lay motionless at the foot of the cliff. She had indeed fainted at the moment she became aware of her deliverer's presence; and no stronger proof could she have given of her firm reliance upon his protection.

Fanshawe was not deterred by the danger, of which he had just received so fearful an evidence, from attempting to descend to her assistance; and, whether owing to his advantage in lightness of frame, or to superior caution, he arrived safely at the base of the precipice.

He lifted the motionless form of Ellen in his arms, and, resting her head against his shoulder, gazed on her cheek of lily paleness with a joy, a triumph, that rose almost to madness. It contained no mixture of hope; it had no reference to the future: it was the perfect bliss of a moment, — an insulated point of happiness. He bent over her, and pressed a kiss — the first, and he knew it would be the last — on her pale lips; then, bearing her to the fountain, he sprinkled its waters profusely over her face, neck, and bosom. She at length opened her eyes, slowly and heavily; but her mind was evidently wandering, till Fanshawe spoke.

" Fear not, Ellen : you are safe," he said.

At the sound of his voice, her arm, which was thrown over his shoulder, involuntarily tightened its embrace, telling him, by that mute motion, with how firm a trust she confided in him. But, as a fuller sense of her situation returned, she raised herself to her feet, though still retaining the support of his arm. It was singular, that, although her insensibility had commenced before the fall of her guide, she turned away her eyes, as if instinctively, from the spot where the mangled body lay; nor did she inquire of Fan-shawe the manner of her deliverance.

"Let us begone from this place," she said in faint, low accents, and with an inward shudder.

They walked along the precipice, seeking some passage by which they might gain its summit, and at length arrived at that by which Ellen and her guide had descended. Chance — for neither Ellen nor Fan-shawe could have discovered the path — led them, after but little wandering, to the cottage. A messenger was sent forward to the town to inform Dr. Melmoth of the recovery of his ward; and the intelligence thus received had interrupted Edward Walcott's conversation with the seaman.

It would have been impossible, in the mangled remains of Ellen's guide, to discover the son of the Widow Butler, except from the evidence of her sister, who became, by his death, the sole inheritrix of the cottage. The history of this evil and unfortunate man must be comprised within very narrow limits. A harsh father, and his own untamable disposition, had driven him from home in his boyhood; and chance had made him the temporary companion of Hugh Crombie. After two years of wandering, when in a foreign country and in circumstances of utmost need, he attracted the notice of Mr. Langton. The merchant took his young countryman under his protection, afforded him advantages of education, and, as his capacity was above mediocrity, gradually trusted him in many affairs of importance. During this period, there was no evidence of dishonesty on his part. On the contrary, he manifested a zeal for Mr. Langton's interest, and a respect for his person, that proved his strong sense of the benefits he had received. But he unfortunately fell into certain youthful indiscretions, which, if not entirely pardonable, might have been palliated by many considerations that would have occurred to a merciful man. Mr. Langton's justice, however, was seldom tempered by mercy; and, on this occasion, he shut the door of repentance against his erring *protégé*, and left him in a situation not less desperate than that from which he had relieved him. The goodness and the nobleness, of which his heart was not destitute, turned, from that time, wholly to evil; and he became irrecoverably ruined and irreclaimably depraved. His wandering life had led him, shortly before the period of this tale, to his native country. Here the erroneous intelligence of Mr. Langton's death had reached him, and suggested the scheme, which circumstances seemed to render practicable, but the fatal termination of which has been related.

The body was buried where it had fallen, close by the huge, gray, moss-grown fragment of rock, — a monument on which centuries can work little change. The eighty years that have elapsed since the death of the widow's son have, however, been sufficient to obliterate an inscription, which some one was at the pains to cut in the smooth surface of the stone. Traces of letters are still discernible; but the writer's many efforts could never discover a connected meaning. The grave, also, is overgrown with fern-bushes, and sunk to a level with the surrounding soil. But the legend, though my version of it may be forgotten, will long be traditionary in that lonely spot, and give to the rock and the precipice and the fountain an interest thrilling to the bosom of the romantic wanderer.

CHAPTER X.

"Sitting then in shelter shady,
  To observe and mark his mone
  Suddenly I saw a lady
  Hasting to him all alone,
  Clad in maiden-white and green,
  Whom I judged the Forest Queen."
                        THE WOODMAN'S BEAR.

DURING several weeks succeeding her danger and deliverance, Ellen Langton was confined to her chamber by illness, resulting from the agitation she had endured. Her father embraced the earliest opportunity to express his deep gratitude to Fanshawe for the inestimable service he had rendered, and to intimate a desire to requite it to the utmost of his power. He had understood that the student's circumstances were not prosperous, and, with the feeling of one who was habituated to give and receive a *quid pro quo*, he would have rejoiced to share his abundance with the deliverer of his daughter. But Fanshawe's flushed brow and haughty eye, when he perceived the thought that was stirring in Mr. Langton's mind, sufficiently proved to the discerning merchant that money was not, in the present instance, a circulating medium. His penetration, in fact, very soon informed him of the motives by which the young man had been actuated in risking his life for Ellen Langton; but he made no allusion to the subject, concealing his intentions, if any he had, in his own bosom.

During Ellen's illness, Edward Walcott had manifested the deepest anxiety respecting her: he had

wandered around and within the house, like a restless
ghost, informing himself of the slightest fluctuation
in her health, and thereby graduating his happiness
or misery. He was at length informed that her con-
valescence had so far progressed, that, on the succeeding day, she would venture below. From that time
Edward's visits to Dr. Melmoth's mansion were relinquished. His cheek grew pale and his eye lost its merry
light; but he resolutely kept himself a banished man.
Multifarious were the conjectures to which this course
of conduct gave rise; but Ellen understood and ap-
proved his motives. The maiden must have been far
more blind than ever woman was in such a matter, if
the late events had not convinced her of Fanshawe's
devoted attachment; and she saw that Edward Walcott, feeling the superior, the irresistible strength of
his rival's claim, had retired from the field. Fanshawe, however, discovered no intention to pursue his
advantage. He paid her no voluntary visit, and even
declined an invitation to tea, with which Mrs. Melmoth, after extensive preparations, had favored him.
He seemed to have resumed all the habits of seclusion by which he was distinguished previous to his
acquaintance with Ellen, except that he still took his
sunset walk on the banks of the stream.

On one of these occasions, he stayed his footsteps
by the old leafless oak which had witnessed Ellen's
first meeting with the angler. Here he mused upon
the circumstances that had resulted from that event,
and upon the rights and privileges (for he was well
aware of them all) which those circumstances had
given him. Perhaps the loveliness of the scene and
the recollections connected with it, perhaps the warm
and mellow sunset, perhaps a temporary weakness in

himself, had softened his feelings, and shaken the
firmness of his resolution, to leave Ellen to be happy
with his rival. His strong affections rose up against
his reason, whispering that bliss — on earth and in
heaven, through time and eternity — might yet be
his lot with her. It is impossible to conceive of the
flood of momentary joy which the bare admission of
such a possibility sent through his frame; and, just
when the tide was highest in his heart, a soft little
hand was laid upon his own, and, starting, he beheld
Ellen at his side.

Her illness, since the commencement of which Fanshawe had not seen her, had wrought a considerable,
but not a disadvantageous, change in her appearance.
She was paler and thinner; her countenance was more
intellectual, more spiritual; and a spirit did the student almost deem her, appearing so suddenly in that
solitude. There was a quick vibration of the delicate
blood in her cheek, yet never brightening to the glow
of perfect health; a tear was glittering on each of
her long, dark eyelashes; and there was a gentle
tremor through all her frame, which compelled her,
for a little space, to support herself against the oak.
Fanshawe's first impulse was to address her in words
of rapturous delight; but he checked himself, and attempted — vainly indeed — to clothe his voice in tones
of calm courtesy. His remark merely expressed pleasure at her restoration to health; and Ellen's low and
indistinct reply had as little relation to the feelings
that agitated her.

" Yet I fear," continued Fanshawe, recovering a degree of composure, and desirous of assigning a motive
(which he felt was not the true one) for Ellen's agitation, — " I fear that your walk has extended too far
for your strength."

"It would have borne me farther with such a motive," she replied, still trembling, — "to express my gratitude to my preserver."

"It was needless, Ellen, it was needless; for the deed brought with it its own reward," exclaimed Fanshawe, with a vehemence that he could not repress. "It was dangerous, for"—

Here he interrupted himself, and turned his face away.

"And wherefore was it dangerous?" inquired Ellen, laying her hand gently on his arm; for he seemed about to leave her.

"Because you have a tender and generous heart, and I a weak one," he replied.

"Not so," answered she, with animation. "Yours is a heart full of strength and nobleness; and if it have a weakness"—

"You know well that it has, Ellen, — one that has swallowed up all its strength," said Fanshawe. "Was it wise, then, to tempt it thus, when, if it yield, the result must be your own misery?"

Ellen did not affect to misunderstand his meaning. On the contrary, with a noble frankness, she answered to what was implied rather than expressed.

"Do me not this wrong," she said, blushing, yet earnestly. "Can it be misery? Will it not be happiness to form the tie that shall connect you to the world? to be your guide — a humble one, it is true, but the one of your choice — to the quiet paths from which your proud and lonely thoughts have estranged you? Oh, I know that there will be happiness in such a lot, from these and a thousand other sources!"

The animation with which Ellen spoke, and, at the same time, a sense of the singular course to which her gratitude had impelled her, caused her beauty to grow brighter and more enchanting with every word. And when, as she concluded, she extended her hand to Fanshawe, to refuse it was like turning from an angel, who would have guided him to heaven. But, had he been capable of making the woman he loved a sacrifice to her own generosity, that act would have rendered him unworthy of her. Yet the struggle was a severe one ere he could reply.

"You have spoken generously and nobly, Ellen," he said. "I have no way to prove that I deserve your generosity, but by refusing to take advantage of it. Even if your heart were yet untouched, if no being more happily constituted than myself had made an impression there, even then, I trust, a selfish passion would not be stronger than my integrity. But now"— He would have proceeded; but the firmness which had hitherto sustained him gave way. He turned aside to hide the tears which all the pride of his nature could not restrain, and which, instead of relieving, added to his anguish. At length he resumed, "No, Ellen, we must part now and forever. Your life will be long and happy. Mine will be short, but not altogether wretched, nor shorter than if we had never met. When you hear that I am in my grave, do not imagine that you have hastened me thither. Think that you scattered bright dreams around my pathway, — an ideal happiness, that you would have sacrificed your own to realize."

He ceased; and Ellen felt that his determination was unalterable. She could not speak; but, taking his hand, she pressed it to her lips, and they saw each other no more. Mr. Langton and his daughter shortly after returned to the seaport, which, for several succeeding years, was their residence.

After Ellen's departure, Fanshawe returned to his studies with the same absorbing ardor that had formerly characterized him. His face was as seldom seen among the young and gay; the pure breeze and the blessed sunshine as seldom refreshed his pale and weary brow; and his lamp burned as constantly from the first shade of evening till the gray morning light began to dim its beams. Nor did he, as weak men will, treasure up his love in a hidden chamber of his breast. He was in reality the thoughtful and earnest student that he seemed. He had exerted the whole might of his spirit over itself, and he was a conqueror. Perhaps, indeed, a summer breeze of sad and gentle thoughts would sometimes visit him; but, in these brief memories of his love, he did not wish that it should be revived, or mourn over its event.

There were many who felt an interest in Fanshawe; but the influence of none could prevail upon him to lay aside the habits, mental and physical, by which he was bringing himself to the grave. His passage thither was consequently rapid, terminating just as he reached his twentieth year. His fellow-students erected to his memory a monument of rough-hewn granite, with a white marble slab for the inscription. This was borrowed from the grave of Nathanael Mather, whom, in his almost insane eagerness for knowledge, and in his early death, Fanshawe resembled.

THE ASHES OF A HARD STUDENT
AND A GOOD SCHOLAR.

Many tears were shed over his grave; but the thoughtful and the wise, though turf never covered a nobler heart, could not lament that it was so soon at rest. He left a world for which he was unfit; and we trust, that, among the innumerable stars of heaven, there is one where he has found happiness.

Of the other personages of this tale, — Hugh Crombie, being exposed to no strong temptations, lived and died an honest man. Concerning Dr. Melmoth, it is unnecessary here to speak. The reader, if he have any curiosity upon the subject, is referred to his Life, which, together with several sermons and other productions of the doctor, was published by his successor in the presidency of Harley College, about the year 1768.

It was not till four years after Fanshawe's death, that Edward Walcott was united to Ellen Langton. Their future lives were uncommonly happy. Ellen's gentle, almost imperceptible, but powerful influence drew her husband away from the passions and pursuits that would have interfered with domestic felicity; and he never regretted the worldly distinction of which she thus deprived him. Theirs was a long life of calm and quiet bliss; and what matters it, that, except in these pages, they have left no name behind them?

SEPTIMIUS FELTON:

OR,

THE ELIXIR OF LIFE.

INTRODUCTORY NOTE.

———————

SEPTIMIUS FELTON.

THE existence of this story, posthumously published, was not known to any one but Hawthorne himself, until some time after his death, when the manuscript was found among his papers. The preparation and copying of his Note-Books for the press occupied the most of Mrs. Hawthorne's available time during the interval from 1864 to 1870; but in the latter year, having decided to publish the unfinished romance, she began the task of putting together its loose sheets and deciphering the handwriting, which, towards the close of Hawthorne's life, had grown somewhat obscure and uncertain. Her death occurred while she was thus engaged, and the transcription was completed by her daughters. The book was then issued simultaneously in America and England, in 1871.

Although "Septimius Felton" appeared so much later than "The Marble Faun," it was conceived and, in another form, begun before the Italian romance had presented itself to the author's mind. The legend of a bloody foot leaving its imprint where it passed, which figures so prominently in the following fiction, was brought to Hawthorne's notice on a visit to Smithell's Hall, Lancashire, England.[1] Only five days after hear-

———————
[1] See *English Note-Books*, April 7, and August 25, 1855.

ing of it, he made a note in his journal, referring to
" my Romance," which had to do with a plot involving
the affairs of a family established both in England
and New England; and it seems likely that he had
already begun to associate the bloody footstep with
this project.   What is extraordinary, and must be regarded as an unaccountable coincidence — one of the
strange premonitions of genius — is that in 1850, before he had ever been to England and before he knew
of the existence of Smithell's Hall, he had jotted down
in his Note-Book, written in America, this suggestion :
" The print in blood of a naked foot to be traced
through the street of a town."   The idea of treating
in fiction the attempt to renew youth or to attain an
earthly immortality had engaged his fancy quite early
in his career, as we discover from " Doctor Heideg-
ger's Experiment," in the " Twice-Told Tales."   In
1840, also, we find in the journal : " If a man were
sure of living forever, he would not care about his offspring."   The " Mosses from an Old Manse " supply
another link in this train of reflection ; for " The Vir-
tuoso's Collection " includes some of the elixir vitæ
" in an antique sepulchral urn."   The narrator there
represents himself as refusing to quaff it.   " ' No ; I
desire not an earthly immortality,' said I.   ' Were
man to live longer on earth, the spiritual would die
out of him. . . . There is a celestial something within
us that requires, after a certain time, the atmosphere
of heaven to preserve it from ruin.' "   On the other
hand, just before hearing, for the first time, the legend
of Smithell's Hall, he wrote in his English journal : —

    " God himself cannot compensate us for being born
for any period short of eternity.   All the misery endured here constitutes a claim for another life, and

still more *all the happiness ;* because all true happiness involves something more than the earth owns, and needs something more than a mortal capacity for the enjoyment of it." It is sufficiently clear that he had meditated on the main theme of " Septimius Felton," at intervals, for many years.

When, in August, 1855, Hawthorne went by invitation to Smithell's Hall, the lady of the manor, on his taking leave, asked him "to write a ghost-story for her house ; " and he observes in his notes, " the legend is a good one." Three years afterwards, in 1858, on the eve of departure for France and Italy, he began to sketch the outline of a romance laid in England, and having for its hero an American who goes thither to assert his inherited rights in an old manor-house possessing the peculiarity of a supposed bloody foot-print on the threshold-stone. This sketch, which appears in the present edition as " The Ancestral Footstep," was in journal form, the story continuing from day to day, with the dates attached. There remains also the manuscript without date, recently edited under the title " Dr. Grimshawe's Secret," which bears a resemblance to some particulars in " Septimius Felton." Nothing further seems to have been done in this direction by the author until he had been to Italy, had written " The Marble Faun," and again returned to The Wayside, his home at Concord. It was then, in 1861, that he took up once more the "Romance of Immortality," as the sub-title of the English edition calls it. " I have not found it possible," he wrote to Mr. Bridge, who remained his confidant, " to occupy my mind with its usual trash and nonsense during these anxious times; but as the autumn advances, I find myself sitting down at my desk and blotting successive sheets of paper as of yore." Concerning this place, The Wayside, he had said in a letter to George William Curtis, in 1852: "I know nothing of the history of the house, except Thoreau's telling me that it was inhabited a generation or two ago by a man who believed he should never die." It was this legendary personage whom he now proceeded to revive and embody as Septimius; and the scene of the story was placed at The Wayside itself and the neighboring house, belonging to Mr. Bronson Alcott, both of which stand at the base of a low ridge running beside the Lexington road, in the village of Concord. Rose Garfield is mentioned as living "in a small house, the site of which is still indicated by the cavity of a cellar, in which I this very summer planted some sunflowers." The cellar-site remains at this day distinctly visible near the boundary of the land formerly owned by Hawthorne.

Attention may here perhaps appropriately be called to the fact that some of the ancestors of President Garfield settled at Weston, not many miles from Concord, and that the name is still borne by dwellers in the vicinity. One of the last letters written by the President was an acceptance of an invitation to visit Concord; and it was his intention to journey thither by carriage, incognito, from Boston, passing through the scenes where those ancestors had lived, and entering the village by the old Lexington road, on which The Wayside faces. It is an interesting coincidence that Hawthorne should have chosen for his first heroine's name, either intentionally or through unconscious association, this one which belonged to the region.

The house upon which the story was thus centred, and where it was written, had been a farm-house, bought and for a time occupied by Hawthorne previous to his departure for Europe. On coming back to it, he made some additions to the old wooden structure, and caused to be built a low tower, which rose above the irregular roofs of the older and newer portions, thus supplying him with a study lifted out of reach of noise or interruption, and in a slight degree recalling the tower in which he had taken so much pleasure at the Villa Montauto. The study was extremely simple in its appointments, being finished chiefly in stained wood, with a vaulted plaster ceiling, and containing, besides a few pictures and some plain furniture, a writing-table, and a shelf at which Hawthorne sometimes wrote standing. A story has gone abroad and is widely believed, that, on mounting the steep stairs leading to this study, he passed through a trap-door and afterwards placed upon it the chair in which he sat, so that intrusion or interruption became physically impossible. It is wholly unfounded. There never was any trap-door, and no precaution of the kind described was ever taken. Immediately behind the house the hill rises in artificial terraces, which, during the romancer's residence, were grassy and planted with fruit-trees. He afterwards had evergreens set out there, and directed the planting of other trees, which still attest his preference for thick verdure. The twelve acres running back over the hill were closely covered with light woods, and across the road lay a level tract of eight acres more, which included a garden and orchard. From his study Hawthorne could overlook a good part of his modest domain; the view embraced a stretch of road lined with trees, wide meadows, and the hills across the shallow valley. The branches of trees rose on all sides as if to embower the house, and birds and bees flew about his casement, through which came the fresh perfumes of the woods, in summer.

In this spot " Septimius Felton " was written ; but the manuscript, thrown aside, was mentioned in the Dedicatory Preface to "Our Old Home" as an "abortive project." As will be found explained in the Introductory Notes to " The Dolliver Romance " and " The Ancestral Footstep," that phase of the same general design which was developed in the "Dolliver" was intended to take the place of this unfinished sketch, since resuscitated.

G. P. L.

PREFACE.

THE following story is the last written by my father. It is printed as it was found among his manuscripts. I believe it is a striking specimen of the peculiarities and charm of his style, and that it will have an added interest for brother artists, and for those who care to study the method of his composition, from the mere fact of its not having received his final revision. In any case, I feel sure that the retention of the passages within brackets (*e. g.* p. 253), which show how my father intended to amplify some of the descriptions and develop more fully one or two of the character studies, will not be regretted by appreciative readers. My earnest thanks are due to Mr. Robert Browning for his kind assistance and advice in interpreting the manuscript, otherwise so difficult to me.

UNA HAWTHORNE.

SEPTIMIUS FELTON;

OR, THE ELIXIR OF LIFE.

———◆———

IT was a day in early spring; and as that sweet, genial time of year and atmosphere calls out tender greenness from the ground, — beautiful flowers, or leaves that look beautiful because so long unseen under the snow and decay, — so the pleasant air and warmth had called out three young people, who sat on a sunny hill-side enjoying the warm day and one another. For they were all friends: two of them young men, and playmates from boyhood; the third, a girl, who, two or three years younger than themselves, had been the object of their boy-love, their little rustic, childish gallantries, their budding affections; until, growing all towards manhood and womanhood, they had ceased to talk about such matters, perhaps thinking about them the more.

These three young people were neighbors' children, dwelling in houses that stood by the side of the great Lexington road, along a ridgy hill that rose abruptly behind them, its brow covered with a wood, and which stretched, with one or two breaks and interruptions, into the heart of the village of Concord, the county town. It was in the side of this hill that, according to tradition, the first settlers of the village had burrowed in caverns which they had dug out for their

shelter, like swallows and woodchucks. As its slope
was towards the south, and its ridge and crowning
woods defended them from the northern blasts and
snow-drifts, it was an admirable situation for the
fierce New England winter; and the temperature was
milder, by several degrees, along this hill-side than on
the unprotected plains, or by the river, or in any other
part of Concord. So that here, during the hundred
years that had elapsed since the first settlement of the
place, dwellings had successively risen close to the
hill's foot, and the meadow that lay on the other side
of the road — a fertile tract — had been cultivated;
and these three young people were the children's children's children of persons of respectability who had
dwelt there, — Rose Garfield, in a small house, the
site of which is still indicated by the cavity of a cellar, in which I this very past summer planted some
sunflowers to thrust their great disks out from the hollow and allure the bee and the humming-bird; Robert
Hagburn, in a house of somewhat more pretension, a
hundred yards or so nearer to the village, standing
back from the road in the broader space which the re-
treating hill, cloven by a gap in that place, afforded;
where some elms intervened between it and the road,
offering a site which some person of a natural taste for
the gently picturesque had seized upon. Those same
elms, or their successors, still flung a noble shade over
the same old house, which the magic hand of Alcott
has improved by the touch that throws grace, amiable-
ness, and natural beauty over scenes that have little
pretension in themselves.

Now, the other young man, Septimius Felton, dwelt
in a small wooden house, then, I suppose, of some
score of years' standing, — a two-story house, gabled

before, but with only two rooms on a floor, crowded upon by the hill behind, — a house of thick walls, as if the projector had that sturdy feeling of permanence in life which incites people to make strong their earthly habitations, as if deluding themselves with the idea that they could still inhabit them ; in short, an ordinary dwelling of a well-to-do New England farmer, such as his race had been for two or three generations past, although there were traditions of ancestors who had led lives of thought and study, and possessed all the erudition that the universities of England could bestow. Whether any natural turn for study had descended to Septimius from these worthies, or how his tendencies came to be different from those of his family, — who, within the memory of the neighborhood, had been content to sow and reap the rich field in front of their homestead, — so it was, that Septimius had early manifested a taste for study. By the kind aid of the good minister of the town he had been fitted for college ; had passed through Cambridge by means of what little money his father had left him and by his own exertions in school-keeping ; and was now a recently decorated baccalaureate, with, as was understood, a purpose to devote himself to the ministry, under the auspices of that reverend and good friend whose support and instruction had already stood him in such stead.

Now here were these young people, on that beautiful spring morning, sitting on the hill - side, a pleasant spectacle of fresh life, — pleasant, as if they had sprouted like green things under the influence of the warm sun. The girl was very pretty, a little freckled, a little tanned, but with a face that glimmered and gleamed with quick and cheerful expressions ; a slender form, not very large, with a quick grace in its movements; sunny hair that had a tendency to curl, which she probably favored at such moments as her household occupation left her; a sociable and pleasant child, as both of the young men evidently thought. Robert Hagburn, one might suppose, would have been the most to her taste; a ruddy, burly young fellow, handsome, and free of manner, six feet high, famous through the neighborhood for strength and athletic skill, the early promise of what was to be a man fit for all offices of active rural life, and to be, in mature age, the selectman, the deacon, the representative, the colonel. As for Septimius, let him alone a moment or two, and then they would see him, with his head bent down, brooding, brooding, his eyes fixed on some chip, some stone, some common plant, any commonest thing, as if it were the clew and index to some mystery; and when, by chance startled out of these meditations, he lifted his eyes, there would be a kind of perplexity, a dissatisfied, foiled look in them, as if of his speculations he found no end. Such was now the case, while Robert and the girl were running on with a gay talk about a serious subject, so that, gay as it was, it was interspersed with little thrills of fear on the girl's part, of excitement on Robert's. Their talk was of public trouble.

" My grandfather says," said Rose Garfield, " that we shall never be able to stand against old England, because the men are a weaker race than he remembers in his day, — weaker than his father, who came from England, — and the women slighter still; so that we are dwindling away, grandfather thinks; only a little sprightlier, he says sometimes, looking at me."

" Lighter, to be sure," said Robert Hagburn; " there

is the lightness of the Englishwomen compressed into little space. I have seen them and know. And as to the men, Rose, if they have lost one spark of courage and strength that their English forefathers brought from the old land, — lost any one good quality without having made it up by as good or better, — then, for my part, I don't want the breed to exist any longer. And this war, that they say is coming on, will be a good opportunity to test the matter. Septimius! don't you think so?"

"Think what?" asked Septimius, gravely, lifting up his head.

"Think! why, that your countrymen are worthy to live," said Robert Hagburn, impatiently. "For there is a question on that point."

"It is hardly worth answering or considering," said Septimius, looking at him thoughtfully. "We live so little while, that (always setting aside the effect on a future existence) it is little matter whether we live or no."

"Little matter!" said Rose, at first bewildered, then laughing, — "little matter! when it is such a comfort to live, so pleasant, so sweet!"

"Yes, and so many things to do," said Robert; "to make fields yield produce; to be busy among men, and happy among the women-folk; to play, work, fight, and be active in many ways."

"Yes; but so soon stilled, before your activity has come to any definite end," responded Septimius, gloomily. "I doubt, if it had been left to my choice, whether I should have taken existence on such terms; so much trouble of preparation to live, and then no life at all; a ponderous beginning, and nothing more."

"Do you find fault with Providence, Septimius?"

asked Rose, a feeling of solemnity coming over her cheerful and buoyant nature. Then she burst out a-laughing. "How grave he looks, Robert; as if he had lived two or three lives already, and knew all about the value of it. But I think it was worth while to be born, if only for the sake of one such pleasant spring morning as this; and God gives us many and better things when these are past."

"We hope so," said Septimius, who was again looking on the ground. "But who knows?"

"I thought you knew," said Robert Hagburn. "You have been to college, and have learned, no doubt, a great many things. You are a student of theology, too, and have looked into these matters. Who should know, if not you?"

"Rose and you have just as good means of ascertaining these points as I," said Septimius; "all the certainty that can be had lies on the surface, as it should, and equally accessible to every man or woman. If we try to grope deeper, we labor for naught, and get less wise while we try to be more so. If life were long enough to enable us thoroughly to sift these matters, then, indeed! — but it is so short!"

"Always this same complaint," said Robert. "Septimius, how long do you wish to live?"

"Forever!" said Septimius. "It is none too long for all I wish to know."

"Forever?" exclaimed Rose, shivering doubtfully. "Ah, there would come many, many thoughts, and after a while we should want a little rest."

"Forever?" said Robert Hagburn. "And what would the people do who wish to fill our places? You are unfair, Septimius. Live and let live! Turn about! Give me my seventy years, and let me go, —

my seventy years of what this life has, — toil, enjoyment, suffering, struggle, fight, rest, — only let me have my share of what's going, and I shall be content."

"Content with leaving everything at odd ends; content with being nothing, as you were before!"

"No, Septimius, content with heaven at last," said Rose, who had come out of her laughing mood into a sweet seriousness. "Oh dear! think what a worn and ugly thing one of these fresh little blades of grass would seem if it were not to fade and wither in its time, after being green in its time."

"Well, well, my pretty Rose," said Septimius apart, "an immortal weed is not very lovely to think of, that is true ; but I should be content with one thing, and that is yourself, if you were immortal, just as you are at seventeen, so fresh, so dewy, so red-lipped, so golden-haired, so gay, so frolicsome, so gentle."

"But I am to grow old, and to be brown and wrinkled, gray-haired and ugly," said Rose, rather sadly, as she thus enumerated the items of her decay, "and then you would think me all lost and gone. But still there might be youth underneath, for one that really loved me to see. Ah, Septimius Felton! such love as would see with ever-new eyes is the true love." And she ran away and left him suddenly, and Robert Hagburn departing at the same time, this little knot of three was dissolved, and Septimius went along the wayside wall, thoughtfully, as was his wont, to his own dwelling. He had stopped for some moments on the threshold, vaguely enjoying, it is probable, the light and warmth of the new spring day and the sweet air, which was somewhat unwonted to the young man, because he was accustomed to spend much of his day in thought and study within doors, and, indeed, like most studious young men, was overfond of the fireside, and of making life as artificial as he could, by fireside heat and lamplight, in order to suit it to the artificial, intellectual, and moral atmosphere which he derived from books, instead of living healthfully in the open air, and among his fellow-beings. Still he felt the pleasure of being warmed through by this natural heat, and, though blinking a little from its superfluity, could not but confess an enjoyment and cheerfulness in this flood of morning light that came aslant the hill-side. While he thus stood, he felt a friendly hand laid upon his shoulder, and, looking up, there was the minister of the village, the old friend of Septimius, to whose advice and aid it was owing that Septimius had followed his instincts by going to college, instead of spending a thwarted and dissatisfied life in the field that fronted the house. He was a man of middle age, or little beyond, of a sagacious, kindly aspect; the experience, the lifelong, intimate acquaintance with many concerns of his people being more apparent in him than the scholarship for which he had been early distinguished. A tanned man, like one who labored in his own grounds occasionally; a man of homely, plain address, which, when occasion called for it, he could readily exchange for the polished manner of one who had seen a more refined world than this about him.

"Well, Septimius," said the minister, kindly, "have you yet come to any conclusion about the subject of which we have been talking?"

"Only so far, sir," replied Septimius, "that I find myself every day less inclined to take up the profession which I have had in view so many years. I do not think myself fit for the sacred desk."

"Surely not; no one is," replied the clergyman; "but if I may trust my own judgment, you have at least many of the intellectual qualifications that should adapt you to it. There is something of the Puritan character in you, Septimius, derived from holy men among your ancestors; as, for instance, a deep, brood-ing turn, such as befits that heavy brow; a disposition to meditate on things hidden; a turn for meditative inquiry,— all these things, with grace to boot, mark you as the germ of a man who might do God service. Your reputation as a scholar stands high at college. You have not a turn for worldly business."

"Ah, but, sir," said Septimius, casting down his heavy brows, "I lack something within."

"Faith, perhaps," replied the minister; "at least, you think so."

"Cannot I know it?" asked Septimius.

"Scarcely, just now," said his friend. "Study for the ministry; bind your thoughts to it; pray; ask a belief, and you will soon find you have it. Doubts may occasionally press in; and it is so with every clergyman. But your prevailing mood will be faith."

"It has seemed to me," observed Septimius, "that it is not the prevailing mood, the most common one, that is to be trusted. This is habit, formality, the shallow covering which we close over what is real, and seldom suffer to be blown aside. But it is the snake-like doubt that thrusts out its head, which gives us a glimpse of reality. Surely such moments are a hun-dred times as real as the dull, quiet moments of faith or what you call such."

"I am sorry for you," said the minister; "yet to a youth of your frame of character, of your ability I will say, and your requisition for something profound in the grounds of your belief, it is not unusual to meet this trouble. Men like you have to fight for their faith. They fight in the first place to win it, and ever afterwards to hold it. The Devil tilts with them daily and often seems to win."

"Yes; but," replied Septimius, "he takes deadly weapons now. If he meet me with the cold pure steel of a spiritual argument, I might win or lose, and still not feel that all was lost; but he takes, as it were, a great clod of earth, massive rocks and mud, soil and dirt, and flings it at me overwhelmingly; so that I am buried under it."

"How is that?" said the minister. "Tell me more plainly."

"May it not be possible," asked Septimius, "to have too profound a sense of the marvellous contrivance and adaptation of this material world to require or believe in anything spiritual? How wonderful it is to see it all alive on this spring day, all growing, budding! Do we exhaust it in our little life? Not so; not in a hundred or a thousand lives. The whole race of man, living from the beginning of time, have not, in all their number and multiplicity and in all their duration, come in the least to know the world they live in! And how is this rich world thrown away upon us, because we live in it such a moment! What mortal work has ever been done since the world began! Because we have no time. No lesson is taught. We are snatched away from our study before we have learned the alphabet. As the world now exists, I confess it to you frankly, my dear pastor and instructor, it seems to me all a failure, because we do not live long enough."

"But the lesson is carried on in another state of being!"

"Not the lesson that we begin here," said Septimius. "We might as well train a child in a primeval forest, to teach him how to live in a European court. No, the fall of man, which Scripture tells us of, seems to me to have its operation in this grievous shortening of earthly existence, so that our life here at all is grown ridiculous."

"Well, Septimius," replied the minister, sadly, yet not as one shocked by what he had never heard before, "I must leave you to struggle through this form of unbelief as best you may, knowing that it is by your own efforts that you must come to the other side of this slough. We will talk further another time. You are getting worn out, my young friend, with much study and anxiety. It were well for you to live more, for the present, in this earthly life that you prize so highly. Cannot you interest yourself in the state of this country, in this coming strife, the voice of which now sounds so hoarsely and so near us? Come out of your thoughts and breathe another air."

"I will try," said Septimius.

"Do," said the minister, extending his hand to him, "and in a little time you will find the change."

He shook the young man's hand kindly, and took his leave, while Septimius entered his house, and turning to the right sat down in his study, where, before the fireplace, stood the table with books and papers. On the shelves around the low-studded walls were more books, few in number but of an erudite appearance, many of them having descended to him from learned ancestors, and having been brought to light by himself after long lying in dusty closets ; works of good and learned divines, whose wisdom he had happened, by help of the Devil, to turn to mischief, reading them by the light of hell-fire. For, indeed, Septimius had but given the clergyman the merest partial glimpse of his state of mind. He was not a new beginner in doubt; but, on the contrary, it seemed to him as if he had never been other than a doubter and questioner, even in his boyhood; believing nothing, although a thin veil of reverence had kept him from questioning some things. And now the new, strange thought of the sufficiency of the world for man, if man were only sufficient for that, kept recurring to him; and with it came a certain sense, which he had been conscious of before, that he, at least, might never die. The feeling was not peculiar to Septimius. It is an instinct, the meaning of which is mistaken. We have strongly within us the sense of an undying principle, and we transfer that true sense to this life and to the body, instead of interpreting it justly as the promise of spiritual immortality.

So Septimius looked up out of his thoughts, and said proudly: " Why should I die? I cannot die, if worthy to live. What if I should say this moment that I will not die, not till ages hence, not till the world is exhausted? Let other men die, if they choose, or yield; let him that is strong enough live! "

After this flush of heroic mood, however, the glow subsided, and poor Septimius spent the rest of the day, as was his wont, poring over his books, in which all the meanings seemed dead and mouldy, and like pressed leaves (some of which dropped out of the books as he opened them), brown, brittle, sapless; so even the thoughts, which when the writers had gathered them seemed to them so brightly colored and full of life. Then he began to see that there must have been some principle of life left out of the book, so that these gathered thoughts lacked something that had given them their only value. Then he suspected that the way truly to live and answer the purposes of life was not to gather up thoughts into books, where they grew so dry, but to live and still be going about, full of green wisdom, ripening ever, not in maxims cut and dry, but a wisdom ready for daily occasions, like a living fountain ; and that to be this, it was necessary to exist long on earth, drink in all its lessons, and not to die on the attainment of some smattering of truth; but to live all the more for that; and apply it to mankind and increase it thereby.

Everything drifted towards the strong, strange eddy into which his mind had been drawn : all his thoughts set hitherward.

So he sat brooding in his study until the shrill-voiced old woman — an aunt, who was his housekeeper and domestic ruler — called him to dinner, — a frugal dinner, — and chided him for seeming inattentive to a dish of early dandelions which she had gathered for him ; but yet tempered her severity with respect for the future clerical rank of her nephew, and for his already being a bachelor of arts. The old woman's voice spoke outside of Septimius, rambling away, and he paying little heed, till at last dinner was over, and Septimius drew back his chair, about to leave the table.

"Nephew Septimius," said the old woman, "you began this meal to-day without asking a blessing, you get up from it without giving thanks, and you soon to be a minister of the Word."

"God bless the meat," replied Septimius (by way of blessing), "and make it strengthen us for the life he means us to bear. Thank God for our food," he

added (by way of grace), "and may it become a portion in us of an immortal body."

"That sounds good, Septimius," said the old lady.
"Ah! you'll be a mighty man in the pulpit, and worthy to keep up the name of your great-grandfather,
who, they say, made the leaves wither on a tree with
the fierceness of his blast against a sin. Some say, to
be sure, it was an early frost that helped him."

"I never heard that before, Aunt Keziah," said
Septimius.

"I warrant you no," replied his aunt. "A man
dies, and his greatness perishes as if it had never been,
and people remember nothing of him only when they
see his gravestone over his old dry bones, and say he
was a good man in his day."

"What truth there is in Aunt Keziah's words!"
exclaimed Septimius. "And how I hate the thought
and anticipation of that contemptuous appreciation of
a man after his death! Every living man triumphs
over every dead one, as he lies, poor and helpless,
under the mould, a pinch of dust, a heap of bones, an
evil odor! I hate the thought! It shall not be so!"

It was strange how every little incident thus brought
him back to that one subject which was taking so
strong hold of his mind; every avenue led thitherward; and he took it for an indication that nature had
intended, by innumerable ways, to point out to us the
great truth that death was an alien misfortune, a prod-
igy, a monstrosity, into which man had only fallen by
defect; and that even now, if a man had a reasonable
portion of his original strength in him, he might live
forever and spurn death.

Our story is an internal one, dealing as little as possible with outward events, and taking hold of these

only where it cannot be helped, in order by means of them to delineate the history of a mind bewildered in certain errors. We would not willingly, if we could, give a lively and picturesque surrounding to this delineation, but it is necessary that we should advert to the circumstances of the time in which this inward history was passing. We will say, therefore, that that night there was a cry of alarm passing all through the succession of country towns and rural communities that lay around Boston, and dying away towards the coast and the wilder forest borders. Horsemen galloped past the line of farm-houses shouting alarm! alarm! There were stories of marching troops coming like dreams through the midnight. Around the little rude meeting-houses there was here and there the beat of a drum, and the assemblage of farmers with their weapons. So all that night there was marching, there was mustering, there was trouble; and, on the road from Boston, a steady march of soldiers' feet onward, onward into the land whose last warlike disturbance had been when the red Indians trod it.

Septimius heard it, and knew, like the rest, that it was the sound of coming war. "Fools that men are!" said he, as he rose from bed and looked out at the misty stars; "they do not live long enough to know the value and purport of life, else they would combine together to live long, instead of throwing away the lives of thousands as they do. And what matters a little tyranny in so short a life? What matters a form of government for such ephemeral creatures?"

As morning brightened, these sounds, this clamor, — or something that was in the air and caused the clamor, — grew so loud that Septimius seemed to feel it even in his solitude. It was in the atmosphere, —

storm, wild excitement, a coming deed. Men hurried
along the usually lonely road in groups, with weapons
in their hands, — the old fowling-piece of seven-foot
barrel, with which the Puritans had shot ducks on the
river and Walden Pond; the heavy harquebus, which
perhaps had levelled one of King Philip's Indians;
the old King gun, that blazed away at the French of
Louisburg or Quebec, — hunter, husbandman, all were
hurrying each other. It was a good time, everybody
felt, to be alive, a nearer kindred, a closer sympathy
between man and man; a sense of the goodness of the
world, of the sacredness of country, of the excellence
of life; and yet its slight account compared with any
truth, any principle; the weighing of the material and
ethereal, and the finding the former not worth considering, when, nevertheless, it had so much to do with
the settlement of the crisis. The ennobling of brute
force; the feeling that it had its godlike side; the
drawing of heroic breath amid the scenes of ordinary
life, so that it seemed as if they had all been transfig-
ured since yesterday. Oh, high, heroic, tremulous juncture, when man felt himself almost an angel; on the
verge of doing deeds that outwardly look so fiendish!
Oh, strange rapture of the coming battle! We know
something of that time now; we that have seen the
muster of the village soldiery on the meeting-house
green, and at railway stations; and heard the drum
and fife, and seen the farewells; seen the familiar
faces that we hardly knew, now that we felt them to
be heroes; breathed higher breath for their sakes;
felt our eyes moistened; thanked them in our souls
for teaching us that nature is yet capable of heroic
moments; felt how a great impulse lifts up a people,
and every cold, passionless, indifferent spectator, —

lifts him up into religion, and makes him join in what becomes an act of devotion, a prayer, when perhaps he but half approves.

Septimius could not study on a morning like this. He tried to say to himself that he had nothing to do with this excitement; that his studious life kept him away from it; that his intended profession was that of peace; but say what he might to himself, there was a tremor, a bubbling impulse, a tingling in his ears, — the page that he opened glimmered and dazzled before him.

"Septimius! Septimius!" cried Aunt Keziah, looking into the room, "in Heaven's name, are you going to sit here to-day, and the redcoats coming to burn the house over our heads? Must I sweep you out with the broomstick? For shame, boy! for shame!"

"Are they coming, then, Aunt Keziah?" asked her nephew. "Well, I am not a fighting-man."

"Certain they are. They have sacked Lexington, and slain the people, and burnt the meeting-house. That concerns even the parsons; and you reckon yourself among them. Go out, go out, I say, and learn the news!"

Whether moved by these exhortations, or by his own stifled curiosity, Septimius did at length issue from his door, though with that reluctance which hampers and impedes men whose current of thought and interest runs apart from that of the world in general; but forth he came, feeling strangely, and yet with a strong impulse to fling himself headlong into the emotion of the moment. It was a beautiful morning, spring-like and summer-like at once. If there had been nothing else to do or think of, such a morning was enough for life only to breathe its air and be conscious of its inspiring influence.

Septimius turned along the road towards the village, meaning to mingle with the crowd on the green, and there learn all he could of the rumors that vaguely filled the air, and doubtless were shaping themselves into various forms of fiction.

As he passed the small dwelling of Rose Garfield, she stood on the doorstep, and bounded forth a little way to meet him, looking frightened, excited, and yet half pleased, but strangely pretty; prettier than ever before, owing to some hasty adornment or other, that she would never have succeeded so well in giving to herself if she had had more time to do it in.

"Septimius — Mr. Felton," cried she, asking information of him who, of all men in the neighborhood, knew nothing of the intelligence afloat; but it showed a certain importance that Septimius had with her. "Do you really think the redcoats are coming? Ah, what shall we do? What shall we do? But you are not going to the village, too, and leave us all alone?"

"I know not whether they are coming or no, Rose," said Septimius, stopping to admire the young girl's fresh beauty, which made a double stroke upon him by her excitement, and, moreover, made her twice as free with him as ever she had been before; for there is nothing truer than that any breaking up of the ordinary state of things is apt to shake women out of their proprieties, break down barriers, and bring them into perilous proximity with the world. "Are you alone here? Had you not better take shelter in the village?"

"And leave my poor, bedridden grandmother! " cried Rose, angrily. "You know I can't, Septimius. But I suppose I am in no danger. Go to the village, if you like. '

" Where is Robert Hagburn?" asked Septimius.

" Gone to the village this hour past, with his grand-father's old firelock on his shoulder," said Rose; " he was running bullets before daylight."

" Rose, I will stay with you," said Septimius.

" Oh gracious, here they come, I'm sure!" cried Rose. " Look yonder at the dust. Mercy! a man at a gallop!"

In fact, along the road, a considerable stretch of which was visible, they heard the clatter of hoofs and saw a little cloud of dust approaching at the rate of a gallop, and disclosing, as it drew near, a hatless coun-tryman in his shirt-sleeves, who, bending over his horse's neck, applied a cart-whip lustily to the animal's flanks, so as to incite him to most unwonted speed. At the same time, glaring upon Rose and Septimius, he lifted up his voice and shouted in a strange, high tone, that communicated the tremor and excitement of the shouter to each auditor: " Alarum! alarum! ala-rum! The redcoats! The redcoats! To arms! ala-rum!"

And trailing this sound far wavering behind him like a pennon, the eager horseman dashed onward to the village.

" Oh dear, what shall we do?" cried Rose, her eyes full of tears, yet dancing with excitement. " They are coming! they are coming! I hear the drum and fife."

"I really believe they are," said Septimius, his cheek flushing and growing pale, not with fear, but the inevitable tremor, half painful, half pleasurable, of the moment. " Hark! there was the shrill note of a fife. Yes, they are coming!"

He tried to persuade Rose to hide herself in the house; but that young person would not be persuaded to do so, clinging to Septimius in a way that flattered while it perplexed him. Besides, with all the girl's fright, she had still a good deal of courage, and much curiosity too, to see what these redcoats were of whom she heard such terrible stories.

" Well, well, Rose," said Septimius ; " I doubt not we may stay here without danger, — you, a woman, and I, whose profession is to be that of peace and good-will to all men. They cannot, whatever is said of them, be on an errand of massacre. We will stand here quietly ; and, seeing that we do not fear them, they will understand that we mean them no harm."

They stood, accordingly, a little in front of the door by the well-curb, and soon they saw a heavy cloud of dust, from amidst which shone bayonets ; and anon, a military band, which had hitherto been silent, struck up, with drum and fife, to which the tramp of a thousand feet fell in regular order ; then came the column, moving massively, and the redcoats who seemed somewhat wearied by a long night-march, dusty, with bedraggled gaiters, covered with sweat which had run down from their powdered locks. Nevertheless, these ruddy, lusty Englishmen marched stoutly, as men that needed only a half-hour's rest, a good breakfast, and a pot of beer apiece, to make them ready to face the world. Nor did their faces look anywise rancorous ; but at most, only heavy, cloddish, good-natured, and humane.

" O heavens, Mr. Felton ! " whispered Rose, " why should we shoot these men, or they us ? they look kind, if homely. Each of them has a mother and sisters, I suppose, just like our men."

" It is the strangest thing in the world that we can think of killing them," said Septimius. " Human life is so precious."

Just as they were passing the cottage, a halt was called by the commanding officer, in order that some little rest might get the troops into a better condition and give them breath before entering the village, where it was important to make as imposing a show as possible. During this brief stop, some of the soldiers approached the well-curb, near which Rose and Septimius were standing, and let down the bucket to satisfy their thirst. A young officer, a petulant boy, extremely handsome, and of gay and buoyant deportment, also came up.

" Get me a cup, pretty one," said he, patting Rose's cheek with great freedom, though it was somewhat and indefinitely short of rudeness ; "a mug, or something to drink out of, and you shall have a kiss for your pains."

"Stand off, sir!" said Septimius, fiercely ; "it is a coward's part to insult a woman."

"I intend no insult in this," replied the handsome young officer, suddenly snatching a kiss from Rose, before she could draw back. "And if you think it so, my good friend, you had better take your weapon and get as much satisfaction as you can, shooting at me from behind a hedge."

Before Septimius could reply or act, — and, in truth, the easy presumption of the young Englishman made it difficult for him, an inexperienced recluse as he was, to know what to do or say, — the drum beat a little tap, recalling the soldiers to their rank and to order. The young officer hastened back, with a laughing glance at Rose, and a light, contemptuous look of defiance at Septimius, the drums rattling out in full beat, and the troops marched on.

" What impertinence ! " said Rose, whose indignant

color made her look pretty enough almost to excuse the offence.

It is not easy to see how Septimius could have shielded her from the insult; and yet he felt inconceivably outraged and humiliated at the thought that this offence had occurred while Rose was under his protection, and he responsible for her. Besides, somehow or other, he was angry with her for having undergone the wrong, though certainly most unreasonably; for the whole thing was quicker done than said.

"You had better go into the house now, Rose," said he, "and see to your bedridden grandmother."

"And what will you do, Septimius?" asked she.

"Perhaps I will house myself, also," he replied. "Perhaps take yonder proud redcoat's counsel, and shoot him behind a hedge."

"But not kill him outright; I suppose he has a mother and a sweetheart, the handsome young officer," murmured Rose pityingly to herself.

Septimius went into his house, and sat in his study for some hours, in that unpleasant state of feeling which a man of brooding thought is apt to experience when the world around him is in a state of intense action, which he finds it impossible to sympathize with. There seemed to be a stream rushing past him, by which, even if he plunged into the midst of it, he could not be wet. He felt himself strangely ajar with the human race, and would have given much either to be in full accord with it, or to be separated from it forever.

"I am dissevered from it. It is my doom to be only a spectator of life; to look on as one apart from it. Is it not well, therefore, that, sharing none of its pleasures and happiness, I should be free of its fatalities, its brevity ? How cold I am now, while this whirlpool of public feeling is eddying around me ! It is as if I had not been born of woman ! "

Thus it was that, drawing wild inferences from phenomena of the mind and heart common to people who, by some morbid action within themselves, are set ajar with the world, Septimius continued still to come round to that strange idea of undyingness which had recently taken possession of him. And yet he was wrong in thinking himself cold, and that he felt no sympathy in the fever of patriotism that was throbbing through his countrymen. He was restless as a flame ; he could not fix his thoughts upon his book ; he could not sit in his chair, but kept pacing to and fro, while through the open window came noises to which his imagination gave diverse interpretation. Now it was a distant drum ; now shouts ; by and by there came the rattle of musketry, that seemed to proceed from some point more distant than the village ; a regular roll, then a ragged volley, then scattering shots. Unable any longer to preserve this unnatural indifference, Septimius snatched his gun, and, rushing out of the house, climbed the abrupt hill-side behind, whence he could see a long way towards the village, till a slight bend hid the uneven road. It was quite vacant, not a passenger upon it. But there seemed to be confusion in that direction ; an unseen and inscrutable trouble, blowing thence towards him, intimated by vague sounds, — by no sounds. Listening eagerly, however, he at last fancied a mustering sound of the drum ; then it seemed as if it were coming towards him ; while in advance rode another horseman, the same kind of headlong messenger, in appearance, who had passed the house with his ghastly cry of alarum ; then appeared scattered countrymen, with guns in their hands, straggling across fields. Then he caught sight of the regular array of British soldiers, filling the road with their front, and marching along as firmly as ever, though at a quick pace, while he fancied that the officers looked watchfully around. As he looked, a shot rang sharp from the hill-side towards the village; the smoke curled up, and Septimius saw a man stagger and fall in the midst of the troops. Septimius shuddered; it was so like murder that he really could not tell the difference; his knees trembled beneath him; his breath grew short, not with terror, but with some new sensation of awe.

Another shot or two came almost simultaneously from the wooded height, but without any effect that Septimius could perceive. Almost at the same moment a company of the British soldiers wheeled from the main body, and, dashing out of the road, climbed the hill, and disappeared into the wood and shrubbery that veiled it. There were a few straggling shots, by whom fired, or with what effect, was invisible, and meanwhile the main body of the enemy proceeded along the road. They had now advanced so nigh that Septimius was strangely assailed by the idea that he might, with the gun in his hand, fire right into the midst of them, and select any man of that now hostile band to be a victim. How strange, how strange it is, this deep, wild passion that nature has implanted in us to be the death of our fellow-creatures, and which co-exists at the same time with horror! Septimius levelled his weapon, and drew it up again; he marked a mounted officer, who seemed to be in chief command, whom he knew that he could kill. But no! he had really no such purpose. Only it was such a temptation. And in a moment the horse would leap, the officer would fall and lie there in the dust of the road, bleeding, gasping, breathing in spasms, breathing no more.

While the young man, in these unusual circumstances, stood watching the marching of the troops, he heard the noise of rustling boughs, and the voices of men, and soon understood that the party, which he had seen separate itself from the main body and ascend the hill, was now marching along on the hill-top, the long ridge which, with a gap or two, extended as much as a mile from the village. One of these gaps occurred a little way from where Septimius stood. They were acting as flank guard, to prevent the uproused people from coming so close to the main body as to fire upon it. He looked and saw that the detachment of British was plunging down one side of this gap, with intent to ascend the other, so that they would pass directly over the spot where he stood; a slight removal to one side, among the small bushes, would conceal him. He stepped aside accordingly, and from his concealment, not without drawing quicker breaths, beheld the party draw near. They were more intent upon the space between them and the main body than upon the dense thicket of birch-trees, pitch-pines, sumach, and dwarf oaks, which, scarcely yet beginning to bud into leaf, lay on the other side, and in which Septimius lurked.

[*Describe how their faces affected him, passing so near; how strange they seemed.*]

They had all passed, except an officer who brought up the rear, and who had perhaps been attracted by some slight motion that Septimius made, — some rustle in the thicket; for he stopped, fixed his eyes pierc-

ingly towards the spot where he stood, and levelled a
light fusil which he carried. "Stand out, or I shoot,"
said he.

Not to avoid the shot, but because his manhood felt
a call upon it not to skulk in obscurity from an open
enemy, Septimius at once stood forth, and confronted.
the same handsome young officer with whom those
fierce words had passed on account of his rudeness to
Rose Garfield. Septimius's fierce Indian blood stirred
in him, and gave a murderous excitement.

"Ah, it is you!" said the young officer, with a
haughty smile. "You meant, then, to take up with
my hint of shooting at me from behind a hedge?
This is better. Come, we have in the first place the
great quarrel between me a king's soldier, and you a
rebel; next our private affair, on account of yonder
pretty girl. Come, let us take a shot on either score!"

The young officer was so handsome, so beautiful, in
budding youth; there was such a free, gay petulance
in his manner; there seemed so little of real evil in
him; he put himself on equal ground with the rustic
Septimius so generously, that the latter, often so morbid and sullen, never felt a greater kindness for fellow-
man than at this moment for this youth.

"I have no enmity towards you," said he; "go in
peace."

"No enmity!" replied the officer. "Then why were
you here with your gun amongst the shrubbery? But
I have a mind to do my first deed of arms on you; so
give up your weapon, and come with me as prisoner."

"A prisoner!" cried Septimius, that Indian fierceness that was in him arousing itself, and thrusting up
its malign head like a snake. "Never! If you would
have me, you must take my dead body."

"Ah well, you have pluck in you, I see, only it needs a considerable stirring. Come, this is a good quarrel of ours. Let us fight it out. Stand where you are, and I will give the word of command. Now; ready, aim, fire!"

As the young officer spoke the three last words, in rapid succession, he and his antagonist brought their firelocks to the shoulder, aimed and fired. Septimius felt, as it were, the sting of a gadfly passing across his temple, as the Englishman's bullet grazed it; but, to his surprise and horror (for the whole thing scarcely seemed real to him), he saw the officer give a great start, drop his fusil, and stagger against a tree, with his hand to his breast. He endeavored to support himself erect, but, failing in the effort, beckoned to Septimius.

"Come, my good friend," said he, with that playful, petulant smile flitting over his face again. "It is my first and last fight. Let me down as softly as you can on mother earth, the mother of both you and me; so we are brothers; and this may be a brotherly act, though it does not look so, nor feel so. Ah! that was a twinge indeed!"

"Good God!" exclaimed Septimius. "I had no thought of this, no malice towards you in the least!"

"Nor I towards you," said the young man. "It was boy's play, and the end of it is that I die a boy, instead of living forever, as perhaps I otherwise might."

"Living forever!" repeated Septimius, his attention arrested, even at that breathless moment, by words that rang so strangely on what had been his brooding thought.

"Yes; but I have lost my chance," said the young

officer. Then, as Septimius helped him to lie against the little hillock of a decayed and buried stump, "Thank you; thank you. If you could only call back one of my comrades to hear my dying words. But I forgot. You have killed me, and they would take your life."

In truth, Septimius was so moved and so astonished, that he probably would have called back the young man's comrades, had it been possible; but, marching at the swift rate of men in peril, they had already gone far onward, in their passage through the shrubbery that had ceased to rustle behind them.

"Yes; I must die here!" said the young man, with a forlorn expression, as of a school-boy far away from home, "and nobody to see me now but you, who have killed me. Could you fetch me a drop of water? I have a great thirst."

Septimius, in a dream of horror and pity, rushed down the hill-side; the house was empty, for Aunt Keziah had gone for shelter and sympathy to some of the neighbors. He filled a jug with cold water, and hurried back to the hill-top, finding the young officer looking paler and more deathlike within those few moments.

"I thank you, my enemy that was, my friend that is," murmured he, faintly smiling. "Methinks, next to the father and mother that gave us birth, the next most intimate relation must be with the man that slays us, who introduces us to the mysterious world to which this is but the portal. You and I are singularly connected, doubt it not, in the scenes of the unknown world."

"Oh, believe me," cried Septimius, "I grieve for you like a brother!"

"I see it, my dear friend," said the young officer; "and though my blood is on your hands, I forgive you freely, if there is anything to forgive. But I am dying, and have a few words to say, which you must hear. You have slain me in fair fight, and my spoils, according to the rules and customs of warfare, belong to the victor. Hang up my sword and fusil over your chimney-place, and tell your children, twenty years hence, how they were won. My purse, keep it or give it to the poor. There is something, here next my heart, which I would fain have sent to the address which I will give you."

Septimius, obeying his directions, took from his breast a miniature that hung round it; but, on examination, it proved that the bullet had passed directly through it, shattering the ivory, so that the woman's face it represented was quite destroyed.

"Ah! that is a pity," said the young man; and yet Septimius thought that there was something light and contemptuous mingled with the pathos in his tones. "Well, but send it; cause it to be transmitted, according to the address."

He gave Septimius, and made him take down on a tablet which he had about him, the name of a hall in one of the midland counties of England.

"Ah, that old place," said he, "with its oaks, and its lawn, and its park, and its Elizabethan gables! I little thought I should die here, so far away, in this barren Yankee land. Where will you bury me?"

As Septimius hesitated to answer, the young man continued: "I would like to have lain in the little old church at Whitnash, which comes up before me now, with its low, gray tower, and the old yew-tree in front, hollow with age, and the village clustering about it, with its thatched houses. I would be loath to lie in one of your Yankee graveyards, for I have a distaste for them, — though I love you, my slayer. Bury me here, on this very spot. A soldier lies best where he falls."

" Here, in secret ? " exclaimed Septimius.

" Yes ; there is no consecration in your Puritan burial-grounds," said the dying youth, some of that queer narrowness of English Churchism coming into his mind. " So bury me here, in my soldier's dress. Ah! and my watch! I have done with time, and you, perhaps, have a long lease of it ; so take it, not as spoil, but as my parting gift. And that reminds me of one other thing. Open that pocket-book which you have in your hand."

Septimius did so, and by the officer's direction took from one of its compartments a folded paper, closely written in a crabbed hand ; it was considerably worn in the outer folds, but not within. There was also a small silver key in the pocket-book.

" I leave it with you," said the officer ; " it was given me by an uncle, a learned man of science, who intended me great good by what he there wrote. Reap the profit, if you can. Sooth to say, I never read beyond the first lines of the paper."

Septimius was surprised, or deeply impressed, to see that through this paper, as well as through the miniature, had gone his fatal bullet, — straight through the midst ; and some of the young man's blood, saturating his dress, had wet the paper all over. He hardly thought himself likely to derive any good from what it had cost a human life, taken (however uncriminally) by his own hands, to obtain.

"Is there anything more that I can do for you?" asked he, with genuine sympathy and sorrow, as he knelt by his fallen foe's side.

"Nothing, nothing, I believe," said he. "There was one thing I might have confessed; if there were a holy man here, I might have confessed, and asked his prayers; for though I have lived few years, it has been long enough to do a great wrong. But I will try to pray in my secret soul. Turn my face towards the trunk of the tree, for I have taken my last look at the world. There, let me be now."

Septimius did as the young man requested, and then stood leaning against one of the neighboring pines, watching his victim with a tender concern that made him feel as if the convulsive throes that passed through his frame were felt equally in his own. There was a murmuring from the youth's lips which seemed to Septimius swift, soft, and melancholy, like the voice of a child when it has some naughtiness to confess to its mother at bedtime; contrite, pleading, yet trusting. So it continued for a few minutes; then there was a sudden start and struggle, as if he were striving to rise; his eyes met those of Septimius with a wild, troubled gaze, but as the latter caught him in his arms, he was dead. Septimius laid the body softly down on the leaf-strewn earth, and tried, as he had heard was the custom with the dead, to compose the features distorted by the dying agony. He then flung himself on the ground at a little distance, and gave himself up to the reflections suggested by the strange occurrences of the last hour.

He had taken a human life; and, however the cir-cumstances might excuse him, — might make the thing even something praiseworthy, and that would be called patriotic, — still, it was not at once that a fresh country youth could see anything but horror in the blood with which his hand was stained. It seemed so dreadful to have reduced this gay, animated, beautiful being to a lump of dead flesh for the flies to settle upon, and which in a few hours would begin to decay; which must be put forthwith into the earth, lest it should be a horror to men's eyes; that delicious beauty for woman to love; that strength and courage to make him famous among men, — all come to nothing; all probabilities of life in one so gifted; the renown, the position, the pleasures, the profits, the keen ecstatic joy, — this never could be made up, — all ended quite; for the dark doubt descended upon Septimius, that, because of the very fitness that was in this youth to enjoy this world, so much the less chance was there of his being fit for any other world. What could it do for him there, — this beautiful grace and elegance of feature, — where there was no form, nothing tangible nor visible? what good that readiness and aptness for associating with all created things, doing his part, acting, enjoying, when, under the changed conditions of another state of being, all this adaptedness would fail? Had he been gifted with permanence on earth, there could not have been a more admirable creature than this young man; but as his fate had turned out, he was a mere grub, an illusion, something that nature had held out in mockery, and then withdrawn. A weed might grow from his dust now; that little spot on the barren hill-top, where he had desired to be buried, would be greener for some years to come, and that was all the difference. Septimius could not get beyond the earthiness; his feeling was as if, by an act of violence, he had forever cut off a happy human ex-

istence. And such was his own love of life and clinging to it, peculiar to dark, sombre natures, and which
lighter and gayer ones can never know, that he shuddered at his deed, and at himself, and could with difficulty bear to be alone with the corpse of his victim,
— trembled at the thought of turning his face towards
him.

Yet he did so, because he could not endure the imagination that the dead youth was turning his eyes
towards him as he lay; so he came and stood beside
him, looking down into his white, upturned face. But
it was wonderful! What a change had come over it
since, only a few moments ago, he looked at that death-
contorted countenance! Now there was a high and
sweet expression upon it, of great joy and surprise,
and yet a quietude diffused throughout, as if the peace
being so very great was what had surprised him. The
expression was like a light gleaming and glowing
within him. Septimius had often, at a certain space
of time after sunset, looking westward, seen a living
radiance in the sky, — the last light of the dead day
that seemed just the counterpart of this death-light in
the young man's face. It was as if the youth were
just at the gate of heaven, which, swinging softly
open, let the inconceivable glory of the blessed city
shine upon his face, and kindle it up with gentle, un-
disturbing astonishment and purest joy. It was an
expression contrived by God's providence to comfort;
to overcome all the dark auguries that the physical
ugliness of death inevitably creates, and to prove by
the divine glory on the face, that the ugliness is a delusion. It was as if the dead man himself showed his
face out of the sky, with heaven's blessing on it, and
bade the afflicted be of good cheer, and believe in immortality.

Septimius remembered the young man's injunctions to bury him there, on the hill, without uncovering the body ; and though it seemed a sin and shame to cover up that beautiful body with earth of the grave, and give it to the worm, yet he resolved to obey.

Be it confessed that, beautiful as the dead form looked, and guiltless as Septimius must be held in causing his death, still he felt as if he should be eased when it was under the ground. He hastened down to the house, and brought up a shovel and a pickaxe, and began his unwonted task of grave-digging, delving earnestly a deep pit, sometimes pausing in his toil, while the sweat-drops poured from him, to look at the beautiful clay that was to occupy it. Sometimes he paused, too, to listen to the shots that pealed in the far distance, towards the east, whither the battle had long since rolled out of reach and almost out of hearing. It seemed to have gathered about itself the whole life of the land, attending it along its bloody course in a struggling throng of shouting, shooting men, so still and solitary was everything left behind it. It seemed the very midland solitude of the world where Septimius was delving at the grave. He and his dead were alone together, and he was going to put the body under the sod, and be quite alone.

The grave was now deep, and Septimius was stooping down into its depths among dirt and pebbles, levelling off the bottom, which he considered to be profound enough to hide the young man's mystery forever, when a voice spoke above him ; a solemn, quiet voice, which he knew well.

" Septimius ! what are you doing here ? "

He looked up and saw the minister.

" I have slain a man in fair fight," answered he.

"and am about to bury him as he requested. I am glad you are come. You, reverend sir, can fitly say a prayer at his obsequies. I am glad for my own sake; for it is very lonely and terrible to be here."

He climbed out of the grave, and, in reply to the minister's inquiries, communicated to him the events of the morning, and the youth's strange wish to be buried here, without having his remains subjected to the hands of those who would prepare it for the grave. The minister hesitated.

"At an ordinary time," said he, " such a singular request would of course have to be refused. Your own safety, the good and wise rules that make it necessary that all things relating to death and burial should be done publicly and in order, would forbid it."

"Yes," replied Septimius; "but, it may be, scores of men will fall to-day, and be flung into hasty graves without funeral rites; without its ever being known, perhaps, what mother has lost her son. I cannot but think that I ought to perform the dying request of the youth whom I have slain. He trusted in me not to uncover his body myself, nor to betray it to the hands of others."

"A singular request," said the good minister, gazing with deep interest at the beautiful dead face, and graceful, slender, manly figure. " What could have been its motive? But no matter. I think, Septimius, that you are bound to obey his request; indeed, having promised him, nothing short of an impossibility should prevent your keeping your faith. Let us lose no time, then."

With few but deeply solemn rites the young stranger was laid by the minister and the youth who slew him in his grave. A prayer was made, and then Septimius, gathering some branches and twigs, spread them over the face that was turned upward from the bottom of the pit, into which the sun gleamed downward, throwing its rays so as almost to touch it. The twigs partially hid it, but still its white shone through. Then the minister threw a handful of earth upon it, and, accustomed as he was to burials, tears fell from his eyes along with the mould.

"It is sad," said he, "this poor young man, coming from opulence, no doubt, a dear English home, to die here for no end, one of the first-fruits of a bloody war, — so much privately sacrificed. But let him rest, Septimius. I am sorry that he fell by your hand, though it involves no shadow of a crime. But death is a thing too serious not to melt into the nature of a man like you."

"It does not weigh upon my conscience, I think," said Septimius; "though I cannot but feel sorrow, and wish my hand were as clean as yesterday. It is, indeed, a dreadful thing to take human life."

"It is a most serious thing," replied the minister; "but perhaps we are apt to over-estimate the importance of death at any particular moment. If the question were whether to die or to live forever, then, indeed, scarcely anything should justify the putting a fellow-creature to death. But since it only shortens his earthly life, and brings a little forward a change which, since God permits it, is, we may conclude, as fit to take place then as at any other time, it alters the case. I often think that there are many things that occur to us in our daily life, many unknown crises, that are more important to us than this mysterious circumstance of death, which we deem the most important of all. All we understand of it is, that it takes the dead person away from our knowledge of him, which, while we live with him, is so very scanty."

"You estimate at nothing, it seems, his earthly life, which might have been so happy."

"At next to nothing," said the minister; "since, as I have observed, it must, at any rate, have closed so soon."

Septimius thought of what the young man, in his last moments, had said of his prospect or opportunity of living a life of interminable length, and which prospect he had bequeathed to himself. But of this he did not speak to the minister, being, indeed, ashamed to have it supposed that he would put any serious weight on such a bequest, although it might be that the dark enterprise of his nature had secretly seized upon this idea, and, though yet sane enough to be influenced by a fear of ridicule, was busy incorporating it with his thoughts.

So Septimius smoothed down the young stranger's earthy bed, and returned to his home, where he hung up the sword over the mantel-piece in his study, and hung the gold watch, too, on a nail, — the first time he had ever had possession of such a thing. Nor did he now feel altogether at ease in his mind about keeping it, — the time-measurer of one whose mortal life he had cut off. A splendid watch it was, round as a turnip. There seems to be a natural right in one who has slain a man to step into his vacant place in all respects ; and from the beginning of man's dealings with man this right has been practically recognized, whether among warriors or robbers, as paramount to every other. Yet Septimius could not feel easy in availing himself of this right. He therefore resolved to keep the watch, and even the sword and fusil, — which were less questionable spoils of war, — only till he should be able to restore them to some representative of the young officer. The contents of the purse, in accordance with the request of the dying youth, he would expend in relieving the necessities of those whom the war (now broken out, and of which no one could see the limit) might put in need of it. The miniature, with its broken and shattered face, that had so vainly interposed itself between its wearer and death, had been sent to its address.

But as to the mysterious document, the written paper, that he had laid aside without unfolding it, but with a care that betokened more interest in it than in either gold or weapon, or even in the golden representative of that earthly time on which he set so high a value. There was something tremulous in his touch of it; it seemed as if he were afraid of it by the mode in which he hid it away, and secured himself from it, as it were.

This done, the air of the room, the low-ceilinged eastern room where he studied and thought, became too close for him, and he hastened out; for he was full of the unshaped sense of all that had befallen, and the perception of the great public event of a broken-out war was intermixed with that of what he had done personally in the great struggle that was beginning. He longed, too, to know what was the news of the battle that had gone rolling onward along the hitherto peaceful country road, converting everywhere (this demon of war, we mean), with one blast of its red sulphurous breath, the peaceful husbandman to a soldier thirsting for blood. He turned his steps, therefore, towards the village, thinking it probable that news must have arrived either of defeat or victory, from messengers or fliers, to cheer or sadden the old men, the women, and the children, who alone perhaps remained there.

But Septimius did not get to the village. As he passed along by the cottage that has been already described, Rose Garfield was standing at the door, peering anxiously forth to know what was the issue of the conflict, — as it has been woman's fate to do from the beginning of the world, and is so still. Seeing Septimius, she forgot the restraint that she had hitherto kept herself under, and, flying at him like a bird, she cried out, " Septimius, dear Septimius, where have you been ? What news do you bring ? You look as if you had seen some strange and dreadful thing."

" Ah, is it so ? Does my face tell such stories ? " exclaimed the young man. " I did not mean it should. Yes, Rose, I have seen and done such things as change a man in a moment."

" Then you have been in this terrible fight," said Rose.

" Yes, Rose, I have had my part in it," answered Septimius.

He was on the point of relieving his overburdened mind by telling her what had happened no farther off than on the hill above them ; but, seeing her excitement, and recollecting her own momentary interview with the young officer, and the forced intimacy and link that had been established between them by the kiss, he feared to agitate her further by telling her that that gay and beautiful young man had since been slain, and deposited in a bloody grave by his hands. And yet the recollection of that kiss caused a thrill of vengeful joy at the thought that the perpetrator had since expiated his offence with his life, and that it was himself that did it, so deeply was Septimius's Indian nature of revenge and blood incorporated with that of more peaceful forefathers, although Septimius had grace enough to chide down that bloody spirit, feeling that it made him, not a patriot, but a murderer.

"Ah," said Rose, shuddering, "it is awful when we must kill one another! And who knows where it will end?"

"With me it will end here, Rose," said Septimius. "It may be lawful for any man, even if he have devoted himself to God, or however peaceful his pursuits, to fight to the death when the enemy's step is on the soil of his home; but only for that perilous juncture, which passed, he should return to his own way of peace. I have done a terrible thing for once, dear Rose, one that might well trace a dark line through all my future life; but henceforth I cannot think it my duty to pursue any further a work for which my studies and my nature unfit me."

"Oh no! Oh no!" said Rose; "never! and you a minister, or soon to be one. There must be some peacemakers left in the world, or everything will turn to blood and confusion; for even women grow dreadfully fierce in these times. My old grandmother laments her bedriddenness, because, she says, she cannot go to cheer on the people against the enemy. But she remembers the old times of the Indian wars, when the women were as much in danger of death as the men, and so were almost as fierce as they, and killed men sometimes with their own hands. But women, nowadays, ought to be gentler; let the men be fierce, if they must, except you, and such as you, Septimius."

"Ah, dear Rose," said Septimius, "I have not the kind and sweet impulses that you speak of. I need something to soften and warm my cold, hard life; something to make me feel how dreadful this time of warfare is. I need you, dear Rose, who are all kindness of heart and mercy."

And here Septimius, hurried away by I know not what excitement of the time, — the disturbed state of the country, his own ebullition of passion, the deed he had done, the desire to press one human being close to his life, because he had shed the blood of another, his half-formed purposes, his shapeless impulses; in short, being affected by the whole stir of his nature, — spoke to Rose of love, and with an energy that, indeed, there was no resisting when once it broke bounds. And Rose, whose maiden thoughts, to say the truth, had long dwelt upon this young man, — admiring him for a certain dark beauty, knowing him familiarly from childhood, and yet having the sense, that is so bewitching, of remoteness, intermixed with intimacy, because he was so unlike herself; having a woman's respect for scholarship, her imagination the more impressed by all in him that she could not comprehend, — Rose yielded to his impetuous suit, and gave him the troth that he requested. And yet it was with a sort of reluctance and drawing back; her whole nature, her secretest heart, her deepest womanhood, perhaps, did not consent. There was something in Septimius, in his wild, mixed nature, the monstrousness that had grown out of his hybrid race, the black infusions, too, which melancholic men had left there, the devilishness that had been symbolized in the popular regard about his family, that made her shiver, even while she came the closer to him for that very dread. And when he gave her the kiss of betrothment her lips grew white. If it had not been in the day of turmoil, if he had asked her in any quiet time, when Rose's heart was in its natural mood, it may well be that, with tears and pity for him, and half-pity for herself, Rose would have told Septimius that she did not think she could love him well enough to be his wife.

And how was it with Septimius? Well; there was a singular correspondence in his feelings to those of Rose Garfield. At first, carried away by a passion that seized him all unawares, and seemed to develop itself all in a moment, he felt, and so spoke to Rose, so pleaded his suit, as if his whole earthly happiness depended on her consent to be his bride. It seemed to him that her love would be the sunshine in the gloomy dungeon of his life. But when her bashful, downcast, tremulous consent was given, then immediately came a strange misgiving into his mind. He felt as if he had taken to himself something good and beautiful doubtless in itself, but which might be the exchange for one more suited to him, that he must now give up. The intellect, which was the prominent point in Septimius, stirred and heaved, crying out vaguely that its own claims, perhaps, were ignored in this contract. Septimius had perhaps no right to love at all; if he did, it should have been a woman of another make, who could be his intellectual companion and helper. And then, perchance, — perchance, — there was destined for him some high, lonely path, in which, to make any progress, to come to any end, he must walk unburdened by the affections. Such thoughts as these depressed and chilled (as many men have found them, or similar ones, to do) the moment of success that should have been the most exulting in the world. And so, in the kiss which these two lovers had exchanged there was, after all, something that repelled; and when they parted they wondered at their strange states of mind, but would not acknowledge that they had done a thing that ought not to have been done. Nothing is surer, however, than that, if we suffer ourselves to be drawn into too close proximity with people, if we over-estimate the degree of our proper tendency towards them, or theirs towards us, a reaction is sure to follow.

Septimius quitted Rose, and resumed his walk towards the village. But now it was near sunset, and there began to be straggling passengers along the road, some of whom came slowly, as if they had received hurts; all seemed wearied. Among them one form appeared which Rose soon found that she recognized. It was Robert Hagburn, with a shattered firelock in his hand, broken at the butt, and his left arm bound with a fragment of his shirt, and suspended in a handkerchief; and he walked weariedly, but brightened up at sight of Rose, as if ashamed to let her see how exhausted and dispirited he was. Perhaps he expected a smile, at least a more earnest reception than he met; for Rose, with the restraint of what had recently passed drawing her back, merely went gravely a few steps to meet him, and said, " Robert, how tired and pale you look! Are you hurt?"

"It is of no consequence," replied Robert Hagburn; "a scratch on my left arm from an officer's sword, with whose head my gunstock made instant acquaintance. It is no matter, Rose; you do not care for it, nor do I either."

"How can you say so, Robert?" she replied. But without more greeting he passed her, and went into his own house, where, flinging himself into a chair, he remained in that despondency that men generally feel after a fight, even if a successful one.

Septimius, the next day, lost no time in writing a letter to the direction given him by the young officer, conveying a brief account of the latter's death and burial, and a signification that he held in readiness to give up certain articles of property, at any future time, to his representatives, mentioning also the amount of money contained in the purse, and his intention, in compliance with the verbal will of the deceased, to expend it in alleviating the wants of prisoners. Having so done, he went up on the hill to look at the grave, and satisfy himself that the scene there had not been a dream; a point which he was inclined to question, in spite of the tangible evidence of the sword and watch, which still hung over the mantel-piece. There was the little mound, however, looking so incontrovertibly a grave, that it seemed to him as if all the world must see it, and wonder at the fact of its being there, and spend their wits in conjecturing who slept within; and, indeed, it seemed to give the affair a questionable character, this secret burial, and he wondered and wondered why the young man had been so earnest about it. Well; there was the grave; and, moreover, on the leafy earth, where the dying youth had lain, there were traces of blood, which no rain had yet washed away. Septimius wondered at the easiness with which he acquiesced in this deed; in fact, he felt in a slight degree the effects of that taste of blood, which makes the slaying of men, like any other abuse, sometimes become a passion. Perhaps it was his Indian trait stirring in him again; at any rate, it is not delightful to observe how readily man becomes a blood-shedding animal.

Looking down from the hill-top, he saw the little
dwelling of Rose Garfield, and caught a glimpse of
the girl herself, passing the windows or the door,
about her household duties, and listened to hear the
singing which usually broke out of her. But Rose,
for some reason or other, did not warble as usual this
morning. She trod about silently, and somehow or
other she was translated out of the ideality in which
Septimius usually enveloped her, and looked little
more than a New England girl, very pretty indeed,
but not enough so perhaps to engross a man's life and
higher purposes into her own narrow circle ; so, at
least, Septimius thought. Looking a little farther, —
down into the green recess where stood Robert Hagburn's house, — he saw that young man, looking very
pale, with his arm in a sling sitting listlessly on a
half-chopped log of wood which was not likely soon to
be severed by Robert's axe. Like other lovers, Septimius had not failed to be aware that Robert Hagburn was sensible to Rose Garfield's attractions ; and
now, as he looked down on them both from his elevated position, he wondered if it would not have been
better for Rose's happiness if her thoughts and virgin
fancies had settled on that frank, cheerful, able, wholesome young man, instead of on himself, who met her
on so few points ; and, in relation to whom, there was
perhaps a plant that had its root in the grave, that
would entwine itself around his whole life, overshadowing it with dark, rich foliage and fruit that he alone
could feast upon.

For the sombre imagination of Septimius, though
he kept it as much as possible away from the subject,
still kept hinting and whispering, still coming back to
the point, still secretly suggesting that the event of

yesterday was to have momentous consequences upon his fate.

He had not yet looked at the paper which the young man bequeathed to him; he had laid it away unopened; not that he felt little interest in it, but, on the contrary, because he looked for some blaze of light which had been reserved for him alone. The young officer had been only the bearer of it to him, and he had come hither to die by his hand, because that was the readiest way by which he could deliver his message. How else, in the infinite chances of human affairs, could the document have found its way to its destined possessor? Thus mused Septimius, pacing to and fro on the level edge of his hill-top, apart from the world, looking down occasionally into it, and seeing its love and interest away from him; while Rose, it might be looking upward, saw occasionally his passing figure, and trembled at the nearness and remoteness that existed between them; and Robert Hagburn looked too, and wondered what manner of man it was who, having won Rose Garfield (for his instinct told him this was so), could keep that distance between her and him, thinking remote thoughts.

Yes; there was Septimius treading a path of his own on the hill-top; his feet began only that morning to wear it in his walking to and fro, sheltered from the lower world, except in occasional glimpses, by the birches and locusts that threw up their foliage from the hill-side. But many a year thereafter he continued to tread that path, till it was worn deep with his footsteps and trodden down hard; and it was believed by some of his superstitious neighbors that the grass and little shrubs shrank away from his path, and made it wider on that account; because there was something in the broodings that urged him to and fro along the path alien to nature and its productions. There was another opinion, too, that an invisible fiend, one of his relatives by blood, walked side by side with him, and so made the pathway wider than his single footsteps could have made it. But all this was idle, and was, indeed, only the foolish babble that hovers like a mist about men who withdraw themselves from the throng, and involve themselves in unintelligible pursuits and interests of their own. For the present, the small world, which alone knew of him, considered Septimius as a studious young man, who was fitting for the ministry, and was likely enough to do credit to the ministerial blood that he drew from his ancestors, in spite of the wild stream that the Indian priest had contributed ; and perhaps none the worse, as a clergyman, for having an instinctive sense of the nature of the Devil from his traditionary claims to partake of his blood. But what strange interest there is in tracing out the first steps by which we enter on a career that influences our life ; and this deep-worn pathway on the hill-top, passing and repassing by a grave, seemed to symbolize it in Septimius's case.

I suppose the morbidness of Septimius's disposition was excited by the circumstances which had put the paper into his possession. Had he received it by post, it might not have impressed him ; he might possibly have looked over it with ridicule, and tossed it aside. But he had taken it from a dying man, and he felt that his fate was in it ; and truly it turned out to be so. He waited for a fit opportunity to open it and read it ; he put it off as if he cared nothing about it ; perhaps it was because he cared so much. Whenever he had a happy time with Rose (and, moody as Sep-

timius was, such happy moments came), he felt that
then was not the time to look into the paper, — it was
not to be read in a happy mood.

Once he asked Rose to walk with him on the hill-
top.

"Why, what a path you have worn here, Septimius!" said the girl. "You walk miles and miles on
this one spot, and get no farther on than when you
started. That is strange walking!"

"I don't know, Rose; I sometimes think I get a
little onward. But it is sweeter — yes, much sweeter,
I find — to have you walking on this path here than
to be treading it alone."

"I am glad of that," said Rose; "for sometimes,
when I look up here, and see you through the
branches, with your head bent down, and your hands
clasped behind you, treading, treading, treading, always in one way, I wonder whether I am at all in your
mind. I don't think, Septimius," added she, looking
up in his face and smiling, "that ever a girl had just
such a young man for a lover."

"No young man ever had such a girl, I am sure,"
said Septimius; "so sweet, so good for him, so prolific
of good influences!"

"Ah, it makes me think well of myself to bring such
a smile into your face! But, Septimius, what is this
little hillock here so close to our path? Have you
heaped it up here for a seat? Shall we sit down upon
it for an instant? — for it makes me more tired to
walk backward and forward on one path than to go
straight forward a much longer distance."

"Well; but we will not sit down on this hillock,"
said Septimius, drawing her away from it. "Farther
out this way, if you please, Rose, where we shall have

a better view over the wide plain, the valley, and the long, tame ridge of hills on the other side, shutting it in like human life. It is a landscape that never tires, though it has nothing striking about it; and I am glad that there are no great hills to be thrusting themselves into my thoughts, and crowding out better things. It might be desirable, in some states of mind, to have a glimpse of water, — to have the lake that once must have covered this green valley, — because water reflects the sky, and so is like religion in life, the spiritual element."

"There is the brook running through it, though we do not see it," replied Rose; "a torpid little brook, to be sure; but, as you say, it has heaven in its bosom, like Walden Pond, or any wider one."

As they sat together on the hill-top, they could look down into Robert Hagburn's enclosure, and they saw him, with his arm now relieved from the sling, walking about, in a very erect manner, with a middle-aged man by his side, to whom he seemed to be talking and explaining some matter. Even at that distance Septimius could see that the rustic stoop and uncouthness had somehow fallen away from Robert, and that he seemed developed.

"What has come to Robert Hagburn?" said he. "He looks like another man than the lout I knew a few weeks ago."

"Nothing," said Rose Garfield, "except what comes to a good many young men nowadays. He has enlisted, and is going to the war. It is a pity for his mother."

"A great pity," said Septimius. "Mothers are greatly to be pitied all over the country just now, and there are some even more to be pitied than the moth-

ers, though many of them do not know or suspect anything about their cause of grief at present."

"Of whom do you speak?" asked Rose.

"I mean those many good and sweet young girls,"
said Septimius, "who would have been happy wives
to the thousands of young men who now, like Robert
Hagburn, are going to the war. Those young men —
many of them at least — will sicken and die in camp,
or be shot down, or struck through with bayonets on
battle-fields, and turn to dust and bones; while the
girls that would have loved them, and made happy
firesides for them, will pine and wither, and tread
along many sour and discontented years, and at last
go out of life without knowing what life is. So you
see, Rose, every shot that takes effect kills two at
least, or kills one and worse than kills the other."

"No woman will live single on account of poor Robert Hagburn being shot," said Rose, with a change of
tone; "for he would never be married were he to stay
at home and plough the field."

"How can you tell that, Rose?" asked Septimius.

Rose did not tell how she came to know so much
about Robert Hagburn's matrimonial purposes; but
after this little talk it appeared as if something had
risen up between them, — a sort of mist, a medium,
in which their intimacy was not increased; for the
flow and interchange of sentiment was balked, and
they took only one or two turns in silence along Septimius's trodden path. I don't know exactly what it
was; but there are cases in which it is inscrutably
revealed to persons that they have made a mistake
in what is of the highest concern to them; and this
truth often comes in the shape of a vague depression
of the spirit, like a vapor settling down on a land-

scape; a misgiving, coming and going perhaps, a lack
of perfect certainty. Whatever it was, Rose and Septimius had no more tender and playful words that day;
and Rose soon went to look after her grandmother,
and Septimius went and shut himself up in his study,
after making an arrangement to meet Rose the next
day.

Septimius shut himself up, and drew forth the document which the young officer, with that singular smile
on his dying face, had bequeathed to him as the reward of his death. It was in a covering of folded
parchment, right through which, as aforesaid, was a
bullet-hole and some stains of blood. Septimius un-
rolled the parchment cover, and found inside a manuscript, closely written in a crabbed hand; so crabbed,
indeed, that Septimius could not at first read a word
of it, nor even satisfy himself in what language it was
written. There seemed to be Latin words, and some
interspersed ones in Greek characters, and here and
there he could doubtfully read an English sentence;
but, on the whole, it was an unintelligible mass, conveying somehow an idea that it was the fruit of vast
labor and erudition, emanating from a mind very full
of books, and grinding and pressing down the great
accumulation of grapes that it had gathered from so
many vineyards, and squeezing out rich viscid juices,—
potent wine,—with which the reader might get drunk.
Some of it, moreover, seemed, for the further mystifi-
cation of the officer, to be written in cipher; a needless
precaution, it might seem, when the writer's natural
chirography was so full of puzzle and bewilderment.

Septimius looked at this strange manuscript, and it
shook in his hands as he held it before his eyes, so

great was his excitement. Probably, doubtless, it was in a great measure owing to the way in which it came to him, with such circumstances of tragedy and mystery; as if — so secret and so important was it — it could not be within the knowledge of two persons at once, and therefore it was necessary that one should die in the act of transmitting it to the hand of another, the destined possessor, inheritor, profiter by it. By the bloody hand, as all the great possessions in this world have been gained and inherited, he had succeeded to the legacy, the richest that mortal man ever could receive. He pored over the inscrutable sentences, and wondered, when he should succeed in reading one, if it might summon up a subject-fiend, appearing with thunder and devilish demonstrations. And by what other strange chance had the document come into the hand of him who alone was fit to receive it? It seemed to Septimius, in his enthusiastic egotism, as if the whole chain of events had been arranged purposely for this end; a difference had come between two kindred peoples; a war had broken out; a young officer, with the traditions of an old family represented in his line, had marched, and had met with a peaceful student, who had been incited from high and noble motives to take his life; then came a strange, brief intimacy, in which his victim made the slayer his heir. All these chances, as they seemed, all these interferences of Providence, as they doubtless were, had been necessary in order to put this manuscript into the hands of Septimius, who now pored over it, and could not with certainty read one word!

But this did not trouble him, except for the momentary delay. Because he felt well assured that the strong, concentrated study that he would bring to it would remove all difficulties, as the rays of a lens melt stones; as the telescope pierces through densest light of stars, and resolves them into their individual brilliancies. He could afford to spend years upon it if it were necessary; but earnestness and application should do quickly the work of years.

Amid these musings he was interrupted by his Aunt Keziah; though generally observant enough of her nephew's studies, and feeling a sanctity in them, both because of his intending to be a minister and because she had a great reverence for learning, even if heathenish, this good old lady summoned Septimius somewhat peremptorily to chop wood for her domestic purposes. How strange it is, — the way in which we are summoned from all high purposes by these little homely necessities; all symbolizing the great fact that the earthly part of us, with its demands, takes up the greater portion of all our available force. So Septimius, grumbling and groaning, went to the woodshed and exercised himself for an hour as the old lady requested; and it was only by instinct that he worked, hardly conscious what he was doing. The whole of passing life seemed impertinent; or if, for an instant, it seemed otherwise, then his lonely speculations and plans seemed to become impalpable, and to have only the consistency of vapor, which his utmost concentration succeeded no further than to make into the likeness of absurd faces, mopping, mowing, and laughing at him.

But that sentence of mystic meaning shone out before him like a transparency, illuminated in the darkness of his mind; he determined to take it for his motto until he should be victorious in his quest. When he took his candle, to retire apparently to bed, he again drew forth the manuscript, and, sitting down by the dim light, tried vainly to read it ; but he could not as yet settle himself to concentrated and regular effort ; he kept turning the leaves of the manuscript, in the hope that some other illuminated sentence might gleam out upon him, as the first had done, and shed a light on the context around it ; and that then another would be discovered, with similar effect, until the whole document would thus be illuminated with separate stars of light, converging and concentrating in one radiance that should make the whole visible. But such was his bad fortune, not another word of the manuscript was he able to read that whole evening ; and, moreover, while he had still an inch of candle left, Aunt Keziah, in her nightcap, — as witch-like a figure as ever went to a wizard meeting in the forest with Septimius's ancestor, — appeared at the door of the room, aroused from her bed, and shaking her finger at him.

"Septimius," said she, "you keep me awake, and you will ruin your eyes, and turn your head, if you study till midnight in this manner. You'll never live to be a minister, if this is the way you go on."

"Well, well, Aunt Keziah," said Septimius, covering his manuscript with a book, "I am just going to bed now."

"Good night, then," said the old woman ; "and God bless your labors."

Strangely enough, a glance at the manuscript, as he hid it from the old woman, had seemed to Septimius to reveal another sentence, of which he had imperfectly caught the purport ; and when she had gone, he in vain sought the place, and vainly, too, endeavored to recall the meaning of what he had read. Doubtless his fancy exaggerated the importance of the sentence, and he felt as if it might have vanished from the book forever. In fact, the unfortunate young man, excited and tossed to and fro by a variety of unusual impulses, was got into a bad way, and was likely enough to go mad, unless the balancing portion of his mind proved to be of greater volume and effect than as yet appeared to be the case.

The next morning he was up, bright and early, poring over the manuscript with the sharpened wits of the new day, peering into its night, into its old, blurred, forgotten dream ; and, indeed, he had been dreaming about it, and was fully possessed with the idea that, in his dream, he had taken up the inscrutable document, and read it off as glibly as he would the page of a modern drama, in a continual rapture with the deep truth that it made clear to his comprehension, and the lucid way in which it evolved the mode in which man might be restored to his originally undying state. So strong was the impression, that when he unfolded the manuscript, it was with almost the belief that the crabbed old handwriting would be plain to him. Such did not prove to be the case, however ; so far from it, that poor Septimius in vain turned over the yellow pages in quest of the one sentence which he had been able, or fancied he had been able, to read yesterday. The illumination that had brought it out was now faded, and all was a blur, an inscrutableness, a scrawl of unintelligible characters alike. So much did this affect him, that he had almost a mind to tear it into a thousand fragments, and scatter it out of the window to the west-wind, that was then blowing past the house ; and if, in that summer season, there had been

a fire on the hearth, it is possible that easy realization
of a destructive impulse might have incited him to
fling the accursed scrawl into the hottest of the flames,
and thus returned it to the Devil, who, he suspected,
was the original author of it. Had he done so, what
strange and gloomy passages would I have been spared
the pain of relating! How different would have been
the life of Septimius, — a thoughtful preacher of God's
word, taking severe but conscientious views of man's
state and relations, a heavy-browed walker and worker
on earth, and, finally, a slumberer in an honored grave,
with an epitaph bearing testimony to his great usefulness in his generation.

But, in the mean time, here was the troublesome day
passing over him, and pestering, bewildering, and trip-
ping him up with its mere sublunary troubles, as the
days will all of us the moment we try to do anything
that we flatter ourselves is of a little more importance
than others are doing. Aunt Keziah tormented him a
great while about the rich field, just across the road, in
front of the house, which Septimius had neglected the
cultivation of, unwilling to spare the time to plough,
to plant, to hoe it himself, but hired a lazy lout of the
village, when he might just as well have employed and
paid wages to the scarecrow which Aunt Keziah dressed
out in ancient habiliments, and set up in the midst of
the corn. Then came an old codger from the village,
talking to Septimius about the war, — a theme of
which he was weary: telling the rumor of skirmishes
that the next day would prove to be false, of battles
that were immediately to take place, of encounters
with the enemy in which our side showed the valor of
twenty-fold heroes, but had to retreat; babbling about
shells and mortars, battalions, manœuvres, angles, fas-

cines, and other items of military art; for war had
filled the whole brain of the people, and enveloped the
whole thought of man in a mist of gunpowder.

In this way, sitting on his doorstep, or in the very
study, haunted by such speculations, this wretched old
man would waste the better part of a summer afternoon, while Septimius listened, returning abstracted
monosyllables, answering amiss, and wishing his perse-
cutor jammed into one of the cannons he talked about,
and fired off, to end his interminable babble in one
roar; [talking] of great officers coming from France
and other countries; of overwhelming forces from
England, to put an end to the war at once; of the un-
likelihood that it ever should be ended; of its hopelessness; of its certainty of a good and speedy end.

Then came limping along the lane a disabled soldier,
begging his way home from the field, which, a little
while ago, he had sought in the full vigor of rustic
health he was never to know again; with whom Septimius had to talk, and relieve his wants as far as he
could (though not from the poor young officer's de-
posit of English gold), and send him on his way.

Then came the minister to talk with his former pupil, about whom he had latterly had much meditation,
not understanding what mood had taken possession of
him; for the minister was a man of insight, and from
conversations with Septimius, as searching as he knew
how to make them, he had begun to doubt whether he
were sufficiently sound in faith to adopt the clerical
persuasion. Not that he supposed him to be anything
like a confirmed unbeliever; but he thought it probable that these doubts, these strange, dark, disheartening suggestions of the Devil, that so surely infect certain temperaments and measures of intellect, were tor-

menting poor Septimius, and pulling him back from the path in which he was capable of doing so much good. So he came this afternoon to talk seriously with him, and to advise him, if the case were as he supposed, to get for a time out of the track of the thought in which he had so long been engaged; to enter into active life; and by and by, when the morbid influences should have been overcome by a change of mental and moral religion, he might return, fresh and healthy, to his original design.

"What can I do," asked Septimius, gloomily, "what business take up, when the whole land lies waste and idle, except for this war?"

"There is the very business, then," said the minister. "Do you think God's work is not to be done in the field as well as in the pulpit? You are strong, Septimius, of a bold character, and have a mien and bearing that gives you a natural command among men. Go to the wars, and do a valiant part for your country, and come back to your peaceful mission when the enemy has vanished. Or you might go as chaplain to a regiment, and use either hand in battle, — pray for success before a battle, help win it with sword or gun, and give thanks to God, kneeling on the bloody field, at its close. You have already stretched one foe on your native soil."

Septimius could not but smile within himself at this warlike and bloody counsel; and, joining it with some similar exhortations from Aunt Keziah, he was inclined to think that women and clergymen are, in matters of war, the most uncompromising and bloodthirsty of the community. However, he replied, coolly, that his moral impulses and his feelings of duty did not exactly impel him in this direction, and that he was of opinion that war was a business in which a man could not engage with safety to his conscience, unless his conscience actually drove him into it; and that this made all the difference between heroic battle and murderous strife. The good minister had nothing very effectual to answer to this, and took his leave, with a still stronger opinion than before that there was something amiss in his pupil's mind.

By this time, this thwarting day had gone on through its course of little and great impediments to his pursuit, — the discouragements of trifling and earthly business, of purely impertinent interruption, of severe and disheartening opposition from the powerful counteraction of different kinds of mind, — until the hour had come at which he had arranged to meet Rose Garfield. I am afraid the poor thwarted youth did not go to his love-tryst in any very amiable mood; but rather, perhaps, reflecting how all things earthly and immortal, and love among the rest, whichever category, of earth or heaven, it may belong to, set themselves against man's progress in any pursuit that he seeks to devote himself to. It is one struggle, the moment he undertakes such a thing, of everything else in the world to impede him.

However, as it turned out, it was a pleasant and happy interview that he had with Rose that afternoon. The girl herself was in a happy, tuneful mood, and met him with such simplicity, threw such a light of sweetness over his soul, that Septimius almost forgot all the wild cares of the day, and walked by her side with a quiet fulness of pleasure that was new to him. She reconciled him, in some secret way, to life as it was, to imperfection, to decay; without any help from her intellect, but through the influence of her charac ter, she seemed, not to solve, but to smooth away, problems that troubled him; merely by being, by womanhood, by simplicity, she interpreted God's ways to him; she softened the stoniness that was gathering about his heart. And so they had a delightful time of talking, and laughing, and smelling to flowers; and when they were parting, Septimius said to her, —

"Rose, you have convinced me that this is a most happy world, and that Life has its two children, Birth and Death, and is bound to prize them equally; and that God is very kind to his earthly children; and that all will go well."

"And have I convinced you of all this?" replied Rose, with a pretty laughter. "It is all true, no doubt, but I should not have known how to argue for it. But you are very sweet, and have not frightened me to-day."

"Do I ever frighten you then, Rose?" asked Septimius, bending his black brow upon her with a look of surprise and displeasure.

"Yes, sometimes," said Rose, facing him with courage, and smiling upon the cloud so as to drive it away; "when you frown upon me like that, I am a little afraid you will beat me, all in good time."

"Now," said Septimius, laughing again, "you shall have your choice, to be beaten on the spot, or suffer another kind of punishment, — which?"

So saying, he snatched her to him, and strove to kiss her, while Rose, laughing and struggling, cried out, "The beating! the beating!" But Septimius relented not, though it was only Rose's cheek that he succeeded in touching. In truth, except for that first one, at the moment of their plighted troths, I doubt whether Septimius ever touched those soft, sweet lips, where the smiles dwelt and the little pouts. He now returned to his study, and questioned with himself whether he should touch that weary, ugly, yellow, blurred, unintelligible, bewitched, mysterious, bullet-penetrated, blood-stained manuscript again. There was an undefinable reluctance to do so, and at the same time an enticement (irresistible, as it proved) drawing him towards it. He yielded, and taking it from his desk, in which the precious, fatal treasure was locked up, he plunged into it again, and this time with a certain degree of success. He found the line which had before gleamed out, and vanished again, and which now started out in strong relief; even as when sometimes we see a certain arrangement of stars in the heavens, and again lose it, by not seeing its individual stars in the same relation as before; even so, looking at the manuscript in a different way, Septimius saw this fragment of a sentence, and saw, moreover, what was necessary to give it a certain meaning. "Set the root in a grave, and wait for what shall blossom. It will be very rich, and full of juice." This was the purport, he now felt sure, of the sentence he had lighted upon; and he took it to refer to the mode of producing something that was essential to the thing to be concocted. It might have only a moral being; or, as is generally the case, the moral and physical truth went hand in hand.

While Septimius was busying himself in this way, the summer advanced, and with it there appeared a new character, making her way into our pages. This was a slender and pale girl, whom Septimius was once startled to find, when he ascended his hill-top, to take his walk to and fro upon the accustomed path, which he had now worn deep.

What was stranger, she sat down close beside the grave, which none but he and the minister knew to be a grave; that little hillock, which he had levelled a little, and had planted with various flowers and shrubs; which the summer had fostered into richness, the poor young man below having contributed what he could, and tried to render them as beautiful as he might, in remembrance of his own beauty. Septimius wished to conceal the fact of its being a grave: not that he was tormented with any sense that he had done wrong in shooting the young man, which had been done in fair battle; but still it was not the pleasantest of thoughts, that he had laid a beautiful human creature, so fit for the enjoyment of life, there, when his own dark brow, his own troubled breast, might better, he could not but acknowledge, have been covered up there. [*Perhaps there might sometimes be something fantastically gay in the language and behavior of the girl.*]

Well; but then, on this flower and shrub-disguised grave, sat this unknown form of a girl, with a slender, pallid, melancholy grace about her, simply dressed in a dark attire, which she drew loosely about her. At first glimpse, Septimius fancied that it might be Rose; but it needed only a glance to undeceive him; her figure was of another character from the vigorous, though slight and elastic beauty of Rose; this was a drooping grace, and when he came near enough to see her face, he saw that those large, dark, melancholy eyes, with which she had looked at him, had never met his gaze before.

"Good-morrow, fair maiden," said Septimius, with such courtesy as he knew how to use (which, to say truth, was of a rustic order, his way of life having brought him little into female society). "There is a nice air here on the hill-top, this sultry morning below the hill!"

As he spoke, he continued to look wonderingly at the strange maiden, half fancying that she might be something that had grown up out of the grave; so unexpected she was, so simply unlike anything that had before come there.

The girl did not speak to him, but as she sat by the grave she kept weeding out the little white blades of faded autumn grass and yellow pine-spikes, peering into the soil as if to see what it was all made of, and everything that was growing there; and in truth, whether by Septimius's care or no, there seemed to be several kinds of flowers, — those little asters that abound everywhere, and golden flowers, such as autumn supplies with abundance. She seemed to be in quest of something, and several times plucked a leaf and examined it carefully; then threw it down again, and shook her head. At last she lifted up her pale face, and, fixing her eyes quietly on Septimius, spoke: "It is not here!"

A very sweet voice it was, — plaintive, low, — and she spoke to Septimius as if she were familiar with him, and had something to do with him. He was greatly interested, not being able to imagine who the strange girl was, or whence she came, or what, of all things, could be her reason for coming and sitting down by this grave, and apparently botanizing upon it, in quest of some particular plant.

"Are you in search of flowers?" asked Septimius. "This is but a barren spot for them, and this is not a good season. In the meadows, and along the margin of the watercourses, you might find the fringed gen-

tian at this time. In the woods there are several
pretty flowers, — the side-saddle flower, the anemone ;
violets are plentiful in spring, and make the whole
hill-side blue. But this hill-top, with its soil strewn
over a heap of pebble-stones, is no place for flowers."

"The soil is fit," said the maiden, "but the flower
has not sprung up."

"What flower do you speak of ?" asked Septimius.

"One that is not here," said the pale girl. "No
matter. I will look for it again next spring."

"Do you, then, dwell hereabout?" inquired Septimius.

"Surely," said the maiden, with a look of surprise ;
"where else should I dwell ? My home is on this hill-
top."

It not a little startled Septimius, as may be supposed, to find his paternal inheritance, of which he
and his forefathers had been the only owners since the
world began (for they held it by an Indian deed),
claimed as a home and abiding-place by this fair, pale,
strange-acting maiden, who spoke as if she had as
much right there as if she had grown up out of the
soil like one of the wild, indigenous flowers which she
had been gazing at and handling. However that
might be, the maiden seemed now about to depart, rising, giving a farewell touch or two to the little ver-
dant hillock, which looked much the neater for her
ministrations.

"Are you going?" said Septimius, looking at her
in wonder.

"For a time," said she.

"And shall I see you again?" asked he.

"Surely," said the maiden, "this is my walk, along
the brow of the hill."

It again smote Septimius with a strange thrill of surprise to find the walk which he himself had made, treading it, and smoothing it, and beating it down with the pressure of his continual feet, from the time when the tufted grass made the sides all uneven, until now, when it was such a pathway as you may see through a wood, or over a field, where many feet pass every day, — to find this track and exemplification of his own secret thoughts and plans and emotions, this writing of his body, impelled by the struggle and movement of his soul, claimed as her own by a strange girl with melancholy eyes and voice, who seemed to have such a sad familiarity with him.

"You are welcome to come here," said he, endeavoring at least to keep such hold on his own property as was implied in making a hospitable surrender of it to another.

"Yes," said the girl, "a person should always be welcome to his own."

A faint smile seemed to pass over her face as she said this, vanishing, however, immediately into the melancholy of her usual expression. She went along Septimius's path, while he stood gazing at her till she reached the brow where it sloped towards Robert Hagburn's house; then she turned, and seemed to wave a slight farewell towards the young man, and began to descend. When her figure had entirely sunk behind the brow of the hill, Septimius slowly followed along the ridge, meaning to watch from that elevated station the course she would take; although, indeed, he would not have been surprised if he had seen nothing, no trace of her in the whole nearness or distance; in short, if she had been a freak, an illusion, of a hard-working mind that had put itself ajar by deeply brood-

ing on abstruse matters, an illusion of eyes that he had
tried too much by poring over the inscrutable manuscript, and of intellect that was mystified and bewildered by trying to grasp things that could not be
grasped. A thing of witchcraft, a sort of fungus-
growth out of the grave, an unsubstantiality altogether; although, certainly, she had weeded the grave
with bodily fingers, at all events. Still he had so
much of the hereditary mysticism of his race in him,
that he might have held her supernatural, only that
on reaching the brow of the hill he saw her feet approach the dwelling of Robert Hagburn's mother, who,
moreover, appeared at the threshold beckoning her to
come, with a motherly, hospitable air, that denoted she
knew the strange girl, and recognized her as human.

It did not lessen Septimius's surprise, however, to
think that such a singular being was established in the
neighborhood without his knowledge; considered as a
real occurrence of this world, it seemed even more unaccountable than if it had been a thing of ghostology
and witchcraft. Continually through the day the incident kept introducing its recollection among his
thoughts and studies; continually, as he paced along
his path, this form seemed to hurry along by his side
on the track that she had claimed for her own, and he
thought of her singular threat or promise, whichever
it were to be held, that he should have a companion
there in future. In the decline of the day, when he
met the schoolmistress coming home from her little
seminary, he snatched the first opportunity to mention
the apparition of the morning, and ask Rose if she
knew anything of her.

"Very little," said Rose, "but she is flesh and
blood, of that you may be quite sure. She is a girl

who has been shut up in Boston by the siege; perhaps
a daughter of one of the British officers, and her
health being frail, she requires better air than they
have there, and so permission was got for her, from
General Washington, to come and live in the country;
as any one may see, our liberties have nothing to fear
from this poor brain-stricken girl. And Robert Hagburn, having to bring a message from camp to the se-
lectmen here, had it in charge to bring the girl, whom
his mother has taken to board."

"Then the poor thing is crazy?" asked Septimius.

"A little brain-touched, that is all," replied Rose,
"owing to some grief that she has had; but she is
quite harmless, Robert was told to say, and needs little or no watching, and will get a kind of fantastic
happiness for herself, if only she is allowed to ramble
about at her pleasure. If thwarted, she might be very
wild and miserable."

"Have you spoken with her?" asked Septimius.

"A word or two this morning, as I was going to my
school," said Rose. "She took me by the hand, and
smiled, and said we would be friends, and that I
should show her where the flowers grew; for that she
had a little spot of her own that she wanted to plant
with them. And she asked me if the *Sanguinea sanguinissima* grew hereabout. I should not have taken
her to be ailing in her wits, only for a kind of free-
spokenness and familiarity, as if we had been acquainted a long while; or as if she had lived in some
country where there are no forms and impediments in
people's getting acquainted."

"Did you like her?" inquired Septimius.

"Yes; almost loved her at first sight," answered
Rose, "and I hope may do her some little good, poor

thing, being of her own age, and the only companion, hereabouts, whom she is likely to find. But she has been well educated, and is a lady, that is easy to see."

"It is very strange," said Septimius, "but I fear I shall be a good deal interrupted in my thoughts and studies, if she insists on haunting my hill-top as much as she tells me. My meditations are perhaps of a little too much importance to be shoved aside for the sake of gratifying a crazy girl's fantasies."

"Ah, that is a hard thing to say!" exclaimed Rose, shocked at her lover's cold egotism, though not giving it that title. "Let the poor thing glide quietly along in the path, though it be yours. Perhaps, after a while, she will help your thoughts."

"My thoughts," said Septimius, "are of a kind that can have no help from any one; if from any, it would only be from some wise, long-studied, and experienced scientific man, who could enlighten me as to the bases and foundation of things, as to mystic writings, as to chemical elements, as to the mysteries of language, as to the principles and system on which we were created. Methinks these are not to be taught me by a girl touched in the wits."

"I fear," replied Rose Garfield with gravity, and drawing imperceptibly apart from him, "that no woman can help you much. You despise woman's thought, and have no need of her affection."

Septimius said something soft and sweet, and in a measure true, in regard to the necessity he felt for the affection and sympathy of one woman at least — the one now by his side — to keep his life warm and to make the empty chambers of his heart comfortable. But even while he spoke, there was something that dragged upon his tongue; for he felt that the solitary pursuit in which he was engaged carried him apart from the sympathy of which he spoke, and that he was concentrating his efforts and interest entirely upon himself, and that the more he succeeded the more remotely he should be carried away, and that his final triumph would be the complete seclusion of himself from all that breathed, — the converting him, from an interested actor into a cold and disconnected spectator of all mankind's warm and sympathetic life. So, as it turned out, this interview with Rose was one of those in which, coming no one knows from whence, a nameless cloud springs up between two lovers, and keeps them apart from one another by a cold, sullen spell. Usually, however, it requires only one word, spoken out of the heart, to break that spell, and compel the invisible, unsympathetic medium which the enemy of love has stretched cunningly between them, to vanish, and let them come closer together than ever ; but, in this case, it might be that the love was the illusive state, and the estrangement the real truth, the disenchanted verity. At all events, when the feeling passed away, in Rose's heart there was no reaction, no warmer love, as is generally the case. As for Septimius, he had other things to think about, and when he next met Rose Garfield, had forgotten that he had been sensible of a little wounded feeling, on her part, at parting.

By dint of continued poring over the manuscript, Septimius now began to comprehend that it was written in a singular mixture of Latin and ancient English, with constantly recurring paragraphs of what he was convinced was a mystic writing ; and these recurring passages of complete unintelligibility seemed to be necessary to the proper understanding of any part of the document. What was discoverable was quaint, curious, but thwarting and perplexing, because it seemed to imply some very great purpose, only to be brought out by what was hidden.

Septimius had read, in the old college library during his pupilage, a work on ciphers and cryptic writing, but being drawn to it only by his curiosity respecting whatever was hidden, and not expecting ever to use his knowledge, he had obtained only the barest idea of what was necessary to the deciphering a secret passage. Judging by what he could pick out, he would have thought the whole essay was upon the moral conduct; all parts of that he could make out seeming to refer to a certain ascetic rule of life; to denial of pleasures; these topics being repeated and insisted on everywhere, although without any discoverable reference to religious or moral motives; and always when the author seemed verging towards a definite purpose, he took refuge in his cipher. Yet withal, imperfectly (or not at all, rather) as Septimius could comprehend its purport, this strange writing had a mystic influence, that wrought upon his imagination, and with the late singular incidents of his life, his continual thought on this one subject, his walk on the hill-top, lonely, or only interrupted by the pale shadow of a girl, combined to set him outside of the living world. Rose Garfield perceived it, knew and felt that he was gliding away from her, and met him with a reserve which she could not overcome.

It was a pity that his early friend, Robert Hagburn, could not at present have any influence over him, having now regularly joined the Continental Army, and being engaged in the expedition of Arnold against Quebec. Indeed, this war, in which the country was so earnestly and enthusiastically engaged, had perhaps an influence on Septimius's state of mind, for it put everybody into an exaggerated and unnatural state, united enthusiasms of all sorts, heightened everybody either into its own heroism or into the peculiar madness to which each person was inclined ; and Septimius walked so much the more wildly on his lonely course, because the people were going enthusiastically on another. In times of revolution and public disturbance all absurdities are more unrestrained ; the measure of calm sense, the habits, the orderly decency, are partially lost. More people become insane, I should suppose ; offences against public morality, female license, are more numerous ; suicides, murders, all ungovernable outbreaks of men's thoughts, embodying themselves in wild acts, take place more frequently, and with less horror to the lookers-on. So [with] Septimius ; there was not, as there would have been at an ordinary time, the same calmness and truth in the public observation, scrutinizing everything with its keen criticism, in that time of seething opinions and overturned principles ; a new time was coming, and Septimius's phase of novelty attracted less attention so far as it was known.

So he continued to brood over the manuscript in his study, and to hide it under lock and key in a recess of the wall, as if it were a secret of murder ; to walk, too, on his hill-top, where at sunset always came the pale, crazy maiden, who still seemed to watch the little hillock with a pertinacious care that was strange to Septimius. By and by came the winter and the deep snows ; and even then, unwilling to give up his habitual place of exercise, the monotonousness of which promoted his wish to keep before his mind one subject of thought, Septimius wore a path through the snow, and still walked there. Here, however. he lost for a time the companionship of the girl; for when the first snow came, she shivered, and looked at its white heap over the hillock, and said to Septimius, " I will look for it again in spring."

[*Septimius is at the point of despair for want of a guide in his studies.*]

The winter swept over, and spring was just begin-ning to spread its green flush over the more favored exposures of the landscape, although on the north side of stone-walls, and the northern nooks of hills, there were still the remnants of snow-drifts. Septimius's hill-top, which was of a soil which quickly rid itself of moisture, now began to be a genial place of resort to him, and he was one morning taking his walk there, meditating upon the still insurmountable difficulties which interposed themselves against the interpretation of the manuscript, yet feeling the new gush of spring bring hope to him, and the energy and elasticity for new effort. Thus pacing to and fro, he was surprised, as he turned at the extremity of his walk, to see a figure advancing towards him; not that of the pale maiden whom he was accustomed to see there, but a figure as widely different as possible. [*He sees a spider dangling from his web, and examines him minutely.*] It was that of a short, broad, somewhat elderly man, dressed in a surtout that had a half-mili-tary air; the cocked hat of the period, well worn, and having a fresher spot in it, whence, perhaps, a cockade had been recently taken off ; and this personage car-ried a well blackened German pipe in his hand, which, as he walked, he applied to his lips, and puffed out volumes of smoke, filling the pleasant western breeze

with the fragrance of some excellent Virginia. He came slowly along, and Septimius, slackening his pace a little, came as slowly to meet him, feeling somewhat indignant, to be sure, that anybody should intrude on his sacred hill; until at last they met, as it happened, close by the memorable little hillock, on which the grass and flower-leaves also had begun to sprout. The stranger looked keenly at Septimius, made a careless salute by putting his hand up, and took the pipe from his mouth.

"Mr. Septimius Felton, I suppose?" said he.

"That is my name," replied Septimius.

"I am Doctor Jabez Portsoaken," said the stranger, "late surgeon of his Majesty's sixteenth regiment, which I quitted when his Majesty's army quitted Boston, being desirous of trying my fortunes in your country, and giving the people the benefit of my scientific knowledge; also to practise some new modes of medical science, which I could not so well do in the army."

"I think you are quite right, Doctor Jabez Portsoaken," said Septimius, a little confused and bewildered, so unused had he become to the society of strangers.

"And as to you, sir," said the doctor, who had a very rough, abrupt way of speaking, "I have to thank you for a favor done me."

"Have you, sir?" said Septimius, who was quite sure that he had never seen the doctor's uncouth figure before.

"Oh, ay, me," said the doctor, puffing coolly, — "me, in the person of my niece, a sickly, poor, nervous little thing, who is very fond of walking on your hill-top, and whom you do not send away."

" You are the uncle of Sibyl Dacy ? " said Septimius.

" Even so, her mother's brother," said the doctor, with a grotesque bow. " So, being on a visit, the first that the siege allowed me to pay, to see how the girl was getting on, I take the opportunity to pay my respects to you ; the more that I understand you to be a young man of some learning, and it is not often that one meets with such in this country."

" No," said Septimius, abruptly, for indeed he had half a suspicion that this queer Doctor Portsoaken was not altogether sincere, — that, in short, he was making game of him. " You have been misinformed. I know nothing whatever that is worth knowing."

" Oho ! " said the doctor, with a long puff of smoke out of his pipe. " If you are convinced of that, you are one of the wisest men I have met with, young as you are. I must have been twice your age before I got so far ; and even now, I am sometimes fool enough to doubt the only thing I was ever sure of knowing. But come, you make me only the more earnest to collogue with you. If we put both our shortcomings together, they may make up an item of positive knowledge."

" What use can one make of abortive thoughts ? " said Septimius.

" Do your speculations take a scientific turn ? " said Doctor Portsoaken. " There I can meet you with as much false knowledge and empiricism as you can bring for the life of you. Have you ever tried to study spiders ? — there is my strong point now ! I have hung my whole interest in life on a spider's web."

" I know nothing of them, sir," said Septimius, " except to crush them when I see them running across the floor, or to brush away the festoons of their webs when they have chanced to escape my Aunt Keziah's broom."

"Crush them! Brush away their webs!" cried the doctor, apparently in a rage, and shaking his pipe at Septimius. "Sir, it is sacrilege! Yes, it is worse than murder. Every thread of a spider's web is worth more than a thread of gold; and before twenty years are passed, a housemaid will be beaten to death with her own broomstick if she disturbs one of these sacred animals. But, come again. Shall we talk of botany, the virtues of herbs?"

"My Aunt Keziah should meet you there, doctor," said Septimius. "She has a native and original acquaintance with their virtues, and can save and kill with any of the faculty. As for myself, my studies have not turned that way."

"They ought! they ought!" said the doctor, looking meaningly at him. "The whole thing lies in the blossom of an herb. Now, you ought to begin with what lies about you; on this little hillock, for instance;" and looking at the grave beside which they were standing, he gave it a kick which went to Septimius's heart, there seemed to be such a spite and scorn in it. "On this hillock I see some specimens of plants which would be worth your looking at."

Bending down towards the grave as he spoke, he seemed to give closer attention to what he saw there; keeping in his stooping position till his face began to get a purple aspect, for the erudite doctor was of that make of man who has to be kept right side uppermost with care. At length he raised himself, muttering, "Very curious! very curious!"

"Do you see anything remarkable there?" asked Septimius, with some interest.

" Yes," said the doctor, bluntly. " No matter what! The time will come when you may like to know it."

" Will you come with me to my residence at the foot of the hill, Doctor Portsoaken ? " asked Septimius. " I am not a learned man, and have little or no title to converse with one, except a sincere desire to be wiser than I am. If you can be moved on such terms to give me your companionship, I shall be thankful."

" Sir, I am with you," said Doctor Portsoaken. " I will tell you what I know, in the sure belief (for I will be frank with you) that it will add to the amount of dangerous folly now in your mind, and help you on the way to ruin. Take your choice, therefore, whether to know me further or not."

" I neither shrink nor fear, — neither hope much," said Septimius, quietly. " Anything that you can communicate — if anything you can — I shall fearlessly receive, and return you such thanks as it may be found to deserve."

So saying, he led the way down the hill, by the steep path that descended abruptly upon the rear of his bare and unadorned little dwelling; the doctor following with much foul language (for he had a terrible habit of swearing) at the difficulties of the way, to which his short legs were ill adapted. Aunt Keziah met them at the door, and looked sharply at the doctor, who returned the gaze with at least as much keenness, muttering between his teeth, as he did so ; and to say the truth, Aunt Keziah was as worthy of being sworn at as any woman could well be, for whatever she might have been in her younger days, she was at this time as strange a mixture of an Indian squaw and herb doctress, with the crabbed old maid, and a mingling of the witch-aspect running through all, as could well be imagined ; and she had a handkerchief over her head, and she was of hue a dusky yellow, and she looked very cross. As Septimius ushered the doctor into his study, and was about to follow him, Aunt Keziah drew him back.

"Septimius, who is this you have brought here?" asked she.

"A man I have met on the hill," answered her nephew ; "a Doctor Portsoaken he calls himself, from the old country. He says he has knowledge of herbs and other mysteries ; in your own line, it may be. If you want to talk with him, give the man his dinner, and find out what there is in him."

"And what do you want of him yourself, Septimius?" asked she.

"I? Nothing! — that is to say, I expect nothing," said Septimius. "But I am astray, seeking everywhere, and so I reject no hint, no promise, no faintest possibility of aid that I may find anywhere. I judge this man to be a quack, but I judge the same of the most learned man of his profession, or any other ; and there is a roughness about this man that may indicate a little more knowledge than if he were smoother. So, as he threw himself in my way, I take him in."

"A grim, ugly-looking old wretch as ever I saw," muttered Aunt Keziah. "Well, he shall have his dinner ; and if he likes to talk about yarb-dishes, I 'm with him."

So Septimius followed the doctor into his study, where he found him with the sword in his hand, which he had taken from over the mantel-piece, and was holding it drawn, examining the hilt and blade with great minuteness ; the hilt being wrought in openwork, with certain heraldic devices, doubtless belonging to the family of its former wearer.

"I have seen this weapon before," said the doctor.

"It may well be," said Septimius. "It was once worn by a person who served in the army of your king."

"And you took it from him?" said the doctor.

"If I did, it was in no way that I need be ashamed of, or afraid to tell, though I choose rather not to speak of it," answered Septimius.

"Have you, then, no desire nor interest to know the family, the personal history, the prospects, of him who once wore this sword, and who will never draw sword again?" inquired Doctor Portsoaken. "Poor Cyril Norton! There was a singular story attached to that young man, sir, and a singular mystery he carried about with him, the end of which, perhaps, is not yet."

Septimius would have been, indeed, well enough pleased to learn the mystery which he himself had seen that there was about the man whom he slew; but he was afraid that some question might be thereby started about the secret document that he had kept possession of; and he therefore would have wished to avoid the whole subject.

"I cannot be supposed to take much interest in English family history. It is a hundred and fifty years, at least, since my own family ceased to be English," he answered. "I care more for the present and future than for the past."

"It is all one," said the doctor, sitting down, taking out a pinch of tobacco and refilling his pipe.

It is unnecessary to follow up the description of the visit of the eccentric doctor through the day. Suffice it to say that there was a sort of charm, or rather fascination, about the uncouth old fellow, in spite of his

strange ways; in spite of his constant puffing of tobacco; and in spite, too, of a constant imbibing of
strong liquor, which he made inquiries for, and of
which the best that could be produced was a certain
decoction, infusion, or distillation, pertaining to Aunt
Keziah, and of which the basis was rum, be it said,
done up with certain bitter herbs of the old lady's own
gathering, at proper times of the moon, and which
was a well-known drink to all who were favored with
Aunt Keziah's friendship; though there was a story
that it was the very drink which used to be passed
round at witch-meetings, being brewed from the Devil's
own recipe. And, in truth, judging from the taste
(for I once took a sip of a draught prepared from the
same ingredients, and in the same way), I should think
this hellish origin might be the veritable one.

[*" I thought,"* quoth the doctor, *" I could drink
anything, but "* —]

But the valiant doctor sipped, and sipped again, and
said with great blasphemy that it was the real stuff,
and only needed henbane to make it perfect. Then,
taking from his pocket a good-sized leathern-covered
flask, with a silver lip fastened on the muzzle, he offered
it to Septimius, who declined, and to Aunt Keziah, who
preferred her own decoction, and then drank it off
himself, with a loud smack of satisfaction, declaring
it to be infernally good brandy.

Well, after this Septimius and he talked; and I
know not how it was, but there was a great deal of imagination in this queer man, whether a bodily or spiritual influence it might be hard to say. On the other
hand Septimius had for a long while held little intercourse with men; none whatever with men who could
comprehend him; the doctor, too, seemed to bring the

discourse singularly in apposition with what his host
was continually thinking about, for he conversed on
occult matters, on people who had had the art of living long, and had only died at last by accident, on the
powers and qualities of common herbs, which he believed to be so great, that all around our feet — growing in the wild forest, afar from man, or following
the footsteps of man wherever he fixes his residence,
across seas, from the old homesteads whence he mi-
grated, following him everywhere, and offering themselves sedulously and continually to his notice, while
he only plucks them away from the comparatively
worthless things which he cultivates, and flings them
aside, blaspheming at them because Providence has
sown them so thickly — grow what we call weeds, only
because all the generations, from the beginning of
time till now, have failed to discover their wondrous
virtues, potent for the curing of all diseases, potent
for procuring length of days.

"Everything good," said the doctor, drinking another dram of brandy, "lies right at our feet, and all
we need is to gather it up."

"That's true," quoth Keziah, taking just a little
sup of her hellish preparation ; "these herbs were all
gathered within a hundred yards of this very spot,
though it took a wise woman to find out their virtues."

The old woman went off about her household duties, and then it was that Septimius submitted to the
doctor the list of herbs which he had picked out of
the old document, asking him, as something apposite
to the subject of their discourse, whether he was acquainted with them, for most of them had very queer
names, some in Latin, some in English.

The bluff doctor put on his spectacles, and looked over the slip of yellow and worn paper scrutinizingly, puffing tobacco-smoke upon it in great volumes, as if thereby to make its hidden purport come out; he mumbled to himself, he took another sip from his flask; and then, putting it down on the table, appeared to meditate.

"This infernal old document," said he, at length, " is one that I have never seen before, yet heard of, nevertheless; for it was my folly in youth (and whether I am any wiser now is more than I take upon me to say, but it was my folly then) to be in quest of certain kinds of secret knowledge, which the fathers of science thought attainable. Now, in several quarters, amongst people with whom my pursuits brought me in contact, I heard of a certain recipe which had been lost for a generation or two, but which, if it could be recovered, would prove to have the true life-giving potency in it. It is said that the ancestor of a great old family in England was in possession of this secret, being a man of science, and the friend of Friar Bacon, who was said to have concocted it himself, partly from the precepts of his master, partly from his own experiments, and it is thought he might have been living to this day, if he had not unluckily been killed in the Wars of the Roses; for you know no recipe for long life would be proof against an old English arrow, or a leaden bullet from one of our own firelocks."

"And what has been the history of the thing after his death?" asked Septimius.

"It was supposed to be preserved in the family," said the doctor, " and it has always been said, that the head and eldest son of that family had it at his option to live forever, if he could only make up his mind to it. But seemingly there were difficulties in the way. There was probably a certain diet and regimen to be observed, certain strict rules of life to be kept, a certain asceticism to be imposed on the person, which was not quite agreeable to young men; and after the period of youth was passed, the human frame became incapable of being regenerated from the seeds of decay and death, which, by that time, had become strongly developed in it. In short, while young, the possessor of the secret found the terms of immortal life too hard to be accepted, since it implied the giving up of most of the things that made life desirable in his view; and when he came to a more reasonable mind, it was too late. And so, in all the generations since Friar Bacon's time, the Nortons have been born, and enjoyed their young days, and worried through their manhood, and tottered through their old age (unless taken off sooner by sword, arrow, ball, fever, or what not), and died in their beds, like men that had no such option; and so this old yellow paper has done not the least good to any mortal. Neither do I see how it can do any good to you, since you know not the rules, moral or dietetic, that are essential to its effect. But how did you come by it?"

"It matters not how," said Septimius, gloomily. "Enough that I am its rightful possessor and inheritor. Can you read these old characters?"

"Most of them," said the doctor; "but let me tell you, my young friend, I have no faith whatever in this secret; and, having meddled with such things myself, I ought to know. The old physicians and chemists had strange ideas of the virtues of plants, drugs, and minerals, and equally strange fancies as to the way of getting those virtues into action. They would

throw a hundred different potencies into a caldron together, and put them on the fire, and expect to brew
a potency containing all their potencies, and having a
different virtue of its own. Whereas, the most likely
result would be that they would counteract one another, and the concoction be of no virtue at all; or
else some more powerful ingredient would tincture
the whole."

He read the paper again, and continued : —

" I see nothing else so remarkable in this recipe, as
that it is chiefly made up of some of the commonest
things that grow ; plants that you set your foot upon
at your very threshold, in your garden, in your wood-
walks, wherever you go. I doubt not old Aunt Keziah knows them, and very likely she has brewed
them up in that hell-drink, the remembrance of which
is still rankling in my stomach. I thought I had swallowed the Devil himself, whom the old woman had
been boiling down. It would be curious enough if the
hideous decoction was the same as old Friar Bacon
and his acolyte discovered by their science ! One ingredient, however, one of those plants, I scarcely think
the old lady can have put into her pot of Devil's
elixir ; for it is a rare plant, that does not grow in
these parts."

" And what is that ? " asked Septimius.

" *Sanguinea sanguinissima*," said the doctor ; " it
has no vulgar name ; but it produces a very beautiful
flower, which I have never seen, though some seeds of
it were sent me by a learned friend in Siberia. The
others, divested of their Latin names, are as common
as plantain, pig-weed, and burdock ; and it stands to
reason that, if vegetable Nature has any such wonderfully efficacious medicine in store for men, and means

them to use it, she would have strewn it everywhere
plentifully within their reach."

"But, after all, it would be a mockery on the old
dame's part," said the young man, somewhat bitterly,
"since she would thus hold the desired thing seemingly within our reach; but because she never tells us
how to prepare and obtain its efficacy, we miss it just
as much as if all the ingredients were hidden from
sight and knowledge in the centre of the earth. We
are the playthings and fools of Nature, which she
amuses herself with during our little lifetime, and then
breaks for mere sport, and laughs in our faces as she
does so."

"Take care, my good fellow," said the doctor, with
his great coarse laugh. "I rather suspect that you
have already got beyond the age when the great medicine could do you good; that speech indicates a great
toughness and hardness and bitterness about the heart
that does not accumulate in our tender years."

Septimius took little or no notice of the raillery of
the grim old doctor, but employed the rest of the time
in getting as much information as he could out of his
guest; and though he could not bring himself to show
him the precious and sacred manuscript, yet he questioned him as closely as possible without betraying his
secret, as to the modes of finding out cryptic writings.
The doctor was not without the perception that his
dark-browed, keen-eyed acquaintance had some purpose not openly avowed in all these pertinacious, distinct questions; he discovered a central reference in
them all, and perhaps knew that Septimius must have
in his possession some writing in hieroglyphics, cipher,
or other secret mode, that conveyed instructions how
to operate with the strange recipe that he had shown
him.

" You had better trust me fully, my good sir," said
he. " Not but what I will give you all the aid I can
without it; for you have done me a greater benefit
than you are aware of, beforehand. No — you will
not? Well, if you can change your mind, seek me
out in Boston, where I have seen fit to settle in the
practice of my profession, and I will serve you according to your folly; for folly it is, I warn you."

Nothing else worthy of record is known to have
passed during the doctor's visit; and in due time he
disappeared, as it were, in a whiff of tobacco-smoke,
leaving an odor of brandy and tobacco behind him,
and a traditionary memory of a wizard that had been
there. Septimius went to work with what items of
knowledge he had gathered from him; but the interview had at least made him aware of one thing, which
was, that he must provide himself with all possible
quantity of scientific knowledge of botany, and perhaps more extensive knowledge, in order to be able to
concoct the recipe. It was the fruit of all the scientific attainment of the age that produced it (so said
the legend, which seemed reasonable enough), a great
philosopher had wrought his learning into it; and this
had been attempered, regulated, improved, by the
quick, bright intellect of his scholar. Perhaps, thought
Septimius, another deep and earnest intelligence added
to these two may bring the precious recipe to still
greater perfection. At least it shall be tried. So
thinking, he gathered together all the books that he
could find relating to such studies; he spent one day,
moreover, in a walk to Cambridge, where he searched
the alcoves of the college library for such works as it
contained; and borrowing them from the war-dis-
turbed institution of learning, he betook himself home

wards, and applied himself to the study with an earnestness of zealous application that perhaps has been seldom equalled in a study of so quiet a character. A month or two of study, with practice upon such plants as he found upon his hill-top, and along the brook and in other neighboring localities, sufficed to do a great deal for him. In this pursuit he was assisted by Sibyl, who proved to have great knowledge in some botanical departments, especially among flowers ; and in her cold and quiet way, she met him on this subject and glided by his side, as she had done so long, a companion, a daily observer and observed of him, mixing herself up with his pursuits, as if she were an attendant sprite upon him.

But this pale girl was not the only associate of his studies, the only instructress, whom Septimius found. The observation which Doctor Portsoaken made about the fantastic possibility that Aunt Keziah might have inherited the same recipe from her Indian ancestry which had been struck out by the science of Friar Bacon and his pupil had not failed to impress Septimius, and to remain on his memory. So, not long after the doctor's departure, the young man took occasion one evening to say to his aunt that he thought his stomach was a little out of order with too much application, and that perhaps she could give him some herb-drink or other that would be good for him.

"That I can, Seppy, my darling," said the old woman, "and I'm glad you have the sense to ask for it at last. Here it is in this bottle; and though that foolish, blaspheming doctor turned up his old brandy nose at it, I'll drink with him any day and come off better than he."

So saying, she took out of the closet her brown jug,

stopped with a cork that had a rag twisted round it to make it tighter, filled a mug half full of the concoction, and set it on the table before Septimius.

"There, child, smell of that ; the smell merely will do you good ; but drink it down, and you 'll live the longer for it."

"Indeed, Aunt Keziah, is that so ? " asked Septimius, a little startled by a recommendation which in some measure tallied with what he wanted in a medicine. " That 's a good quality."

He looked into the mug, and saw a turbid, yellow concoction, not at all attractive to the eye; he smelt of it, and was partly of opinion that Aunt Keziah had mixed a certain unfragrant vegetable, called skunk-cabbage, with the other ingredients of her witch-drink. He tasted it ; not a mere sip, but a good, genuine gulp, being determined to have real proof of what the stuff was in all respects. The draught seemed at first to burn in his mouth, unaccustomed to any drink but water, and to go scorching all the way down into his stomach, making him sensible of the depth of his inwards by a track of fire, far, far down ; and then, worse than the fire, came a taste of hideous bitterness and nauseousness, which he had not previously conceived to exist, and which threatened to stir up his bowels into utter revolt ; but knowing Aunt Keziah's touchiness with regard to this concoction, and how sacred she held it, he made an effort of real heroism, squelched down his agony, and kept his face quiet, with the exception of one strong convulsion, which he allowed to twist across it for the sake of saving his life.

"It tastes as if it might have great potency in it, Aunt Keziah," said this unfortunate young man ; " I wish you would tell me what it is made of, and how you brew it; for I have observed you are very strict and secret about it."

"Aha! you have seen that, have you?" said Aunt Keziah, taking a sip of her beloved liquid, and grinning at him with a face and eyes as yellow as that she was drinking. In fact the idea struck him, that in temper, and all appreciable qualities, Aunt Keziah was a good deal like this drink of hers, having probably become saturated by them while she drank of it. And then, having drunk, she gloated over it, and tasted, and smelt of the cup of this hellish wine, as a wine-bibber does of that which is most fragrant and delicate. "And you want to know how I make it? But first, child, tell me honestly, do you love this drink of mine? Otherwise, here, and at once, we stop talking about it."

"I love it for its virtues," said Septimius, temporizing with his conscience, "and would prefer it on that account to the rarest wines."

"So far good," said Aunt Keziah, who could not well conceive that her liquor should be otherwise than delicious to the palate. "It is the most virtuous liquor that ever was; and therefore one need not fear drinking too much of it. And you want to know what it is made of? Well; I have often thought of telling you, Seppy, my boy, when you should come to be old enough; for I have no other inheritance to leave you, and you are all of my blood, unless I should happen to have some far-off uncle among the Cape Indians. But first, you must know how this good drink, and the faculty of making it, came down to me from the chiefs, and sachems, and Peow-wows, that were your ancestors and mine, Septimius, and from the old wizard who was my great-grandfather and yours, and who, they say, added the fire-water to the other ingredients, and so gave it the only one thing that it wanted to make it perfect."

And so Aunt Keziah, who had now put herself into a most comfortable and jolly state by sipping again, and after pressing Septimius to mind his draught (who declined, on the plea that one dram at a time was enough for a new beginner, its virtues being so strong, as well as admirable), the old woman told him a legend strangely wild and uncouth, and mixed up of savage and civilized life, and of the superstitions of both, but which yet had a certain analogy, that impressed Septimius much, to the story that the doctor had told him.

She said that, many ages ago, there had been a wild sachem in the forest, a king among the Indians, and from whom, the old lady said, with a look of pride, she and Septimius were lineally descended, and were probably the very last who inherited one drop of that royal, wise, and warlike blood. The sachem had lived very long, longer than anybody knew, for the Indians kept no record, and could only talk of a great number of moons ; and they said he was as old, or older, than the oldest trees ; as old as the hills almost, and could remember back to the days of godlike men, who had arts then forgotten. He was a wise and good man, and could foretell as far into the future as he could remember into the past ; and he continued to live on, till his people were afraid that he would live forever, and so disturb the whole order of nature ; and they thought it time that so good a man, and so great a warrior and wizard, should be gone to the happy hunting-grounds, and that so wise a counsellor should go and tell his experience of life to the Great Father, and give him an account of matters here, and perhaps lead him to make some changes in the conduct of the lower world. And so, all these things duly considered, they very reverently assassinated the great, never-dying sachem ; for though safe against disease, and undecayable by age, he was capable of being killed by violence, though the hardness of his skull broke to fragments the stone tomahawk with which they at first tried to kill him.

So a deputation of the best and bravest of the tribe went to the great sachem, and told him their thought, and reverently desired his consent to be put out of the world ; and the undying one agreed with them that it was better for his own comfort that he should die, and that he had long been weary of the world, having learned all that it could teach him, and having, chiefly, learned to despair of ever making the red race much better than they now were. So he cheerfully consented, and told them to kill him if they could ; and first they tried the stone hatchet, which was broken against his skull ; and then they shot arrows at him, which could not pierce the toughness of his skin ; and finally they plastered up his nose and mouth (which kept uttering wisdom to the last) with clay, and set him to bake in the sun ; so at last his life burnt out of his breast, tearing his body to pieces, and he died.

[*Make this legend grotesque, and express the weariness of the tribe at the intolerable control the undying one had of them ; his always bringing up precepts from his own experience, never consenting to anything new, and so impeding progress ; his habits hardening into him, his ascribing to himself all wisdom, and depriving everybody of his right to succes*

sive command; his endless talk, and dwelling on the
past, so that the world could not bear him. De-
scribe his ascetic and severe habits, his rigid calm-
ness, etc.]

But before the great sagamore died he imparted to
a chosen one of his tribe, the next wisest to himself,
the secret of a potent and delicious drink, the constant
imbibing of which, together with his abstinence from
luxury and passion, had kept him alive so long, and
would doubtless have compelled him to live forever.
This drink was compounded of many ingredients, all
of which were remembered and handed down in tradition, save one, which, either because it was nowhere to
be found, or for some other reason, was forgotten; so
that the drink ceased to give immortal life as before.
They say it was a beautiful purple flower. [*Perhaps*
the Devil taught him the drink, or else the Great
Spirit, — doubtful which.] But it still was a most
excellent drink, and conducive to health, and the cure
of all diseases; and the Indians had it at the time of
the settlement by the English; and at one of those
wizard meetings in the forest, where the Black Man
used to meet his red children and his white ones, and
be jolly with them, a great Indian wizard taught the
secret to Septimius's great-grandfather, who was a
wizard, and died for it; and he, in return, taught the
Indians to mix it with rum, thinking that this might
be the very ingredient that was missing, and that by
adding it he might give endless life to himself and all
his Indian friends, among whom he had taken a wife.

"But your great-grandfather, you know, had not a
fair chance to test its virtues, having been hanged for
a wizard; and as for the Indians, they probably mixed
too much fire-water with their liquid, so that it burnt

them up, and they all died ; and my mother, and her
mother, — who taught the drink to me, — and her
mother afore her, thought it a sin to try to live longer
than the Lord pleased, so they let themselves die.
And though the drink is good, Septimius, and tooth-
some, as you see, yet I sometimes feel as if I were getting old, like other people, and may die in the course
of the next half-century ; so perhaps the rum was not
just the thing that was wanting to make up the recipe.
But it is very good! Take a drop more of it, dear."

"Not at present, I thank you, Aunt Keziah," said
Septimius, gravely ; " but will you tell me what the
ingredients are, and how you make it ? "

"Yes, I will, my boy, and you shall write them
down," said the old woman ; " for it 's a good drink,
and none the worse, it may be, for not making you live
forever. I sometimes think I had as lief go to heaven
as keep on living here."

Accordingly, making Septimius take pen and ink,
she proceeded to tell him a list of plants and herbs,
and forest productions, and he was surprised to find
that it agreed most wonderfully with the recipe contained in the old manuscript, as he had puzzled it out,
and as it had been explained by the doctor. There
were a few variations, it is true ; but even here there
was a close analogy, plants indigenous to America
being substituted for cognate productions, the growth
of Europe. Then there was another difference in the
mode of preparation, Aunt Keziah's nostrum being a
concoction, whereas the old manuscript gave a process
of distillation. This similarity had a strong effect on
Septimius's imagination. Here was, in one case, a
drink suggested, as might be supposed, to a primitive
people by something similar to that instinct by which

the brute creation recognizes the medicaments suited to its needs, so that they mixed up fragrant herbs for reasons wiser than they knew, and made them into a salutary potion ; and here, again, was a drink contrived by the utmost skill of a great civilized philosopher, searching the whole field of science for his purpose ; and these two drinks proved, in all essential particulars, to be identically the same.

"O Aunt Keziah," said he, with a longing earnestness, "are you sure that you cannot remember that one ingredient ? "

"No, Septimius, I cannot possibly do it," said she. "I have tried many things, skunk-cabbage, wormwood, and a thousand things ; for it is truly a pity that the chief benefit of the thing should be lost for so little. But the only effect was, to spoil the good taste of the stuff, and, two or three times, to poison myself, so that I broke out all over blotches, and once lost the use of my left arm, and got a dizziness in the head, and a rheumatic twist in my knee, a hardness of hearing, and a dimness of sight, and the trembles ; all of which I certainly believe to have been caused by my putting something else into this blessed drink besides the good New England rum. Stick to that, Seppy, my dear."

So saying, Aunt Keziah took yet another sip of the beloved liquid, after vainly pressing Septimius to do the like ; and then lighting her old clay pipe, she sat down in the chimney-corner, meditating, dreaming, muttering pious prayers and ejaculations, and sometimes looking up the wide flue of the chimney, with thoughts, perhaps, how delightful it must have been to fly up there, in old times, on excursions by midnight into the forest, where was the Black Man, and the Puritan deacons and ladies, and those wild Indian ancestors of hers; and where the wildness of the forest was so grim and delightful, and so unlike the commonplaceness in which she spent her life. For thus did the savage strain of the woman, mixed up as it was with the other weird and religious parts of her composition, sometimes snatch her back into barbarian life and its instincts; and in Septimius, though further diluted, and modified likewise by higher cultivation, there was the same tendency.

Septimius escaped from the old woman, and was glad to breathe the free air again; so much had he been wrought upon by her wild legends and wild character, the more powerful by its analogy with his own; and perhaps, too, his brain had been a little bewildered by the draught of her diabolical concoction which she had compelled him to take. At any rate, he was glad to escape to his hill-top, the free air of which had doubtless contributed to keep him in health through so long a course of morbid thought and estranged study as he had addicted himself to.

Here, as it happened, he found both Rose Garfield and Sibyl Dacy, whom the pleasant summer evening had brought out. They had formed a friendship, or at least society; and there could not well be a pair more unlike, — the one so natural, so healthy, so fit to live in the world; the other such a morbid, pale thing. So there they were, walking arm in arm, with one arm round each other's waist, as girls love to do. They greeted the young man in their several ways, and began to walk to and fro together, looking at the sunset as it came on, and talking of things on earth and in the clouds.

"When has Robert Hagburn been heard from?" asked Septimius, who, involved in his own pursuits was altogether behindhand in the matters of the war, — shame to him for it!

"There came news, two days past," said Rose, blushing. "He is on his way home with the remnant of General Arnold's command, and will be here soon."

"He is a brave fellow, Robert," said Septimius, carelessly. "And I know not, since life is so short, that anything better can be done with it than to risk it as he does."

"I truly think not," said Rose Garfield, composedly.

"What a blessing it is to mortals," said Sibyl Dacy, "what a kindness of Providence, that life is made so uncertain; that death is thrown in among the possibilities of our being; that these awful mysteries are thrown around us, into which we may vanish! For, without it, how would it be possible to be heroic, how should we plod along in commonplaces forever, never dreaming high things, never risking anything? For my part, I think man is more favored than the angels, and made capable of higher heroism, greater virtue, and of a more excellent spirit than they, because we have such a mystery of grief and terror around us; whereas they, being in a certainty of God's light, seeing his goodness and his purposes more perfectly than we, cannot be so brave as often poor weak man, and weaker woman, has the opportunity to be, and sometimes makes use of it. God gave the whole world to man, and if he is left alone with it, it will make a clod of him at last; but, to remedy that, God gave man a grave, and it redeems all, while it seems to destroy all, and makes an immortal spirit of him in the end."

"Dear Sibyl, you are inspired," said Rose, gazing in her face.

" I think you ascribe a great deal too much potency to the grave," said Septimius, pausing involuntarily alone by the little hillock, whose contents he knew so well. " The grave seems to me a vile pitfall, put right in our pathway, and catching most of us, — all of us, — causing us to tumble in at the most inconvenient opportunities, so that all human life is a jest and a farce, just for the sake of this inopportune death; for I observe it never waits for us to accomplish anything: we may have the salvation of a country in hand, but we are none the less likely to die for that. So that, being a believer, on the whole, in the wisdom and graciousness of Providence, I am convinced that dying is a mistake, and that by and by we shall overcome it. I say there is no use in the grave."

" I still adhere to what I said," answered Sibyl Dacy; " and besides, there is another use of a grave which I have often observed in old English graveyards, where the moss grows green, and embosses the letters of the gravestones; and also graves are very good for flower-beds."

Nobody ever could tell when the strange girl was going to say what was laughable, — when what was melancholy; and neither of Sibyl's auditors knew quite what to make of this speech. Neither could Septimius fail to be a little startled by seeing her, as she spoke of the grave as a flower-bed, stoop down to the little hillock to examine the flowers, which, indeed, seemed to prove her words by growing there in strange abundance, and of many sorts; so that, if they could all have bloomed at once, the spot would have looked like a bouquet by itself, or as if the earth were richest in beauty there, or as if seeds had been lavished by some florist. Septimius could not account for it, for though the hill-side did produce certain flowers, — the aster, the golden-rod, the violet, and other such simple and common things, — yet this seemed as if a carpet of bright colors had been thrown down there and covered the spot.

"This is very strange," said he.

"Yes," said Sibyl Dacy, "there is some strange richness in this little spot of soil."

"Where could the seeds have come from? — that is the greatest wonder," said Rose. "You might almost teach me botany, methinks, on this one spot."

"Do you know this plant?" asked Sibyl of Septimius, pointing to one not yet in flower, but of singular leaf, that was thrusting itself up out of the ground, on the very centre of the grave, over where the breast of the sleeper below might seem to be. "I think there is no other here like it."

Septimius stooped down to examine it, and was convinced that it was unlike anything he had seen of the flower kind; a leaf of a dark green, with purple veins traversing it, it had a sort of questionable aspect, as some plants have, so that you would think it very likely to be poison, and would not like to touch or smell very intimately, without first inquiring who would be its guarantee that it should do no mischief. That it had some richness or other, either baneful or beneficial, you could not doubt.

"I think it poisonous," said Rose Garfield, shuddering, for she was a person so natural she hated poisonous things, or anything speckled especially, and did not, indeed, love strangeness. "Yet I should not wonder if it bore a beautiful flower by and by. Nevertheless, if I were to do just as I feel inclined, I should root it up and fling it away."

"Shall she do so?" said Sibyl to Septimius.

"Not for the world," said he, hastily. "Above all things, I desire to see what will come of this plant."

"Be it as you please," said Sibyl. "Meanwhile, if you like to sit down here and listen to me, I will tell you a story that happens to come into my mind just now, — I cannot tell why. It is a legend of an old hall that I know well, and have known from my childhood, in one of the northern counties of England, where I was born. Would you like to hear it, Rose?"

"Yes, of all things," said she. "I like all stories of hall and cottage in the old country, though now we must not call it our country any more."

Sibyl looked at Septimius, as if to inquire whether he, too, chose to listen to her story, and he made answer: —

"Yes, I shall like to hear the legend, if it is a genuine one that has been adopted into the popular belief, and came down in chimney-corners with the smoke and soot that gathers there; and incrusted over with humanity, by passing from one homely mind to another. Then, such stories get to be true, in a certain sense, and indeed in that sense may be called true throughout, for the very nucleus, the fiction in them, seems to have come out of the heart of man in a way that cannot be imitated of malice aforethought. Nobody can make a tradition; it takes a century to make it."

"I know not whether this legend has the character you mean," said Sibyl, "but it has lived much more than a century; and here it is.

"On the threshold of one of the doors of —— Hall there is a bloody footstep impressed into the doorstep, and ruddy as if the bloody foot had just trodden there;

and it is averred that, on a certain night of the year, and at a certain hour of the night, if you go and look at that doorstep you will see the mark wet with fresh blood. Some have pretended to say that this appearance of blood was but dew; but can dew redden a cambric handkerchief? Will it crimson the finger-tips when you touch it? And that is what the bloody footstep will surely do when the appointed night and hour come round, this very year, just as it would three hundred years ago.

"Well; but how did it come there? I know not precisely in what age it was, but long ago, when light was beginning to shine into what were called the dark ages, there was a lord of —— Hall who applied himself deeply to knowledge and science, under the guidance of the wisest man of that age, — a man so wise that he was thought to be a wizard; and, indeed, he may have been one, if to be a wizard consists in having command over secret powers of nature, that other men do not even suspect the existence of, and the control of which enables one to do feats that seem as wonderful as raising the dead. It is needless to tell you all the strange stories that have survived to this day about the old Hall; and how it is believed that the master of it, owing to his ancient science, has still a sort of residence there, and control of the place; and how, in one of the chambers, there is still his antique table, and his chair, and some rude old instruments and machinery, and a book, and everything in readiness, just as if he might still come back to finish some experiment. What it is important to say is, that one of the chief things to which the old lord applied himself was to discover the means of prolonging his own life, so that its duration should be indefinite, if not

infinite ; and such was his science, that he was believed
to have attained this magnificent and awful purpose.

"So, as you may suppose, the man of science had
great joy in having done this thing, both for the
pride of it, and because it was so delightful a thing to
have before him the prospect of endless time, which
he might spend in adding more and more to his science, and so doing good to the world ; for the chief
obstruction to the improvement of the world and the
growth of knowledge is, that mankind cannot go
straightforward in it, but continually there have to be
new beginnings, and it takes every new man half his
life, if not the whole of it, to come up to the point
where his predecessor left off. And so this noble man
— this man of a noble purpose — spent many years
in finding out this mighty secret ; and at last, it is
said, he succeeded. But on what terms ?

"Well, it is said that the terms were dreadful and
horrible ; insomuch that the wise man hesitated whether
it were lawful and desirable to take advantage of
them, great as was the object in view.

"You see, the object of the lord of —— Hall was
to take a life from the course of Nature, and Nature
did not choose to be defrauded ; so that, great as was
the power of this scientific man over her, she would
not consent that he should escape the necessity of dying at his proper time, except upon condition of sacrificing some other life for his ; and this was to be
done once for every thirty years that he chose to live,
thirty years being the account of a generation of man ;
and if in any way, in that time, this lord could be the
death of a human being, that satisfied the requisition,
and he might live on. There is a form of the legend
which says, that one of the ingredients of the drink

which the nobleman brewed by his science was the heart's blood of a pure young boy or girl. But this I reject, as too coarse an idea; and, indeed, I think it may be taken to mean symbolically, that the person who desires to engross to himself more than his share of human life must do it by sacrificing to his selfishness some dearest interest of another person, who has a good right to life, and may be as useful in it as he.

"Now, this lord was a just man by nature, and if he had gone astray, it was greatly by reason of his earnest wish to do something for the poor, wicked, struggling, bloody, uncomfortable race of man, to which he belonged. He bethought himself whether he would have a right to take the life of one of those creatures, without their own consent, in order to prolong his own; and after much arguing to and fro, he came to the conclusion that he should not have the right, unless it were a life over which he had control, and which was the next to his own. He looked round him; he was a lonely and abstracted man, secluded by his studies from human affections, and there was but one human being whom he cared for; — that was a beautiful kinswoman, an orphan, whom his father had brought up, and, dying, left her to his care. There was great kindness and affection — as great as the abstracted nature of his pursuits would allow — on the part of this lord towards the beautiful young girl; but not what is called love, — at least, he never acknowledged it to himself. But, looking into his heart, he saw that she, if any one, was to be the person whom the sacrifice demanded, and that he might kill twenty others without effect, but if he took the life of this one, it would make the charm strong and good.

"My friends, I have meditated many a time on this ugly feature of my legend, and am unwilling to take it in the literal sense; so I conceive its spiritual meaning (for everything, you know, has its spiritual meaning, which to the literal meaning is what the soul is to the body), — its spiritual meaning was, that to the deep pursuit of science we must sacrifice great part of the joy of life; that nobody can be great, and do great things, without giving up to death, so far as he regards his enjoyment of it, much that he would gladly enjoy; and in that sense I choose to take it. But the earthly old legend will have it that this mad, high-minded, heroic, murderous lord did insist upon it with himself that he must murder this poor, loving, and beloved child.

"I do not wish to delay upon this horrible matter, and to tell you how he argued it with himself; and how, the more and more he argued it, the more reasonable it seemed, the more absolutely necessary, the more a duty that the terrible sacrifice should be made. Here was this great good to be done to mankind, and all that stood in the way of it was one little delicate life, so frail that it was likely enough to be blown out, any day, by the mere rude blast that the rush of life creates, as it streams along, or by any slightest accident; so good and pure, too, that she was quite unfit for this world, and not capable of any happiness in it; and all that was asked of her was to allow herself to be transported to a place where she would be happy, and would find companions fit for her, — which he, her only present companion, certainly was not. In fine, he resolved to shed the sweet, fragrant blood of this little violet that loved him so.

"Well; let us hurry over this part of the story as

fast as we can. He did slay this pure young girl; he took her into the wood near the house, an old wood that is standing yet, with some of its magnificent oaks; and then he plunged a dagger into her heart, after they had had a very tender and loving talk together, in which he had tried to open the matter tenderly to her, and make her understand that, though he was to slay her, it was really for the very reason that he loved her better than anything else in the world, and that he would far rather die himself, if that would answer the purpose at all. Indeed, he is said to have offered her the alternative of slaying him, and taking upon herself the burden of indefinite life, and the studies and pursuits by which he meant to benefit mankind. But she, it is said, — this noble, pure, loving child, — she looked up into his face and smiled sadly, and then snatching the dagger from him, she plunged it into her own heart. I cannot tell whether this be true, or whether she waited to be killed by him; but this I know, that in the same circumstances I think I should have saved my lover or my friend the pain of killing me. There she lay dead, at any rate, and he buried her in the wood, and returned to the house; and, as it happened, he had set his right foot in her blood, and his shoe was wet in it, and by some miraculous fate it left a track all along the wood-path, and into the house, and on the stone steps of the threshold, and up into his chamber, all along; and the servants saw it the next day, and wondered, and whispered, and missed the fair young girl, and looked askance at their lord's right foot, and turned pale, all of them, as death.

" And next, the legend says, that Sir Forrester was struck with horror at what he had done, and could not bear the laboratory where he had toiled so long, and was sick to death of the object that he had pursued, and was most miserable, and fled from his old Hall, and was gone full many a day.   But all the while he was gone there was the mark of a bloody footstep impressed upon the stone doorstep of the Hall.   The track had lain all along through the wood-path, and across the lawn, to the old Gothic door of the Hall; but the rain, the English rain, that is always falling, had come the next day, and washed it all away.   The track had lain, too, across the broad hall, and up the stairs, and into the lord's study; but there it had lain on the rushes that were strewn there, and these the servants had gathered carefully up, and thrown them away, and spread fresh ones.   So that it was only on the threshold that the mark remained.

"But the legend says, that wherever Sir Forrester went, in his wanderings about the world, he left a bloody track behind him.   It was wonderful, and very inconvenient, this phenomenon.   When he went into a church, you would see the track up the broad aisle, and a little red puddle in the place where he sat or knelt.   Once he went to the king's court, and there being a track up to the very throne, the king frowned upon him, so that he never came there any more. Nobody could tell how it happened; his foot was not seen to bleed, only there was the bloody track behind him, wherever he went; and he was a horror-stricken man, always looking behind him to see the track, and then hurrying onward, as if to escape his own tracks; but always they followed him as fast.

"In the hall of feasting, there was the bloody track to his chair.   The learned men whom he consulted about this strange difficulty conferred with one another, and with him, who was equal to any of them, and pished and pshawed, and said, ' Oh, there is nothing miraculous in this; it is only a natural infirmity, which can easily be put an end to, though, perhaps, the stoppage of such an evacuation will cause damage to other parts of the frame.' Sir Forrester always said, ' Stop it, my learned brethren, if you can; no matter what the consequences.' And they did their best, but without result; so that he was still compelled to leave his bloody track on their college-rooms and combination-rooms, the same as elsewhere; and in street and in wilderness; yes, and in the battle-field, they said, his track looked freshest and reddest of all. So, at last, finding the notice he attracted inconvenient, this unfortunate lord deemed it best to go back to his own Hall, where, living among faithful old servants born in the family, he could hush the matter up better than elsewhere, and not be stared at continually, or, glancing round, see people holding up their hands in terror at seeing a bloody track behind him. And so home he came, and there he saw the bloody track on the doorstep, and dolefully went into the hall, and up the stairs, an old servant ushering him into his chamber, and half a dozen others following behind, gazing, shuddering, pointing with quivering fingers, looking horror-stricken in one another's pale faces, and the moment he had passed, running to get fresh rushes, and to scour the stairs. The next day, Sir Forrester went into the wood, and by the aged oak he found a grave, and on the grave he beheld a beautiful crimson flower; the most gorgeous and beautiful, surely, that ever grew; so rich it looked, so full of potent juice. That flower he gathered; and the spirit of his scientific pursuits coming upon him, he knew that this was the flower, produced out of a human life, that was essential to the perfection of his recipe for immortality ; and he made the drink, and drank it, and became immortal in woe and agony, still studying, still growing wiser and more wretched in every age. By and by he vanished from the old Hall, but not by death ; for, from generation to generation, they say that a bloody track is seen around that house, and sometimes it is tracked up into the chambers, so freshly that you see he must have passed a short time before ; and he grows wiser and wiser, and lonelier and lonelier, from age to age. And this is the legend of the bloody footstep, which I myself have seen at the Hall door. As to the flower, the plant of it continued for several years to grow out of the grave ; and after a while, perhaps a century ago, it was transplanted into the garden of —— Hall, and preserved with great care, and is so still. And as the family attribute a kind of sacredness, or cursedness, to the flower, they can hardly be prevailed upon to give any of the seeds, or allow it to be propagated elsewhere, though the king should send to ask it. It is said, too, that there is still in the family the old lord's recipe for immortality, and that several of his collateral descendants have tried to concoct it, and instil the flower into it, and so give indefinite life ; but unsuccessfully, because the seeds of the flower must be planted in a fresh grave of bloody death, in order to make it effectual."

So ended Sibyl's legend ; in which Septimius was struck by a certain analogy to Aunt Keziah's Indian legend, — both referring to a flower growing out of a grave ; and also he did not fail to be impressed with the wild coincidence of this disappearance of an an-

cestor of the family long ago, and the appearance, at
about the same epoch, of the first known ancestor of
his own family, the man with wizard's attributes, with
the bloody footstep, and whose sudden disappearance
became a myth, under the idea that the Devil carried
him away. Yet, on the whole, this wild tradition,
doubtless becoming wilder in Sibyl's wayward and morbid fancy, had the effect to give him a sense of the fan-
tasticalness of his present pursuit, and that in adopt-
ing it, he had strayed into a region long abandoned
to superstition, and where the shadows of forgotten
dreams go when men are done with them ; where past
worships are ; where great Pan went when he died to
the outer world ; a limbo into which living men sometimes stray when they think themselves sensiblest and
wisest, and whence they do not often find their way
back into the real world. Visions of wealth, visions
of fame, visions of philanthropy, — all visions find
room here, and glide about without jostling. When
Septimius came to look at the matter in his present
mood, the thought occurred to him that he had perhaps got into such a limbo, and that Sibyl's legend,
which looked so wild, might be all of a piece with his
own present life ; for Sibyl herself seemed an illusion,
and so, most strangely, did Aunt Keziah, whom he
had known all his life, with her homely and quaint
characteristics ; the grim doctor, with his brandy and
his German pipe, impressed him in the same way ;
and these, altogether, made his homely cottage by the
wayside seem an unsubstantial edifice, such as castles
in the air are built of, and the ground he trod on unreal ; and that grave, which he knew to contain the
decay of a beautiful young man, but a fictitious swell
formed by the fantasy of his eyes. All unreal ; all

illusion! Was Rose Garfield a deception too, with
her daily beauty, and daily cheerfulness, and daily
worth? In short, it was such a moment as I suppose
all men feel (at least, I can answer for one), when
the real scene and picture of life swims, jars, shakes,
seems about to be broken up and dispersed, like the
picture in a smooth pond, when we disturb its tranquil
mirror by throwing in a stone; and though the scene
soon settles itself, and looks as real as before, a haunting doubt keeps close at hand, as long as we live, asking, " Is it stable? Am I sure of it? Am I certainly
not dreaming? See; it trembles again, ready to dis-
solve."

Applying himself with earnest diligence to his attempt to decipher and interpret the mysterious manuscript, working with his whole mind and strength,
Septimius did not fail of some flattering degree of
success.

A good deal of the manuscript, as has been said,
was in an ancient English script, although so uncouth
and shapeless were the characters, that it was not easy
to resolve them into letters, or to believe that they
were anything but arbitrary and dismal blots and
scrawls upon the yellow paper; without meaning,
vague, like the misty and undefined germs of thought
as they exist in our minds before clothing themselves
in words. These, however, as he concentrated his
mind upon them, took distincter shape, like cloudy
stars at the power of the telescope, and became sometimes English, sometimes Latin, strangely patched together, as if, so accustomed was the writer to use that
language in which all the science of that age was usually embodied, that he really mixed it unconsciously

with the vernacular, or used both indiscriminately. There was some Greek, too, but not much. Then frequently came in the cipher, to the study of which Septimius had applied himself for some time back, with the aid of the books borrowed from the college library, and not without success. Indeed, it appeared to him, on close observation, that it had not been the intention of the writer really to conceal what he had written from any earnest student, but rather to lock it up for safety in a sort of coffer, of which diligence and insight should be the key, and the keen intelligence with which the meaning was sought should be the test of the seeker's being entitled to possess the secret treasure.

Amid a great deal of misty stuff, he found the document to consist chiefly, contrary to his supposition beforehand, of certain rules of life; he would have taken it, on a casual inspection, for an essay of counsel, addressed by some great and sagacious man to a youth in whom he felt an interest, — so secure and good a doctrine of life was propounded, such excellent maxims there were, such wisdom in all matters that came within the writer's purview. It was as much like a digested synopsis of some old philosopher's wise rules of conduct, as anything else. But on closer inspection, Septimius, in his unsophisticated consideration of this matter, was not so well satisfied. True, everything that was said seemed not discordant with the rules of social morality; not unwise: it was shrewd, sagacious; it did not appear to infringe upon the rights of mankind; but there was something left out, something unsatisfactory, — what was it? There was certainly a cold spell in the document; a magic, not of fire, but of ice; and Septimius the more exemplified its power, in that he soon began to be insensible of it. It affected him as if it had been written by some greatly wise and worldly-experienced man, like the writer of Ecclesiastes; for it was full of truth. It was a truth that does not make men better, though perhaps calmer; and beneath which the buds of happiness curl up like tender leaves in a frost. What was the matter with this document, that the young man's youth perished out of him as he read? What icy hand had written it, so that the heart was chilled out of the reader? Not that Septimius was sensible of this character; at least, not long, — for as he read, there grew upon him a mood of calm satisfaction, such as he had never felt before. His mind seemed to grow clearer; his perceptions most acute; his sense of the reality of things grew to be such, that he felt as if he could touch and handle all his thoughts, feel round about all their outline and circumference, and know them with a certainty, as if they were material things. Not that all this was in the document itself; but by studying it so earnestly, and, as it were, creating its meaning anew for himself, out of such illegible materials, he caught the temper of the old writer's mind, after so many ages as that tract had lain in the mouldy and musty manuscript. He was magnetized with him; a powerful intellect acted powerfully upon him; perhaps, even, there was a sort of spell and mystic influence imbued into the paper, and mingled with the yellow ink, that steamed forth by the effort of this young man's earnest rubbing, as it were, and by the action of his mind, applied to it as intently as he possibly could; and even his handling the paper, his bending over it, and breathing upon it, had its effect.

It is not in our power, nor in our wish, to produce

the original form, nor yet the spirit, of a production which is better lost to the world : because it was the expression of a human intellect originally greatly gifted and capable of high things, but gone utterly astray, partly by its own subtlety, partly by yielding to the temptations of the lower part of its nature, by yielding the spiritual to a keen sagacity of lower things, until it was quite fallen ; and·yet fallen in such a way, that it seemed not only to itself, but to mankind, not fallen at all, but wise and good, and fulfilling all the ends of intellect in such a life as ours, and proving, moreover, that earthly life was good, and all that the development of our nature demanded. All this is better forgotten ; better burnt ; better never thought over again ; and all the more, because its aspect was so wise, and even praiseworthy. But what we must preserve of it were certain rules of life and moral diet, not exactly expressed in the document, but which, as it were, on its being duly received into Septimius's mind, were precipitated from the rich solution, and crystallized into diamonds, and which he found to be the moral dietetics, so to speak, by observing which he was to achieve the end of earthly immortality, whose physical nostrum was given in the recipe which, with the help of Doctor Portsoaken and his Aunt Keziah, he had already pretty satisfactorily made out.

"Keep thy heart at seventy throbs in a minute ; all more than that wears away life too quickly. If thy respiration be too quick, think with thyself that thou hast sinned against natural order and moderation.

"Drink not wine nor strong drink ; and observe that this rule is worthiest in its symbolic meaning.

"Bask daily in the sunshine and let it rest on thy heart.

"Run not; leap not; walk at a steady pace, and count thy paces per day.

"If thou feelest, at any time, a throb of the heart, pause on the instant, and analyze it; fix thy mental eye steadfastly upon it, and inquire why such commotion is.

"Hate not any man nor woman; be not angry, unless at any time thy blood seem a little cold and torpid; cut out all rankling feelings, they are poisonous to thee. If, in thy waking moments, or in thy dreams, thou hast thoughts of strife or unpleasantness with any man, strive quietly with thyself to forget him.

"Have no friendships with an imperfect man, with a man in bad health, of violent passions, of any characteristic that evidently disturbs his own life, and so may have disturbing influence on thine. Shake not any man by the hand, because thereby, if there be any evil in the man, it is likely to be communicated to thee.

"Kiss no woman if her lips be red; look not upon her if she be very fair. Touch not her hand if thy finger-tips be found to thrill with hers ever so little. On the whole, shun woman, for she is apt to be a disturbing influence. If thou love her, all is over, and thy whole past and remaining labor and pains will be in vain.

"Do some decent degree of good and kindness in thy daily life, for the result is a slight pleasurable sense that will seem to warm and delectate thee with felicitous self-laudings; and all that brings thy thoughts to thyself tends to invigorate that central principle by the growth of which thou art to give thyself indefinite life.

"Do not any act manifestly evil; it may grow upon

thee, and corrode thee in after-years. Do not any foolish good act; it may change thy wise habits.

"Eat no spiced meats. Young chickens, new-fallen lambs, fruits, bread four days old, milk, freshest butter, will make thy fleshy tabernacle youthful.

"From sick people, maimed wretches, afflicted people, — all of whom show themselves at variance with things as they should be, — from people beyond their wits, from people in a melancholic mood, from people in extravagant joy, from teething children, from dead corpses, turn away thine eyes and depart elsewhere.

"If beggars haunt thee, let thy servants drive them away, thou withdrawing out of ear-shot.

"Crying and sickly children, and teething children, as aforesaid, carefully avoid. Drink the breath of wholesome infants as often as thou conveniently canst, — it is good for thy purpose; also the breath of buxom maids, if thou mayest without undue disturbance of the flesh, drink it as a morning-draught, as medicine; also the breath of cows as they return from rich pasture at eventide.

"If thou seest human poverty, or suffering, and it trouble thee, strive moderately to relieve it, seeing that thus thy mood will be changed to a pleasant self-laudation.

"Practise thyself in a certain continual smile, for its tendency will be to compose thy frame of being, and keep thee from too much wear.

"Search not to see if thou hast a gray hair; scrutinize not thy forehead to find a wrinkle; nor the corners of thy eyes to discover if they be corrugated. Such things, being gazed at, daily take heart and grow.

"Desire nothing too fervently, not even life : yet

keep thy hold upon it mightily, quietly, unshakably, for as long as thou really art resolved to live, Death, with all his force, shall have no power against thee.

"Walk not beneath tottering ruins, nor houses being put up, nor climb to the top of a mast, nor approach the edge of a precipice, nor stand in the way of the lightning, nor cross a swollen river, nor voyage at sea, nor ride a skittish horse, nor be shot at by an arrow, nor confront a sword, nor put thyself in the way of violent death; for this is hateful, and breaketh through all wise rules.

"Say thy prayers at bedtime, if thou deemest it will give thee quieter sleep; yet let it not trouble thee if thou forgettest them.

"Change thy shirt daily; thereby thou castest off yesterday's decay, and imbibest the freshness of the morning's life, which enjoy with smelling to roses, and other healthy and fragrant flowers, and live the longer for it. Roses are made to that end.

"Read not great poets; they stir up thy heart; and the human heart is a soil which, if deeply stirred, is apt to give out noxious vapors."

Such were some of the precepts which Septimius gathered and reduced to definite form out of this wonderful document; and he appreciated their wisdom, and saw clearly that they must be absolutely essential to the success of the medicine with which they were connected. In themselves, almost, they seemed capable of prolonging life to an indefinite period, so wisely were they conceived, so well did they apply to the causes which almost invariably wear away this poor short life of men, years and years before even the shattered constitutions that they received from their forefathers need compel them to die. He deemed himself well rewarded for all his labor and pains, should nothing else follow but his reception and proper appreciation of these wise rules; but continually, as he read the manuscript, more truths, and, for aught I know, profounder and more practical ones, developed themselves; and, indeed, small as the manuscript looked, Septimius thought that he should find a volume as big as the most ponderous folio in the college library too small to contain its wisdom. It seemed to drip and distil with precious fragrant drops, whenever he took it out of his desk; it diffused wisdom like those vials of perfume which, small as they look, keep diffusing an airy wealth of fragrance for years and years together, scattering their virtue in incalculable volumes of invisible vapor, and yet are none the less in bulk for all they give; whenever he turned over the yellow leaves, bits of gold, diamonds of good size, precious pearls, seemed to drop out from between them.

And now ensued a surprise which, though of a happy kind, was almost too much for him to bear; for it made his heart beat considerably faster than the wise rules of his manuscript prescribed. Going up on his hill-top, as summer wore away (he had not been there for some time), and walking by the little flowery hillock, as so many a hundred times before, what should he see there but a new flower, that during the time he had been poring over the manuscript so sedulously had developed itself, blossomed, put forth its petals, bloomed into full perfection, and now, with the dew of the morning upon it, was waiting to offer itself to Septimius? He trembled as he looked at it, it was too much almost to bear, — it was so very beautiful, so very stately, so very rich, so very mysterious and wonderful. It was like a person, like a life! Whence did it come? He stood apart from it, gazing in wonder; tremulously taking in its aspect, and thinking of the legends he had heard from Aunt Keziah and from Sibyl Dacy; and how that this flower, like the one that their wild traditions told of, had grown out of a grave, — out of a grave in which he had laid one slain by himself.

The flower was of the richest crimson, illuminated with a golden centre of a perfect and stately beauty. From the best descriptions that I have been able to gain of it, it was more like a dahlia than any other flower with which I have acquaintance; yet it does not satisfy me to believe it really of that species, for the dahlia is not a flower of any deep characteristics, either lively or malignant, and this flower, which Septimius found so strangely, seems to have had one or the other. If I have rightly understood, it had a fragrance which the dahlia lacks; and there was something hidden in its centre, a mystery, even in its fullest bloom, not developing itself so openly as the heartless, yet not dishonest, dahlia. I remember in England to have seen a flower at Eaton Hall, in Cheshire, in those magnificent gardens, which may have been like this, but my remembrance of it is not sufficiently distinct to enable me to describe it better than by saying that it was crimson, with a gleam of gold in its centre, which yet was partly hidden. It had many petals of great richness.

Septimius, bending eagerly over the plant, saw that this was not to be the only flower that it would produce that season; on the contrary, there was to be a great abundance of them, a luxuriant harvest; as if the crimson offspring of this one plant would cover the whole hillock, — as if the dead youth beneath had burst into a resurrection of many crimson flowers ! And in its veiled heart, moreover, there was a mystery like death, although it seemed to cover something bright and golden.

Day after day the strange crimson flower bloomed more and more abundantly, until it seemed almost to cover the little hillock, which became a mere bed of it, apparently turning all its capacity of production to this flower ; for the other plants, Septimius thought, seemed to shrink away, and give place to it, as if they were unworthy to compare with the richness, glory, and worth of this their queen. The fervent summer burned into it, the dew and the rain ministered to it ; the soil was rich, for it was a human heart contributing its juices, — a heart in its fiery youth sodden in its own blood, so that passion, unsatisfied loves and longings, ambition that never won its object, tender dreams and throbs, angers, lusts, hates, all concentrated by life, came sprouting in it, and its mysterious being, and streaks and shadows, had some meaning in each of them.

The two girls, when they next ascended the hill, saw the strange flower, and Rose admired it, and wondered at it, but stood at a distance, without showing an attraction towards it, rather an undefined aversion, as if she thought it might be a poison flower ; at any rate she would not be inclined to wear it in her bosom. Sibyl Dacy examined it closely, touched its leaves, smelt it, looked at it with a botanist's eye, and at last remarked to Rose, " Yes, it grows well in this new soil ; methinks it looks like a new human life."

" What is the strange flower ? " asked Rose.

" The *Sanguinea sanguinissima*," said Sibyl.

It so happened about this time that poor Aunt Keziah, in spite of her constant use of that bitter mixture of hers, was in a very bad state of health. She looked all of an unpleasant yellow, with bloodshot eyes; she complained terribly of her inwards. She had an ugly rheumatic hitch in her motion from place to place, and was heard to mutter many wishes that she had a broomstick to fly about upon, and she used to bind up her head with a dishclout, or what looked to be such, and would sit by the kitchen fire even in the warm days, bent over it, crouching as if she wanted to take the whole fire into her poor cold heart or gizzard, — groaning regularly with each breath a spiteful and resentful groan, as if she fought womanfully with her infirmities; and she continually smoked her pipe, and sent out the breath of her complaint visibly in that evil odor; and sometimes she murmured a little prayer, but somehow or other the evil and bitterness, acridity, pepperiness, of her natural disposition overcame the acquired grace which compelled her to pray, insomuch that, after all, you would have thought the poor old woman was cursing with all her rheumatic might. All the time an old, broken-nosed, brown earthen jug, covered with the lid of a black teapot, stood on the edge of the embers, steaming forever, and sometimes bubbling a little, and giving a great puff, as if it were sighing and groaning in sympathy with poor Aunt Keziah, and when it sighed there came a great steam of herby fragrance, not particularly pleasant, into the kitchen. And ever and anon, — half a dozen times it might be, — of an afternoon, Aunt Keziah took a certain bottle from a private receptacle of hers, and also a teacup, and likewise a little, old-fashioned silver teaspoon, with which she measured three teaspoonfuls of some spirituous liquor into the teacup, half filled the cup with the hot decoction, drank it off, gave a grunt of content, and for the space of half an hour appeared to find life tolerable.

But one day poor Aunt Keziah found herself unable, partly from rheumatism, partly from other sickness or weakness, and partly from dolorous ill-spirits, to keep about any longer, so she betook herself to her bed; and betimes in the forenoon Septimius heard a tremendous knocking on the floor of her bedchamber, which happened to be the room above his own. He was the only person in or about the house; so with great reluctance, he left his studies, which were upon the recipe, in respect to which he was trying to make out the mode of concoction, which was told in such a mysterious way that he could not well tell either the quantity of the ingredients, the mode of trituration, nor in what way their virtue was to be extracted and combined.

Running hastily up stairs, he found Aunt Keziah lying in bed, and groaning with great spite and bitterness; so that, indeed, it seemed not improvidential that such an inimical state of mind towards the human race was accompanied with an almost inability of motion, else it would not be safe to be within a considerable distance of her.

"Seppy, you good-for-nothing, are you going to see me lying here, dying, without trying to do anything for me?"

"Dying, Aunt Keziah?" repeated the young man. "I hope not! What can I do for you? Shall I go for Rose? or call a neighbor in? or the doctor?"

"No, no, you fool!" said the afflicted person. "You can do all that anybody can for me; and that is to put my mixture on the kitchen fire till it steams, and is just ready to bubble ; then measure three teaspoon-fuls — or it may be four, as I am very bad — of spirit into a teacup, fill it half full, — or it may be quite full, for I am very bad, as I said afore; six teaspoonfuls of spirit into a cup of mixture, and let me have it as soon as may be ; and don't break the cup, nor spill the precious mixture, for goodness knows when I can go into the woods to gather any more. Ah me! ah me! it 's a wicked, miserable world, and I am the most mis-erable creature in it. Be quick, you good-for-nothing, and do as I say ! ' "

Septimius hastened down ; but as he went a thought came into his head, which it occurred to him might re-sult in great benefit to Aunt Keziah, as well as to the great cause of science and human good, and to the promotion of his own purpose, in the first place. A day or two ago, he had gathered several of the beauti-ful flowers, and laid them in the fervid sun to dry ; and they now seemed to be in about the state in which the old woman was accustomed to use her herbs, so far as Septimius had observed. Now if these flowers were really, as there was so much reason for supposing, the one ingredient that had for hundreds of years been missing out of Aunt Keziah's nostrum, — if it was this which that strange Indian sagamore had mingled with his drink with such beneficial effect, — why should not Septimius now restore it, and if it would not make his beloved aunt young again, at least as-suage the violent symptoms, and perhaps prolong her valuable life some years, for the solace and delight of her numerous friends? Septimius, like other people of investigating and active minds, had a great ten-dency to experiment, and so good an opportunity as the

present, where (perhaps he thought) there was so little
to be risked at worst, and so much to be gained, was
not to be neglected ; so, without more ado, he stirred
three of the crimson flowers into the earthen jug, set
it on the edge of the fire, stirred it well, and when it
steamed, threw up little scarlet bubbles, and was about
to boil, he measured out the spirits, as Aunt Keziah
had bidden him and then filled the teacup.

" Ah, this will do her good ; little does she think,
poor old thing, what a rare and costly medicine is
about to be given her. This will set her on her feet
again."

The hue was somewhat changed, he thought, from
what he had observed of Aunt Keziah's customary decoction ; instead of a turbid yellow, the crimson petals of the flower had tinged it, and made it almost red ;
not a brilliant red, however, nor the least inviting in
appearance. Septimius smelt it, and thought he could
distinguish a little of the rich odor of the flower, but
was not sure. He considered whether to taste it ; but
the horrible flavor of Aunt Keziah's decoction recurred strongly to his remembrance, and he concluded
that were he evidently at the point of death, he might
possibly be bold enough to taste it again ; but that
nothing short of the hope of a century's existence at
least would repay another taste of that fierce and
nauseous bitterness. Aunt Keziah loved it ; and as she
brewed, so let her drink.

He went up stairs, careful not to spill a drop of the
brimming cup, and approached the old woman's bedside, where she lay, groaning as before, and breaking
out into a spiteful croak the moment he was within
ear-shot.

" You don't care whether I live or die," said she.

"You 've been waiting in hopes I shall die, and so save yourself further trouble."

"By no means, Aunt Keziah," said Septimius. "Here is the medicine, which I have warmed, and measured out, and mingled, as well as I knew how; and I think it will do you a great deal of good."

"Won't you taste it, Seppy, my dear?" said Aunt Keziah, mollified by the praise of her beloved mixture. "Drink first, dear, so that my sick old lips need not taint it. You look pale, Septimius; it will do you good."

"No, Aunt Keziah, I do not need it; and it were a pity to waste your precious drink," said he.

"It does not look quite the right color," said Aunt Keziah, as she took the cup in her hand. "You must have dropped some soot into it." Then, as she raised it to her lips, "It does not smell quite right. But, woe 's me! how can I expect anybody but myself to make this precious drink as it should be?"

She drank it off at two gulps; for she appeared to hurry it off faster than usual, as if not tempted by the exquisiteness of its flavor to dwell upon it so long.

"You have not made it just right, Seppy," said she in a milder tone than before, for she seemed to feel the customary soothing influence of the draught, "but you 'll do better the next time. It had a queer taste, methought; or is it that my mouth is getting out of taste? Hard times it will be for poor Aunt Kezzy, if she 's to lose her taste for the medicine that, under Providence, has saved her life for so many years."

She gave back the cup to Septimius, after looking a little curiously at the dregs.

"It looks like bloodroot, don't it?" said she. "Perhaps it 's my own fault after all. I gathered a fresh bunch of the yarbs yesterday afternoon, and put them to steep, and it may be I was a little blind, for it was between daylight and dark, and the moon shone on me before I had finished. I thought how the witches used to gather their poisonous stuff at such times, and what pleasant uses they made of it, — but those are sinful thoughts, Seppy, sinful thoughts! so I 'll say a prayer and try to go to sleep. I feel very noddy all at once."

Septimius drew the bedclothes up about her shoulders, for she complained of being very chilly, and, carefully putting her stick within reach, went down to his own room, and resumed his studies, trying to make out from those aged hieroglyphics, to which he was now so well accustomed, what was the precise method of making the elixir of immortality. Sometimes, as men in deep thought do, he rose from his chair, and walked to and fro the four or five steps or so that conveyed him from end to end of his little room. At one of these times he chanced to look in the little looking-glass that hung between the windows, and was startled at the paleness of his face. It was quite white, indeed. Septimius was not in the least a foppish young man ; careless he was in dress, though often his apparel took an unsought picturesqueness that set off his slender, agile figure, perhaps from some quality of spontaneous arrangement that he had inherited from his Indian ancestry. Yet many women might have found a charm in that dark, thoughtful face, with its hidden fire and energy, although Septimius never thought of its being handsome, and seldom looked at it. Yet now he was drawn to it by seeing how strangely white it was, and, gazing at it, he observed that since he considered it last, a very

deep furrow, or corrugation, or fissure, it might al
most be called, had indented his brow, rising from the
commencement of his nose towards the centre of the
forehead.   And he knew it was his brooding thought,
his fierce, hard determination, his intense concentra-
tiveness for so many months, that had been digging
that furrow ; and it must prove indeed a potent spe-
cific of the life-water that would smooth that away,
and restore him all the youth and elasticity that he
had buried in that profound grave.

But why was he so pale ?   He could have supposed
himself startled by some ghastly thing that he had just
seen ; by a corpse in the next room, for instance ; or
else by the foreboding that one would soon be there ;
but yet he was conscious of no tremor in his frame, no
terror in his heart ; as why should there be any ?
Feeling his own pulse, he found the strong, regular
beat that should be there.   He was not ill, nor affrighted ; not expectant of any pain.   Then why so
ghastly pale ?   And why, moreover, Septimius, did
you listen so earnestly for any sound in Aunt Keziah's
chamber ?   Why did you creep on tiptoe, once, twice,
three times, up to the old woman's chamber, and put
your ear to the keyhole, and listen breathlessly ?
Well ; it must have been that he was subconscious
that he was trying a bold experiment, and that he
had taken this poor old woman to be the medium of
it, in the hope, of course, that it would turn out well ;
yet with other views than her interest in the matter.
What was the harm of that ?   Medical men, no doubt,
are always doing so, and he was a medical man for the
time.   Then why was he so pale ?

He sat down and fell into a reverie, which perhaps
was partly suggested by that chief furrow which he

had seen, and which we have spoken of, in his brow. He considered whether there was anything in this pursuit of his that used up life particularly fast; so that, perhaps, unless he were successful soon, he should be incapable of renewal; for, looking within himself, and considering his mode of being, he had a singular fancy that his heart was gradually drying up, and that he must continue to get some moisture for it, or else it would soon be like a withered leaf. Supposing his pursuit were vain, what a waste he was making of that little treasure of golden days, which was his all! Could this be called life, which he was leading now? How unlike that of other young men! How unlike that of Robert Hagburn, for example! There had come news yesterday of his having performed a gallant part in the battle of Monmouth, and being promoted to be a captain for his brave conduct. Without thinking of long life, he really lived in heroic actions and emotions; he got much life in a little, and did not fear to sacrifice a lifetime of torpid breaths, if necessary, to the ecstasy of a glorious death!

[*It appears from a written sketch by the author of this story, that he changed his first plan of making Septimius and Rose lovers, and she was to be represented as his half-sister, and in the copy for publication this alteration would have been made.* — Ed.]

And then Robert loved, too, loved his sister Rose, and felt, doubtless, an immortality in that passion. Why could not Septimius love too? It was forbidden! Well, no matter; whom could he have loved? Who, in all this world would have been suited to his secret, brooding heart, that he could have let her into its mysterious chambers, and walked with her from one cavernous gloom to another, and said, "Here are my treasures. I make thee mistress of all these; with all these goods I thee endow." And then, revealing to her his great secret and purpose of gaining immortal life, have said: "This shall be thine, too. Thou shalt share with me. We will walk along the endless path together, and keep one another's hearts warm, and so be content to live."

Ah, Septimius! but now you are getting beyond those rules of yours, which, cold as they are, have been drawn out of a subtle philosophy, and might, were it possible to follow them out, suffice to do all that you ask of them; but if you break them, you do it at the peril of your earthly immortality. Each warmer and quicker throb of the heart wears away so much of life. The passions, the affections, are a wine not to be indulged in. Love, above all, being in its essence an immortal thing, cannot be long contained in an earthly body, but would wear it out with its own secret power, softly invigorating as it seems. You must be cold, therefore, Septimius; you must not even earnestly and passionately desire this immortality that seems so necessary to you. Else the very wish will prevent the possibility of its fulfilment.

By and by, to call him out of these rhapsodies, came Rose home; and finding the kitchen hearth cold, and Aunt Keziah missing, and no dinner by the fire, which was smouldering, — nothing but the portentous earthen jug, which fumed, and sent out long, ill-flavored sighs, she tapped at Septimius's door, and asked him what was the matter.

"Aunt Keziah has had an ill turn," said Septimius, "and has gone to bed."

"Poor auntie!" said Rose, with her quick sympathy. "I will this moment run up and see if she needs anything."

"No, Rose," said Septimius, "she has doubtless gone to sleep, and will awake as well as usual. It would displease her much were you to miss your afternoon school; so you had better set the table with whatever there is left of yesterday's dinner, and leave me to take care of auntie."

"Well," said Rose, "she loves you best; but if she be really ill, I shall give up my school and nurse her."

"No doubt," said Septimius, "she will be about the house again to-morrow."

So Rose ate her frugal dinner (consisting chiefly of purslain, and some other garden herbs, which her thrifty aunt had prepared for boiling), and went away as usual to her school; for Aunt Keziah, as aforesaid, had never encouraged the tender ministrations of Rose, whose orderly, womanly character, with its well-defined orb of daily and civilized duties, had always appeared to strike her as tame; and she once said to her, "You are no squaw, child, and you'll never make a witch." Nor would she even so much as let Rose put her tea to steep, or do anything whatever for herself personally; though, certainly, she was not backward in requiring of her a due share of labor for the general housekeeping.

Septimius was sitting in his room, as the afternoon wore away; because, for some reason or other, or, quite as likely, for no reason at all, he did not air himself and his thoughts, as usual, on the hill; so he was sitting musing, thinking, looking into his mysterious manuscript, when he heard Aunt Keziah moving in the chamber above. First she seemed to rattle a chair; then she began a slow, regular beat with the stick which Septimius had left by her bedside, and which startled him strangely, — so that, indeed, his heart beat faster than the five-and-seventy throbs to which he was restricted by the wise rules that he had digested. So he ran hastily up stairs, and behold, Aunt Keziah was sitting up in bed, looking very wild, — so wild that you would have thought she was going to fly up chimney the next minute; her gray hair all dishevelled, her eyes staring, her hands clutching for ward, while she gave a sort of howl, what with pain and agitation.

"Seppy! Seppy!" said she, — "Seppy, my darling! are you quite sure you remember how to make that precious drink?"

"Quite well, Aunt Keziah," said Septimius, inwardly much alarmed by her aspect, but preserving a true Indian composure of outward mien. "I wrote it down, and could say it by heart besides. Shall I make you a fresh pot of it? for I have thrown away the other."

"That was well, Seppy," said the poor old woman, "for there is something wrong about it; but I want no more, for, Seppy dear, I am going fast out of this world, where you and that precious drink were my only treasures and comforts. I wanted to know if you remembered the recipe; it is all I have to leave you, and the more you drink of it, Seppy, the better. Only see to make it right!"

"Dear auntie, what can I do for you?" said Septimius, in much consternation, but still calm. "Let me run for the doctor, — for the neighbors? something must be done!"

The old woman contorted herself as if there were a fearful time in her insides: and grinned, and twisted the yellow ugliness of her face, and groaned, and howled; and yet there was a tough and fierce kind of endurance with which she fought with her anguish, and would not yield to it a jot, though she allowed herself the relief of shrieking savagely at it, — much more like a defiance than a cry for mercy.

"No doctor! no woman!" said she; "if my drink could not save me, what would a doctor's foolish pills and powders do? And a woman! If old Martha Denton, the witch, were alive, I would be glad to see her. But other women! Pah! Ah! Ai! Oh! Phew! Ah, Seppy, what a mercy it would be now if I could set to and blaspheme a bit, and shake my fist at the sky! But I'm a Christian woman, Seppy, — a Christian woman."

"Shall I send for the minister, Aunt Keziah?" asked Septimius. "He is a good man, and a wise one."

"No minister for me, Seppy," said Aunt Keziah, howling as if somebody were choking her. "He may be a good man, and a wise one, but he's not wise enough to know the way to my heart, and never a man as was! Eh, Seppy, I'm a Christian woman, but I'm not like other Christian women; and I'm glad I'm going away from this stupid world. I've not been a bad woman, and I deserve credit for it, for it would have suited me a great deal better to be bad. Oh, what a delightful time a witch must have had, starting off up chimney on her broomstick at midnight, and looking down from aloft in the sky on the sleeping village far below, with its steeple pointing up at her, so that she might touch the golden weathercock! You, meanwhile, in such an ecstasy, and all below you the dull, innocent, sober humankind; the wife sleeping by her husband, or mother by her child, squalling with wind in its stomach; the goodman driving up his cattle and his plough, — all so innocent, all so stupid, with their dull days just alike, one after another. And you up in the air, sweeping away to some nook in the forest! Ha! What's that? A wizard! Ha! ha! Known below as a deacon! There is Goody Chickering! How quietly she sent the young people to bed after prayers! There is an Indian; there a nigger; they all have equal rights and privileges at a witch-meeting. Phew! the wind blows cold up here! Why does not the Black Man have the meeting at his own kitchen hearth? Ho! ho! Oh dear me! But I'm a Christian woman and no witch; but those must have been gallant times!"

Doubtless it was a partial wandering of the mind that took the poor old woman away on this old-witch flight; and it was very curious and pitiful to witness the compunction with which she returned to herself and took herself to task for the preference which, in her wild nature, she could not help giving to harum-scarum wickedness over tame goodness. Now she tried to compose herself, and talk reasonably and godly.

"Ah, Septimius, my dear child, never give way to temptation, nor consent to be a wizard, though the Black Man persuade you ever so hard. I know he will try. He has tempted me, but I never yielded, never gave him his will; and never do you, my boy, though you, with your dark complexion, and your brooding brow, and your eye veiled, only when it suddenly looks out with a flash of fire in it, are the sort of man he seeks most, and that afterwards serves him. But don't do it, Septimius. But if you could be an Indian, methinks it would be better than this tame life we lead. 'T would have been better for me, at all events. Oh, how pleasant 't would have been to spend my life wandering in the woods, smelling the pines and

the hemlock all day, and fresh things of all kinds, and
no kitchen work to do, — not to rake up the fire, nor
sweep the room, nor make the beds, — but to sleep on
fresh boughs in a wigwam, with the leaves still on the
branches that made the roof! And then to see the
deer brought in by the red hunter, and the blood
streaming from the arrow-dart! Ah! and the fight
too! and the scalping! and, perhaps, a woman might
creep into the battle, and steal the wounded enemy
away of her tribe and scalp him, and be praised for
it! O Seppy, how I hate the thought of the dull life
women lead! A white woman's life is so dull! Thank
Heaven, I'm done with it! If I'm ever to live again,
may I be whole Indian, please my Maker!"

After this goodly outburst, Aunt Keziah lay quietly
for a few moments, and her skinny claws being clasped
together, and her yellow visage grinning, as pious an
aspect as was attainable by her harsh and pain-dis-
torted features, Septimius perceived that she was in
prayer. And so it proved by what followed, for the
old woman turned to him with a grim tenderness on
her face, and stretched out her hand to be taken in his
own. He clasped the bony talon in both his hands.

"Seppy, my dear, I feel a great peace, and I don't
think there is so very much to trouble me in the other
world. It won't be all house-work, and keeping decent, and doing like other people there. I suppose I
need n't expect to ride on a broomstick, — that would
be wrong in any kind of a world, — but there may be
woods to wander in, and a pipe to smoke in the air of
heaven; trees to hear the wind in, and to smell of,
and all such natural, happy things; and by and by I
shall hope to see you there, Seppy, my darling boy!
Come by and by; 't is n't worth your while to live for

ever, even if you should find out what's wanting in the drink I've taught you. I can see a little way into the next world now, and I see it to be far better than this heavy and wretched old place. You'll die when your time comes; won't you, Seppy, my darling?"

"Yes, dear auntie, when my time comes," said Septimius. "Very likely I shall want to live no longer by that time."

"Likely not," said the old woman. "I'm sure I don't. It is like going to sleep on my mother's breast to die. So good night, dear Seppy!"

"Good night, and God bless you, auntie!" said Septimius, with a gush of tears blinding him, spite of his Indian nature.

The old woman composed herself, and lay quite still and decorous for a short time; then, rousing herself a little, "Septimius," said she, "is there just a little drop of my drink left? Not that I want to live any longer, but if I could sip ever so little, I feel as if I should step into the other world quite cheery, with it warm in my heart, and not feel shy and bashful at going among strangers."

"Not one drop, auntie."

"Ah, well, no matter! It was not quite right, that last cup. It had a queer taste. What could you have put into it, Seppy, darling? But no matter, no matter! It's a precious stuff, if you make it right. Don't forget the herbs, Septimius. Something wrong had certainly got into it."

These, except for some murmurings, some groanings and unintelligible whisperings, were the last utterances of poor Aunt Keziah, who did not live a great while longer, and at last passed away in a great sigh, like a gust of wind among the trees, she having just before stretched out her hand again and grasped that of Septimius; and he sat watching her and gazing at her, wondering and horrified, touched, shocked by death, of which he had so unusual a terror, — and by the death of this creature especially, with whom he felt a sympathy that did not exist with any other person now living. So long did he sit, holding her hand, that at last he was conscious that it was growing cold within his own, and that the stiffening fingers clutched him, as if they were disposed to keep their hold, and not forego the tie that had been so peculiar.

Then rushing hastily forth, he told the nearest available neighbor, who was Robert Hagburn's mother; and she summoned some of her gossips, and came to the house, and took poor Aunt Keziah in charge. They talked of her with no great respect, I fear, nor much sorrow, nor sense that the community would suffer any great deprivation in her loss; for, in their view, she was a dram-drinking, pipe-smoking, cross-grained old maid, and, as some thought, a witch; and, at any rate, with too much of the Indian blood in her to be of much use; and they hoped that now Rose Garfield would have a pleasanter life, and Septimius study to be a minister, and all things go well, and the place be cheerfuller. They found Aunt Keziah's bottle in the cupboard, and tasted and smelt of it.

"Good West Indjy as ever I tasted," said Mrs. Hagburn; "and there stands her broken pitcher, on the hearth. Ah, empty! I never could bring my mind to taste it; but now I 'm sorry I never did, for I suppose nobody in the world can make any more of it."

Septimius, meanwhile, had betaken himself to the hill-top, which was his place of refuge on all occasions when the house seemed too stifled to contain him; and there he walked to and fro, with a certain kind of calmness and indifference that he wondered at; for there is hardly anything in this world so strange as the quiet surface that spreads over a man's mind in his greatest emergencies: so that he deems himself perfectly quiet, and upbraids himself with not feeling anything, when indeed he is passion-stirred. As Septimius walked to and fro, he looked at the rich crimson flowers, which seemed to be blooming in greater profusion and luxuriance than ever before. He had made an experiment with these flowers, and he was curious to know whether that experiment had been the cause of Aunt Keziah's death. Not that he felt any remorse therefor, in any case, or believed himself to have committed a crime, having really intended and desired nothing but good. I suppose such things (and he must be a lucky physician, methinks, who has no such mischief within his own experience) never weigh with deadly weight on any man's conscience. Something must be risked in the cause of science, and in desperate cases something must be risked for the patient's self. Septimius, much as he loved life, would not have hesitated to put his own life to the same risk that he had imposed on Aunt Keziah; or, if he did hesitate, it would have been only because, if the experiment turned out disastrously in his own person, he would not be in a position to make another and more successful trial; whereas, by trying it on others, the man of science still reserves himself for new efforts, and does not put all the hopes of the world, so far as involved in his success, on one cast of the die.

By and by he met Sibyl Dacy, who had ascended the hill, as was usual with her, at sunset, and came towards him, gazing earnestly in his face.

"They tell me poor Aunt Keziah is no more," said
she.

"She is dead," said Septimius.

"The flower is a very famous medicine," said the
girl, "but everything depends on its being applied in
the proper way."

"Do you know the way, then?" asked Septimius.

"No; you should ask Doctor Portsoaken about that,"
said Sibyl.

Doctor Portsoaken! And so he should consult him.
That eminent chemist and scientific man had evidently
heard of the recipe, and at all events would be acquainted with the best methods of getting the virtues
out of flowers and herbs, some of which, Septimius
had read enough to know, were poison in one phase
and shape of preparation, and possessed of richest virtues in others; their poison, as one may say, serving
as a dark and terrible safeguard, which Providence
has set to watch over their preciousness; even as a
dragon, or some wild and fiendish spectre, is set to
watch and keep hidden gold and heaped-up diamonds.
A dragon always waits on everything that is very good.
And what would deserve the watch and ward of danger of a dragon, or something more fatal than a dragon,
if not this treasure of which Septimius was in quest,
and the discovery and possession of which would enable him to break down one of the strongest barriers of
nature? It ought to be death, he acknowledged it, to
attempt such a thing; for how changed would be life
if he should succeed; how necessary it was that mankind should be defended from such attempts on the
general rule on the part of all but him. How could
Death be spared? — then the sire would live forever,
and the heir never come to his inheritance, and so he

would at once hate his own father, from the perception that he would never be out of his way, Then the same class of powerful minds would always rule the state, and there would never be a change of policy.

[*Here several pages are missing.* — Ed.]

Through such scenes Septimius sought out the direction that Doctor Portsoaken had given him, and came to the door of a house in the olden part of the town. The Boston of those days had very much the aspect of provincial towns in England, such as may still be seen there, while our own city has undergone such wonderful changes that little likeness to what our ancestors made it can now be found. The streets, crooked and narrow; the houses, many gabled, projecting, with latticed windows and diamond panes; without sidewalks; with rough pavements.

Septimius knocked loudly at the door, nor had long to wait before a serving-maid appeared, who seemed to be of English nativity; and in reply to his request for Doctor Portsoaken bade him come in, and led him up a staircase with broad landing-places; then tapped at the door of a room, and was responded to by a gruff voice saying, "Come in!" The woman held the door open, and Septimius saw the veritable Doctor Portsoaken in an old, faded morning-gown, and with a nightcap on his head, his German pipe in his mouth, and a brandy-bottle, to the best of our belief, on the table by his side.

"Come in, come in," said the gruff doctor, nodding to Septimius. "I remember you. Come in, man, and tell me your business."

Septimius did come in, but was so struck by the aspect of Dr Portsoaken's apartment, and his gown, that he did not immediately tell his business. In the first place, everything looked very dusty and dirty, so that evidently no woman had ever been admitted into this sanctity of a place; a fact made all the more evident by the abundance of spiders, who had spun their webs about the walls and ceiling in the wildest apparent confusion, though doubtless each individual spider knew the cordage which he had lengthened out of his own miraculous bowels. But it was really strange. They had festooned their cordage on whatever was stationary in the room, making a sort of gray, dusky tapestry, that waved portentously in the breeze, and flapped, heavy and dismal, each with its spider in the centre of his own system. And what was most marvellous was a spider over the doctor's head; a spider, I think, of some South American breed, with a circumference of its many legs as big, unless I am misinformed, as a teacup, and with a body in the midst as large as a dollar; giving the spectator horrible qualms as to what would be the consequence if this spider should be crushed, and, at the same time, suggesting the poisonous danger of suffering such a monster to live. The monster, however, sat in the midst of the stalwart cordage of his web, right over the doctor's head; and he looked, with all those complicated lines, like the symbol of a conjurer or crafty politician in the midst of the complexity of his scheme; and Septimius wondered if he were not the type of Dr. Portsoaken himself, who, fat and bloated as the spider, seemed to be the centre of some dark contrivance. And could it be that poor Septimius was typified by the fascinated fly, doomed to be entangled by the web?

"Good day to you," said the gruff doctor, taking his pipe from his mouth. "Here I am, with my brother spiders, in the midst of my web. I told you, you remember, the wonderful efficacy which I had discovered in spiders' webs; and this is my laboratory, where I have hundreds of workmen concocting my panacea for me. Is it not a lovely sight?"

"A wonderful one, at least," said Septimius. "That one above your head, the monster, is calculated to give a very favorable idea of your theory. What a quantity of poison there must be in him!"

"Poison, do you call it?" quoth the grim doctor. "That's entirely as it may be used. Doubtless his bite would send a man to kingdom come; but, on the other hand, no one need want a better life-line than that fellow's web. He and I are firm friends, and I believe he would know my enemies by instinct. But come, sit down, and take a glass of brandy. No? Well, I'll drink it for you. And how is the old aunt yonder, with her infernal nostrum, the bitterness and nauseousness of which my poor stomach has not yet forgotten?"

"My Aunt Keziah is no more," said Septimius.

"No more! Well, I trust in Heaven she has carried her secret with her," said the doctor. "If anything could comfort you for her loss, it would be that. But what brings you to Boston?"

"Only a dried flower or two," said Septimius, producing some specimens of the strange growth of the grave. "I want you to tell me about them."

The naturalist took the flowers in his hand, one of which had the root appended, and examined them with great minuteness and some surprise; two or three times looking in Septimius's face with a puzzled and inquiring air; then examined them again.

"Do you tell me," said he, "that the plant has been

found indigenous in this country, and in your part of it? And in what locality?"

"Indigenous, so far as I know," answered Septimius. "As to the locality," — he hesitated a little, — "it is on a small hillock, scarcely bigger than a mole hill, on the hill-top behind my house."

The naturalist looked steadfastly at him with red, burning eyes, under his deep, impending, shaggy brows; then again at the flower.

"Flower, do you call it?" said he, after a reëxamination. "This is no flower, though it so closely resembles one, and a beautiful one, — yes, most beautiful. But it is no flower. It is a certain very rare fungus, — so rare as almost to be thought fabulous; and there are the strangest superstitions, coming down from ancient times, as to the mode of production. What sort of manure had been put into that hillock? Was it merely dried leaves, the refuse of the forest, or something else?"

Septimius hesitated a little; but there was no reason why he should not disclose the truth, — as much of it as Doctor Portsoaken cared to know.

"The hillock where it grew," answered he, "was a grave."

"A grave! Strange! strange!" quoth Doctor Portsoaken. "Now these old superstitions sometimes prove to have a germ of truth in them, which some philosopher has doubtless long ago, in forgotten ages, discovered and made known; but in process of time his learned memory passes away, but the truth, undiscovered, survives him, and the people get hold of it, and make it the nucleus of all sorts of folly. So it grew out of a grave! Yes, yes; and probably it would have grown out of any other dead flesh, as well as that of a human being; a dog would have answered the purpose as well as a man. You must know that the seeds of fungi are scattered so universally over the world that, only comply with the conditions, and you will produce them everywhere. Prepare the bed it loves, and a mushroom will spring up spontaneously, an excellent food, like manna from heaven. So superstition says, kill your deadliest enemy, and plant him, and he will come up in a delicious fungus, which I presume to be this; steep him, or distil him, and he will make an elixir of life for you. I suppose there is some foolish symbolism or other about the matter; but the fact I affirm to be nonsense. Dead flesh under some certain conditions of rain and sunshine, not at present ascertained by science, will produce the fungus, whether the manure be friend, or foe, or cattle."

"And as to its medical efficacy?" asked Septimius.

"That may be great for aught I know," said Portsoaken; "but I am content with my cobwebs. You may seek it out for yourself. But if the poor fellow lost his life in the supposition that he might be a useful ingredient in a recipe, you are rather an unscrupulous practitioner."

"The person whose mortal relics fill that grave," said Septimius, "was no enemy of mine (no private enemy, I mean, though he stood among the enemies of my country), nor had I anything to gain by his death. I strove to avoid aiming at his life, but he compelled me."

"Many a chance shot brings down the bird," said Doctor Portsoaken. "You say you had no interest in his death. We shall see that in the end."

Septimius did not try to follow the conversation among the mysterious hints with which the doctor chose to involve it; but he now sought to gain some information from him as to the mode of preparing the recipe, and whether he thought it would be most efficacious as a decoction, or as a distillation. The learned chemist supported most decidedly the latter opinion, and showed Septimius how he might make for himself a simpler apparatus, with no better aids than Aunt Keziah's teakettle, and one or two trifling things, which the doctor himself supplied, by which all might be done with every necessary scrupulousness.

"Let me look again at the formula," said he. "There are a good many minute directions that appear trifling, but it is not safe to neglect any minutiæ in the preparation of an affair like this; because, as it is all mysterious and unknown ground together, we cannot tell which may be the important and efficacious part. For instance, when all else is done, the recipe is to be exposed seven days to the sun at noon. That does not look very important, but it may be. Then again, 'Steep it in moonlight during the second quarter.' That 's all moonshine, one would think; but there 's no saying. It is singular, with such preciseness, that no distinct directions are given whether to infuse, decoct, distil, or what other way; but my advice is to distil."

"I will do it," said Septimius, "and not a direction shall be neglected."

"I shall be curious to know the result," said Doctor Portsoaken, "and am glad to see the zeal with which you enter into the matter. A very valuable medicine may be recovered to science through your agency, and you may make your fortune by it; though, for my part, I prefer to trust to my cobwebs. This spider,

now, is not he a lovely object? See, he is quite capa
ble of knowledge and affection."

There seemed, in fact, to be some mode of communication between the doctor and his spider, for on some
sign given by the former, imperceptible to Septimius,
the many-legged monster let himself down by a cord,
which he extemporized out of his own bowels, and
came dangling his huge bulk down before his master's
face, while the latter lavished many epithets of endear-
ment upon him, ludicrous, and not without horror, as
applied to such a hideous production of nature.

" I assure you," said Dr. Portsoaken, " I run some
risk from my intimacy with this lovely jewel, and if I
behave not all the more prudently, your countrymen
will hang me for a wizard, and annihilate this precious
spider as my familiar. There would be a loss to the
world; not small in my own case, but enormous in the
case of the spider. Look at him now, and see if the
mere uninstructed observation does not discover a wonderful value in him."

In truth, when looked at closely, the spider really
showed that a care and art had been bestowed upon
his make, not merely as regards curiosity, but absolute
beauty, that seemed to indicate that he must be a
rather distinguished creature in the view of Providence; so variegated was he with a thousand minute
spots, spots of color, glorious radiance, and such a
brilliance was attained by many conglomerated brilliancies; and it was very strange that all this care was
bestowed on a creature that, probably, had never been
carefully considered except by the two pair of eyes
that were now upon it; and that, in spite of its beauty
and magnificence, could only be looked at with an effort to overcome the mysterious repulsiveness of its

presence ; for all the time that Septimius looked and
admired, he still hated the thing, and thought it
wrong that it was ever born, and wished that it could
be annihilated.   Whether the spider was conscious of
the wish, we are unable to say ; but certainly Septimius felt as if he were hostile to him, and had a mind
to sting him ; and, in fact, Dr. Portsoaken seemed of
the same opinion.

"Aha, my friend," said he, " I would advise you
not to come too near Orontes!   He is a lovely beast,
it is true ; but in a certain recess of this splendid
form of his he keeps a modest supply of a certain potent and piercing poison, which would produce a wonderful effect on any flesh to which he chose to apply
it.   A powerful fellow is Orontes ; and he has a great
sense of his own dignity and importance, and will not
allow it to be imposed on."

Septimius moved from the vicinity of the spider,
who, in fact, retreated, by climbing up his cord, and
ensconced himself in the middle of his web, where he
remained waiting for his prey.   Septimius wondered
whether the doctor were symbolized by the spider, and
was likewise waiting in the middle of his web for his
prey.   As he saw no way, however, in which the doctor could make a profit out of himself, or how he could
be victimized, the thought did not much disturb his
equanimity.   He was about to take his leave, but the
doctor, in a derisive kind of way, bade him sit still,
for he purposed keeping him as a guest, that night, at
least.

"I owe you a dinner," said he, " and will pay it
with a supper and knowledge ; and before we part I
have certain inquiries to make, of which you may not
at first see the object, but yet are not quite purpose-

less. My familiar, up aloft there, has whispered me
something about you, and I rely greatly on his intima-
tions."

Septimius, who was sufficiently common-sensible,
and invulnerable to superstitious influences on every
point except that to which he had surrendered himself,
was easily prevailed upon to stay ; for he found the
singular, charlatanic, mysterious lore of the man curious, and he had enough of real science to at least
make him an object of interest to one who knew nothing of the matter; and Septimius's acuteness, too, was
piqued in trying to make out what manner of man he
really was, and how much in him was genuine science
and self-belief, and how much quackery and pretension
and conscious empiricism. So he stayed, and supped
with the doctor at a table heaped more bountifully,
and with rarer dainties, than Septimius had ever before conceived of ; and in his simpler cognizance, heretofore, of eating merely to live, he could not but wonder to see a man of thought caring to eat of more than
one dish, so that most of the meal, on his part, was
spent in seeing the doctor feed and hearing him discourse upon his food.

"If man lived only to eat," quoth the doctor, "one
life would not suffice, not merely to exhaust the pleasure of it, but even to get the rudiments of it."

When this important business was over, the doctor
and his guest sat down again in his laboratory, where
the former took care to have his usual companion, the
black bottle, at his elbow, and filled his pipe, and
seemed to feel a certain sullen, genial, fierce, brutal,
kindly mood enough, and looked at Septimius with a
sort of friendship, as if he had as lief shake hands
with him as knock him down.

" Now for a talk about business," said he.

Septimius thought, however, that the doctor's talk began, at least, at a sufficient remoteness from any practical business ; for he began to question about his remote ancestry, what he knew, or what record had been preserved, of the first emigrant from England ; whence, from what shire or part of England, that ancestor had come ; whether there were any memorial of any kind remaining of him, any letters or written documents, wills, deeds, or other legal paper; in short, all about him.

Septimius could not satisfactorily see whether these inquiries were made with any definite purpose, or from a mere general curiosity to discover how a family of early settlement in America might still be linked with the old country; whether there were any tendrils stretching across the gulf of a hundred and fifty years by which the American branch of the family was separated from the trunk of the family tree in England. The doctor partly explained this.

" You must know," said he, " that the name you bear, Felton, is one formerly of much eminence and repute in my part of England, and, indeed, very recently possessed of wealth and station. I should like to know if you are of that race."

Septimius answered with such facts and traditions as had come to his knowledge respecting his family history ; a sort of history that is quite as liable to be mythical, in its early and distant stages, as that of Rome, and, indeed, seldom goes three or four generations back without getting into a mist really impenetrable, though great, gloomy, and magnificent shapes of men often seem to loom in it, who, if they could be brought close to the naked eye, would turn out as com-

monplace as the descendants who wonder at and admire them. He remembered Aunt Keziah's legend,
and said he had reason to believe that his first ancestor came over at a somewhat earlier date than the
first Puritan settlers, and dwelt among the Indians,
where (and here the young man cast down his eyes,
having the customary American abhorrence for any
mixture of blood) he had intermarried with the daughter of a sagamore, and succeeded to his rule.   This
might have happened as early as the end of Elizabeth's
reign, perhaps later. It was impossible to decide dates
on such a matter. There had been a son of this connection, perhaps more than one, but certainly one son,
who, on the arrival of the Puritans, was a youth, his
father appearing to have been slain in some outbreak
of the tribe, perhaps owing to the jealousy of prominent chiefs at seeing their natural authority abrogated
or absorbed by a man of different race. He slightly
alluded to the supernatural attributes that gathered
round this predecessor, but in a way to imply that he
put no faith in them; for Septimius's natural keen
sense and perception kept him from betraying his
weaknesses to the doctor, by the same instinctive and
subtle caution with which a madman can so well conceal his infirmity.

On the arrival of the Puritans, they had found
among the Indians a youth partly of their own blood,
able, though imperfectly, to speak their language, —
having, at least, some early recollections of it, — in-
heriting, also, a share of influence over the tribe on
which his father had grafted him. It was natural that
they should pay especial attention to this youth, consider it their duty to give him religious instruction in
the faith of his fathers, and try to use him as a means

of influencing his tribe. They did so, but did not succeed in swaying the tribe by his means, their success
having been limited to winning the half-Indian from
the wild ways of his mother's people, into a certain
partial, but decent accommodation to those of the English. A tendency to civilization was brought out in
his character by their rigid training; at least, his savage wildness was broken. He built a house among
them, with a good deal of the wigwam, no doubt, in its
style of architecture, but still a permanent house, near
which he established a corn-field, a pumpkin-garden,
a melon-patch, and became farmer enough to be entitled to ask the hand of a Puritan maiden. There he
spent his life, with some few instances of temporary
relapse into savage wildness, when he fished in the
river Musquehannah, or in Walden, or strayed in the
woods, when he should have been planting or hoeing;
but, on the whole, the race had been redeemed from
barbarism in his person, and in the succeeding generations had been tamed more and more. The second
generation had been distinguished in the Indian wars
of the provinces, and then intermarried with the stock
of a distinguished Puritan divine, by which means
Septimius could reckon great and learned men, scholars of old Cambridge, among his ancestry on one side,
while on the other it ran up to the early emigrants,
who seemed to have been remarkable men, and to that
strange wild lineage of Indian chiefs, whose blood was
like that of persons not quite human, intermixed with
civilized blood.

"I wonder," said the doctor, musingly, "whether
there are really no documents to ascertain the epoch
at which that old first emigrant came over, and whence
he came, and precisely from what English family.

Often the last heir of some respectable name dies in England, and we say that the family is extinct; whereas, very possibly, it may be abundantly flourishing in the New World, revived by the rich infusion of new blood in a new soil, instead of growing feebler, heavier, stupider, each year by sticking to an old soil, intermarrying over and over again with the same respectable families, till it has made common stock of all their vices, weaknesses, madnesses. Have you no documents, I say, no muniment deed?"

"None," said Septimius.

"No old furniture, desks, trunks, chests, cabinets?"

"You must remember," said Septimius, "that my Indian ancestor was not very likely to have brought such things out of the forest with him. A wandering Indian does not carry a chest of papers with him. I do remember, in my childhood, a little old iron-bound chest, or coffer, of which the key was lost, and which my Aunt Keziah used to say came down from her great-great-grandfather. I don't know what has become of it, and my poor old aunt kept it among her own treasures."

"Well, my friend, do you hunt up that old coffer, and, just as a matter of curiosity, let me see the contents."

"I have other things to do," said Septimius.

"Perhaps so," quoth the doctor, "but no other, as it may turn out, of quite so much importance as this. I'll tell you fairly: the heir of a great English house is lately dead, and the estate lies open to any well-sustained, perhaps to any plausible, claimant. If it should appear from the records of that family, as I have some reason to suppose, that a member of it, who would now represent the older branch, disap-

peared mysteriously and unaccountably, at a date corresponding with what might be ascertained as that of
your ancestor's first appearance in this country; if
any reasonable proof can be brought forward, on the
part of the representatives of that white sagamore, that
wizard pow-wow, or however you call him, that he was
the disappearing Englishman, why, a good case is made
out. Do you feel no interest in such a prospect?"

"Very little, I confess," said Septimius.

"Very little!" said the grim doctor, impatiently.
"Do not you see that, if you make good your claim,
you establish for yourself a position among the English aristocracy, and succeed to a noble English estate, an ancient hall, where your forefathers have
dwelt since the Conqueror; splendid gardens, hereditary woods and parks, to which anything America can
show is despicable, — all thoroughly cultivated and
adorned, with the care and ingenuity of centuries;
and an income, a month of which would be greater
wealth than any of your American ancestors, raking
and scraping for his lifetime, has ever got together,
as the accumulated result of the toil and penury by
which he has sacrificed body and soul?"

"That strain of Indian blood is in me yet," said
Septimius, "and it makes me despise, — no, not despise; for I can see their desirableness for other people, — but it makes me reject for myself what you think
so valuable. I do not care for these common aims.
I have ambition, but it is for prizes such as other men
cannot gain, and do not think of aspiring after. I
could not live in the habits of English life, as I conceive it to be, and would not, for my part, be burdened
with the great estate you speak of. It might answer
my purpose for a time. It would suit me well enough

to try that mode of life, as well as a hundred others, but only for a time. It is of no permanent importance."

" I 'll tell you what it is, young man," said the doctor, testily, " you have something in your brain that makes you talk very foolishly ; and I have partly a suspicion what it is, — only I can't think that a fellow who is really gifted with respectable sense, in other directions, should be such a confounded idiot in this."

Septimius blushed, but held his peace, and the conversation languished after this ; the doctor grimly smoking his pipe, and by no means increasing the milkiness of his mood by frequent applications to the black bottle, until Septimius intimated that he would like to go to bed. The old woman was summoned, and ushered him to his chamber.

At breakfast, the doctor partially renewed the subject which he seemed to consider most important in yesterday's conversation.

" My young friend," said he, " I advise you to look in cellar and garret, or wherever you consider the most likely place, for that iron-bound coffer. There may be nothing in it; it may be full of musty love-letters, or old sermons, or receipted bills of a hundred years ago ; but it may contain what will be worth to you an estate of five thousand pounds a year. It is a pity the old woman with the damnable decoction is gone off. Look it up, I say."

" Well, well," said Septimius, abstractedly, " when I can find time."

So saying, he took his leave, and retraced his way back to his home. He had not seemed like himself during the time that elapsed since he left it, and it appeared an infinite space that he had lived through and travelled over, and he fancied it hardly possible that he could ever get back again. But now, with every step that he took, he found himself getting miserably back into the old enchanted land. The mist rose up about him, the pale mist-bow of ghostly promise curved before him; and he trod back again, poor boy, out of the clime of real effort, into the land of his dreams and shadowy enterprise.

"How was it," said he, "that I can have been so untrue to my convictions? Whence came that dark and dull despair that weighed upon me? Why did I let the mocking mood which I was conscious of in that brutal, brandy-burnt sceptic have such an influence on me? Let him guzzle! He shall not tempt me from my pursuit, with his lure of an estate and name among those heavy English beef-eaters of whom he is a brother. My destiny is one which kings might envy, and strive in vain to buy with principalities and kingdoms."

So he trod on air almost, in the latter parts of his journey, and instead of being wearied, grew more airy with the latter miles that brought him to his wayside home.

So now Septimius sat down and began in earnest his endeavors and experiments to prepare the medicine, according to the mysterious terms of the recipe It seemed not possible to do it, so many rebuffs and disappointments did he meet with. No effort would produce a combination answering to the description of the recipe, which propounded a brilliant, gold-colored liquid, clear as the air itself, with a certain fragrance which was peculiar to it, and also, what was the more individual test of the correctness of the mixture, a certain coldness of the feeling, a chillness which was

described as peculiarly refreshing and invigorating.
With all his trials, he produced nothing but turbid
results, clouded generally, or lacking something in
color, and never that fragrance, and never that coldness which was to be the test of truth. He studied
all the books of chemistry which at that period were
attainable, — a period when, in the world, it was a
science far unlike what it has since become ; and when
Septimius had no instruction in this country, nor could
obtain any beyond the dark, mysterious charlatanic
communications of Doctor Portsoaken. So that, in
fact, he seemed to be discovering for himself the science through which he was to work. He seemed to
do everything that was stated in the recipe, and yet
no results came from it ; the liquid that he produced
was nauseous to the smell, — to taste it he had a horrible repugnance, turbid, nasty, reminding him in most
respects of poor Aunt Keziah's elixir ; and it was a
body without a soul, and that body dead. And so
it went on ; and the poor, half-maddened Septimius
began to think that his immortal life was preserved
by the mere effort of seeking for it, but was to be
spent in the quest, and was therefore to be made an
eternity of abortive misery. He pored over the document that had so possessed him, turning its crabbed
meanings every way, trying to get out of it some new
light, often tempted to fling it into the fire which he
kept under his retort, and let the whole thing go ; but
then again, soon rising out of that black depth of despair, into a determination to do what he had so long
striven for. With such intense action of mind as he
brought to bear on this paper, it is wonderful that it
was not spiritually distilled ; that its essence did not
arise, purified from all alloy of falsehood, from all

turbidness of obscurity and ambiguity, and form a pure essence of truth and invigorating motive, if of any it were capable. In this interval, Septimius is said by tradition to have found out many wonderful secrets that were almost beyond the scope of science. It was said that old Aunt Keziah used to come with a coal of fire from unknown furnaces, to light his distilling apparatus; it was said, too, that the ghost of the old lord, whose ingenuity had propounded this puzzle for his descendants, used to come at midnight and strive to explain to him this manuscript; that the Black Man, too, met him on the hill-top, and promised him an immediate release from his difficulties, provided he would kneel down and worship him, and sign his name in his book, an old, iron-clasped, much-worn volume, which he produced from his ample pockets, and showed him in it the names of many a man whose name has become historic, and above whose ashes kept watch an inscription testifying to his virtues and devotion, — old autographs, — for the Black Man was the original autograph collector.

But these, no doubt, were foolish stories, conceived and propagated in chimney-corners, while yet there were chimney-corners and firesides, and smoky flues. There was no truth in such things, I am sure; the Black Man had changed his tactics, and knew better than to lure the human soul thus to come to him with his musty autograph-book. So Septimius fought with his difficulty by himself, as many a beginner in science has done before him; and to his efforts in this way are popularly attributed many herb-drinks, and some kinds of spruce-beer, and nostrums used for rheumatism, sore throat, and typhus fever; but I rather think they all came from Aunt Keziah; or perhaps, like

jokes to Joe Miller, all sorts of quack medicines, flock
ing at large through the community, are assigned to
him or her. The people have a little mistaken the
character and purpose of poor Septimius, and remember him as a quack doctor, instead of a seeker for a
secret, not the less sublime and elevating because it
happened to be unattainable.

I know not through what medium or by what
means, but it got noised abroad that Septimius was
engaged in some mysterious work; and, indeed, his
seclusion, his absorption, his indifference to all that
was going on in that weary time of war, looked strange
enough to indicate that it must be some most important business that engrossed him. On the few occasions when he came out from his immediate haunts into
the village, he had a strange, owl-like appearance, un-
combed, unbrushed, his hair long and tangled; his
face, they said, darkened with smoke; his cheeks pale;
the indentation of his brow deeper than ever before;
an earnest, haggard, sulking look; and so he went
hastily along the village street, feeling as if all eyes
might find out what he had in his mind from his appearance; taking by-ways where they were to be found,
going long distances through woods and fields, rather
than short ones where the way lay through the frequented haunts of men. For he shunned the glances
of his fellow-men, probably because he had learnt to
consider them not as fellows, because he was seeking
to withdraw himself from the common bond and destiny, — because he felt, too, that on that account his
fellow-men would consider him as a traitor, an enemy,
one who had deserted their cause, and tried to withdraw his feeble shoulder from under that great burden of death which is imposed on all men to bear,

and which, if one could escape, each other would feel his load proportionably heavier. With these beings of a moment he had no longer any common cause; they must go their separate ways, yet apparently the same, — they on the broad, dusty, beaten path, that seemed always full, but from which continually they so strangely vanished into invisibility, no one knowing, nor long inquiring, what had become of them; he on his lonely path, where he should tread secure, with no trouble but the loneliness, which would be none to him. For a little while he would seem to keep them company, but soon they would all drop away, the minister, his accustomed towns-people, Robert Hagburn, Rose, Sibyl Dacy, — all leaving him in blessed unknownness to adopt new temporary relations, and take a new course.

Sometimes, however, the prospect a little chilled him. Could he give them all up, — the sweet sister; the friend of his childhood; the grave instructor of his youth; the homely, life-known faces? Yes; there were such rich possibilities in the future: for he would seek out the noblest minds, the deepest hearts in every age, and be the friend of human time. Only it might be sweet to have one unchangeable companion; for, unless he strung the pearls and diamonds of life upon one unbroken affection, he sometimes thought that his life would have nothing to give it unity and identity; and so the longest life would be but an aggregate of insulated fragments, which would have no relation to one another. And so it would not be one life, but many unconnected ones. Unless he could look into the same eyes, through the mornings of future time, opening and blessing him with the fresh gleam of love and joy; unless the same sweet voice could melt his thoughts together ; unless some sympathy of a life side by side with his could knit them into one ; looking back upon the same things, looking forward to the same ; the long, thin thread of an individual life, stretching onward and onward, would cease to be visible, cease to be felt, cease, by and by, to have any real bigness in proportion to its length, and so be virtually non-existent, except in the mere inconsiderable Now. If a group of chosen friends, chosen out of all the world for their adaptedness, could go on in endless life together, keeping themselves mutually warm on the high, desolate way, then none of them need ever sigh to be comforted in the pitiable snugness of the grave. If one especial soul might be his companion, then how complete the fence of mutual arms, the warmth of close-pressing breast to breast ! Might there be one ! O Sibyl Dacy !

Perhaps it could not be. Who but himself could undergo that great trial, and hardship, and self-denial, and firm purpose, never wavering, never sinking for a moment, keeping his grasp on life like one who holds up by main force a sinking and drowning friend ? — how could a woman do it ! He must then give up the thought. There was a choice, — friendship, and the love of woman, — the long life of immortality. There was something heroic and ennobling in choosing the latter. And so he walked with the mysterious girl on the hill-top, and sat down beside her on the grave, which still ceased not to redden, portentously beautiful, with that unnatural flower, — and they talked together ; and Septimius looked on her weird beauty, and often said to himself, " This, too, will pass away she is not capable of what I am ; she is a woman. It must be a manly and courageous and forcible spirit

vastly rich in all three particulars, that has strength
enough to live! Ah, is it surely so? There is such
a dark sympathy between us, she knows me so well,
she touches my inmost so at unawares, that I could
almost think I had a companion here. Perhaps not
so soon. At the end of centuries I might wed one;
not now."

But once he said to Sibyl Dacy, "Ah, how sweet it
would be — sweet for me, at least — if this intercourse might last forever!"

"That is an awful idea that you present," said
Sibyl, with a hardly perceptible, involuntary shudder;
"always on this hill-top, always passing and repassing
this little hillock; always smelling these flowers! I
always looking at this deep chasm in your brow; you
always seeing my bloodless cheek! — doing this till
these trees crumble away, till perhaps a new forest
grew up wherever this white race had planted, and a
race of savages again possess the soil. I should not
like it. My mission here is but for a short time, and
will soon be accomplished, and then I go."

"You do not rightly estimate the way in which the
long time might be spent," said Septimius. "We
would find out a thousand uses of this world, uses
and enjoyments which now men never dream of, because the world is just held to their mouths, and then
snatched away again, before they have time hardly to
taste it, instead of becoming acquainted with the deli-
ciousness of this great world-fruit. But you speak of
a mission, and as if you were now in performance of
it. Will you not tell me what it is?"

"No," said Sibyl Dacy, smiling on him. "But one
day you shall know what it is, — none sooner nor better than you, — so much I promise you."

"Are we friends?" asked Septimius, somewhat puzzled by her look.

"We have an intimate relation to one another," replied Sibyl.

"And what is it?" demanded Septimius.

"That will appear hereafter," answered Sibyl, again smiling on him.

He knew not what to make of this, nor whether to be exalted or depressed; but, at all events, there seemed to be an accordance, a striking together, a mutual touch of their two natures, as if, somehow or other, they were performing the same part of solemn music; so that he felt his soul thrill, and at the same time shudder. Some sort of sympathy there surely was, but of what nature he could not tell; though often he was impelled to ask himself the same question he asked Sibyl, "Are we friends?" because of a sudden shock and repulsion that came between them, and passed away in a moment; and there would be Sibyl, smiling askance on him.

And then he toiled away again at his chemical pursuits; tried to mingle things harmoniously that apparently were not born to be mingled; discovering a science for himself, and mixing it up with absurdities that other chemists had long ago flung aside; but still there would be that turbid aspect, still that lack of fragrance, still that want of the peculiar temperature, that was announced as the test of the matter. Over and over again he set the crystal vase in the sun, and let it stay there the appointed time, hoping that it would digest in such a manner as to bring about the desired result.

One day, as it happened, his eyes fell upon the silver key which he had taken from the breast of the dead young man, and he thought within himself that this might have something to do with the seemingly unattainable success of his pursuit. He remembered, for the first time, the grim doctor's emphatic injunction to search for the little iron-bound box of which he had spoken, and which had come down with such legends attached to it ; as, for instance, that it held the Devil's bond with his great-great-grandfather, now cancelled by the surrender of the latter's soul ; that it held the golden key of Paradise ; that it was full of old gold, or of the dry leaves of a hundred years ago ; that it had a familiar fiend in it, who would be exorcised by the turning of the lock, but would otherwise remain a prisoner till the solid oak of the box mouldered, or the iron rusted away ; so that between fear and the loss of the key, this curious old box had remained unopened, till itself was lost.

But now Septimius, putting together what Aunt Keziah had said in her dying moments, and what Doctor Portsoaken had insisted upon, suddenly came to the conclusion that the possession of the old iron box might be of the greatest importance to him. So he set himself at once to think where he had last seen it. Aunt Keziah, of course, had put it away in some safe place or other, either in cellar or garret, no doubt ; so Septimius, in the intervals of his other occupations, devoted several days to the search ; and not to weary the reader with the particulars of the quest for an old box, suffice it to say that he at last found it, amongst various other antique rubbish, in a corner of the garret.

It was a very rusty old thing, not more than a foot in length, and half as much in height and breadth ; but most ponderously iron-bound, with bars, and corners,

and all sorts of fortification; looking very much like
an ancient alms-box, such as are to be seen in the older
rural churches of England, and which seem to intimate
great distrust of those to whom the funds are committed. Indeed, there might be a shrewd suspicion
that some ancient church beadle among Septimius's
forefathers, when emigrating from England, had taken
the opportunity of bringing the poor-box along with
him. On looking close, too, there were rude embellish-
ments on the lid and sides of the box in long-rusted
steel, designs such as the Middle Ages were rich in;
a representation of Adam and Eve, or of Satan and a
soul, nobody could tell which; but, at any rate, an
illustration of great value and interest. Septimius
looked at this ugly, rusty, ponderous old box, so worn
and battered with time, and recollected with a scorn-
ful smile the legends of which it was the object; all
of which he despised and discredited, just as much as
he did that story in the "Arabian Nights," where a
demon comes out of a copper vase, in a cloud of smoke
that covers the sea-shore; for he was singularly invulnerable to all modes of superstition, all nonsense,
except his own. But that one mode was ever in full
force and operation with him. He felt strongly convinced that inside the old box was something that ap-
pertained to his destiny; the key that he had taken
from the dead man's breast, had that come down
through time, and across the sea, and had a man died
to bring and deliver it to him, merely for nothing?
It could not be.

He looked at the old, rusty, elaborated lock of the
little receptacle. It was much flourished about with
what was once polished steel; and certainly, when
thus polished, and the steel bright with which it was

hooped, defended, and inlaid, it must have been a thing fit to appear in any cabinet; though now the oak was worm-eaten as an old coffin, and the rust of the iron came off red on Septimius's fingers, after he had been fumbling at it. He looked at the curious old silver key, too, and fancied that he discovered in its elaborate handle some likeness to the ornaments about the box; at any rate, this he determined was the key of fate, and he was just applying it to the lock when somebody tapped familiarly at the door, having opened the outer one, and stepped in with a manly stride. Septimius, inwardly blaspheming, as secluded men are apt to do when any interruption comes, and especially when it comes at some critical moment of projection, left the box as yet unbroached, and said, "Come in."

The door opened, and Robert Hagburn entered; looking so tall and stately, that Septimius hardly knew him for the youth with whom he had grown up familiarly. He had on the Revolutionary dress of buff and blue, with decorations that to the initiated eye denoted him an officer, and certainly there was a kind of authority in his look and manner, indicating that heavy responsibilities, critical moments, had educated him, and turned the ploughboy into a man.

"Is it you?" exclaimed Septimius. "I scarcely knew you. How war has altered you!"

"And I may say, Is it you? for you are much altered likewise, my old friend. Study wears upon you terribly. You will be an old man, at this rate, before you know you are a young one. You will kill yourself, as sure as a gun!"

"Do you think so?" said Septimius, rather startled, for the queer absurdity of the position struck him, if he should so exhaust and wear himself as to die, just at the moment when he should have found out the secret of everlasting life. "But though I look pale, I am very vigorous. Judging from that scar, slanting down from your temple, you have been nearer death than you now think me, though in another way."

"Yes," said Robert Hagburn; "but in hot blood, and for a good cause, who cares for death? And yet I love life; none better, while it lasts, and I love it in all its looks and turns and surprises, — there is so much to be got out of it, in spite of all that people say. Youth is sweet, with its fiery enterprise, and I suppose mature manhood will be just as much so, though in a calmer way, and age, quieter still, will have its own merits, — the thing is only to do with life what we ought, and what is suited to each of its stages; do all, enjoy all, — and I suppose these two rules amount to the same thing. Only catch real earnest hold of life, not play with it, and not defer one part of it for the sake of another, then each part of life will do for us what was intended. People talk of the hardships of military service, of the miseries that we undergo fighting for our country. I have undergone my share, I believe, — hard toil in the wilderness, hunger, extreme weariness, pinching cold, the torture of a wound, peril of death; and really I have been as happy through it as ever I was at my mother's cosey fireside of a winter's evening. If I had died, I doubt not my last moments would have been happy. There is no use of life, but just to find out what is fit for us to do; and, doing it, it seems to be little matter whether we live or die in it. God does not want our work, but only our willingness to work; at least, the last seems to answer all his purposes."

"This is a comfortable philosophy of yours," said Septimius, rather contemptuously, and yet enviously. "Where did you get it, Robert?"

"Where? Nowhere; it came to me on the march; and though I can't say that I thought it when the bullets pattered into the snow about me, in those narrow streets of Quebec, yet, I suppose, it was in my mind then; for, as I tell you, I was very cheerful and contented. And you, Septimius? I never saw such a discontented, unhappy-looking fellow as you are. You have had a harder time in peace than I in war. You have not found what you seek, whatever that may be. Take my advice. Give yourself to the next work that comes to hand. The war offers place to all of us; we ought to be thankful, — the most joyous of all the generations before or after us, — since Providence gives us such good work to live for, or such a good opportunity to die. It is worth living for, just to have the chance to die so well as a man may in these days. Come, be a soldier. Be a chaplain, since your education lies that way; and you will find that nobody in peace prays so well as we do, we soldiers; and you shall not be debarred from fighting, too; if war is holy work, a priest may lawfully do it, as well as pray for it. Come with us, my old friend Septimius, be my comrade, and, whether you live or die, you will thank me for getting you out of the yellow forlornness in which you go on, neither living nor dying."

Septimius looked at Robert Hagburn in surprise; so much was he altered and improved by this brief experience of war, adventure, responsibility, which he had passed through. Not less than the effect produced on his loutish, rustic air and deportment, developing his figure, seeming to make him taller, setting free the manly graces that lurked within his awkward frame, — not less was the effect on his mind and moral nature, giving freedom of ideas, simple perception of great thoughts, a free natural chivalry; so that the knight, the Homeric warrior, the hero, seemed to be here, or possible to be here, in the young New England rustic; and all that history has given, and hearts throbbed and sighed and gloried over, of patriotism and heroic feeling and action, might be repeated, perhaps, in the life and death of this familiar friend and playmate of his, whom he had valued not over highly, — Robert Hagburn. He had merely followed out his natural heart, boldly and singly, — doing the first good thing that came to hand, — and here was a hero.

"You almost make me envy you, Robert," said he, sighing.

"Then why not come with me?" asked Robert.

"Because I have another destiny," said Septimius.

"Well, you are mistaken; be sure of that," said Robert. "This is not a generation for study, and the making of books; that may come by and by. This great fight has need of all men to carry it on, in one way or another; and no man will do well, even for himself, who tries to avoid his share in it. But I have said my say. And now, Septimius, the war takes much of a man, but it does not take him all, and what it leaves is all the more full of life and health thereby. I have something to say to you about this."

"Say it then, Robert," said Septimius, who, having got over the first excitement of the interview, and the sort of exhilaration produced by the healthful glow of Robert's spirit, began secretly to wish that it might close, and to be permitted to return to his solitary thoughts again. "What can I do for you?"

"Why, nothing," said Robert, looking rather confused, "since all is settled. The fact is, my old friend, as perhaps you have seen, I have very long had an eye upon your sister Rose ; yes, from the time we went together to the old school-house, where she now teaches children like what we were then. The war took me away, and in good time, for I doubt if Rose would ever have cared enough for me to be my wife, if I had stayed at home, a country lout, as I was getting to be, in shirt-sleeves and bare feet. But now, you see, I have come back, and this whole great war, to her woman's heart, is represented in me, and makes me heroic, so to speak, and strange, and yet her old familiar lover. So I found her heart tenderer for me than it was ; and, in short, Rose has consented to be my wife, and we mean to be married in a week ; my furlough permits little delay."

"You surprise me," said Septimius, who, immersed in his own pursuits, had taken no notice of the growing affection between Robert and his sister. "Do you think it well to snatch this little lull that is allowed you in the wild striving of war to try to make a peaceful home ? Shall you like to be summoned from it soon ? Shall you be as cheerful among dangers afterwards, when one sword may cut down two happinesses ? "

"There is something in what you say, and I have thought of it," said Robert, sighing. "But I can't tell how it is ; but there is something in this uncertainty, this peril, this cloud before us, that makes it sweeter to love and to be loved than amid all seeming quiet and serenity. Really, I think, if there were to be no death, the beauty of life would be all tame. So we take our chance, or our dispensation of Providence, and are going to love, and to be married, just as confidently as if we were sure of living forever."

"Well, old fellow," said Septimius, with more cordiality and outgush of heart than he had felt for a long while, "there is no man whom I should be happier to call brother. Take Rose, and all happiness along with her. She is a good girl, and not in the least like me. May you live out your threescore years and ten, and every one of them be happy."

Little more passed, and Robert Hagburn took his leave with a hearty shake of Septimius's hand, too conscious of his own happiness to be quite sensible how much the latter was self-involved, strange, anxious, separated from healthy life and interests; and Septimius, as soon as Robert had disappeared, locked the door behind him, and proceeded at once to apply the silver key to the lock of the old strong box.

The lock resisted somewhat, being rusty, as might well be supposed after so many years since it was opened; but it finally allowed the key to turn, and Septimius, with a good deal of flutter at his heart, opened the lid. The interior had a very different aspect from that of the exterior; for, whereas the latter looked so old, this, having been kept from the air, looked about as new as when shut up from light and air two centuries ago, less or more. It was lined with ivory, beautifully carved in figures, according to the art which the mediæval people possessed in great perfection; and probably the box had been a lady's jewel-casket formerly, and had glowed with rich lustre and bright colors at former openings. But now there was nothing in it of that kind, — nothing in keeping with those figures carved in the ivory representing some mythical subjects, — nothing but some papers in the bottom of the box written over in an ancient hand, which Septimius at once fancied that he recognized as

that of the manuscript and recipe which he had found
on the breast of the young soldier. He eagerly seized
them, but was infinitely disappointed to find that they
did not seem to refer at all to the subjects treated by
the former, but related to pedigrees and genealogies,
and were in reference to an English family and some
member of it who, two centuries before, had crossed
the sea to America, and who, in this way, had sought
to preserve his connection with his native stock, so as
to be able, perhaps, to prove it for himself or his descendants ; and there was reference to documents and
records in England in confirmation of the genealogy.
Septimius saw that this paper had been drawn up by
an ancestor of his own, the unfortunate man who had
been hanged for witchcraft; but so earnest had been
his expectation of something different, that he flung
the old papers down with bitter indifference.

Then again he snatched them up, and contemptuously read them, — those proofs of descent through
generations of esquires and knights, who had been re-
nowned in war ; and there seemed, too, to be running
through the family a certain tendency to letters, for
three were designated as of the colleges of Oxford or
Cambridge ; and against one there was the note, " he
that sold himself to Sathan ; " and another seemed to
have been a follower of Wickliffe ; and they had murdered kings, and been beheaded, and banished, and
what not ; so that the age-long life of this ancient family had not been after all a happy or very prosperous one, though they had kept their estate, in one or
another descendant, since the Conquest. It was not
wholly without interest that Septimius saw that this
ancient descent, this connection with noble families,
and intermarriages with names, some of which he rec-

ognized as known in English history, all referred to his own family, and seemed to centre in himself, the last of a poverty - stricken line, which had dwindled down into obscurity, and into rustic labor and humble toil, reviving in him a little ; yet how little, unless he fulfilled his strange purpose. Was it not better worth his while to take this English position here so strangely offered him ? He had apparently slain unwittingly the only person who could have contested his rights, — the young man who had so strangely brought him the hope of unlimited life at the same time that he was making room for him among his forefathers. What a change in his lot would have been here, for there seemed to be some pretensions to a title, too, from a barony which was floating about and occasionally moving out of abeyancy !

"Perhaps," said Septimius to himself, "I may hereafter think it worth while to assert my claim to these possessions, to this position amid an ancient aristocracy, and try that mode of life for one generation. Yet there is something in my destiny incompatible, of course, with the continued possession of an estate. I must be, of necessity, a wanderer on the face of the earth, changing place at short intervals, disappearing suddenly and entirely ; else the foolish, short-lived multitude and mob of mortals will be enraged with one who seems their brother, yet whose countenance will never be furrowed with his age, nor his knees totter, nor his force be abated ; their little brevity will be rebuked by his age-long endurance, above whom the oaken roof-tree of a thousand years would crumble, while still he would be hale and strong. So that this house, or any other, would be but a resting-place of a day, and then I must away into another obscurity."

With almost a regret, he continued to look over the documents until he reached one of the persons recorded in the line of pedigree, — a worthy, apparently, of the reign of Elizabeth, to whom was attributed a title of Doctor in Utriusque Juris; and against his name was a verse of Latin written, for what purpose Septimius knew not, for, on reading it, it appeared to have no discoverable appropriateness; but suddenly he remembered the blotted and imperfect hieroglyphical passage in the recipe. He thought an instant, and was convinced this was the full expression and outwriting of that crabbed little mystery; and that here was part of that secret writing for which the Age of Elizabeth was so famous and so dexterous. His mind had a flash of light upon it, and from that moment he was enabled to read not only the recipe but the rules, and all the rest of that mysterious document, in a way which he had never thought of before; to discern that it was not to be taken literally and simply, but had a hidden process involved in it that made the whole thing infinitely deeper than he had hitherto deemed it to be. His brain reeled, he seemed to have taken a draught of some liquor that opened infinite depths before him, he could scarcely refrain from giving a shout of triumphant exultation, the house could not contain him, he rushed up to his hill-top, and there, after walking swiftly to and fro, at length flung himself on the little hillock, and burst forth, as if addressing him who slept beneath.

"O brother, O friend!" said he, "I thank thee for thy matchless beneficence to me; for all which I rewarded thee with this little spot on my hill-top. Thou wast very good, very kind. It would not have been well for thee, a youth of fiery joys and passions, loving to laugh, loving the lightness and sparkling brilliancy of life, to take this boon to thyself; for, O brother! I see, I see, it requires a strong spirit, capable of much lonely endurance, able to be sufficient to itself, loving not too much, dependent on no sweet ties of affection, to be capable of the mighty trial which now devolves on me. I thank thee, O kinsman! Yet thou, I feel, hast the better part, who didst so soon lie down to rest, who hast done forever with this troublesome world, which it is mine to contemplate from age to age, and to sum up the meaning of it. Thou art disporting thyself in other spheres. I enjoy the high, severe, fearful office of living here, and of being the minister of Providence from one age to many successive ones."

In this manner he raved, as never before, in a strain of exalted enthusiasm, securely treading on air, and sometimes stopping to shout aloud, and feeling as if he should burst if he did not do so; and his voice came back to him again from the low hills on the other side of the broad, level valley, and out of the woods afar, mocking him; or as if it were airy spirits, that knew how it was all to be, confirming his cry, saying "It shall be so," "Thou hast found it at last," "Thou art immortal." And it seemed as if Nature were inclined to celebrate his triumph over herself; for above the woods that crowned the hill to the northward, there were shoots and streams of radiance, a white, a red, a many-colored lustre, blazing up high towards the zenith, dancing up, flitting down, dancing up again; so that it seemed as if spirits were keeping a revel there. The leaves of the trees on the hill-side, all except the evergreens, had now mostly fallen with the autumn; so that Septimius was seen by the few pass-

ers-by, in the decline of the afternoon, passing to and
fro along his path, wildly gesticulating; and heard to
shout so that the echoes came from all directions to
answer him.   After nightfall, too, in the harvest moonlight, a shadow was still seen passing there, waving
its arms in shadowy triumph; so, the next day, there
were various goodly stories afloat and astir, coming
out of successive mouths, more wondrous at each birth;
the simplest form of the story being, that Septimius
Felton had at last gone raving mad on the hill-top
that he was so fond of haunting; and those who listened to his shrieks said that he was calling to the
Devil; and some said that by certain exorcisms he
had caused the appearance of a battle in the air, charg-
ing squadrons, cannon-flashes, champions encounter-
ing; all of which foreboded some real battle to be
fought with the enemies of the country; and as the
battle of Monmouth chanced to occur, either the very
next day, or about that time, this was supposed to be
either caused or foretold by Septimius's eccentricities;
and as the battle was not very favorable to our arms,
the patriotism of Septimius suffered much in popular
estimation.

But he knew nothing, thought nothing, cared nothing about his country, or his country's battles; he
was as sane as he had been for a year past, and was
wise enough, though merely by instinct, to throw off
some of his superfluous excitement by these wild gestures, with wild shouts, and restless activity; and when
he had partly accomplished this he returned to the
house, and, late as it was, kindled his fire, and began
anew the processes of chemistry, now enlightened by
the late teachings.   A new agent seemed to him to
mix itself up with his toil and to forward his pur-

pose; something helped him along; everything became facile to his manipulation, clear to his thought. In this way he spent the night, and when at sunrise he let in the eastern light upon his study, the thing was done.

Septimius had achieved it. That is to say, he had succeeded in amalgamating his materials so that they acted upon one another, and in accordance; and had produced a result that had a subsistence in itself, and a right to be; a something potent and substantial; each ingredient contributing its part to form a new essence, which was as real and individual as anything it was formed from. But in order to perfect it, there was necessity that the powers of nature should act quietly upon it through a month of sunshine; that the moon, too, should have its part in the production; and so he must wait patiently for this. Wait! surely he would! Had he not time for waiting? Were he to wait till old age, it would not be too much; for all future time would have it in charge to repay him.

So he poured the inestimable liquor into a glass vase, well secured from the air, and placed it in the sunshine, shifting it from one sunny window to another, in order that it might ripen; moving it gently lest he should disturb the living spirit that he knew to be in it. And he watched it from day to day, watched the reflections in it, watched its lustre, which seemed to him to grow greater day by day, as if it imbibed the sunlight into it. Never was there anything so bright as this. It changed its hue, too, gradually, being now a rich purple, now a crimson, now a violet, now a blue; going through all these prismatic colors without losing any of its brilliance, and never was there such a hue as the sunlight took in falling through

it and resting on his floor. And strange and beautiful it was, too, to look through this medium at the
outer world, and see how it was glorified and made
anew, and did not look like the same world, although
there were all its familiar marks. And then, past his
window, seen through this, went the farmer and his
wife, on saddle and pillion, jogging to meeting-house
or market; and the very dog, the cow coming home
from pasture, the old familiar faces of his childhood,
looked differently. And so at last, at the end of the
month, it settled into a most deep and brilliant crimson, as if it were the essence of the blood of the young
man whom he had slain ; the flower being now triumphant, it had given its own hue to the whole mass, and
had grown brighter every day ; so that it seemed to
have inherent light, as if it were a planet by itself, a
heart of crimson fire burning within it.

And when this had been done, and there was no
more change, showing that the digestion was perfect,
then he took it and placed it where the changing moon
would fall upon it; and then again he watched it,
covering it in darkness by day, revealing it to the
moon by night; and watching it here, too, through
more changes. And by and by he perceived that the
deep crimson hue was departing, — not fading ; we
cannot say that, because of the prodigious lustre which
still pervaded it, and was not less strong than ever ;
but certainly the hue became fainter, now a rose-color,
now fainter, fainter still, till there was only left the
purest whiteness of the moon itself ; a change that
somewhat disappointed and grieved Septimius, though
still it seemed fit that the water of life should be of no
one richness, because it must combine all. As the absorbed young man gazed through the lonely nights at

his beloved liquor, he fancied sometimes that he could see wonderful things in the crystal sphere of the vase; as in Doctor Dee's magic crystal used to be seen, which now lies in the British Museum ; representations, it might be, of things in the far past, or in the further future, scenes in which he himself was to act, persons yet unborn, the beautiful and the wise, with whom he was to be associated, palaces and towers, modes of hitherto unseen architecture, that old hall in England to which he had a hereditary right, with its gables, and its smooth lawn ; the witch-meetings in which his ancestor used to take part; Aunt Keziah on her death-bed ; and, flitting through all, the shade of Sibyl Dacy, eying him from secret nooks, or some remoteness, with her peculiar mischievous smile, beckoning him into the sphere. All such visions would he see, and then become aware that he had been in a dream, superinduced by too much watching, too intent thought; so that living among so many dreams, he was almost afraid that he should find himself waking out of yet another, and find that the vase itself and the liquid it contained were also dream-stuff. But no ; these were real.

There was one change that surprised him, although he accepted it without doubt, and, indeed, it did imply a wonderful efficacy, at least singularity, in the newly converted liquid. It grew strangely cool in temperature in the latter part of his watching it. It appeared to imbibe its coldness from the cold, chaste moon, until it seemed to Septimius that it was colder than ice itself ; the mist gathered upon the crystal vase as upon a tumbler of iced water in a warm room. Some say it actually gathered thick with frost, crystallized into a thousand fantastic and beautiful shapes, but this I do not know so well. Only it was very cold. Septimius pondered upon it, and thought he saw that life itself was cold, individual in its being, a high, pure essence, chastened from all heats ; cold, therefore, and therefore invigorating.

Thus much, inquiring deeply, and with painful research into the liquid which Septimius concocted, have I been able to learn about it, — its aspect, its properties ; and now I suppose it to be quite perfect, and that nothing remains but to put it to such use as he had so long been laboring for. But this, somehow or other, he found in himself a strong reluctance to do ; he paused, as it were, at the point where his pathway separated itself from that of other men, and meditated whether it were worth while to give up everything that Providence had provided, and take instead only this lonely gift of immortal life. Not that he ever really had any doubt about it ; no, indeed ; but it was his security, his consciousness that he held the bright sphere of all futurity in his hand, that made him dally a little, now that he could quaff immortality as soon as he liked.

Besides, now that he looked forward from the verge of mortal destiny, the path before him seemed so very lonely. Might he not seek some one own friend — one single heart — before he took the final step? There was Sibyl Dacy ! Oh, what bliss, if that pale girl might set out with him on his journey! how sweet, how sweet, to wander with her through the places else so desolate ! for he could but half see, half know things, without her to help him. And perhaps it might be so. She must already know, or strongly suspect, that he was engaged in some deep, mysterious research ; it might be that, with her sources of myste rious knowledge among her legendary lore, she knew of this. Then, oh, to think of those dreams which lovers have always had, when their new love makes the old earth seem so happy and glorious a place, that not a thousand nor an endless succession of years can exhaust it, — all those realized for him and her! If this could not be, what should he do? Would he venture onward into such a wintry futurity, symbolized, perhaps, by the coldness of the crystal goblet? He shivered at the thought.

Now, what had passed between Septimius and Sibyl Dacy is not upon record, only that one day they were walking together on the hill-top, or sitting by the little hillock, and talking earnestly together. Sibyl's face was a little flushed with some excitement, and really she looked very beautiful; and Septimius's dark face, too, had a solemn triumph in it that made him also beautiful; so rapt he was after all those watchings, and emaciations, and the pure, unworldly, self-denying life that he had spent. They talked as if there were some foregone conclusion on which they based what they said.

"Will you not be weary in the time that we shall spend together?" asked he.

"Oh no," said Sibyl, smiling, "I am sure that it will be very full of enjoyment."

"Yes," said Septimius, "though now I must remould my anticipations; for I have only dared, hitherto, to map out a solitary existence."

"And how did you do that?" asked Sibyl.

"Oh, there is nothing that would come amiss," answered Septimius; "for, truly, as I have lived apart from men, yet it is really not because I have no taste for whatever humanity includes: but I would fain, if

I might, live everybody's life at once, or, since that may not be, each in succession. I would try the life of power, ruling men ; but that might come later, after I had had long experience of men, and had lived through much history, and had seen, as a disinterested observer, how men might best be influenced for their own good. I would be a great traveller at first ; and as a man newly coming into possession of an estate goes over it, and views each separate field and wood-lot, and whatever features it contains, so will I, whose the world is, because I possess it forever ; whereas all others are but transitory guests. So will I wander over this world of mine, and be acquainted with all its shores, seas, rivers, mountains, fields, and the various peoples who inhabit them, and to whom it is my purpose to be a benefactor ; for think not, dear Sibyl, that I suppose this great lot of mine to have devolved upon me without great duties, — heavy and difficult to fulfil, though glorious in their adequate fulfilment. But for all this there will be time. In a century I shall partially have seen this earth, and known at least its boundaries, — have gotten for myself the outline, to be filled up hereafter."

"And I, too," said Sibyl, "will have my duties and labors ; for while you are wandering about among men, I will go among women, and observe and converse with them, from the princess to the peasant-girl ; and will find out what is the matter, that woman gets so large a share of human misery laid on her weak shoulders. I will see why it is that, whether she be a royal princess, she has to be sacrificed to matters of state, or a cottage-girl, still somehow the thing not fit for her is done ; and whether there is or no some deadly curse on woman, so that she has nothing to do, and nothing to enjoy, but only to be wronged by man, and still to love him, and despise herself for it, — to be shaky in her revenges. And then if, after all this investigation, it turns out — as I suspect — that woman is not capable of being helped, that there is something inherent in herself that makes it hopeless to struggle for her redemption, then what shall I do? Nay, I know not, unless to preach to the sisterhood that they all kill their female children as fast as they are born, and then let the generations of men manage as they can! Woman, so feeble and crazy in body, fair enough sometimes, but full of infirmities; not strong, with nerves prone to every pain; ailing, full of little weaknesses, more contemptible than great ones!"

"That would be a dreary end, Sibyl," said Septimius. "But I trust that we shall be able to hush up this weary and perpetual wail of womankind on easier terms than that. Well, dearest Sibyl, after we have spent a hundred years in examining into the real state of mankind, and another century in devising and putting in execution remedies for his ills, until our maturer thought has time to perfect his cure, we shall then have earned a little playtime, — a century of pastime, in which we will search out whatever joy can be had by thoughtful people, and that childlike sportiveness which comes out of growing wisdom, and enjoyment of every kind. We will gather about us everything beautiful and stately, a great palace, for we shall then be so experienced that all riches will be easy for us to get; with rich furniture, pictures, statues, and all royal ornaments; and side by side with this life we will have a little cottage, and see which is the happiest, for this has always been a dispute. For this century we will neither toil nor spin, nor think of anything beyond the day that is passing over us. There is time enough to do all that we have to do."

"A hundred years of play! Will not that be tiresome?" said Sibyl.

"If it is," said Septimius, "the next century shall make up for it; for then we will contrive deep philosophies, take up one theory after another, and find out its hollowness and inadequacy, and fling it aside, the rotten rubbish that they all are, until we have strewn the whole realm of human thought with the broken fragments, all smashed up. And then, on this great mound of broken potsherds (like that great Monte Testaccio, which we will go to Rome to see), we will build a system that shall stand, and by which mankind shall look far into the ways of Providence, and find practical uses of the deepest kind in what it has thought merely speculation. And then, when the hundred years are over, and this great work done, we will still be so free in mind, that we shall see the emptiness of our own theory, though men see only its truth. And so, if we like more of this pastime, then shall another and another century, and as many more as we like, be spent in the same way."

"And after that another play-day?" asked Sibyl Dacy.

"Yes," said Septimius, "only it shall not be called so; for the next century we will get ourselves made rulers of the earth; and knowing men so well, and having so wrought our theories of government and what not, we will proceed to execute them, — which will be as easy to us as a child's arrangement of its dolls. We will smile superior, to see what a facile thing it is to make a people happy. In our reign of

a hundred years, we shall have time to extinguish
errors, and make the world see the absurdity of them ;
to substitute other methods of government for the old,
bad ones ; to fit the people to govern itself, to do with
little government, to do with none ; and when this is
effected, we will vanish from our loving people, and
be seen no more, but be reverenced as gods, — we,
meanwhile, being overlooked, and smiling to ourselves,
amid the very crowd that is looking for us."

" I intend," said Sibyl, making this wild talk wilder
by that petulance which she so often showed, — " I
intend to introduce a new fashion of dress when I am
queen, and that shall be my part of the great reform
which you are going to make. And for my crown, I
intend to have it of flowers, in which that strange
crimson one shall be the chief ; and when I vanish,
this flower shall remain behind, and perhaps they shall
have a glimpse of me wearing it in the crowd. Well,
what next ? "

" After this," said Septimius, " having seen so much
of affairs, and having lived so many hundred years, I
will sit down and write a history, such as histories
ought to be, and never have been. And it shall be
so wise, and so vivid, and so self-evidently true, that
people shall be convinced from it that there is some
undying one among them, because only an eye-witness
could have written it, or could have gained so much
wisdom as was needful for it."

" And for my part in the history," said Sibyl, " I
will record the various lengths of women's waists, and
the fashion of their sleeves. What next ? "

" By this time," said Septimius, — " how many hundred years have we now lived ? — by this time, I shall
have pretty well prepared myself for what I have been

contemplating from the first. I will become a religious teacher, and promulgate a faith, and prove it by prophecies and miracles; for my long experience will enable me to do the first, and the acquaintance which I shall have formed with the mysteries of science will put the latter at my fingers' ends. So I will be a prophet, a greater than Mahomet, and will put all man's hopes into my doctrine, and make him good, holy, happy; and he shall put up his prayers to his Creator, and find them answered, because they shall be wise, and accompanied with effort. This will be a great work, and may earn me another rest and pastime."

[*He would see, in one age, the column raised in memory of some great deed of his in a former one.*]

"And what shall that be?" asked Sibyl Dacy.

"Why," said Septimius, looking askance at her, and speaking with a certain hesitation, " I have learned, Sibyl, that it is a weary toil for a man to be always good, holy, and upright. In my life as a sainted prophet, I shall have somewhat too much of this; it will be enervating and sickening, and I shall need another kind of diet. So, in the next hundred years, Sibyl, — in that one little century, — methinks I would fain be what men call wicked. How can I know my brethren, unless I do that once? I would experience all. Imagination is only a dream. I can imagine myself a murderer, and all other modes of crime; but it leaves no real impression on the heart. I must live these things."

[*The rampant unrestraint, which is the characteristic of wickedness.*]

"Good," said Sibyl, quietly; "and I too."

"And thou too!" exclaimed Septimius. "Not so,

Sibyl. I would reserve thee, good and pure, so that there may be to me the means of redemption, — some stable hold in the moral confusion that I will create around myself, whereby I shall by and by get back into order, virtue, and religion. Else all is lost, and I may become a devil, and make my own hell around me ; so, Sibyl, do thou be good forever, and not fall nor slip a moment. Promise me!"

"We will consider about that in some other century," replied Sibyl, composedly. "There is time enough yet. What next?"

"Nay, this is enough for the present," said Septimius. "New vistas will open themselves before us continually, as we go onward. How idle to think that one little lifetime would exhaust the world! After hundreds of centuries, I feel as if we might still be on the threshold. There is the material world, for instance, to perfect ; to draw out the powers of nature, so that man shall, as it were, give life to all modes of matter, and make them his ministering servants. Swift ways of travel, by earth, sea, and air ; machines for doing whatever the hand of man now does, so that we shall do all but put souls into our wheel-work and watch-work ; the modes of making night into day ; of getting control over the weather and the seasons ; the virtues of plants, — these are some of the easier things thou shalt help me do."

"I have no taste for that," said Sibyl, "unless I could make an embroidery worked of steel."

"And so, Sibyl," continued Septimius, pursuing his strain of solemn enthusiasm, intermingled as it was with wild, excursive vagaries, "we will go on as many centuries as we choose. Perhaps, — yet I think not so, — perhaps, however, in the course of lengthened time, we may find that the world is the same always, and mankind the same, and all possibilities of human fortune the same; so that by and by we shall discover that the same old scenery serves the world's stage in all ages, and that the story is always the same; yes, and the actors always the same, though none but we can be aware of it; and that the actors and spectators would grow weary of it, were they not bathed in forgetful sleep, and so think themselves new made in each successive lifetime. We may find that the stuff of the world's drama, and the passions which seem to play in it, have a monotony, when once we have tried them; that in only once trying them, and viewing them, we find out their secret, and that afterwards the show is too superficial to arrest our attention. As dramatists and novelists repeat their plots, so does man's life repeat itself, and at length grows stale. This is what, in my desponding moments, I have sometimes suspected. What to do, if this be so?"

"Nay, that is a serious consideration," replied Sibyl, assuming an air of mock alarm, "if you really think we shall be tired of life, whether or no."

"I do not think it, Sibyl," replied Septimius. "By much musing on this matter, I have convinced myself that man is not capable of debarring himself utterly from death, since it is evidently a remedy for many evils that nothing else would cure. This means that we have discovered of removing death to an indefinite distance is not supernatural; on the contrary, it is the most natural thing in the world, — the very perfection of the natural, since it consists in applying the powers and processes of Nature to the prolongation of the existence of man, her most perfect handiwork; and this could only be done by entire accordance and co-effort with Nature. Therefore Nature is not changed, and death remains as one of her steps, just as heretofore. Therefore, when we have exhausted the world, whether by going through its apparently vast variety, or by satisfying ourselves that it is all a repetition of one thing, we will call death as the friend to introduce us to something new."

[*He would write a poem, or other great work, inappreciable at first, and live to see it famous, — himself among his own posterity.*]

"Oh, insatiable love of life!" exclaimed Sibyl, looking at him with strange pity. "Canst thou not conceive that mortal brain and heart might at length be content to sleep?"

"Never, Sibyl!" replied Septimius, with horror. "My spirit delights in the thought of an infinite eternity. Does not thine?"

"One little interval — a few centuries only — of dreamless sleep," said Sibyl, pleadingly. "Cannot you allow me that?"

"I fear," said Septimius, "our identity would change in that repose; it would be a Lethe between the two parts of our being, and with such disconnection a continued life would be equivalent to a new one, and therefore valueless."

In such talk, snatching in the fog at the fragments of philosophy, they continued fitfully; Septimius calming down his enthusiasm thus, which otherwise might have burst forth in madness, affrighting the quiet little village with the marvellous things about which they mused. Septimius could not quite satisfy himself whether Sibyl Dacy shared in his belief of the success of his experiment, and was confident, as he was, that he held in his control the means of unlimited life ; neither was he sure that she loved him, — loved him well enough to undertake with him the long march that he propounded to her, making a union an affair of so vastly more importance than it is in the brief lifetime of other mortals. But he determined to let her drink the invaluable draught along with him, and to trust to the long future, and the better opportunities that time would give him, and his outliving all rivals, and the loneliness which an undying life would throw around her, without him, as the pledges of his success.

And now the happy day had come for the celebration of Robert Hagburn's marriage with pretty Rose Garfield, the brave with the fair ; and, as usual, the ceremony was to take place in the evening, and at the house of the bride ; and preparations were made accordingly : the wedding-cake, which the bride's own fair hands had mingled with her tender hopes, and seasoned it with maiden fears, so that its composition was as much ethereal as sensual ; and the neighbors and friends were invited, and came with their best wishes and good-will. For Rose shared not at all the distrust, the suspicion, or whatever it was, that had waited on the true branch of Septimius's family, in one shape or another, ever since the memory of man ; and all — except, it might be, some disappointed damsels who had hoped to win Robert Hagburn for themselves — rejoiced at the approaching union of this fit couple, and wished them happiness.

Septimius, too, accorded his gracious consent to the union, and while he thought within himself that such a brief union was not worth the trouble and feeling which

his sister and her lover wasted on it, still he wished
them happiness. As he compared their brevity with
his long duration, he smiled at their little fancies of
loves, of which he seemed to see the end ; the flower
of a brief summer, blooming beautifully enough, and
shedding its leaves, the fragrance of which would linger a little while in his memory, and then be gone.
He wondered how far in the coming centuries he
should remember this wedding of his sister Rose ; perhaps he would meet, five hundred years hence, some
descendant of the marriage, — a fair girl, bearing the
traits of his sister's fresh beauty ; a young man, recalling the strength and manly comeliness of Robert
Hagburn, — and could claim acquaintance and kindred. He would be the guardian, from generation to
generation, of this race ; their ever-reappearing friend
at times of need ; and meeting them from age to age,
would find traditions of himself growing poetical in
the lapse of time ; so that he would smile at seeing his
features look so much more majestic in their fancies
than in reality. So all along their course, in the history of the family, he would trace himself, and by his
traditions he would make them acquainted with all
their ancestors, and so still be warmed by kindred
blood.

And Robert Hagburn, full of the life of the moment, warm with generous blood, came in a new uniform, looking fit to be the founder of a race who
should look back to a hero sire. He greeted Septimius as a brother. The minister, too, came, of course,
and mingled with the throng, with decorous aspect,
and greeted Septimius with more formality than he
had been wont ; for Septimius had insensibly withdrawn himself from the minister's intimacy, as he got

deeper and deeper into the enthusiasm of his own cause. Besides, the minister did not fail to see that his once devoted scholar had contracted habits of study into the secrets of which he himself was not admitted, and that he no longer alluded to studies for the ministry; and he was inclined to suspect that Septimius had unfortunately allowed infidel ideas to assail, at least, if not to overcome, that fortress of firm faith, which he had striven to found and strengthen in his mind, — a misfortune frequently befalling speculative and imaginative and melancholic persons, like Septimius, whom the Devil is all the time planning to assault, because he feels confident of having a traitor in the garrison. The minister had heard that this was the fashion of Septimius's family, and that even the famous divine, who, in his eyes, was the glory of it, had had his season of wild infidelity in his youth, before grace touched him; and had always thereafter, throughout his long and pious life, been subject to seasons of black and sulphurous despondency, during which he disbelieved the faith which, at other times, he preached powerfully."

"Septimius, my young friend," said he, "are you yet ready to be a preacher of the truth?"

"Not yet, reverend pastor," said Septimius, smiling at the thought of the day before, that the career of a prophet would be one that he should some time assume. "There will be time enough to preach the truth when I better know it."

"You do not look as if you knew it so well as formerly, instead of better," said his reverend friend, looking into the deep furrows of his brow, and into his wild and troubled eyes.

"Perhaps not," said Septimius. "There is time yet."

These few words passed amid the bustle and murmur of the evening, while the guests were assembling, and all were awaiting the marriage with that interest which the event continually brings with it, common as it is, so that nothing but death is commoner. Everybody congratulated the modest Rose, who looked quiet and happy; and so she stood up at the proper time, and the minister married them with a certain fervor and individual application, that made them feel they were married indeed. Then there ensued a salutation of the bride, the first to kiss her being the minister, and then some respectable old justices and farmers, each with his friendly smile and joke. Then went round the cake and wine, and other good cheer, and the hereditary jokes with which brides used to be assailed in those days. I think, too, there was a dance, though how the couples in the reel found space to foot it in the little room, I cannot imagine; at any rate, there was a bright light out of the windows, gleaming across the road, and such a sound of the babble of numerous voices and merriment, that travellers passing by, on the lonely Lexington road, wished they were of the party; and one or two of them stopped and went in, and saw the new-made bride, drank to her health, and took a piece of the wedding-cake home to dream upon.

[*It is to be observed that Rose had requested of her friend, Sibyl Dacy, to act as one of her bridesmaids, of whom she had only the modest number of two; and the strange girl declined, saying that her intermeddling would bring ill-fortune to the marriage.*]

"Why do you talk such nonsense, Sibyl?" asked Rose. "You love me, I am sure, and wish me well; and your smile, such as it is, will be the promise of prosperity, and I wish for it on my wedding-day."

"I am an ill-fate, a sinister demon, Rose; a thing that has sprung out of a grave; and you had better not entreat me to twine my poison tendrils round your destinies. You would repent it."

"Oh, hush, hush!" said Rose, putting her hand over her friend's mouth. "Naughty one! you can bless me, if you will, only you are wayward."

"Bless you, then, dearest Rose, and all happiness on your marriage!"

Septimius had been duly present at the marriage, and kissed his sister with moist eyes, it is said, and a solemn smile, as he gave her into the keeping of Robert Hagburn; and there was something in the words he then used that afterwards dwelt on her mind, as if they had a meaning in them that asked to be sought into, and needed reply.

"There, Rose," he had said, "I have made myself ready for my destiny. I have no ties any more, and may set forth on my path without scruple."

"Am I not your sister still, Septimius?" said she, shedding a tear or two.

"A married woman is no sister; nothing but a married woman till she becomes a mother; and then what shall I have to do with you?"

He spoke with a certain eagerness to prove his case, which Rose could not understand, but which was probably to justify himself in severing, as he was about to do, the link that connected him with his race, and making for himself an exceptional destiny, which, if it did not entirely insulate him, would at least create new relations with all. There he stood, poor fellow, looking on the mirthful throng, not in exultation, as might have been supposed, but with a strange sadness upon him. It seemed to him, at that final moment,

as if it were Death that linked together all; yes, and
so gave the warmth to all. Wedlock itself seemed a
brother of Death; wedlock, and its sweetest hopes, its
holy companionship, its mysteries, and all that warm
mysterious brotherhood that is between men; passing
as they do from mystery to mystery in a little gleam
of light; that wild, sweet charm of uncertainty and
temporariness, — how lovely it made them all, how innocent, even the worst of them; how hard and prosaic
was his own situation in comparison to theirs. He
felt a gushing tenderness for them, as if he would
have flung aside his endless life, and rushed among
them, saying, —

"Embrace me! I am still one of you, and will not
leave you! Hold me fast!"

After this it was not particularly observed that both
Septimius and Sibyl Dacy had disappeared from the
party, which, however, went on no less merrily without them. In truth, the habits of Sibyl Dacy were so
wayward, and little squared by general rules, that nobody wondered or tried to account for them; and as
for Septimius, he was such a studious man, so little
accustomed to mingle with his fellow-citizens on any
occasion, that it was rather wondered at that he should
have spent so large a part of a sociable evening with
them, than that he should now retire.

After they were gone the party received an unexpected addition, being no other than the excellent
Doctor Portsoaken, who came to the door, announcing
that he had just arrived on horseback from Boston,
and that, his object being to have an interview with
Sibyl Dacy, he had been to Robert Hagburn's house
in quest of her; but, learning from the old grand
mother that she was here, he had followed.

Not finding her, he evinced no alarm, but was easily induced to sit down among the merry company, and partake of some brandy, which, with other liquors. Robert had provided in sufficient abundance; and that being a day when man had not learned to fear the glass, the doctor found them all in a state of hilarious chat. Taking out his German pipe, he joined the group of smokers in the great chimney-corner, and entered into conversation with them, laughing and joking, and mixing up his jests with that mysterious suspicion which gave so strange a character to his intercourse.

"It is good fortune, Mr. Hagburn," quoth he, "that brings me here on this auspicious day. And how has been my learned young friend Dr. Septimius, — for so he should be called, — and how have flourished his studies of late? The scientific world may look for great fruits from that decoction of his."

"He'll never equal Aunt Keziah for herb-drinks," said an old woman, smoking her pipe in the corner, "though I think likely he'll make a good doctor enough by and by. Poor Kezzy, she took a drop too much of her mixture, after all. I used to tell her how it would be; for Kezzy and I were pretty good friends once, before the Indian in her came out so strongly, — the squaw and the witch, for she had them both in her blood, poor yellow Kezzy!"

"Yes! had she indeed?" quoth the doctor; "and I have heard an odd story, that if the Feltons chose to go back to the old country, they'd find a home and an estate there ready for them."

The old woman mused, and puffed at her pipe. "Ah, yes," muttered she, at length, "I remember to have heard something about that; and how, if Felton chose to strike into the woods, he'd find a tribe of wild Indians there ready to take him for their sagamore, and conquer the whites; and how, if he chose to go to England, there was a great old house all ready for him, and a fire burning in the hall, and a dinner-table spread, and the tall - posted bed ready, with clean sheets, in the best chamber, and a man waiting at the gate to show him in. Only there was a spell of a bloody footstep left on the threshold by the last that came out, so that none of his posterity could ever cross it again. But that was all nonsense!"

"Strange old things one dreams in a chimney-corner," quoth the doctor. "Do you remember any more of this?"

"No, no; I'm so forgetful nowadays," said old Mrs. Hagburn; "only it seems as if I had my memories in my pipe, and they curl up in smoke. I've known these Feltons all along, or it seems as if I had; for I'm nigh ninety years old now, and I was two year old in the witch's time, and I have seen a piece of the halter that old Felton was hung with."

Some of the company laughed.

"That must have been a curious sight," quoth the doctor.

"It is not well," said the minister seriously to the doctor, "to stir up these old remembrances, making the poor old lady appear absurd. I know not that she need to be ashamed of showing the weaknesses of the generation to which she belonged; but I do not like to see old age put at this disadvantage among the young."

"Nay, my good and reverend sir," returned the doctor, "I mean no such disrespect as you seem to think. Forbid it, ye upper powers, that I should cast any ridicule on beliefs, — superstitions, do you call them? — that are as worthy of faith, for aught I know, as any that are preached in the pulpit. If the old lady would tell me any secret of the old Felton's science, I shall treasure it sacredly; for I interpret these stories about his miraculous gifts as meaning that he had a great command over natural science, the virtues of plants, the capacities of the human body."

While these things were passing, or before they passed, or some time in that eventful night, Septimius had withdrawn to his study, when there was a low tap at the door, and, opening it, Sibyl Dacy stood before him. It seemed as if there had been a previous arrangement between them; for Septimius evinced no surprise, only took her hand and drew her in.

"How cold your hand is!" he exclaimed. "Nothing is so cold, except it be the potent medicine. It makes me shiver."

"Never mind that," said Sibyl. "You look frightened at me."

"Do I?" said Septimius. "No, not that; but this is such a crisis; and methinks it is not yourself. Your eyes glare on me strangely."

"Ah, yes; and you are not frightened at me? Well, I will try not to be frightened at myself. Time was, however, when I should have been."

She looked round at Septimius's study, with its few old books, its implements of science, crucibles, retorts, and electrical machines; all these she noticed little; but on the table drawn before the fire, there was something that attracted her attention; it was a vase that seemed of crystal, made in that old fashion in which the Venetians made their glasses, — a most pure kind of glass, with a long stalk, within which was a curved elaboration of fancy-work, wreathed and twisted. This old glass was an heirloom of the Feltons, a relic that had come down with many traditions, bringing its frail fabric safely through all the perils of time, that had shattered empires; and, if space sufficed, I could tell many stories of this curious vase, which was said, in its time, to have been the instrument both of the Devil's sacrament in the forest, and of the Christian in the village meeting-house. But, at any rate, it had been a part of the choice household gear of one of Septimius's ancestors, and was engraved with his arms, artistically done.

"Is that the drink of immortality?" said Sibyl.

"Yes, Sibyl," said Septimius. "Do but touch the goblet; see how cold it is."

She put her slender, pallid fingers on the side of the goblet, and shuddered, just as Septimius did when he touched her hand.

"Why should it be so cold?" said she, looking at Septimius.

"Nay, I know not, unless because endless life goes round the circle and meets death, and is just the same with it. O Sibyl, it is a fearful thing that I have accomplished! Do you not feel it so? What if this shiver should last us through eternity?"

"Have you pursued this object so long," said Sibyl, "to have these fears respecting it now? In that case, methinks I could be bold enough to drink it alone, and look down upon you, as I did so, smiling at your fear to take the life offered you."

"I do not fear," said Septimius; "but yet I acknowledge there is a strange, powerful abhorrence in me towards this draught, which I know not how to account for, except as the reaction, the revulsion of feeling, consequent upon its being too long overstrained in one direction. I cannot help it. The meannesses, the littlenesses, the perplexities, the general irksomeness of life, weigh upon me strangely. Thou didst refuse to drink with me. That being the case, methinks I could break the jewelled goblet now, untasted, and choose the grave as the wiser part."

"The beautiful goblet! What a pity to break it!" said Sibyl, with her characteristic malign and mysterious smile. "You cannot find it in your heart to do it."

"I could, — I can. So thou wilt not drink with me?"

"Do you know what you ask?" said Sibyl. "I am a being that sprung up, like this flower, out of a grave; or, at least, I took root in a grave, and, growing there, have twined about your life, until you cannot possibly escape from me. Ah, Septimius! you know me not. You know not what is in my heart towards you. Do you remember this broken miniature? would you wish to see the features that were destroyed when that bullet passed? Then look at mine!"

"Sibyl! what do you tell me? Was it you — were they your features — which that young soldier kissed as he lay dying?"

"They were," said Sibyl. "I loved him, and gave him that miniature, and the face they represented. I had given him all, and you slew him."

"Then you hate me," whispered Septimius.

"Do you call it hatred?" asked Sibyl, smiling. "Have I not aided you, thought with you, encouraged you, heard all your wild ravings when you dared to tell no one else? kept up your hopes; suggested; helped you with my legendary lore to useful hints;

helped you, also, in other ways, which you do not suspect? And now you ask me if I hate you. Does this
look like it?"

"No," said Septimius. "And yet, since first I knew
you, there has been something whispering me of harm,
as if I sat near some mischief. There is in me the
wild, natural blood of the Indian, the instinctive, the
animal nature, which has ways of warning that civilized life polishes away and cuts out; and so, Sibyl,
never did I approach you, but there were reluctances,
drawings back, and, at the same time, a strong impulse to come closest to you; and to that I yielded.
But why, then, knowing that in this grave lay the man
you loved, laid there by my hand, — why did you aid
me in an object which you must have seen was the
breath of my life?"

"Ah, my friend, — my enemy, if you will have it
so, — are you yet to learn that the wish of a man's inmost heart is oftenest that by which he is ruined and
made miserable? But listen to me, Septimius. No
matter for my earlier life; there is no reason why I
should tell you the story, and confess to you its weakness, its shame. It may be, I had more cause to hate
the tenant of that grave, than to hate you who unconsciously avenged my cause; nevertheless, I came here
in hatred, and desire of revenge, meaning to lie in
wait, and turn your dearest desire against you, to eat
into your life, and distil poison into it, I sitting on
this grave, and drawing fresh hatred from it; and at
last, in the hour of your triumph, I meant to make the
triumph mine."

"Is this still so?" asked Septimius, with pale lips;
"or did your fell purpose change?"

"Septimius, I am weak, — a weak, weak girl, —

only a girl, Septimius; only eighteen yet," exclaimed Sibyl. "It is young, is it not? I might be forgiven much. You know not how bitter my purpose was to you. But look, Septimius, — could it be worse than this? Hush, be still! Do not stir!"

She lifted the beautiful goblet from the table, put it to her lips, and drank a deep draught from it; then, smiling mockingly, she held it towards him.

"See; I have made myself immortal before you. Will you drink?"

He eagerly held out his hand to receive the goblet, but Sibyl, holding it beyond his reach a moment, deliberately let it fall upon the hearth, where it shivered into fragments, and the bright, cold water of immortality was all spilt, shedding its strange fragrance around.

"Sibyl, what have you done?" cried Septimius in rage and horror.

"Be quiet! See what sort of immortality I win by it, — then, if you like, distil your drink of eternity again, and quaff it."

"It is too late, Sibyl; it was a happiness that may never come again in a lifetime. I shall perish as a dog does. It is too late!"

"Septimius," said Sibyl, who looked strangely beautiful, as if the drink, giving her immortal life, had likewise the potency to give immortal beauty answering to it, "listen to me. You have not learned all the secrets that lay in those old legends, about which we have talked so much. There were two recipes, discovered or learned by the art of the studious old Gaspar Felton. One was said to be that secret of immortal life which so many old sages sought for, and which some were said to have found; though, if that were the case, it is strange some of them have not lived till our day. Its essence lay in a certain rare flower, which, mingled properly with other ingredients of great potency in themselves, though still lacking the crowning virtue till the flower was supplied, produced the drink of immortality."

"Yes, and I had the flower, which I found in a grave," said Septimius, "and distilled the drink which you have spilt."

"You had a flower, or what you called a flower," said the girl. "But, Septimius, there was yet another drink, in which the same potent ingredients were used; all but the last. In this, instead of the beautiful flower, was mingled the semblance of a flower, but really a baneful growth out of a grave. This I sowed there, and it converted the drink into a poison, famous in old science, — a poison which the Borgias used, and Mary de Medicis, — and which has brought to death many a famous person, when it was desirable to his enemies. This is the drink I helped you to distil. It brings on death with pleasant and delightful thrills of the nerves. O Septimius, Septimius, it is worth while to die, to be so blest, so exhilarated as I am now."

"Good God, Sibyl, is this possible?"

"Even so, Septimius. I was helped by that old physician, Doctor Portsoaken, who, with some private purpose of his own, taught me what to do; for he was skilled in all the mysteries of those old physicians, and knew that their poisons at least were efficacious, whatever their drinks of immortality might be. But the end has not turned out as I meant. A girl's fancy is so shifting, Septimius. I thought I loved that youth in the grave yonder; but it was you I loved, — and I am dying. Forgive me for my evil purposes, for I am dying."

"Why hast thou spilt the drink?" said Septimius, bending his dark brows upon her, and frowning over her. "We might have died together."

"No, live, Septimius," said the girl, whose face appeared to grow bright and joyous, as if the drink of death exhilarated her like an intoxicating fluid. "I would not let you have it, not one drop. But to think," and here she laughed, "what a penance, — what months of wearisome labor thou hast had, — and what thoughts, what dreams, and how I laughed in my sleeve at them all the time! Ha, ha, ha! Then thou didst plan out future ages, and talk poetry and prose to me. Did I not take it very demurely, and answer thee in the same style? and so thou didst love me, and kindly didst wish to take me with thee in thy immortality. O Septimius, I should have liked it well! Yes, latterly, only, I knew how the case stood. Oh, how I surrounded thee with dreams, and instead of giving thee immortal life, so kneaded up the little life allotted thee with dreams and vaporing stuff, that thou didst not really live even that. Ah, it was a pleasant pastime, and pleasant is now the end of it. Kiss me, thou poor Septimius, one kiss!"

[*She gives the ridiculous aspect to his scheme, in an airy way.*]

But as Septimius, who seemed stunned, instinctively bent forward to obey her, she drew back. "No, there shall be no kiss! There may a little poison linger on my lips. Farewell! Dost thou mean still to seek for thy liquor of immortality? — ah, ah! It was a good jest. We will laugh at it when we meet in the other world."

And here poor Sibyl Dacy's laugh grew fainter, and dying away, she seemed to die with it; for there she

was, with that mirthful, half-malign expression still on
her face, but motionless; so that however long Septimius's life was likely to be, whether a few years
or many centuries, he would still have her image in
his memory so. And here she lay among his broken
hopes, now shattered as completely as the goblet which
held his draught, and as incapable of being formed
again.

The next day, as Septimius did not appear, there
was research for him on the part of Doctor Portsoaken.
His room was found empty, the bed untouched. Then
they sought him on his favorite hill-top; but neither
was he found there, although something was found
that added to the wonder and alarm of his disappearance. It was the cold form of Sibyl Dacy, which was
extended on the hillock so often mentioned, with her
arms thrown over it; but, looking in the dead face,
the beholders were astonished to see a certain malign
and mirthful expression, as if some airy part had been
played out, — some surprise, some practical joke of
a peculiarly airy kind had burst with fairy shoots of
fire among the company.

"Ah, she is dead! Poor Sibyl Dacy!" exclaimed
Doctor Portsoaken. "Her scheme, then, has turned
out amiss."

This exclamation seemed to imply some knowledge
of the mystery; and it so impressed the auditors,
among whom was Robert Hagburn, that they thought
it not inexpedient to have an investigation; so the
learned doctor was not uncivilly taken into custody and
examined. Several interesting particulars, some of
which throw a certain degree of light on our narrative,
were discovered. For instance, that Sibyl Dacy, who

was a niece of the doctor, had been beguiled from her home and led over the sea by Cyril Norton, and that the doctor, arriving in Boston with another regiment, had found her there, after her lover's death. Here there was some discrepancy or darkness in the doctor's narrative. He appeared to have consented to, or instigated (for it was not quite evident how far his concurrence had gone) this poor girl's scheme of going and brooding over her lover's grave, and living in close contiguity with the man who had slain him. The doctor had not much to say for himself on this point ; but there was found reason to believe that he was acting in the interest of some English claimant of a great estate that was left without an apparent heir by the death of Cyril Norton, and there was even a suspicion that he, with his fantastic science and antiquated empiricism, had been at the bottom of the scheme of poisoning, which was so strangely intertwined with Septimius's notion, in which he went so nearly crazed, of a drink of immortality. It was observable, however, that the doctor — such a humbug in scientific matters, that he had perhaps bewildered himself — seemed to have a sort of faith in the efficacy of the recipe which had so strangely come to light, provided the true flower could be discovered ; but that flower, according to Doctor Portsoaken, had not been seen on earth for many centuries, and was banished probably forever. The flower, or fungus, which Septimius had mistaken for it, was a sort of earthly or devilish counterpart of it, and was greatly in request among the old poisoners for its admirable uses in their art. In fine, no tangible evidence being found against the worthy doctor, he was permitted to depart, and disappeared from the neighborhood, to the scandal of many people, unhanged; leaving behind him few available effects beyond the web and empty skin of an enormous spider.

As to Septimius, he returned no more to his cottage by the wayside, and none undertook to tell what had become of him; crushed and annihilated, as it were, by the failure of his magnificent and most absurd dreams. Rumors there have been, however, at various times, that there had appeared an American claimant, who had made out his right to the great estate of Smithell's Hall, and had dwelt there, and left posterity, and that in the subsequent generation an ancient baronial title had been revived in favor of the son and heir of the American. Whether this was our Septimius, I cannot tell; but I should be rather sorry to believe that after such splendid schemes as he had entertained, he should have been content to settle down into the fat substance and reality of English life, and die in his due time, and be buried like any other man.

A few years ago, while in England, I visited Smithell's Hall, and was entertained there, not knowing at the time that I could claim its owner as my countryman by descent; though, as I now remember, I was struck by the thin, sallow, American cast of his face, and the lithe slenderness of his figure, and seem now (but this may be my fancy) to recollect a certain Indian glitter of the eye and cast of feature.

As for the Bloody Footstep, I saw it with my own eyes, and will venture to suggest that it was a mere natural reddish stain in the stone, converted by superstition into a Bloody Footstep.

APPENDIX.

THE ANCESTRAL FOOTSTEP

THE ANCESTRAL FOOTSTEP:

OUTLINES OF AN ENGLISH ROMANCE.

INTRODUCTORY NOTE.

"SEPTIMIUS FELTON" was the outgrowth of a project, formed by Hawthorne during his residence in England, of writing a romance, the scene of which should be laid in that country; but this project was afterwards abandoned, giving place to a new conception in which the visionary search for means to secure an earthly immortality was to form the principal interest. The new conception took shape in the uncompleted "Dolliver Romance." The two themes, of course, were distinct, but, by a curious process of thought, one grew directly out of the other: the whole history constitutes, in fact, a chapter in what may be called the genealogy of a romance. There remained, after "Septimius Felton" had been published, certain manuscripts connected with the scheme of an English story. One of these manuscripts was written in the form of a journalized narrative; the author merely noting the date of what he wrote, as he went along. The other was a more extended sketch, of much greater bulk, and without date, but probably produced several years later. It was not originally intended by those who at the time had charge of Hawthorne's papers that either of these incomplete writings should be laid before the public; because they manifestly had not been left by him in a form which he would have considered as warranting such a course. But since the second and larger manuscript has been published under the title of "Dr. Grimshawe's Secret," it has been thought best to issue the present sketch, so that the two documents may be examined together. Their appearance places in the hands of readers the entire process of development leading to the "Septimius" and "The Dolliver Romance." They speak for themselves much more efficiently than any commentator can expect to do; and little, therefore, remains to be said beyond a few words of explanation in regard to the following pages.

The Note-Books show that the plan of an English romance, turning upon the fact that an emigrant to America had carried away a family secret which should give his descendant the power to ruin the family in the mother country, had occurred to Hawthorne as early as April, 1855. In August of the same year he visited Smithell's Hall, in Bolton le Moors, concerning which he had already heard its legend of "The Bloody Footstep," and from that time on, the idea of this footprint on the threshold-stone of the ancestral mansion seems to have associated itself inextricably with the dreamy substance of his yet unshaped romance. Indeed, it leaves its mark broadly upon Sibyl Dacy's wild legend in "Septimius Felton," and reappears in the last paragraph of that story. But, so far as we can know at this day, nothing definite was done until after his departure for Italy. It was then, while staying in Rome, that he began to put upon paper that plot which had first occupied his thoughts three years before, in the scant leisure allowed him by his duties at the Liverpool consulate. Of leisure there was not a great deal at Rome, either; for, as the "French and Italian Note-Books" show, sight-seeing and social intercourse took up a good deal of his time, and the daily record in his journal likewise had to be kept up. But he set to work resolutely to embody, so far as he might, his stray imaginings upon the haunting English theme, and to give them connected form. April 1, 1858, he began; and then nearly two weeks passed before he found an opportunity to resume; April 13th being the date of the next passage. By May he gets fully into swing, so that day after day, with but slight breaks, he carries on the story, always increasing in interest for us who read as for him who improvised. Thus it continues until May 19th, by which time he has made a tolerably complete outline, filled in with a good deal of detail here and there. Although the sketch is cast in the form of a regular narrative, one or two gaps occur, indicating that the author had thought out certain points which he then took for granted without making note of them. Brief scenes, passages of conversation and of narration, follow one another after the manner of a finished story, alternating with synopses of the plot, and queries concerning particulars that needed further study; confidences of the romancer to himself which form certainly a valuable contribution to literary history. The manuscript closes with a rapid sketch of the conclusion, and the way in which it is to be executed. Succinctly, what we have here is a romance in embryo; one, moreover, that never attained to a viable stature and constitution. During his lifetime it naturally would not have been put forward as demanding public attention; and, in consideration of that fact, it has since been withheld from the press by the decision of his daughter, in whom the title to it vests. Students of literary art, however, and many more general readers will, I think, be likely to discover in it a charm all the greater for its being in parts only indicated; since, as it stands, it presents the precise condition of a work of fiction in its first stage. The unfinished "Grimshawe" was another development of the same theme, and the "Septimius" a later sketch, with a new element introduced. But the present experimental fragment, to which it has been decided to give the title of "The Ancestral Footstep," possesses a freshness and spontaneity recalling the peculiar fascination of those chalk or pencil outlines with which great masters in the graphic art have been wont to arrest their fleeting glimpses of a composition still unwrought.

It would not be safe to conclude, from the large amount

of preliminary writing done with a view to that romance, that Hawthorne always adopted this laborious mode of making several drafts of a book. On the contrary, it is understood that his habit was to mature a design so thoroughly in his mind before attempting to give it actual existence on paper that but little rewriting was needed. The circumstance that he was obliged to write so much that did not satisfy him in this case may account partly for his relinquishing the theme, as one which for him had lost its seductiveness through too much recasting.

It need be added only that the original manuscript, from which the following pages are printed through the medium of an exact copy, is singularly clear and fluent. Not a single correction occurs throughout; but here and there a word is omitted, obviously by mere accident, and these omissions have been supplied. The correction in each case is marked by brackets, in this printed reproduction. The sketch begins abruptly; but there is no reason to suppose that anything preceded it except the unrecorded musings in the author's mind, and one or two memoranda in the "English Note-Books." We must therefore imagine the central figure, Middleton, who is the American descendant of an old English family, as having been properly introduced, and then pass at once to the opening sentences. The rest will explain itself. G. P. L.

THE ANCESTRAL FOOTSTEP.

OUTLINES OF AN ENGLISH ROMANCE.

I.

APRIL 1, 1858. *Thursday.*—He had now been travelling long in those rich portions of England where he would most have wished to find the object of his pursuit; and many had been the scenes which he would willingly have identified with that mentioned in the ancient, time-yellowed record which he bore about with him. It is to be observed that, undertaken at first half as the amusement, the unreal object, of a grown man's play-day, it had become more and more real to him with every step of the way that he followed it up; along those green English lanes it seemed as if everything would bring him close to the mansion that he sought; every morning he went on with renewed hopes, nor did the evening, though it brought with it no success, bring with it the gloom and heaviness of a real disappointment. In all his life, including its earliest and happiest days, he had never known such a spring and zest as now filled his veins, and gave lightsomeness to his limbs; this spirit gave to the beautiful country which he trod a still richer beauty than it had ever borne, and he sought his ancient home as if he had found his way into Paradise and were there endeavoring to trace out the sight [site] of Eve's bridal bower, the birthplace of the human race and its glorious possibilities of happiness and high performance.

In these sweet and delightful moods of mind, varying from one dream to another, he loved indeed the solitude of his way; but likewise he loved the facility which his pursuit afforded him, of coming in contact with many varieties of

men, and he took advantage of this facility to an extent
which it was not usually his impulse to do. But now he
came forth from all reserves, and offered himself to whom-
ever the chances of the way offered to him, with a ready
sensibility that made its way through every barrier that even
English exclusiveness, in whatever rank of life, could set
up. The plastic character of Middleton was perhaps a variety of American nature only presenting itself under an
individual form; he could throw off the man of our day,
and put on a ruder nature, but then it was with a certain
fineness, that made this only [a] distinction between it and
the central truth. He found less variety of form in the English character than he had been accustomed to see at home;
but perhaps this was in consequence of the external nature
of his acquaintance with it; for the view of one well accustomed to a people, and of a stranger to them, differs in this
— that the latter sees the homogeneity, the one universal
character, the groundwork of the whole, while the former
sees a thousand little differences, which distinguish the individual men apart, to such a degree that they seem hardly to
have any resemblance among themselves.

But just at the period of his journey when we take him
up, Middleton had been for two or three days the companion of an old man who interested him more than most of
his wayside companions; the more especially as he seemed
to be wandering without an object, or with such a dreamy
object as that which led Middleton's own steps onward. He
was a plain old man enough, but with a pale, strong-featured
face and white hair, a certain picturesqueness and venerableness, which Middleton fancied might have befitted a richer
garb than he now wore. In much of their conversation,
too, he was sensible that, though the stranger betrayed no
acquaintance with literature, nor seemed to have conversed
with cultivated minds, yet the results of such acquaintance
and converse were here. Middleton was inclined to think
him, however, an old man, one of those itinerants, such as

Wordsworth represented in the " Excursion," who smooth themselves by the attrition of the world and gain a knowledge equivalent to or better than that of books from the actual intellect of man awake and active around them.

Often, during the short period since their companionship originated, Middleton had felt impelled to disclose to the old man the object of his journey, and the wild tale by which, after two hundred years, he had been blown as it were across the ocean, and drawn onward to commence this search. The old man's ordinary conversation was of a nature to draw forth such a confidence as this ; frequently turning on the traditions of the wayside ; the reminiscences that lingered on the battle-fields of the Roses, or of the Parliament, like flowers nurtured by the blood of the slain, and prolonging their race through the centuries for the wayfarer to pluck them ; or the family histories of the castles, manor-houses, and seats which, of various epochs, had their park-gates along the roadside and would be seen with dark gray towers or ancient gables, or more modern forms of architecture, rising up among clouds of ancient oaks. Middleton watched earnestly to see if, in any of these tales, there were circumstances resembling those striking and singular ones which he had borne so long in his memory, and on which he was now acting in so strange a manner ; but [though] there was a good deal of variety of incident in them, there never was any combination of incidents having the peculiarity of this.

" I suppose," said he to the old man, " the settlers in my country may have carried away with them traditions long since forgotten in this country, but which might have an interest and connection, and might even piece out the broken relics of family history, which have remained perhaps a mystery for hundreds of years. I can conceive, even, that this might be of importance in settling the heirships of estates; but which now, only the two insulated parts of the story being known, remain a riddle, although the solution of it is actually in the world, if only these two parts could be united across the sea, like the wires of an electric telegraph."

"It is an impressive idea," said the old man. "Do you know any such tradition as you have hinted at?"

April 13th. — Middleton could not but wonder at the singular chance that had established him in such a place, and in such society, so strangely adapted to the purposes with which he had been wandering through England. He had come hither, hoping as it were to find the past still alive and in action; and here it was so in this one only spot, and these few persons into the midst of whom he had suddenly been cast. With these reflections he looked forth from his window into the old-fashioned garden, and at the stone sundial, which had numbered all the hours — all the daylight and serene ones, at least — since his mysterious ancestor left the country. And [is] this, then, he thought to himself, the establishment of which some rumor had been preserved? Was it here that the secret had its hiding-place in the old coffer, in the cupboard, in the secret chamber, or whatever was indicated by the apparently idle words of the document which he had preserved? He still smiled at the idea, but it was with a pleasant, mysterious sense that his life had at last got out of the dusty real, and that strangeness had mixed itself up with his daily experience.

With such feelings he prepared himself to go down to dinner with his host. He found him alone at table, which was placed in a dark old room modernized with every English comfort and the pleasant spectacle of a table set with the whitest of napery and the brightest of glass and china. The friendly old gentleman, as he had found him from the first, became doubly and trebly so in that position which brings out whatever warmth of heart an Englishman has, and gives it to him if he has none. The impressionable and sympathetic character of Middleton answered to the kindness of his host; and by the time the meal was concluded, the two were conversing with almost as much zest and friendship as if they were similar in age, even fellow-countrymen, and had known one another all their life-time. Middleton's secret, it may be supposed, came often to the tip of his tongue; but still he kept it within, from a natural repugnance to bring out the one romance of his life. The talk, however, necessarily ran much upon topics among which this one would have come in without any extra attempt to introduce it.

"This decay of old families," said the Master, "is much greater than would appear on the surface of things. We have such a reluctance to part with them, that we are content to see them continued by any fiction, through any indirections, rather than to dispense with old names. In your country, I suppose, there is no such reluctance; you are willing that one generation should blot out all that preceded it, and be itself the newest and only age of the world."

"Not quite so," answered Middleton; "at any rate, if there be such a feeling in the people at large, I doubt whether, even in England, those who fancy themselves possessed of claims to birth, cherish them more as a treasure than we do. It is, of course, a thousand times more difficult for us to keep alive a name amid a thousand difficulties sedulously thrown around it by our institutions, than for you to do, where your institutions are anxiously calculated to promote the contrary purpose. It has occasionally struck me, however, that the ancient lineage might often be found in America, for a family which has been compelled to prolong itself here through the female line, and through alien stocks."

"Indeed, my young friend," said the Master, "if that be the case, I should like to [speak?] further with you upon it; for, I can assure you, there are sometimes vicissitudes in old families that make me grieve to think that a man cannot be made for the occasion."

All this while, the young lady at table had remained almost silent; and Middleton had only occasionally been reminded of her by the necessity of performing some of those

offices which put people at table under a Christian necessity
of recognizing one another. He was, to say the truth, somewhat interested in her, yet not strongly attracted by the
neutral tint of her dress, and the neutral character of her
manners. She did not seem to be handsome, although, with
her face full before him, he had not quite made up his mind
on this point.

April 14th. — So here was Middleton, now at length seeing indistinctly a thread, to which the thread that he had so
long held in his hand — the hereditary thread that ancestor
after ancestor had handed down — might seem ready to join
on. He felt as if they were the two points of an electric
chain, which being joined, an instantaneous effect must follow. Earnestly, as he would have looked forward to this
moment (had he in sober reason ever put any real weight
on the fantasy in pursuit of which he had wandered so far)
he now, that it actually appeared to be realizing itself,
paused with a vague sensation of alarm. The mystery was
evidently one of sorrow, if not of crime, and he felt as if
that sorrow and crime might not have been annihilated even
by being buried out of human sight and remembrance so
long. He remembered to have heard or read, how that
once an old pit had been dug open, in which were found the
remains of persons that, as the shuddering by-standers traditionally remembered, had died of an ancient pestilence;
and out of that old grave had come a new plague, that slew
the far-off progeny of those who had first died by it. Might
not some fatal treasure like this, in a moral view, be brought
to light by the secret into which he had so strangely been
drawn? Such were the fantasies with which he awaited the
return of Alice, whose light footsteps sounded afar along the
passages of the old mansion; and then all was silent.

At length he heard the sound, a great way off, as he concluded, of her returning footstep, approaching from chamber
to chamber, and along the staircases, closing the doors behind her. At first, he paid no great attention to the char-

acter of these sounds, but as they drew nearer, he became
aware that the footstep was unlike those of Alice; indeed, as
unlike as could be, very regular, slow, yet not firm, so that
it seemed to be that of an aged person, sauntering listlessly
through the rooms. We have often alluded to Middleton's
sensitiveness, and the quick vibrations of his sympathies;
and there was something in this slow approach that produced
a strange feeling within him; so that he stood breathlessly,
looking towards the door by which these slow footsteps were
to enter. At last, there appeared in the doorway a venerable figure, clad in a rich, faded dressing-gown, and standing on the threshold looked fixedly at Middleton, at the
same time holding up a light in his left hand. In his right
was some object that Middleton did not distinctly see. But
he knew the figure, and recognized the face. It was the old
man, his long since companion on the journey hitherward.

"So," said the old man, smiling gravely, "you have
thought fit, at last, to accept the hospitality which I offered
you so long ago. It might have been better for both of us
— for all parties — if you had accepted it then!"

"You here!" exclaimed Middleton. "And what can
be your connection with all the error and trouble, and involuntary wrong, through which I have wandered since our
last meeting? And is it possible that you even then held
the clue which I was seeking?"

"No, — no," replied Rothermel. "I was not conscious,
at least, of so doing. And yet had we two sat down there
by the wayside, or on that English stile, which attracted
your attention so much; had we sat down there and thrown
forth each his own dream, each his own knowledge, it would
have saved much that we must now forever regret. Are
you even now ready to confide wholly in me?"

"Alas," said Middleton, with a darkening brow, "there
are many reasons, at this moment, which did not exist then,
to incline me to hold my peace. And why has not Alice
returned? — and what is your connection with her?"

"Let her answer for herself," said Rothermel; and he called her, shouting through the silent house as if she were at the furthest chamber, and he were in instant need: "Alice!—Alice!—Alice!—here is one who would know what is the link between a maiden and her father!"

Amid the strange uproar which he made Alice came flying back, not in alarm but only in haste, and put her hand within his own. "Hush, father," said she. "It is not time."

Here is an abstract of the plot of this story. The Middleton who emigrated to America, more than two hundred years ago, had been a dark and moody man; he came with a beautiful though not young woman for his wife, and left a family behind him. In this family a certain heirloom had been preserved, and with it a tradition that grew wilder and stranger with the passing generations. The tradition had lost, if it ever had, some of its connecting links; but it referred to a murder, to the expulsion of a brother from the hereditary house, in some strange way, and to a Bloody Footstep which he had left impressed into the threshold, as he turned about to make a last remonstrance. It was rumored, however, or vaguely understood, that the expelled brother was not altogether an innocent man; but that there had been wrong done, as well as crime committed, insomuch that his reasons were strong that led him, subsequently, to imbibe the most gloomy religious views, and to bury himself in the Western wilderness. These reasons he had never fully imparted to his family; but had necessarily made allusions to them, which had been treasured up and doubtless enlarged upon. At last, one descendant of the family determines to go to England, with the purpose of searching out whatever ground there may be for these traditions, carrying with him certain ancient documents, and other relics; and goes about the country, half in earnest, and half in sport of fancy, in quest of the old family mansion. He makes singular discoveries, all of which bring the book to an end unexpected by everybody, and not satisfactory to the natural yearnings of novel readers. In the traditions that he brought over, there was a key to some family secrets that were still unsolved, and that controlled the descent of estates and titles. His influence upon these matters involves [him] in divers strange and perilous adventures; and at last it turns out that he himself is the rightful heir to the titles and estate, that had passed into another name within the last half-century. But he respects both, feeling that it is better to make a virgin soil than to try to make the old name grow in a soil that had been darkened with so much blood and misfortune as this.

April 27th. Tuesday. — It was with a delightful feeling of release from ordinary rules, that Middleton found himself brought into this connection with Alice; and he only hoped that this play-day of his life might last long enough to rest him from all that he had suffered. In the enjoyment of his position he almost forgot the pursuit that occupied him, nor might he have remembered for a long space if, one evening, Alice herself had not alluded to it. " You are wasting precious days," she suddenly said. " Why do not you renew your quest ? "

" To what do you allude ? " said Middleton, in surprise. " What object do you suppose me to have ? "

Alice smiled ; nay, laughed outright. " You suppose yourself to be a perfect mystery, no doubt," she replied. " But do not I know you — have not I known you long — as the holder of the talisman, the owner of the mysterious cabinet that contains the blood-stained secret ? "

" Nay, Alice, this is certainly a strange coincidence, that you should know even thus much of a foolish secret that makes me employ this little holiday time, which I have stolen out of a weary life, in a wild-goose chase. But, believe me, you allude to matters that are more a mystery to me than my affairs appear to be to you. Will you explain what you would suggest by this badinage ? "

Alice shook her head. "You have no claim to know what I know, even if it would be any addition to your own knowledge. I shall not, and must not enlighten you. You must burrow for the secret with your own tools, in your own manner, and in a place of your own choosing. I am bound not to assist you."

"Alice, this is wilful, wayward, unjust," cried Middleton, with a flushed cheek. "I have not told you — yet you know well — the deep and real importance which this subject has for me. We have been together as friends, yet, the instant when there comes up an occasion when the slightest friendly feeling would induce you to do me a good office, you assume this altered tone."

"My tone is not in the least altered in respect to you," said Alice. "All along, as you know, I have reserved myself on this very point; it being, I candidly tell you, impossible for me to act in your interest in the matter alluded to. If you choose to consider this unfriendly, as being less than the terms on which you conceive us to have stood give you a right to demand of me — you must resent it as you please. I shall not the less retain for you the regard due to one who has certainly befriended me in very untoward circumstances."

This conversation confirmed the previous idea of Middleton, that some mystery of a peculiarly dark and evil character was connected with the family secret with which he was himself entangled; but it perplexed him to imagine in what way this, after the lapse of so many years, should continue to be a matter of real importance at the present day. All the actors in the original guilt — if guilt it were — must have been long ago in their graves; some in the churchyard of the village, with those moss-grown letters embossing their names; some in the church itself, with mural tablets recording their names over the family-pew, and one, it might be, far over the sea, where his grave was first made under the forest leaves, though now a city had grown up around it. Yet here was he, the remote descendant of that family, setting his foot at last in the country, and as secretly as might be ; and all at once his mere presence seemed to revive the buried secret, almost to awake the dead who partook of that secret and had acted it. There was a vibration from the other world, continued and prolonged into this, the instant that he stepped upon the mysterious and haunted ground.

He knew not in what way to proceed. He could not but feel that there was something not exactly within the limits of propriety in being here, disguised — at least, not known in his true character — prying into the secrets of a proud and secluded Englishman. But then, as he said to himself on his own side of the question, the secret belonged to himself by exactly as ancient a tenure and by precisely as strong a claim, as to the Englishman. His rights here were just as powerful and well-founded as those of his ancestor had been, nearly three centuries ago ; and here the same feeling came over him that he was that very personage, returned after all these ages, to see if his foot would fit this bloody footstep left of old upon the threshold. The result of all his cogitation was, as the reader will have foreseen, that he decided to continue his researches, and, his proceedings being pretty defensible, let the result take care of itself.

For this purpose he went next day to the hospital, and ringing at the Master's door, was ushered into the old-fashioned, comfortable library, where he had spent that well-remembered evening which threw the first ray of light on the pursuit that now seemed developing into such strange and unexpected consequences. Being admitted, he was desired by the domestic to wait, as his Reverence was at that moment engaged with a gentleman on business. Glancing through the ivy that mantled over the window, Middleton saw that this interview was taking place in the garden, where the Master and his visitor were walking to and fro in the avenue of box, discussing some matter, as it seemed to him, with considerable earnestness on both sides. He observed, too, that there was warmth, passion, a disturbed feeling on the stranger's part; while, on that of the Master, it was a calm, serious, earnest representation of whatever view he was endeavoring to impress on the other. At last, the interview appeared to come toward a climax, the Master addressing some words to his guest, still with undisturbed calmness, to which the latter replied by a violent and even fierce gesture, as it should seem of menace, not towards the Master, but some unknown party; and then hastily turning, he left the garden and was soon heard riding away. The Master looked after him awhile, and then, shaking his white head, returned into the house and soon entered the parlor.

He looked somewhat surprised, and, as it struck Middleton, a little startled, at finding him there; yet he welcomed him with all his former cordiality — indeed, with a friendship that thoroughly warmed Middleton's heart even to its coldest corner.

" This is strange ! " said the old gentleman. " Do you remember our conversation on that evening when I first had the unlooked-for pleasure of receiving you as a guest into my house? At that time I spoke to you of a strange family story, of which there was no denouement, such as a novelwriter would desire, and which had remained in that unfinished posture for more than two hundred years ! Well; perhaps it will gratify you to know that there seems a prospect of that wanting termination being supplied ! "

" Indeed ! " said Middleton.

" Yes," replied the Master. " A gentleman has just parted with me who was indeed the representative of the family concerned in the story. He is the descendant of a younger son of that family, to whom the estate devolved about a century ago, although at that time there was search for the heirs of the elder son, who had disappeared after the bloody incident which I related to you. Now, singular as it may appear, at this late day, a person claiming to be the descendant and heir of that eldest son has appeared, and if I may credit my friend's account, is disposed not only to claim the estate, but the dormant title which Eldredge himself has been so long preparing to claim for himself. Singularly enough, too, the heir is an American."

May 2d, Sunday. — "I believe," said Middleton, "that many English secrets might find their solution in America, if the two threads of a story could be brought together, disjoined as they have been by time and the ocean. But are you at liberty to tell me the nature of the incidents to which you allude?"

"I do not see any reason to the contrary," answered the Master; "for the story has already come in an imperfect way before the public, and the full and authentic particulars are likely soon to follow. It seems that the younger brother was ejected from the house on account of a love affair; the elder having married a young woman with whom the younger was in love, and, it is said, the wife disappeared on the bridal night, and was never heard of more. The elder brother remained single during the rest of his life; and dying childless, and there being still no news of the second brother, the inheritance and representation of the family devolved upon the third brother and his posterity. This branch of the family has ever since remained in possession; and latterly the representation has become of more importance, on account of a claim to an old title, which, by the failure of another branch of this ancient family, has devolved upon the branch here settled. Now, just at this juncture, comes another heir from America, pretending that he is the descendant of a marriage between the second son, supposed to have been murdered on the threshold of the manor-house, and the missing bride! Is it not a singular story?"

"It would seem to require very strong evidence to prove

it," said Middleton. "And methinks a Republican should care little for the title, however he might value the estate."

"Both — both," said the Master, smiling, "would be equally attractive to your countryman. But there are further curious particulars in connection with this claim. You must know, they are a family of singular characteristics, humorists, sometimes developing their queer traits into something like insanity; though oftener, I must say, spending stupid hereditary lives here on their estates, rusting out and dying without leaving any biography whatever about them. And yet there has always been one very queer thing about this generally very commonplace family. It is that each father, on his death-bed, has had an interview with his son, at which he has imparted some secret that has evidently had an influence on the character and after life of the son, making him ever after a discontented man, aspiring for something he has never been able to find. Now the American, I am told, pretends that he has the clue which has always been needed to make the secret available; the key whereby the lock may be opened; the something that the lost son of the family carried away with him, and by which through these centuries he has impeded the progress of the race. And, wild as the story seems, he does certainly seem to bring something that looks very like the proof of what he says."

"And what are those proofs?" inquired Middleton, wonder-stricken at the strange reduplication of his own position and pursuits.

"In the first place," said the Master, "the English marriage-certificate by a clergyman of that day in London, after publication of the banns, with a reference to the register of the parish church where the marriage is recorded. Then, a certified genealogy of the family in New England, where such matters can be ascertained from town and church records, with at least as much certainty, it would appear, as in this country. He has likewise a manuscript in his ancestor's autograph, containing a brief account of the events which banished him from his own country; the circumstances which favored the idea that he had been slain, and which he himself was willing should be received as a belief; the fortune that led him to America, where he wished to found a new race wholly disconnected with the past; and this manuscript he sealed up, with directions that it should not be opened till two hundred years after his death, by which time, as it was probable to conjecture, it would matter little to any mortal whether the story was told or not. A whole generation has passed since the time when the paper was at last unsealed and read, so long it had no operation; yet now, at last, here comes the American, to disturb the succession of an ancient family!"

"There is something very strange in all this," said Middleton.

And indeed there was something stranger in his view of the matter than he had yet communicated to the Master. For, taking into consideration the relation in which he found himself with the present recognized representative of the family, the thought struck him that his coming hither had dug up, as it were, a buried secret that immediately assumed life and activity the moment that it was above ground again. For seven generations the family had vegetated in the quietude of English country gentility, doing nothing to make itself known, passing from the cradle to the tomb amid the same old woods that had waved over it before his ancestor had impressed the bloody footstep; and yet the instant that he came back, an influence seemed to be at work that was likely to renew the old history of the family. He questioned with himself whether it were not better to leave all as it was; to withdraw himself into the secrecy from which he had but half emerged, and leave the family to keep on, to the end of time perhaps, in its rusty innocence, rather than to interfere with his wild American character to disturb it. The smell of that dark crime — that brotherly hatred and attempted murder — seemed to breathe out of the ground as he dug it up. Was it not better that it should remain forever buried, for what to him was this old English title — what this estate, so far from his own native land, located amidst feelings and manners which would never be his own? It was late, to be sure — yet not too late for him to turn back: the vibration, the fear, which his footsteps had caused, would subside into peace! Meditating in this way, he took a hasty leave of the kind old Master, promising to see him again at an early opportunity. By chance, or however it was, his footsteps turned to the woods of —— Chace, and there he wandered through its glades, deep in thought, yet always with a strange sense that he was treading on the soil where his ancestors had trodden, and where he himself had best right of all men to be. It was just in this state of feeling that he found his course arrested by a hand upon his shoulder.

"What business have you here?" was the question sounded in his ear; and, starting, he found himself in the grasp, as his blood tingled to know, of a gentleman in a shooting-dress, who looked at him with a wrathful brow. "Are you a poacher, or what?"

Be the case what it might, Middleton's blood boiled at the grasp of that hand, as it never before had done in the course of his impulsive life. He shook himself free, and stood fiercely before his antagonist, confronting him with his uplifted stick, while the other, likewise, appeared to be shaken by a strange wrath.

"Fellow," muttered he — "Yankee blackguard! — impostor — take yourself off these grounds. Quick, or it will be the worse for you!"

Middleton restrained himself. "Mr. Eldredge," said he, "for I believe I speak to the man who calls himself owner of this land on which we stand, — Mr. Eldredge, you are acting under a strange misapprehension of my character. I have come hither with no sinister purpose, and am entitled, at the hands of a gentleman, to the consideration of an honorable antagonist, even if you deem me one at all. And perhaps, if you think upon the blue chamber and the ebony cabinet, and the secret connected with it," —

"Villain, no more!" said Eldredge; and utterly mad with rage, he presented his gun at Middleton; but even at the moment of doing so, he partly restrained himself, so far as, instead of shooting him, to raise the butt of his gun, and strike a blow at him. It came down heavily on Middleton's shoulder, though aimed at his head; and the blow was terribly avenged, even by itself, for the jar caused the hammer to come down; the gun went off, sending the bullet downwards through the heart of the unfortunate man, who fell dead upon the ground. Eldredge [1] stood stupefied, looking at the catastrophe which had so suddenly occurred.

May 3d, Monday. — So here was the secret suddenly made safe in this so terrible way; its keepers reduced from two parties to one interest; the other who alone knew of this age-long mystery and trouble now carrying it into eternity, where a long line of those who partook of the knowledge, in each successive generation, might now be waiting to inquire of him how he had held his trust. He had kept it well, there was no doubt of it; for there he lay dead upon the ground, having betrayed it to no one, though by a method which none could have foreseen, the whole had come into the possession of him who had brought hither but half of it. Middleton looked down in horror upon the form that had just been so full of life and wrathful vigor — and now lay so quietly. Being wholly unconscious of any purpose to bring about the catastrophe, it had not at first struck him that his own position was in any manner affected by the violent death, under such circumstances, of the unfortunate man. But now it suddenly occurred to him, that there had been a train of incidents all calculated to make him the object of suspicion; and he felt that he could not, under the

[1] Evidently a slip of the pen: Middleton being intended.

English administration of law, be suffered to go at large without rendering a strict account of himself and his relations with the deceased. He might, indeed, fly; he might still remain in the vicinity, and possibly escape notice. But was not the risk too great? Was it just even to be aware of this event, and not relate fully the manner of it, lest a suspicion of blood-guiltiness should rest upon some innocent head? But while he was thus cogitating, he heard footsteps approaching along the wood-path; and half-impulsively, half on purpose, he stept aside into the shrubbery, but still where he could see the dead body, and what passed near it.

The footsteps came on, and at the turning of the path, just where Middleton had met Eldredge, the new-comer appeared in sight. It was Hoper, in his usual dress of velveteen, looking now seedy, poverty-stricken, and altogether in ill-case, trudging moodily along, with his hat pulled over his brows, so that he did not see the ghastly object before him till his foot absolutely trod upon the dead man's hand. Being thus made aware of the proximity of the corpse, he started back a little, yet evincing such small emotion as did credit to his English reserve; then uttering a low exclamation, — cautiously low, indeed, — he stood looking at the corpse a moment or two, apparently in deep meditation. He then drew near, bent down, and without evincing any horror at the touch of death in this horrid shape, he opened the dead man's vest, inspected the wound, satisfied himself that life was extinct, and then nodded his head and smiled gravely. He next proceeded to examine seriatim the dead man's pockets, turning each of them inside out and taking the contents, where they appeared adapted to his needs: for instance, a silken purse, through the interstices of which some gold was visible; a watch, which however had been injured by the explosion, and had stopt just at the moment — twenty-one minutes past five — when the catastrophe took place. Hoper ascertained, by putting the watch to his ear, that this was the case; then pocketing it, he continued his researches. He likewise secured a note-book, on examining which he found several bank-notes, and some other papers. And having done this, the thief stood considering what to do next; nothing better occurring to him, he thrust the pockets back, gave the corpse as nearly as he could the same appearance that it had worn before he found it, and hastened away, leaving the horror there on the wood-path.

He had been gone only a few minutes when another step, a light woman's step, [was heard] coming along the pathway, and Alice appeared, having on her usual white mantle, straying along with that fearlessness which characterized her so strangely, and made her seem like one of the denizens of nature. She was singing in a low tone some one of those airs which have become so popular in England, as negro melodies; when suddenly, looking before her, she saw the blood-stained body on the grass, the face looking ghastly upward. Alice pressed her hand upon her heart; it was not her habit to scream, not the habit of that strong, wild, self-dependent nature; and the exclamation which broke from her was not for help, but the voice of her heart crying out to herself. For an instant she hesitated, as [if] not knowing what to do; then approached, and with her white, maiden hand felt the brow of the dead man, tremblingly, but yet firm, and satisfied herself that life had wholly departed. She pressed her hand, that had just touched the dead man's, on her forehead, and gave a moment to thought.

What her decision might have been, we cannot say, for while she stood in this attitude, Middleton stept from his seclusion, and at the noise of his approach she turned suddenly round, looking more frightened and agitated than at the moment when she had first seen the dead body. She faced Middleton, however, and looked him quietly in the eye. " You see this ! " said she, gazing fixedly at him. " It is not at this moment that you first discover it."

"No," said Middleton, frankly. " It is not. I was present at the catastrophe. In one sense, indeed, I was the cause of it; but, Alice, I need not tell you that I am no murderer."

"A murderer? — no," said Alice, still looking at him with the same fixed gaze. "But you and this man were at deadly variance. He would have rejoiced at any chance that would have laid you cold and bloody on the earth, as he is now; nay, he would most eagerly have seized on any fair-looking pretext that would have given him a chance to stretch you there. The world will scarcely believe, when it knows all about your relations with him, that his blood is not on your hand. Indeed," said she, with a strange smile, "I see some of it there now!"

And, in very truth, so there was; a broad blood-stain that had dried on Middleton's hand. He shuddered at it, but essayed vainly to rub it off.

"You see," said she. "It was foreordained that you should shed this man's blood; foreordained that, by digging into that old pit of pestilence, you should set the contagion loose again. You should have left it buried forever. But now what do you mean to do?"

"To proclaim this catastrophe," replied Middleton. "It is the only honest and manly way. What else can I do?"

"You can and ought to leave him on the wood-path, where he has fallen," said Alice, "and go yourself to take advantage of the state of things which Providence has brought about. Enter the old house, the hereditary house, where — now, at least — you alone have a right to tread. Now is the hour. All is within your grasp. Let the wrong of three hundred years be righted, and come back thus to your own, to these hereditary fields, this quiet, long-descended home; to title, to honor."

Yet as the wild maiden spoke thus, there was a sort of mockery in her eyes; on her brow; gleaming through all her face, as if she scorned what she thus pressed upon him, the spoils of the dead man who lay at their feet. Middleton, with his susceptibility, could not [but] be sensible of a wild and strange charm, as well as horror, in the situation; it seemed such a wonder that here, in formal, orderly, well-governed England, so wild a scene as this should have occurred; that they too [two?] should stand here, deciding on the descent of an estate, and the inheritance of a title, holding a court of their own.

"Come, then, " said he, at length. "Let us leave this poor fallen antagonist in his blood, and go whither you will lead me. I will judge for myself. At all events, I will not leave my hereditary home without knowing what my power is."

"Come," responded Alice; and she turned back; but then returned and threw a handkerchief over the dead man's face, which while they spoke had assumed that quiet, ecstatic expression of joy which often is observed to overspread the faces of those who die of gunshot wounds, however fierce the passion in which the spirits took their flight. With this strange, grand, awful joy did the dead man gaze upward into the very eyes and hearts, as it were, of the two that now bent over him. They looked at one another.

"Whence comes this expression?" said Middleton, thoughtfully. "Alice, methinks he is reconciled to us now; and that we are members of one reconciled family, all of whom are in heaven but me."

Tuesday, May 4th. — "How strange is this whole situation between you and me," said Middleton, as they went up the winding pathway that led towards the house. "Shall I ever understand it? Do you mean ever to explain it to me? That I should find you here with that old man,[1] so mysteri-

---

[1] The allusion here is apparently to the old man who proclaims himself Alice's father, in the portion dated April 14th. He figures hereafter as the old Hospitaller, Hammond. The reader must not take this present passage as referring to the death of Eldredge, which has just taken place in the preceding section. The author is now beginning to elaborate the relation of Middleton and Alice. As will be seen, farther on, the death of Eldredge is ignored and abandoned; Eldredge is revived, and the story proceeds in another way. — G. P. L.

ous, apparently so poor, yet so powerful! What [is] his relation to you?"

"A close one," replied Alice sadly. "He was my father!"

"Your father!" repeated Middleton, starting back. "It does but heighten the wonder! Your father! And yet, by all the tokens that birth and breeding, and habits of thought and native character can show, you are my country-woman. That wild, free spirit was never born in the breast of an Englishwoman; that slight frame, that slender beauty, that frail envelopment of a quick, piercing, yet stubborn and patient spirit, — are those the properties of an English maiden?"

"Perhaps not," replied Alice quietly. "I am your coun-trywoman. My father was an American, and one of whom you have heard — and no good, alas! — for many a year."

"And who then was he?" asked Middleton.

"I know not whether you will hate me for telling you," replied Alice, looking him sadly though firmly in the face. "There was a man — long years since, in your childhood — whose plotting brain proved the ruin of himself and many another; a man whose great designs made him a sort of potentate, whose schemes became of national importance, and produced results even upon the history of the country in which he acted. That man was my father; a man who sought to do great things, and, like many who have had sim-ilar aims, disregarded many small rights, strode over them, on his way to effect a gigantic purpose. Among other men, your father was trampled under foot, ruined, done to death, even, by the effects of his ambition."

"How is it possible!" exclaimed Middleton. "Was it Wentworth?"

"Even so," said Alice, still with the same sad calmness and not withdrawing her steady eyes from his face. "After his ruin; after the catastrophe that overwhelmed him and hundreds more, he took to flight; guilty, perhaps, but guilty as a fallen conqueror is; guilty to such an extent that he ceased to be a cheat, as a conqueror ceases to be a murderer. He came to England. My father had an original nobility of nature; and his life had not been such as to debase it, but rather such as to cherish and heighten that self-esteem which at least keeps the possessor of it from many meaner vices. He took nothing with him; nothing beyond the bare means of flight, with the world before him, although thousands of gold would not have been missed out of the scattered fragments of ruin that lay around him. He found his way hither, led, as you were, by a desire to reconnect himself with the place whence his family had originated; for he, too, was of a race which had something to do with the ancient story which has now been brought to a close. Arrived here, there were circumstances that chanced to make his talents and habits of business available to this Mr. Eldredge, a man ignorant and indolent, unknowing how to make the best of the property that was in his hands. By degrees, he took the estate into his management, acquiring necessarily a preponderating influence over such a man."

"And you," said Middleton. "Have you been all along in England? For you must have been little more than an infant at the time."

"A mere infant," said Alice, "and I remained in our own country under the care of a relative who left me much to my own keeping; much to the influences of that wild culture which the freedom of our country gives to its youth. It is only two years that I have been in England."

"This, then," said Middleton thoughtfully, "accounts for much that has seemed so strange in the events through which we have passed; for the knowledge of my identity and my half-defined purpose which has always glided before me, and thrown so many strange shapes of difficulty in my path. But whence, — whence came that malevolence which your father's conduct has so unmistakably shown? I had done him no injury, though I had suffered much."

"I have often thought," replied Alice, "that my father,

though retaining a preternatural strength and acuteness of
intellect, was really not altogether sane. And, besides, he
had made it his business to keep this estate, and all the
complicated advantages of the representation of this old
family, secure to the person who was deemed to have inherited them. A succession of ages and generations might be
supposed to have blotted out your claims from existence;
for it is not just that there should be no term of time which
can make security for lack of fact and a few formalities.
At all events, he had satisfied himself that his duty was to
act as he has done."

"Be it so! I do not seek to throw blame on him," said
Middleton. "Besides, Alice, he was your father!"

"Yes," said she, sadly smiling; "let him [have] what
protection that thought may give him, even though I lose
what he may gain. And now here we are at the house.
At last, come in! It is your own; there is none that can
longer forbid you!"

They entered the door of the old mansion, now a farm-
house, and there were its old hall, its old chambers, all before them. They ascended the staircase, and stood on the
landing-place above; while Middleton had again that feeling that had so often made him dizzy, — that sense of being
in one dream and recognizing the scenery and events of a
former dream. So overpowering was this feeling, that he
laid his hand on the slender arm of Alice, to steady himself; and she comprehended the emotion that agitated him,
and looked into his eyes with a tender sympathy, which she
had never before permitted to be visible, — perhaps never
before felt. He steadied himself and followed her till they
had entered an ancient chamber, but one that was finished
with all the comfortable luxury customary to be seen in
English homes.

"Whither have you led me now?" inquired Middleton.

"Look round," said Alice. "Is there nothing here that
you ought to recognize? — nothing that you kept the memory of, long ago?"

He looked round the room again and again, and at last, in a somewhat shadowy corner, he espied an old cabinet made of ebony and inlaid with pearl; one of those tall, stately, and elaborate pieces of furniture that are rather articles of architecture than upholstery; and on which a higher skill, feeling, and genius than now is ever employed on such things, was expended. Alice drew near the stately cabinet and threw wide the doors, which, like the portals of a palace, stood between two pillars; it all seemed to be unlocked, showing within some beautiful old pictures in the panel of the doors, and a mirror, that opened a long succession of mimic halls, reflection upon reflection, extending to an interminable nowhere.

"And what is this?" said Middleton, — "a cabinet? Why do you draw my attention so strongly to it?"

"Look at it well," said she. "Do you recognize nothing there? Have you forgotten your description? The stately palace with its architecture, each pillar with its architecture, those pilasters, that frieze; you ought to know them all. Somewhat less than you imagined in size, perhaps; a fairy reality, inches for yards; that is the only difference. And you have the key?"

And there then was that palace, to which tradition, so false at once and true, had given such magnitude and magnificence in the traditions of the Middleton family, around their shifting fireside in America. Looming afar through the mists of time, the little fact had become a gigantic vision. Yes, here it was in miniature, all that he had dreamed of; a palace of four feet high!

"You have the key of this palace," said Alice; "it has waited — that is, its secret and precious chamber has, for you to open it, these three hundred years. Do you know how to find that secret chamber?"

Middleton, still in that dreamy mood, threw open an inner door of the cabinet, and applying the old-fashioned key at his watch-chain to a hole in the mimic pavement within, pressed one of the mosaics, and immediately the whole floor of the apartment sank, and revealed a receptacle within. Alice had come forward eagerly, and they both looked into the hiding-place, expecting what should be there. It was empty! They looked into each other's faces with blank astonishment. Everything had been so strangely true, and so strangely false, up to this moment, that they could not comprehend this failure at the last moment. It was the strangest, saddest jest! It brought Middleton up with such a sudden revulsion that he grew dizzy, and the room swam round him and the cabinet dazzled before his eyes. It had been magnified to a palace; it had dwindled down to Liliputian size; and yet, up till now, it had seemed to contain in its diminutiveness all the riches which he had attributed to its magnitude. This last moment had utterly subverted it; the whole great structure seemed to vanish.

"See; here are the dust and ashes of it," observed Alice, taking something that was indeed only a pinch of dust out of the secret compartment. "There is nothing else."

II.

May 5th, Wednesday. — The father of these two sons, an aged man at the time, took much to heart their enmity; and after the catastrophe, he never held up his head again. He was not told that his son had perished, though such was the belief of the family; but imbibed the opinion that he had left his home and native land to become a wanderer on the face of the earth, and that some time or other he might return. In this idea he spent the remainder of his days; in this idea he died. It may be that the influence of this idea might be traced in the way in which he spent some of the latter years of his life, and a portion of the wealth which had become of little value in his eyes, since it had caused dissension and bloodshed between the sons of one household.

It was a common mode of charity in those days — a common thing for rich men to do — to found an almshouse or a hospital, and endow it, for the support of a certain number of old and destitute men or women, generally such as had some claim of blood upon the founder, or at least were natives of the parish, the district, the county, where he dwelt. The Eldredge Hospital was founded for the benefit of twelve old men, who should have been wanderers upon the face of the earth; men, they should be, of some education, but defeated and hopeless, cast off by the world for misfortune, but not for crime. And this charity had subsisted, on terms varying little or nothing from the original ones, from that day to this; and, at this very time, twelve old men were not wanting, of various countries, of various fortunes, but all ending finally in ruin, who had centred here, to live on the poor pittance that had been assigned to them, three hundred years ago. What a series of chronicles it would have been if each of the beneficiaries of this charity, since its foundation, had left a record of the events which finally led him hither. Middleton often, as he talked with these old men, regretted that he himself had no turn for authorship, so rich a volume might he have compiled from the experience, sometimes sunny and triumphant, though always ending in shadow, which he gathered here. They were glad to talk to him, and would have been glad and grateful for any auditor, as they sat on one or another of the stone benches, in the sunshine of the garden; or at evening, around the great fireside, or within the chimney-corner, with their pipes and ale.

There was one old man who attracted much of his attention, by the venerableness of his aspect; by something dignified, almost haughty and commanding, in his air. Whatever might have been the intentions and expectations of the founder, it certainly had happened in these latter days that there was a difficulty in finding persons of education, of good manners, of evident respectability, to put into the places made vacant by deaths of members; whether that the paths of life are surer now than they used to be, and that men so arrange their lives as not to be left, in any event, quite without resources as they draw near its close; at any rate, there was a little tincture of the vagabond running through these twelve quasi gentlemen, — through several of them, at least. But this old man could not well be mistaken; in his manners, in his tones, in all his natural language and deportment, there was evidence that he had been more than respectable; and, viewing him, Middleton could not help wondering what statesman had suddenly vanished out of public life and taken refuge here, for his head was of the statesman-class, and his demeanor that of one who had exercised influence over large numbers of men. He sometimes endeavored to set on foot a familiar relation with this old man, but there was even a sternness in the manner in which he repelled these advances, that gave little encouragement for their renewal. Nor did it seem that his companions of the Hospital were more in his confidence than Middleton himself. They regarded him with a kind of awe, a shyness, and in most cases with a certain dislike, which denoted an imperfect understanding of him. To say the truth, there was not generally much love lost between any of the members of this family; they had met with too much disappointment in the world to take kindly, now, to one another or to anything or anybody. I rather suspect that they really had more pleasure in burying one another, when the time came, than in any other office of mutual kindness and brotherly love which it was their part to do; not out of hardness of heart, but merely from soured temper, and because, when people have met disappointment and have settled down into final unhappiness, with no more gush and spring of good spirits, there is nothing any more to create amiability out of.

So the old people were unamiable and cross to one another, and unamiable and cross to old Hammond, yet always with a certain respect; and the result seemed to be such as treated the old man well enough. And thus he moved about among them, a mystery; the histories of the others, in the general outline, were well enough known, and perhaps not very uncommon; this old man's history was known to none, except, of course, to the trustees of the charity, and to the Master of the Hospital, to whom it had necessarily been revealed, before the beneficiary could be admitted as an inmate. It was judged, by the deportment of the Master, that the old man had once held some eminent position in society; for, though bound to treat them all as gentlemen, he was thought to show an especial and solemn courtesy to Hammond.

Yet by the attraction which two strong and cultivated minds inevitably have for one another, there did spring up an acquaintanceship, an intercourse, between Middleton and this old man, which was followed up in many a conversation which they held together on all subjects that were supplied by the news of the day, or the history of the past. Middleton used to make the newspaper the opening for much discussion; and it seemed to him that the talk of his companion had much of the character of that of a retired statesman, on matters which, perhaps, he would look at all the more wisely, because it was impossible he could ever more have a personal agency in them. Their discussions sometimes turned upon the affairs of his own country, and its relations with the rest of the world, especially with England; and Middleton could not help being struck with the accuracy of the old man's knowledge respecting that country, which so few Englishmen know anything about; his shrewd appreciation of the American character, — shrewd and caustic, yet not without a good degree of justice; the sagacity of his remarks on the past, and prophecies of what was likely to happen, — prophecies which, in one instance, were singularly verified, in regard to a complexity which was then arresting the attention of both countries.

"You must have been in the United States," said he, one day.

"Certainly ; my remarks imply personal knowledge," was the reply. "But it was before the days of steam."

"And not, I should imagine, for a brief visit," said Middleton. "I only wish the administration of this government had the benefit to-day of your knowledge of my countrymen. It might be better for both of these kindred nations."

"Not a whit," said the old man. "England will never understand America ; for England never does understand a foreign country ; and whatever you may say about kindred, America is as much a foreign country as France itself. These two hundred years of a different climate and circumstances — of life on a broad continent instead of in an island, to say nothing of the endless intermixture of nationalities in every part of the United States, except New England — have created a new and decidedly original type of national character. It is as well for both parties that they should not aim at any very intimate connection. It will never do."

"I should be sorry to think so," said Middleton ; "they are at all events two noble breeds of men, and ought to appreciate one another. And America has the breadth of idea to do this for England, whether reciprocated or not."

Thursday, May 6th. — Thus Middleton was established in a singular way among these old men, in one of the surroundings most unlike anything in his own country. So old it was that it seemed to him the freshest and newest thing that he had ever met with. The residence was made infinitely the more interesting to him by the sense that he was near the place — as all the indications warned him — which he sought, whither his dreams had tended from his childhood ; that he could wander each day round the park within which were the old gables of what he believed was his hereditary home. He had never known anything like the dreamy enjoyment of these days ; so quiet, such a contrast to the tur-

bulent life from which he had escaped across the sea. And
here he set himself, still with that sense of shadowiness in
what he saw and in what he did, in making all the researches possible to him, about the neighborhood ; visiting
every little church that raised its square battlemented Norman tower of gray stone, for several miles round about;
making himself acquainted with each little village and ham-
let that surrounded these churches, clustering about the
graves of those who had dwelt in the same cottages afore-
time. He visited all the towns within a dozen miles ; and
probably there were few of the inhabitants who had so good
an acquaintance with the neighborhood as this native American attained within a few weeks after his coming thither.

In course of these excursions he had several times met
with a young woman, — a young lady, one might term her,
but in fact he was in some doubt what rank she might hold,
in England, — who happened to be wandering about the
country with a singular freedom. She was always alone,
always on foot; he would see her sketching some picturesque old church, some ivied ruin, some fine drooping elm.
She was a slight figure, much more so than English women
generally are ; and, though healthy of aspect, had not the
ruddy complexion, which he was irreverently inclined to
call the coarse tint, that is believed the great charm of English beauty. There was a freedom in her step and whole
little womanhood, an elasticity, an irregularity, so to speak,
that made her memorable from first sight ; and when he
had encountered her three or four times, he felt in a certain
way acquainted with her. She was very simply dressed,
and quite as simple in her deportment ; there had been one
or two occasions, when they had both smiled at the same
thing ; soon afterwards a little conversation had taken place
between them ; and thus, without any introduction, and in a
way that somewhat puzzled Middleton himself, they had become acquainted. It was so unusual that a young English
girl should be wandering about the country entirely alone —

so much less usual that she should speak to a stranger — that Middleton scarcely knew how to account for it, but meanwhile accepted the fact readily and willingly, for in truth he found this mysterious personage a very likely and entertaining companion. There was a strange quality of boldness in her remarks, almost of brusqueness, that he might have expected to find in a young countrywoman of his own, if bred up among the strong-minded, but was astonished to find in a young Englishwoman. Somehow or other she made him think more of home than any other person or thing he met with; and he could not but feel that she was in strange contrast with everything about her. She was no beauty; very piquant; very pleasing; in some points of view and at some moments pretty; always good-humored, but somewhat too self-possessed for Middleton's taste. It struck him that she had talked with him as if she had some knowledge of him and of the purposes with which he was there; not that this was expressed, but only implied by the fact that, on looking back to what had passed, he found many strange coincidences in what she had said with what he was thinking about.

He perplexed himself much with thinking whence this young woman had come, where she belonged, and what might be her history; when, the next day, he again saw her, not this time rambling on foot, but seated in an open barouche with a young lady. Middleton lifted his hat to her, and she nodded and smiled to him; and it appeared to Middleton that a conversation ensued about him with the young lady, her companion. Now, what still more interested him was the fact that, on the panel of the barouche were the arms of the family now in possession of the estate of Smithell's; so that the young lady, his new acquaintance, or the young lady, her seeming friend, one or the other, was the sister of the present owner of that estate. He was inclined to think that his acquaintance could not be the Miss Eldredge, of whose beauty he had heard many tales among the people of the neighborhood. The other young lady, a tall, reserved, fair-haired maiden, answered the description considerably better. He concluded, therefore, that his acquaintance must be a visitor, perhaps a dependent and companion; though the freedom of her thought, action, and way of life seemed hardly consistent with this idea. However, this slight incident served to give him a sort of connection with the family, and he could but hope that some further chance would introduce him within what he fondly called his hereditary walls. He had come to think of this as a dreamland; and it seemed even more a dreamland now than before it rendered itself into actual substance, an old house of stone and timber standing within its park, shaded about with its ancestral trees.

But thus, at all events, he was getting himself a little wrought into the net-work of human life around him, secluded as his position had at first seemed to be, in the farm-house where he had taken up his lodgings. For, there was the Hospital and its old inhabitants, in whose monotonous existence he soon came to pass for something, with his liveliness of mind, his experience, his good sense, his patience as a listener, his comparative youth even — his power of adapting himself to these stiff and crusty characters, a power learned among other things in his political life, where he had acquired something of the faculty (good or bad as might be) of making himself all things to all men. But though he amused himself with them all, there was in truth but one man among them in whom he really felt much interest; and that one, we need hardly say, was Hammond. It was not often that he found the old gentleman in a conversible mood; always courteous, indeed, but generally cool and reserved; often engaged in his one room, to which Middleton had never yet been admitted, though he had more than once sent in his name, when Hammond was not apparent upon the bench which, by common consent of the Hospital, was appropriated to him.

One day, however, notwithstanding that the old gentleman was confined to his room by indisposition, he ventured to inquire at the door, and, considerably to his surprise, was admitted. He found Hammond in his easy-chair, at a table, with writing-materials before him : and as Middleton entered, the old gentleman looked at him with a stern, fixed regard, which, however, did not seem to imply any particular displeasure towards this visitor, but rather a severe way of regarding mankind in general. Middleton looked curiously around the small apartment, to see what modification the character of the man had had upon the customary furniture of the Hospital, and how much of individuality he had given to that general type. There was a shelf of books, and a row of them on the mantel-piece ; works of political economy, they appeared to be, statistics and things of that sort ; very dry reading, with which, however, Middleton's experience as a politician had made him acquainted. Besides these there were a few works on local antiquities, a county-history borrowed from the Master's library, in which Hammond appeared to have been lately reading.

" They are delightful reading," observed Middleton, " these old county-histories, with their great folio volumes and their minute account of the affairs of families and the genealogies, and descents of estates, bestowing as much blessed space on a few hundred acres as other historians give to a principality. I fear that in my own country we shall never have anything of this kind. Our space is so vast that we shall never come to know and love it, inch by inch, as the English antiquarians do the tracts of country with which they deal; and besides, our land is always likely to lack the interest that belongs to English estates; for where land changes its ownership every few years, it does not become imbued with the personalities of the people who live on it. It is but so much grass ; so much dirt, where a succession of people have dwelt too little to make it really their own. But I have found a pleasure that I had no conception of before, in reading some of the English local histories."

"It is not a usual course of reading for a transitory visitor," said Hammond. "What could induce you to undertake it?"

"Simply the wish, so common and natural with Americans," said Middleton — "the wish to find out something about my kindred — the local origin of my own family."

"You do not show your wisdom in this," said his visitor. "America had better recognize the fact that it has nothing to do with England, and look upon itself as other nations and people do, as existing on its own hook. I never heard of any people looking back to the country of their remote origin in the way the Anglo-Americans do. For instance, England is made up of many alien races, German, Danish, Norman, and what not: it has received large accessions of population at a later date than the settlement of the United States. Yet these families melt into the great homogeneous mass of Englishmen, and look back no more to any other country. There are in this vicinity many descendants of the French Huguenots; but they care no more for France than for Timbuctoo, reckoning themselves only Englishmen, as if they were descendants of the aboriginal Britons. Let it be so with you."

"So it might be," replied Middleton, "only that our relations with England remain far more numerous than our disconnections, through the bonds of history, of literature, of all that makes up the memories, and much that makes up the present interests of a people. And therefore I must still continue to pore over these old folios, and hunt around these precincts, spending thus the little idle time I am likely to have in a busy life. Possibly finding little to my purpose; but that is quite a secondary consideration."

"If you choose to tell me precisely what your aims are," said Hammond, "it is possible I might give you some little assistance."

May 7th, Friday. — Middleton was in fact more than half ashamed of the dreams which he had cherished before

coming to England, and which since, at times, had been
very potent with him, assuming as strong a tinge of reality
as those [scenes?] into which he had strayed. He could not
prevail with himself to disclose fully to this severe, and, as
he thought, cynical old man how strong within him was the
sentiment that impelled him to connect himself with the old
life of England, to join on the broken thread of ancestry
and descent, and feel every link well established. But it
seemed to him that he ought not to lose this fair opportunity
of gaining some light on the abstruse field of his researches ;
and he therefore explained to Hammond that he had reason,
from old family traditions, to believe that he brought with
him a fragment of a history that, if followed out, might
lead to curious results. He told him, in a tone half serious,
what he had heard respecting the quarrel of the two brothers, and the Bloody Footstep, the impress of which was said
to remain, as a lasting memorial of the tragic termination
of that enmity. At this point, Hammond interrupted him.
He had indeed, at various points of the narrative, nodded
and smiled mysteriously, as if looking into his mind and
seeing something there analogous to what he was listening
to. He now spoke.

"This is curious," said he. "Did you know that there
is a manor-house in this neighborhood, the family of which
prides itself on having such a blood-stained threshold as you
have now described ? "

"No, indeed ! " exclaimed Middleton, greatly interested.
"Where ? "

"It is the old manor-house of Smithell's," replied Hammond, "one of those old wood and timber [plaster ?] mansions, which are among the most ancient specimens of domestic architecture in England. The house has now passed
into the female line, and by marriage has been for two or
three generations in possession of another family. But the
blood of the old inheritors is still in the family. The house
itself, or portions of it, are thought to date back quite as far
as the Conquest."

"Smithell's?" said Middleton. "Why, I have seen that old house from a distance, and have felt no little interest in its antique aspect. And it has a Bloody Footstep! Would it be possible for a stranger to get an opportunity to inspect it?"

"Unquestionably," said Hammond; "nothing easier. It is but a moderate distance from here, and if you can moderate your young footsteps, and your American quick walk, to an old man's pace, I would go there with you some day. In this languor and ennui of my life, I spend some time in local antiquarianism, and perhaps I might assist you in tracing out how far these traditions of yours may have any connection with reality. It would be curious, would it not, if you had come, after two hundred years, to piece out a story which may have been as much a mystery in England as there in America?"

An engagement was made for a walk to Smithell's the ensuing day; and meanwhile Middleton entered more fully into what he had received from family traditions and what he had thought out for himself on the matter in question.

"Are you aware," asked Hammond, "that there was formerly a title in this family, now in abeyance, and which the heirs have at various times claimed, and are at this moment claiming? Do you know, too, — but you can scarcely know it, — that it has been surmised by some that there is an insecurity in the title to the estate, and has always been; so that the possessors have lived in some apprehension, from time immemorial, that another heir would appear and take from them the fair inheritance? It is a singular coincidence."

"Very strange," exclaimed Middleton. "No; I was not aware of it; and, to say the truth, I should not altogether like to come forward in the light of a claimant. But this is a dream, surely!"

"I assure you, sir," continued the old man, "that you come here in a very critical moment; and singularly enough there is a perplexity, a difficulty, that has endured for as long a time as when your ancestors emigrated, that is still rampant within the bowels, as I may say, of the family. Of course, it is too like a romance that you should be able to establish any such claim as would have a valid influence on this matter; but still, being here on the spot, it may be worth while, if merely as a matter of amusement, to make some researches into this matter."

"Surely I will," said Middleton, with a smile, which concealed more earnestness than he liked to show; "as to the title, a Republican cannot be supposed to think twice about such a bagatelle. The estate! — that might be a more serious consideration."

They continued to talk on the subject; and Middleton learned that the present possessor of the estates was a gentleman nowise distinguished from hundreds of other English gentlemen; a country squire modified in accordance with the type of to-day, a frank, free, friendly sort of a person enough, who had travelled on the Continent, who employed himself much in field-sports, who was unmarried, and had a sister who was reckoned among the beauties of the county.

While the conversation was thus going on, to Middleton's astonishment there came a knock at the door of the room, and, without waiting for a response, it was opened, and there appeared at it the same young woman whom he had already met. She came in with perfect freedom and familiarity, and was received quietly by the old gentleman; who, however, by his manner towards Middleton, indicated that he was now to take his leave. He did so, after settling the hour at which the excursion of the next day was to take place. This arranged, he departed, with much to think of, and a light glimmering through the confused labyrinth of thoughts which had been unilluminated hitherto.

To say the truth, he questioned within himself whether it were not better to get as quickly as he could out of the vicinity; and, at any rate, not to put anything of earnest in

what had hitherto been nothing more than a romance to
him. There was something very dark and sinister in the
events of family history, which now assumed a reality that
they had never before worn; so much tragedy, so much
hatred, had been thrown into that deep pit, and buried
under the accumulated débris, the fallen leaves, the rust
and dust of more than two centuries, that it seemed not
worth while to dig it up; for perhaps the deadly influences,
which it had taken so much time to hide, might still be lurk-
ing there, and become potent if he now uncovered them.
There was something that startled him, in the strange, wild
light, which gleamed from the old man's eyes, as he threw
out the suggestions which had opened this prospect to him.
What right had he — an American, Republican, disconnected with this country so long, alien from its habits of
thought and life, reverencing none of the things which Englishmen reverenced — what right had he to come with these
musty claims from the dim past, to disturb them in the life
that belonged to them? There was a higher and a deeper
law than any connected with ancestral claims which he
could assert; and he had an idea that the law bade him
keep to the country which his ancestor had chosen and to
its institutions, and not meddle nor make with England.
The roots of his family tree could not reach under the
ocean; he was at most but a seedling from the parent tree.
While thus meditating he found that his footsteps had
brought him unawares within sight of the old manor-house
of Smithell's; and that he was wandering in a path which,
if he followed it further, would bring him to an entrance in
one of the wings of the mansion. With a sort of shame
upon him, he went forward, and, leaning against a tree,
looked at what he considered the home of his ancestors.

May 9th, Sunday. — At the time appointed, the two companions set out on their little expedition, the old man in his
Hospital uniform, the long black mantle, with the bear and
ragged staff engraved in silver on the breast, and Middle-

ton in the plain costume which he had adopted in these wanderings about the country. On their way, Hammond was not very communicative, occasionally dropping some shrewd remark with a good deal of acidity in it ; now and then, too, favoring his companion with some reminiscence of local antiquity ; but oftenest silent. Thus they went on, and entered the park of Pemberton Manor by a by-path, over a stile and one of those footways, which are always so well worth threading out in England, leading the pedestrian into picturesque and characteristic scenes, when the high-road would show him nothing except what was common-place and uninteresting. Now the gables of the old manor-house appeared before them, rising amidst the hereditary woods, which doubtless dated from a time beyond the days which Middleton fondly recalled, when his ancestors had walked beneath their shade. On each side of them were thickets and copses of fern, amidst which they saw the hares peeping out to gaze upon them, occasionally running across the path, and comporting themselves like creatures that felt themselves under some sort of protection from the outrages of man, though they knew too much of his destructive character to trust him too far. Pheasants, too, rose close beside them, and winged but a little way before they alighted ; they likewise knew, or seemed to know, that their hour was not yet come. On all sides in these woods, these wastes, these beasts and birds, there was a character that was neither wild nor tame. Man had laid his grasp on them all, and done enough to redeem them from barbarism, but had stopped short of domesticating them ; although Nature, in the wildest thing there, acknowledged the powerful and pervading influence of cultivation.

Arriving at a side door of the mansion, Hammond rang the bell, and a servant soon appeared. He seemed to know the old man, and immediately acceded to his request to be permitted to show his companion the house ; although it was not precisely a show-house, nor was this the hour when strangers were usually admitted. They entered; and the servant did not give himself the trouble to act as a cicerone to the two visitants, but carelessly said to the old gentleman that he knew the rooms, and that he would leave him to discourse to his friend about them. Accordingly, they went into the old hall, a dark oaken-panelled room, of no great height, with many doors opening into it. There was a fire burning on the hearth; indeed, it was the custom of the house to keep it up from morning to night; and in the damp, chill climate of England, there is seldom a day in some part of which a fire is not pleasant to feel. Hammond here pointed out a stuffed fox, to which some story of a famous chase was attached; a pair of antlers of enormous size; and some old family pictures, so blackened with time and neglect that Middleton could not well distinguish their features, though curious to do so, as hoping to see there the lineaments of some with whom he might claim kindred. It was a venerable apartment, and gave a good foretaste of what they might hope to find in the rest of the mansion.

But when they had inspected it pretty thoroughly, and were ready to proceed, an elderly gentleman entered the hall, and, seeing Hammond, addressed him in a kindly, familiar way; not indeed as an equal friend, but with a pleasant and not irksome conversation. "I am glad to see you here again," said he. "What? I have an hour of leisure; for, to say the truth, the day hangs rather heavy till the shooting season begins. Come; as you have a friend with you, I will be your cicerone myself about the house, and show you whatever mouldy objects of interest it contains."

He then graciously noticed the old man's companion, but without asking or seeming to expect an introduction; for, after a careless glance at him, he had evidently set him down as a person without social claims, a young man in the rank of life fitted to associate with an inmate of Pemberton's Hospital. And it must be noticed that his treatment of Middleton was not on that account the less kind, though far from being so elaborately courteous as if he had met him as an equal. "You have had something of a walk," said he, "and it is a rather hot day. The beer of Pemberton Manor has been reckoned good these hundred years; will you taste it?"

Hammond accepted the offer, and the beer was brought in a foaming tankard; but Middleton declined it, for in truth there was a singular emotion in his breast, as if the old enmity, the ancient injuries, were not yet atoned for, and as if he must not accept the hospitality of one who represented his hereditary foe. He felt, too, as if there were something unworthy, a certain want of fairness, in entering clandestinely the house, and talking with its occupant under a veil, as it were; and had he seen clearly how to do it, he would perhaps at that moment have fairly told Mr. Eldredge that he brought with him the character of kinsman, and must be received on that grade or none. But it was not easy to do this; and after all, there was no clear reason why he should do it; so he let the matter pass, merely declining to take the refreshment, and keeping himself quiet and retired.

Squire Eldredge seemed to be a good, ordinary sort of gentleman, reasonably well educated, and with few ideas beyond his estate and neighborhood, though he had once held a seat in Parliament for part of a term. Middleton could not but contrast him, with an inward smile, with the shrewd, alert politicians, their faculties all sharpened to the utmost, whom he had known and consorted with in the American Congress. Hammond had slightly informed him that his companion was an American; and Mr. Eldredge immediately gave proof of the extent of his knowledge of that country, by inquiring whether he came from the State of New England, and whether Mr. Webster was still President of the United States; questions to which Middleton returned answers that led to no further conversation. These little preliminaries over, they continued their ramble through the house, going through tortuous passages, up and down little flights of steps, and entering chambers that had all the charm of discoveries of hidden regions; loitering about, in short, in a labyrinth calculated to put the head into a delightful confusion. Some of these rooms contained their time-honored furniture, all in the best possible repair, heavy, dark, polished; beds that had been marriage beds and dying beds over and over again; chairs with carved backs; and all manner of old world curiosities; family pictures, and samplers, and embroidery; fragments of tapestry; an inlaid floor; everything having a story to it, though, to say the truth, the possessor of these curiosities made but a bungling piece of work in telling the legends connected with them. In one or two instances Hammond corrected him.

By and by they came to what had once been the principal bed-room of the house; though its gloom, and some circumstances of family misfortune that had happened long ago, had caused it to fall into disrepute in latter times; and it was now called the Haunted Chamber, or the Ghost's Chamber. The furniture of this room, however, was particularly rich in its antique magnificence; and one of the principal objects was a great black cabinet of ebony and ivory, such as may often be seen in old English houses, and perhaps often in the palaces of Italy, in which country they perhaps originated. This present cabinet was known to have been in the house as long ago as the reign of Queen Elizabeth, and how much longer neither tradition nor record told. Hammond particularly directed Middleton's attention to it.

"There is nothing in this house," said he, "better worth your attention than that cabinet. Consider its plan; it represents a stately mansion, with pillars, an entrance, with a lofty flight of steps, windows, and everything perfect. Examine it well."

There was such an emphasis in the old man's way of

speaking *hat* Middleton turned suddenly round from all
that he had been looking at, and fixed his whole attention
on the cabinet ; and strangely enough, it seemed to be the
representative, in small, of something that he had seen in a
dream.   To say the truth, if some cunning workman had
been employed to copy his idea of the old family mansion,
on a scale of half an inch to a yard, and in ebony and ivory
instead of stone, he could not have produced a closer imitation.   Everything was there.

"This is miraculous ! " exclaimed he.   " I do not understand it."

"Your friend seems to be curious in these matters,"
said Mr. Eldredge graciously.   "Perhaps he is of some
trade that makes this sort of manufacture particularly interesting to him.   You are quite at liberty, my friend, to
open the cabinet and inspect it as minutely as you wish.
It is an article that has a good deal to do with an obscure
portion of our family history.   Look, here is the key, and
the mode of opening the outer door of the palace, as we
may well call it."   So saying, he threw open the outer
door, and disclosed within the mimic likeness of a stately
entrance hall, with a floor chequered of ebony and ivory.
There were other doors that seemed to open into apartments
in the interior of the palace ; but when Mr. Eldredge threw
them likewise wide, they proved to be drawers and secret
receptacles, where papers, jewels, money, anything that it
was desirable to store away secretly, might be kept.

"You said, sir," said Middleton, thoughtfully, " that your
family history contained matter of interest in reference to
this cabinet.   Might I inquire what those legends are ? "

"Why, yes," said Mr. Eldredge, musing a little.   "I
see no reason why I should have any idle concealment
about the matter, especially to a foreigner and a man whom
I am never likely to see again.   You must know, then, my
friend, that there was once a time when this cabinet was
known to contain the fate of the estate and its possessors ;

and if it had held all that it was supposed to hold, I should not now be the lord of Pemberton Manor, nor the claimant of an ancient title. But my father, and his father before him, and his father besides, have held the estate and prospered on it ; and I think we may fairly conclude now that the cabinet contains nothing except what we see."

And he rapidly again threw open one after another all the numerous drawers and receptacles of the cabinet.

"It is an interesting object," said Middleton, after looking very closely and with great attention at it, being pressed thereto, indeed, by the owner's good natured satisfaction in possessing this rare article of vertu. "It is admirable work," repeated he, drawing back. "That mosaic floor, especially, is done with an art and skill that I never saw equalled."

There was something strange and altered in Middleton's tones, that attracted the notice of Mr. Eldredge. Looking at him, he saw that he had grown pale, and had a rather bewildered air.

"Is your friend ill ? " said he. " He has not our English ruggedness of look. He would have done better to take a sip of the cool tankard, and a slice of the cold beef. He finds no such food and drink as that in his own country, I warrant."

"His color has come back," responded Hammond, briefly. "He does not need any refreshment, I think, except, perhaps, the open air."

In fact, Middleton, recovering himself, apologized to Mr. Hammond [Eldredge ?] ; and as they had now seen nearly the whole of the house, the two visitants took their leave, with many kindly offers on Mr. Eldredge's part to permit the young man to view the cabinet whenever he wished. As they went out of the house (it was by another door than that which gave them entrance), Hammond laid his hand on Middleton's shoulder and pointed to a stone on the threshold, on which he was about to set his foot. "Take care ! " said he. "It is the Bloody Footstep."

Middleton looked down and saw something, indeed, very like the shape of a footprint, with a hue very like that of blood. It was a twilight sort of a place, beneath a porch, which was much overshadowed by trees and shrubbery. It might have been blood; but he rather thought, in his wicked skepticism, that it was a natural, reddish stain in the stone. He measured his own foot, however, in the Bloody Footstep, and went on.

May 10th, Monday. — This is the present aspect of the story: Middleton is the descendant of a family long settled in the United States; his ancestor having emigrated to New England with the Pilgrims; or, perhaps, at a still earlier date, to Virginia with Raleigh's colonists. There had been a family dissension, — a bitter hostility between two brothers in England; on account, probably, of a love affair, the two both being attached to the same lady. By the influence of the family on both sides, the young lady had formed an engagement with the elder brother, although her affections had settled on the younger. The marriage was about to take place when the younger brother and the bride both disappeared, and were never heard of with any certainty afterwards; but it was believed at the time that he had been killed, and in proof of it a bloody footstep remained on the threshold of the ancestral mansion. There were rumors, afterwards, traditionally continued to the present day, that the younger brother and the bride were seen, and together, in England; and that some voyager across the sea had found them living together, husband and wife, on the other side of the Atlantic. But the elder brother became a moody and reserved man, never married, and left the inheritance to the children of a third brother, who then became the representative of the family in England; and the better authenticated story was that the second brother had really been slain, and that the young lady (for all the parties may have been Catholic) had gone to the Continent and taken the veil there. Such was the family history as known or surmised in England, and in the neighborhood of the manor-house, where the Bloody Footstep still remained on the threshold; and the posterity of the third brother still held the estate, and perhaps were claimants of an ancient baronage, long in abeyance.

Now, on the other side of the Atlantic, the second brother and the young lady had really been married, and became the parents of a posterity, still extant, of which the Middleton of the romance is the surviving male. Perhaps he had changed his name, being so much tortured with the evil and wrong that had sprung up in his family, so remorseful, so outraged, that he wished to disconnect himself with all the past, and begin life quite anew in a new world. But both he and his wife, though happy in one another, had been remorsefully and sadly so; and, with such feelings, they had never again communicated with their respective families, nor had given their children the means of doing so. There must, I think, have been something nearly approaching to guilt on the second brother's part, and the bride should have broken a solemnly plighted troth to the elder brother, breaking away from him when almost his wife. The elder brother had been known to have been wounded at the time of the second brother's disappearance; and it had been the surmise that he had received this hurt in the personal conflict in which the latter was slain. But in truth the second brother had stabbed him in the emergency of being discovered in the act of escaping with the bride; and this was what weighed upon his conscience throughout life in America. The American family had prolonged itself through various fortunes, and all the ups and downs incident to our institutions, until the present day. They had some old family documents, which had been rather carelessly kept; but the present representative, being an educated man, had looked over them, and found one which interested him strongly. It was — what was it? — perhaps a copy of a letter written by his ancestor on his death-

bed, telling his real name, and relating the above incidents.
These incidents had come down in a vague, wild way, traditionally, in the American family, forming a wondrous and
incredible legend, which Middleton had often laughed at,
yet been greatly interested in; and the discovery of this
document seemed to give a certain aspect of veracity and
reality to the tradition. Perhaps, however, the document
only related to the change of name, and made reference to
certain evidences by which, if any descendant of the family
should deem it expedient, he might prove his hereditary
identity. The legend must be accounted for by having been
gathered from the talk of the first ancestor and his wife.
There must be in existence, in the early records of the col-
ony, an authenticated statement of this change of name, and
satisfactory proofs that the American family, long known as
Middleton, were really a branch of the English family of
Eldredge, or whatever. And in the legend, though not in
the written document, there must be an account of a certain magnificent, almost palatial residence, which Middleton
shall presume to be the ancestral home; and in this palace
there shall be said to be a certain secret chamber, or receptacle, where is reposited a document that shall complete the
evidence of the genealogical descent.

Middleton is still a young man, but already a distinguished one in his own country; he has entered early into
politics, been sent to Congress, but having met with some
disappointments in his ambitious hopes, and being disgusted
with the fierceness of political contests in our country, he
has come abroad for recreation and rest. His imagination
has dwelt much, in his boyhood, on the legendary story of
his family; and the discovery of the document has revived
these dreams. He determines to search out the family
mansion; and thus he arrives, bringing half of a story,
being the only part known in America, to join it on to the
other half, which is the only part known in England. In
an introduction I must do the best I can to state his side

of the matter to the reader, he having communicated it to me in a friendly way, at the Consulate; as many people have communicated quite as wild pretensions to English genealogies.

He comes to the midland counties of England, where he conceives his claims to lie, and seeks for his ancestral home; but there are difficulties in the way of finding it, the estates having passed into the female line, though still remaining in the blood. By and by, however, he comes to an old town where there is one of the charitable institutions bearing the name of his family, by whose beneficence it had indeed been founded, in Queen Elizabeth's time. He of course becomes interested in this Hospital; he finds it still going on, precisely as it did in the old days; and all the character and life of the establishment must be picturesquely described. Here he gets acquainted with an old man, an inmate of the Hospital, who (if the uncontrollable fatality of the story will permit) must have an active influence on the ensuing events. I suppose him to have been an American, but to have fled his country and taken refuge in England; he shall have been a man of the Nicholas Biddle stamp, a mighty speculator, the ruin of whose schemes had crushed hundreds of people, and Middleton's father among the rest. Here he had quitted the activity of his mind, as well as he could, becoming a local antiquary, etc., and he has made himself acquainted with the family history of the Eldredges, knowing more about it than the members of the family themselves do. He had known in America (from Middleton's father, who was his friend) the legends preserved in this branch of the family, and perhaps had been struck by the way in which they fit into the English legends; at any rate, this strikes him when Middleton tells him his story and shows him the document respecting the change of name. After various conversations together (in which, however, the old man keeps the secret of his own identity, and indeed acts as mysteriously as possible), they go together to visit the ancestral mansion. Perhaps it should not be in their first visit that the cabinet, representing the stately mansion, shall be seen. But the Bloody Footstep may; which shall interest Middleton much, both because Hammond has told him the English tradition respecting it, and because too the legends of the American family made some obscure allusions to his ancestor having left blood — a bloody footstep — on the ancestral threshold. This is the point to which the story has now been sketched out. Middleton finds a commonplace old English country gentleman in possession of the estate, where his forefathers have lived in peace for many generations; but there must be circumstances contrived which shall cause Middleton's conduct to be attended by no end of turmoil and trouble. The old Hospitaller, I suppose, must be the malicious agent in this; and his malice must be motived in some satisfactory way. The more serious question, what shall be the nature of this tragic trouble, and how can it be brought about?

May 11*th, Tuesday.* — How much better would it have been if this secret, which seemed so golden, had remained in the obscurity in which two hundred years had buried it! That deep, old, grass-grown grave being opened, out from it streamed into the sunshine the old fatalities, the old crimes, the old misfortunes, the sorrows, that seemed to have departed from the family forever. But it was too late now to close it up; he must follow out the thread that led him on, — the thread of fate, if you choose to call it so; but rather the impulse of an evil will, a stubborn self-interest, a desire for certain objects of ambition which were preferred to what yet were recognized as real goods. Thus reasoned, thus raved, Eldredge, as he considered the things that he had done, and still intended to do; nor did these perceptions make the slightest difference in his plans, nor in the activity with which he set about their performance. For this purpose he sent for his lawyer, and consulted him on the feasibility of the design which he had already communicated to him respecting Middleton. But the man of law shook his head, and, though deferentially, declined to have any active concern with the matter that threatened to lead him beyond the bounds which he allowed himself, into a seductive but perilous region.

"My dear sir," said he, with some earnestness, "you had much better content yourself with such assistance as I can professionally and consistently give you. Believe [me], I am willing to do a lawyer's utmost, and to do more would be as unsafe for the client as for the legal adviser."

Thus left without an agent and an instrument, this unfortunate man had to meditate on what means he would use to gain his ends through his own unassisted efforts. In the struggle with himself through which he had passed, he had exhausted pretty much all the feelings that he had to bestow on this matter; and now he was ready to take hold of almost any temptation that might present itself, so long as it showed a good prospect of success and a plausible chance of impunity. While he was thus musing, he heard a female voice chanting some song, like a bird's among the pleasant foliage of the trees, and soon he saw at the end of a woodwalk Alice, with her basket on her arm, passing on toward the village. She looked towards him as she passed, but made no pause nor yet hastened her steps, not seeming to think it worth her while to be influenced by him. He hurried forward and overtook her.

So there was this poor old gentleman, his comfort utterly overthrown, decking his white hair and wrinkled brow with the semblance of a coronet, and only hoping that the reality might crown and bless him before he was laid in the ancestral tomb. It was a real calamity; though by no means the greatest that had been fished up out of the pit of domestic discord that had been opened anew by the advent of the American; and by the use which had been made of it by the cantankerous old man of the Hospital. Middleton, as he looked at these evil consequences, sometimes regretted that he had not listened to those forebodings which had warned him back on the eve of his enterprise ; yet such was the strange entanglement and interest which had wound about him, that often he rejoiced that for once he was engaged in something that absorbed him fully, and the zeal for the development of which made him careless for the result in respect to its good or evil, but only desirous that it show itself. As for Alice, she seemed to skim lightly through all these matters, whether as a spirit of good or ill he could not satisfactorily judge. He could not think her wicked ; yet her actions seemed unaccountable on the plea that she was otherwise. It was another characteristic thread in the wild web of madness that had spun itself about all the prominent characters of our story. And when Middleton thought of these things, he felt as if it might be his duty (supposing he had the power) to shovel the earth again into the pit that he had been the means of opening ; but also felt that, whether duty or not, he would never perform it.

For, you see, on the American's arrival he had found the estate in the hands of one of the descendants ; but some disclosures consequent on his arrival had thrown it into the hands of another ; or, at all events, had seemed to make it apparent that justice required that it should be so disposed of. No sooner was the discovery made than the possessor put on a coronet ; the new heir had commenced legal proceedings ; the sons of the respective branches had come to blows and blood ; and the devil knows what other devilish consequences had ensued. Besides this, there was much falling in love at cross-purposes, and a general animosity of everybody against everybody else, in proportion to the closeness of the natural ties and their obligation to love one another.

The moral, if any moral were to be gathered from these petty and wretched circumstances, was, " Let the past alone : do not seek to renew it ; press on to higher and better things, — at all events, to other things; and be assured that the right way can never be that which leads you back to the identical shapes that you long ago left behind. Onward, onward, onward!"

"What have you to do here?" said Alice. "Your lot is in another land. You have seen the birthplace of your forefathers, and have gratified your natural yearning for it; now return, and cast in your lot with your own people, let it be what it will. I fully believe that it is such a lot as the world has never yet seen, and that the faults, the weaknesses, the errors, of your countrymen will vanish away like morning mists before the rising sun. You can do nothing better than to go back."

"This is strange advice, Alice," said Middleton, gazing at her and smiling. "Go back, with such a fair prospect before me; that were strange indeed! It is enough to keep me here, that here only I shall see you, — enough to make me rejoice to have come, that I have found you here."

"Do not speak in this foolish way," cried Alice, panting. "I am giving you the best advice, and speaking in the wisest way I am capable of, — speaking on good grounds too, — and you turn me aside with a silly compliment. I tell you that this is no comedy in which we are performers, but a deep, sad tragedy; and that it depends most upon you whether or no it shall be pressed to a catastrophe. Think well of it."

"I have thought, Alice," responded the young man, "and I must let things take their course; if, indeed, it depends at all upon me, which I see no present reason to suppose. Yet I wish you would explain to me what you mean."

To take up the story from the point where we left it: by the aid of the American's revelations, some light is thrown upon points of family history, which induce the English possessor of the estate to suppose that the time has come for asserting his claim to a title which has long been in abeyance. He therefore sets about it, and engages in

great expenses, besides contracting the enmity of many persons, with whose interests he interferes. A further compli-
cation is brought about by the secret interference of the old
Hospitaller, and Alice goes singing and dancing through
the whole, in a way that makes her seem like a beautiful
devil, though finally it will be recognized that she is an
angel of light. Middleton, half bewildered, can scarcely
tell how much of this is due to his own agency; how much
is independent of him and would have happened had he
stayed on his own side of the water. By and by a further
and unexpected development presents the singular fact that
he himself is the heir to whatever claims there are, whether
of property or rank, — all centring in him as the representative of the eldest brother. On this discovery there ensues
a tragedy in the death of the present possessor of the estate,
who has staked everything upon the issue; and Middleton,
standing amid the ruin and desolation of which he has been
the innocent cause, resigns all the claims which he might
now assert, and retires, arm in arm with Alice, who has encouraged him to take this course, and to act up to his character. The estate takes a passage into the female line, and
the old name becomes extinct, nor does Middleton seek to
continue it by resuming it in place of the one long ago assumed by his ancestor. Thus he and his wife become the
Adam and Eve of a new epoch, and the fitting missionaries
of a new social faith, of which there must be continual hints
through the book.

A knot of characters may be introduced as gathering
around Middleton, comprising expatriated Americans of all
sorts: the wandering printer who came to me so often at
the Consulate, who said he was a native of Philadelphia,
and could not go home in the thirty years that he had been
trying to do so, for lack of the money to pay his passage;
the large banker; the consul of Leeds; the woman asserting her claims to half Liverpool; the gifted literary lady,
maddened by Shakespeare, &c., &c. The Yankee who had

been driven insane by the Queen's notice, slight as it was, of the photographs of his two children which he had sent her. I have not yet struck the true key-note of this Romance, and until I do, and unless I do, I shall write nothing but tediousness and nonsense. I do not wish it to be a picture of life, but a Romance, grim, grotesque, quaint, of which the Hospital might be the fitting scene. It might have so much of the hues of life that the reader should sometimes think it was intended for a picture, yet the atmosphere should be such as to excuse all wildness. In the Introduction, I might disclaim all intention to draw a real picture, but say that the continual meetings I had with Americans bent on such errands had suggested this wild story. The descriptions of scenery, &c., and of the Hospital, might be correct, but there should be a tinge of the grotesque given to all the characters and events. The tragic and the gentler pathetic need not be excluded by the tone and treatment. If I could but write one central scene in this vein, all the rest of the Romance would readily arrange itself around that nucleus. The begging-girl would be another American character; the actress too; the caravan people. It must be humorous work, or nothing.

III.

May 12th, Wednesday. — Middleton found his abode here becoming daily more interesting; and he sometimes thought that it was the sympathies with the place and people, buried under the supergrowth of so many ages, but now coming forth with the life and vigor of a fountain, that, long hidden beneath earth and ruins, gushes out singing into the sunshine, as soon as these are removed. He wandered about the neighborhood with insatiable interest; sometimes, and often, lying on a hill-side and gazing at the gray tower of the church; sometimes coming into the village clustered round that same church, and looking at the old timber and plaster houses, the same, except that the thatch had probably been often renewed, that they used to be in his ancestor's days. In those old cottages still dwelt the families, the ——s, the Prices, the Hopnorts, the Copleys, that had dwelt there when America was a scattered progeny of infant colonies; and in the churchyard were the graves of all the generations since — including the dust of those who had seen his ancestor's face before his departure.

The graves, outside the church walls indeed, bore no marks of this antiquity; for it seems not to have been an early practice in England to put stones over such graves; and where it has been done, the climate causes the inscriptions soon to become obliterated and unintelligible. But, within the church, there were rich words of the personages and times with whom Middleton's musings held so much converse.

But one of his greatest employments and pastimes was to ramble through the grounds of Smithell's, making himself as well acquainted with its wood paths, its glens, its woods, its venerable trees, as if he had been bred up there from infancy. Some of those old oaks his ancestor might have been acquainted with, while they were already sturdy and well-grown trees; might have climbed them in boyhood; might have mused beneath them as a lover; might have flung himself at full length on the turf beneath them, in the bitter anguish that must have preceded his departure forever from the home of his forefathers. In order to secure an uninterrupted enjoyment of his rambles here, Middleton had secured the good-will of the game-keepers and other underlings whom he was likely to meet about the grounds, by giving them a shilling or a half-crown; and he was now free to wander where he would, with only the advice rather than the caution, to keep out of the way of their old master, — for there might be trouble, if he should meet a stranger on the grounds, in any of his tantrums. But, in fact, Mr.

Eldredge was not much in the habit of walking about the grounds; and there were hours of every day, during which it was altogether improbable that he would have emerged from his own apartments in the manor-house. These were the hours, therefore, when Middleton most frequented the estate; although, to say the truth, he would gladly have so timed his visits as to meet and form an acquaintance with the lonely lord of this beautiful property, his own kinsman, though with so many ages of dark oblivion between. For Middleton had not that feeling of infinite distance in the relationship, which he would have had if his branch of the family had continued in England, and had not intermarried with the other branch, through such a long waste of years; he rather felt as if he were the original emigrant who, long resident on a foreign shore, had now returned, with a heart brimful of tenderness, to revisit the scenes of his youth, and renew his tender relations with those who shared his own blood.

There was not, however, much in what he heard of the character of the present possessor of the estate — or indeed in the strong family characteristic that had become hereditary — to encourage him to attempt any advances. It is very probable that the religion of Mr. Eldredge, as a Catholic, may have excited a prejudice against him, as it certainly had insulated the family, in a great degree, from the sympathies of the neighborhood. Mr. Eldredge, moreover, had resided long on the Continent; long in Italy; and had come back with habits that little accorded with those of the gentry of the neighborhood; so that, in fact, he was almost as much of a stranger, and perhaps quite as little of a real Englishman, as Middleton himself. Be that as it might, Middleton, when he sought to learn something about him, heard the strangest stories of his habits of life, of his temper, and of his employments, from the people with whom he conversed. The old legend, turning upon the monomania of the family, was revived in full force in reference to this

poor gentleman; and many a time Middleton's interlocutors
shook their wise heads, saying with a knowing look and
under their breath that the old gentleman was looking for
the track of the Bloody Footstep. They fabled — or said,
for it might not have been a false story — that every descendant of this house had a certain portion of his life, during which he sought the track of that footstep which was left
on the threshold of the mansion; that he sought it far and
wide, over every foot of the estate; not only on the estate,
but throughout the neighborhood; not only in the neighborhood but all over England; not only throughout England
but all about the world. It was the belief of the neighborhood — at least of some old men and women in it — that the
long period of Mr. Eldredge's absence from England had
been spent in the search for some trace of those departing
footsteps that had never returned. It is very possible —
probable, indeed — that there may have been some ground
for this remarkable legend; not that it is to be credited that
the family of Eldredge, being reckoned among sane men,
would seriously have sought, years and generations after the
fact, for the first track of those bloody footsteps which the
first rain of drippy England must have washed away; to
say nothing of the leaves that had fallen and the growth
and decay of so many seasons, that covered all traces of
them since. But nothing is more probable than that the
continual recurrence to the family genealogy, which had
been necessitated by the matter of the dormant peerage,
had caused the Eldredges, from father to son, to keep alive
an interest in that ancestor who had disappeared, and who
had been supposed to carry some of the most important
family papers with him. But yet it gave Middleton a
strange thrill of pleasure, that had something fearful in it,
to think that all through these ages he had been waited for,
sought for, anxiously expected, as it were; it seemed as if
the very ghosts of his kindred, a long shadowy line, held
forth their dim arms to welcome him; a line stretching back

to the ghosts of those who had flourished in the old, old times ; the doubletted and beruffled knightly shades of Queen Elizabeth's time ; a long line, stretching from the mediæval ages, and their duskiness, downward, downward, with only one vacant space, that of him who had left the Bloody Footstep. There was an inexpressible pleasure (airy and evanescent, gone in a moment if he dwelt upon it too thoughtfully, but very sweet) to Middleton's imagination, in this idea. When he reflected, however, that his revelations, if they had any effect at all, might serve only to quench the hopes of these long expectants, it of course made him hesitate to declare himself.

One afternoon, when he was in the midst of musings such as this, he saw at a distance through the park, in the direction of the manor-house, a person who seemed to be walking slowly and seeking for something upon the ground. He was a long way off when Middleton first perceived him ; and there were two clumps of trees and underbrush, with interspersed tracts of sunny lawn, between them. The person, whoever he was, kept on, and plunged into the first clump of shrubbery, still keeping his eyes on the ground, as if intensely searching for something. When he emerged from the concealment of the first clump of shrubbery, Middleton saw that he was a tall, thin person, in a dark dress ; and this was the chief observation that the distance enabled him to make, as the figure kept slowly onward, in a somewhat wavering line, and plunged into the second clump of shrubbery. From that, too, he emerged ; and soon appeared to be a thin elderly figure, of a dark man with gray hair, bent, as it seemed to Middleton, with infirmity, for his figure still stooped even in the intervals when he did not appear to be tracking the ground. But Middleton could not but be surprised at the singular appearance the figure had of setting its foot, at every step, just where a previous footstep had been made, as if he wanted to measure his whole pathway in the track of somebody who had recently gone over the ground in advance of him. Middleton was sitting at the foot of an oak; and he began to feel some awkwardness in the consideration of what he would do if Mr. Eldredge — for he could not doubt that it was he — were to be led just to this spot, in pursuit of his singular occupation. And even so it proved.

Middleton could not feel it manly to fly and hide himself, like a guilty thing; and indeed the hospitality of the English country gentleman in many cases gives the neighborhood and the stranger a certain degree of freedom in the use of the broad expanse of ground in which they and their forefathers have loved to sequester their residences. The figure kept on, showing more and more distinctly the tall, meagre, not unvenerable features of a gentleman in the decline of life, apparently in ill-health; with a dark face, that might once have been full of energy, but now seemed enfeebled by time, passion, and perhaps sorrow. But it was strange to see the earnestness with which he looked on the ground, and the accuracy with which he at last set his foot, apparently adjusting it exactly to some footprint before him; and Middleton doubted not that, having studied and re-studied the family records and the judicial examinations which described exactly the track that was seen the day after the memorable disappearance of his ancestor, Mr. Eldredge was now, in some freak, or for some purpose best known to himself, practically following it out. And follow it out he did, until at last he lifted up his eyes, muttering to himself: "At this point the footsteps wholly disappear."

Lifting his eyes, as we have said, while thus regretfully and despairingly muttering these words, he saw Middleton against the oak, within three paces of him.

May 13*th, Thursday.* — Mr. Eldredge (for it was he) first kept his eyes fixed full on Middleton's face, with an expression as if he saw him not; but gradually — slowly, at first — he seemed to become aware of his presence; then, with a sudden flush, he took in the idea that he was encountered by a stranger in his secret mood. A flush of anger or shame, perhaps both, reddened over his face; his eyes gleamed; and he spoke hastily and roughly.

"Who are you?" he said. "How come you here? I allow no intruders in my park. Begone, fellow!"

"Really, sir, I did not mean to intrude upon you," said Middleton blandly. "I am aware that I owe you an apology; but the beauties of your park must plead my excuse; and the constant kindness of [the] English gentleman, which admits a stranger to the privilege of enjoying so much of the beauty in which he himself dwells as the stranger's taste permits him to enjoy."

"An artist, perhaps," said Mr. Eldredge, somewhat less uncourteously. "I am told that they love to come here and sketch those old oaks and their vistas, and the old mansion yonder. But you are an intrusive set, you artists, and think that a pencil and a sheet of paper may be your passport anywhere. You are mistaken, sir. My park is not open to strangers."

"I am sorry, then, to have intruded upon you," said Middleton, still in good humor; for in truth he felt a sort of kindness, a sentiment, ridiculous as it may appear, of kindred towards the old gentleman, and besides was not unwilling in any way to prolong a conversation in which he found a singular interest. "I am sorry, especially as I have not even the excuse you kindly suggest for me. I am not an artist, only an American, who have strayed hither to enjoy this gentle, cultivated, tamed nature which I find in English parks, so contrasting with the wild, rugged nature of my native land. I beg your pardon, and will retire."

"An American," repeated Mr. Eldredge, looking curiously at him. "Ah, you are wild men in that country, I suppose, and cannot conceive that an English gentleman encloses his grounds — or that his ancestors have done so before him — for his own pleasure and convenience, and does not calculate on having it infringed upon by everybody, like your own forests, as you say. It is a curious country, that of yours; and in Italy I have seen curious people from it."

"True, sir," said Middleton, smiling. "We send queer specimens abroad; but Englishmen should consider that we spring from them, and that we present after all only a picture of their own characteristics, a little varied by climate and in situation."

Mr. Eldredge looked at him with a certain kind of interest, and it seemed to Middleton that he was not unwilling to continue the conversation, if a fair way to do so could only be offered to him. A secluded man often grasps at any opportunity of communicating with his kind, when it is casually offered to him, and for the nonce is surprisingly familiar, running out towards his chance-companion with the gush of a dammed-up torrent, suddenly unlocked. As Middleton made a motion to retire, he put out his hand with an air of authority to restrain him.

"Stay," said he. "Now that you are here, the mischief is done, and you cannot repair it by hastening away. You have interrupted me in my mood of thought, and must pay the penalty by suggesting other thoughts. I am a lonely man here, having spent most of my life abroad, and am separated from my neighbors by various circumstances. You seem to be an intelligent man. I should like to ask you a few questions about your country."

He looked at Middleton as he spoke, and seemed to be considering in what rank of life he should place him; his dress being such as suited a humble rank. He seemed not to have come to any very certain decision on this point.

"I remember," said he, "you have no distinctions of rank in your country; a convenient thing enough, in some respects. When there are no gentlemen, all are gentlemen. So let it be. You speak of being Englishmen; and it has often occurred to me that Englishmen have left this country and been much missed and sought after, who might perhaps be sought there successfully."

"It is certainly so, Mr. Eldredge," said Middleton, lifting his eyes to his face as he spoke, and then turning them aside. "Many footsteps, the track of which is lost in England, might be found reappearing on the other side of the Atlantic ; ay, though it be hundreds of years since the track was lost here."

Middleton, though he had refrained from looking full at Mr. Eldredge as he spoke, was conscious that he gave a great start ; and he remained silent for a moment or two, and when he spoke there was the tremor in his voice of a nerve that had been struck and still vibrated.

"That is a singular idea of yours," he at length said ; "not singular in itself, but strangely coincident with something that happened to be occupying my mind. Have you ever heard any such instances as you speak of ? "

"Yes," replied Middleton, "I have had pointed out to me the rightful heir to a Scottish earldom, in the person of an American farmer, in his shirt-sleeves. There are many Americans who believe themselves to hold similar claims. And I have known one family, at least, who had in their possession, and had had for two centuries, a secret that might have been worth wealth and honors if known in England. Indeed, being kindred as we are, it cannot but be the case."

Mr. Eldredge appeared to be much struck by these last words, and gazed wistfully, almost wildly, at Middleton, as if debating with himself whether to say more. He made a step or two aside ; then returned abruptly, and spoke.

"Can you tell me the name of the family in which this secret was kept ? " said he ; "and the nature of the secret ? "

"The nature of the secret," said Middleton, smiling, "was not likely to be extended to any one out of the family. The name borne by the family was Middleton. There is no member of it, so far as I am aware, at this moment remaining in America."

" And has the secret died with them?" asked Mr. El-dredge.

" They communicated it to none," said Middleton.

" It is a pity! It was a villainous wrong," said Mr. El-dredge. " And so, it may be, some ancient line, in the old country, is defrauded of its rights for want of what might have been obtained from this Yankee, whose democracy has demoralized them to the perception of what is due to the antiquity of descent, and of the bounden duty that there is, in all ranks, to keep up the honor of a family that has had potence enough to preserve itself in distinction for a thousand years."

" Yes," said Middleton, quietly, " we have sympathy with what is strong and vivacious to-day; none with what was so yesterday."

The remark seemed not to please Mr. Eldredge; he frowned, and muttered something to himself; but recovering himself, addressed Middleton with more courtesy than at the commencement of their interview; and, with this graciousness, his face and manner grew very agreeable, almost fascinating: he [was] still haughty, however.

" Well, sir," said he, " I am not sorry to have met you. I am a solitary man, as I have said, and a little communication with a stranger is a refreshment, which I enjoy seldom enough to be sensible of it. Pray, are you staying hereabouts?"

Middleton signified to him that he might probably spend some little time in the village.

" Then, during your stay," said Mr. Eldredge, " make free use of the walks in these grounds; and though it is not probable that you will meet me in them again, you need apprehend no second questioning of your right to be here. My house has many points of curiosity that may be of interest to a stranger from a new country. Perhaps you have heard of some of them."

" I have heard some wild legend about a Bloody Footstep," answered Middleton; "indeed, I think I remember hearing something about it in my own country ; and having a fanciful sort of interest in such things, I took advantage of the hospitable custom which opens the doors of curious old houses to strangers, to go to see it. It seemed to me, I confess, only a natural stain in the old stone that forms the doorstep."

"There, sir," said Mr. Eldredge, "let me say that you came to a very foolish conclusion ; and so, good-by, sir."

And without further ceremony, he cast an angry glance at Middleton, who perceived that the old gentleman reck-oned the Bloody Footstep among his ancestral honors, and would probably have parted with his claim to the peerage almost as soon as have given up the legend.

Present aspect of the story : Middleton on his arrival be-comes acquainted with the old Hospitaller, and is familiar-ized at the Hospital. He pays a visit in his company to the manor-house, but merely glimpses at its remarkable things, at this visit, among others at the old cabinet, which does not, at first view, strike him very strongly. But, on musing about his visit afterwards, he finds the recollection of the cabinet strangely identifying itself with his previous im-aginary picture of the palatial mansion ; so that at last he begins to conceive the mistake he has made. At this first [visit], he does not have a personal interview with the pos-sessor of the estate ; but, as the Hospitaller and himself go from room to room, he finds that the owner is preceding them, shyly flitting like a ghost, so as to avoid them. Then there is a chapter about the character of the Eldredge of the day, a Catholic, a morbid, shy man, representing all the peculiarities of an old family, and generally thought to be insane. And then comes the interview between him and Middleton, where the latter excites such an interest that he dwells upon the old man's mind, and the latter probably takes pains to obtain further intercourse with him, and per-haps invites him to dinner, and [to] spend a night in his house. If so, this second meeting must lead to the examination of the cabinet, and the discovery of some family documents in it. Perhaps the cabinet may be in Middleton's sleeping-chamber, and he examines it by himself, before going to bed; and finds out a secret which will perplex him how to deal with it.

May 14th, Friday. — We have spoken several times already of a young girl, who was seen at this period about the little antiquated village of Smithells; a girl in manners and in aspect unlike those of the cottages amid which she dwelt. Middleton had now so often met her, and in solitary places, that an acquaintance had inevitably established itself between them. He had ascertained that she had lodgings at a farm-house near by, and that she was connected in some way with the old Hospitaller, whose acquaintance had proved of such interest to him; but more than this he could not learn either from her or others. But he was greatly attracted and interested by the free spirit and fearlessness of this young woman; nor could he conceive where, in staid and formal England, she had grown up to be such as she was, so without manner, so without art, yet so capable of doing and thinking for herself. She had no reserve, apparently, yet never seemed to sin against decorum; it never appeared to restrain her that anything she might wish to do was contrary to custom; she had nothing of what could be called shyness in her intercourse with him; and yet he was conscious of an unapproachableness in Alice. Often, in the old man's presence, she mingled in the conversation that went on between him and Middleton, and with an acuteness that betokened a sphere of thought much beyond what could be customary with young English maidens; and Middleton was often reminded of the theories of those in our own country, who believe that the amelioration of society depends greatly on the part that women shall hereafter take, according to their individual capacity, in all the various pursuits of life. These deeper thoughts, these higher qualities, sur-

prised him as they showed themselves, whenever occasion
called them forth, under the light, gay, and frivolous exterior which she had at first seemed to present. Middleton
often amused himself with surmises in what rank of life
Alice could have been bred, being so free of all conventional
rule, yet so nice and delicate in her perception of the true
proprieties that she never shocked him.

One morning, when they had met in one of Middleton's
rambles about the neighborhood, they began to talk of
America; and Middleton described to Alice the stir that
was being made in behalf of women's rights; and he said
that whatever cause was generous and disinterested always,
in that country, derived much of its power from the sympathy of women, and that the advocates of every such cause
were in favor of yielding the whole field of human effort to
be shared with women.

"I have been surprised," said he, "in the little I have
seen and heard of English women, to discover what a difference there is between them and my own countrywomen."

"I have heard," said Alice, with a smile, "that your
countrywomen are a far more delicate and fragile race than
Englishwomen; pale, feeble hot-house plants, unfit for the
wear and tear of life, without energy of character, or any
slightest degree of physical strength to base it upon. If,
now, you had these large-framed Englishwomen, you might,
I should imagine, with better hopes, set about changing the
system of society, so as to allow them to struggle in the
strife of politics, or any other strife, hand to hand, or side
by side with men."

"If any countryman of mine has said this of our women,"
exclaimed Middleton, indignantly, "he is a slanderous villain, unworthy to have been borne by an American mother;
if an Englishman has said it — as I know many of them
have and do — let it pass as one of the many prejudices only
half believed, with which they strive to console themselves
for the inevitable sense that the American race is destined to

higher purposes than their own. But pardon me; I forgot that I was speaking to an Englishwoman, for indeed you do not remind me of them. But, I assure you, the world has not seen such women as make up, I had almost said the mass of womanhood in my own country; slight in aspect, slender in frame, as you suggest, but yet capable of bringing forth stalwart men; they themselves being of inexhaustible courage, patience, energy; soft and tender, deep of heart, but high of purpose. Gentle, refined, but bold in every good cause."

"Oh, you have said quite enough," replied Alice, who had seemed ready to laugh outright, during this encomium. "I think I see one of these paragons now, in a Bloomer, I think you call it, swaggering along with a Bowie knife at her girdle, smoking a cigar, no doubt, and tippling sherry-cobblers and mint-juleps. It must be a pleasant life."

"I should think you, at least, might form a more just idea of what women become," said Middleton, considerably piqued, "in a country where the rules of conventionalism are somewhat relaxed; where woman, whatever you may think, is far more profoundly educated than in England, where a few ill-taught accomplishments, a little geography, a catechism of science, make up the sum, under the superintendence of a governess; the mind being kept entirely inert as to any capacity for thought. They are cowards, except within certain rules and forms; they spend a life of old proprieties, and die, and if their souls do not die with them, it is Heaven's mercy."

Alice did not appear in the least moved to anger, though considerably to mirth, by this description of the character of English females. She laughed as she replied, "I see there is little danger of your leaving your heart in England." She added more seriously, "And permit me to say, I trust, Mr. Middleton, that you remain as much American in other respects as in your preference of your own race of women. The American who comes hither and persuades himself that

he is one with Englishmen, it seems to me, makes a great
mistake ; at least, if he is correct in such an idea he is not
worthy of his own country, and the high development that
awaits it. There is much that is seductive in our life, but
I think it is not upon the higher impulses of our nature that
such seductions act. I should think ill of the American
who, for any causes of ambition, — any hope of wealth or
rank, — or even for the sake of any of those old, delightful ideas of the past, the associations of ancestry, the loveliness of an age-long home, — the old poetry and romance
that haunt these ancient villages and estates of England,
— would give up the chance of acting upon the unmoulded
future of America."

"And you, an Englishwoman, speak thus ! " exclaimed
Middleton. "You perhaps speak truly ; and it may be that
your words go to a point where they are especially appli-
cable at this moment. But where have you learned these
ideas ? And how is it that you know how to awake these
sympathies, that have slept perhaps too long ? "

"Think only if what I have said be truth," replied Alice.
" It is no matter who or what I am that speak it."

" Do you speak," asked Middleton, from a sudden impulse, "with any secret knowledge affecting a matter now
in my mind ? "

Alice shook her head, as she turned away ; but Middleton could not determine whether the gesture was meant as
a negative to his question, or merely as declining to answer
it. She left him ; and he found himself strangely disturbed
with thoughts of his own country, of the life that he ought
to be leading there, the struggles in which he ought to be
taking part ; and, with these motives in his impressible
mind, the motives that had hitherto kept him in England
seemed unworthy to influence him.

May 15th, Saturday. — It was not long after Middleton's
meeting with Mr. Eldredge in the park of Smithells, that he
received — what it is precisely the most common thing to

receive — an invitation to dine at the manor - house and spend the night. The note was written with much appearance of cordiality, as well as in a respectful style ; and Middleton could not but perceive that Mr. Eldredge must have been making some inquiries as to his social status, in order to feel him justified in putting him on this footing of equality. He had no hesitation in accepting the invitation, and on the appointed day was received in the old house of his forefathers as a guest. The owner met him, not quite on the frank and friendly footing expressed in his note, but still with a perfect and polished courtesy, which however could not hide from the sensitive Middleton a certain coldness, a something that seemed to him Italian rather than English ; a symbol of a condition of things between them, undecided, suspicious, doubtful very likely. Middleton's own manner corresponded to that of his host, and they made few advances towards more intimate acquaintance. Middleton was however recompensed for his host's unapproachableness by the society of his daughter, a young lady born indeed in Italy, but who had been educated in a Catholic family in England ; so that here was another relation — the first female one — to whom he had been introduced. She was a quiet, shy, undemonstrative young woman, with a fine bloom and other charms which she kept as much in the background as possible, with maiden reserve. (There is a Catholic priest at table.)

Mr. Eldredge talked chiefly, during dinner, of art, with which his long residence in Italy had made him thoroughly acquainted, and for which he seemed to have a genuine taste and enjoyment. It was a subject on which Middleton knew little ; but he felt the interest in it which appears to be not uncharacteristic of Americans, among the earliest of their developments of cultivation ; nor had he failed to use such few opportunities as the English public or private galleries offered him to acquire the rudiments of a taste. He was surprised at the depth of some of Mr. Eldredge's remarks

on the topics thus brought up, and at the sensibility which
appeared to be disclosed by his delicate appreciation of
some of the excellences of those great masters who wrote
their epics, their tender sonnets, or their simple ballads, upon
canvas; and Middleton conceived a respect for him which
he had not hitherto felt, and which possibly Mr. Eldredge
did not quite deserve. Taste seems to be a department of
moral sense; and yet it is so little identical with it, and so
little implies conscience, that some of the worst men in the
world have been the most refined.

After Miss Eldredge had retired, the host appeared to
desire to make the dinner a little more social than it had
hitherto been; he called for a peculiar species of wine from
Southern Italy, which he said was the most delicious production of the grape, and had very seldom, if ever before
been imported pure into England. A delicious perfume
came from the cradled bottle, and bore an ethereal, evanescent testimony to the truth of what he said: and the taste,
though too delicate for wine quaffed in England, was nevertheless delicious, when minutely dwelt upon.

"It gives me pleasure to drink your health, Mr. Middleton," said the host. "We might well meet as friends in
England, for I am hardly more an Englishman than yourself; bred up, as I have been, in Italy, and coming back
hither at my age, unaccustomed to the manners of the country, with few friends, and insulated from society by a faith
which makes most people regard me as an enemy. I seldom welcome people here, Mr. Middleton; but you are welcome."

"I thank you, Mr. Eldredge, and may fairly say that the
circumstances to which you allude make me accept your
hospitality with a warmer feeling than I otherwise might.
Strangers, meeting in a strange land, have a sort of tie in
their foreignness to those around them, though there be no
positive relation between themselves."

"We are friends, then?" said Mr. Eldredge, looking

keenly at Middleton, as if to discover exactly how much was meant by the compact. He continued, " You know, I suppose, Mr. Middleton, the situation in which I find myself on returning to my hereditary estate, which has devolved to me somewhat unexpectedly by the death of a younger man than myself. There is an old flaw here, as perhaps you have been told, which keeps me out of a property long kept in the guardianship of the crown, and of a barony, one of the oldest in England. There is an idea — a tradition — a legend, founded, however, on evidence of some weight, that there is still in existence the possibility of finding the proof which we need, to confirm our cause."

" I am most happy to hear it, Mr. Eldredge," said Middleton.

" But," continued his host, " I am bound to remember and to consider that for several generations there seems to have been the same idea, and the same expectation; whereas nothing has ever come of it. Now, among other suppositions — perhaps wild ones — it has occurred to me that this testimony, the desirable proof, may exist on your side of the Atlantic; for it has long enough been sought here in vain."

" As I said in our meeting in your park, Mr. Eldredge," replied Middleton, " such a suggestion may very possibly be true; yet let me point out that the long lapse of years, and the continual melting and dissolving of family institutions — the consequent scattering of family documents, and the annihilation of traditions from memory, all conspire against its probability."

" And yet, Mr. Middleton," said his host, "when we talked together at our first singular interview, you made use of an expression — of one remarkable phrase — which dwelt upon my memory and now recurs to it."

" And what was that, Mr. Eldredge ? " asked Middleton.

" You spoke," replied his host, "of the Bloody Footstep reappearing on the threshold of the old palace of S——,

Now where, let me ask you, did you ever hear this strange name, which you then spoke, and which I have since spoken ? "

"From my father's lips, when a child, in America," responded Middleton.

"It is very strange," said Mr. Eldredge, in a hasty, dissatisfied tone. "I do not see my way through this."

May 16th, Sunday. — Middleton had been put into a chamber in the oldest part of the house, the furniture of which was of antique splendor, well befitting to have come down for ages, well befitting the hospitality shown to noble and even royal guests. It was the same room in which, at his first visit to the house, Middleton's attention had been drawn to the cabinet, which he had subsequently remembered as the palatial residence in which he had harbored so many dreams. It still stood in the chamber, making the principal object in it, indeed ; and when Middleton was left alone, he contemplated it not without a certain awe, which at the same time he felt to be ridiculous. He advanced towards it, and stood contemplating the mimic façade, wondering at the singular fact of this piece of furniture having been preserved in traditionary history, when so much had been forgotten, — when even the features and architectural characteristics of the mansion in which it was merely a piece of furniture had been forgotten. And, as he gazed at it, he half thought himself an actor in a fairy portal [tale ?] ; and would not have been surprised — at least, he would have taken it with the composure of a dream — if the mimic portal had unclosed, and a form of pigmy majesty had appeared within, beckoning him to enter and find the revelation of what had so long perplexed him. The key of the cabinet was in the lock, and knowing that it was not now the receptacle of anything in the shape of family papers, he threw it open ; and there appeared the mosaic floor, the representation of a stately, pillared hall, with the doors on either side, opening, as would seem, into various apartments. And here should have stood the visionary figures of his ancestry, waiting to welcome the descendant of their race, who had so long delayed his coming. After looking and musing a considerable time, — even till the old clock from the turret of the house told twelve, he turned away with a sigh, and went to bed. The wind moaned through the ancestral trees; the old house creaked as with ghostly footsteps; the curtains of his bed seemed to waver. He was now at home; yes, he had found his home, and was sheltered at last under the ancestral roof after all those long, long wanderings, — after the little log-built hut of the early settlement, after the straight roof of the American house, after all the many roofs of two hundred years, here he was at last under the one which he had left, on that fatal night, when the Bloody Footstep was so mysteriously impressed on the threshold. As he drew nearer and nearer towards sleep, it seemed more and more to him as if he were the very individual — the self-same one throughout the whole — who had done, seen, suffered, all these long toils and vicissitudes, and were now come back to rest, and found his weariness so great that there could be no rest.

Nevertheless, he did sleep; and it may be that his dreams went on, and grew vivid, and perhaps became truer in proportion to their vividness. When he awoke he had a perception, an intuition, that he had been dreaming about the cabinet, which, in his sleeping imagination, had again assumed the magnitude and proportions of a stately mansion, even as he had seen it afar from the other side of the Atlantic. Some dim associations remained lingering behind, the dying shadows of very vivid ones which had just filled his mind; but as he looked at the cabinet, there was some idea that still seemed to come so near his consciousness that, every moment, he felt on the point of grasping it. During the process of dressing, he still kept his eyes turned involuntarily towards the cabinet, and at last he approached it, and looked within the mimic portal, still endeavoring to recollect what it was that he had heard or dreamed about it, — what half obliterated remembrance from childhood, what fragmentary last night's dream it was, that thus haunted him. It must have been some association of one or the other nature that led him to press his finger on one particular square of the mosaic pavement; and as he did so, the thin plate of polished marble slipt aside. It disclosed, indeed, no hollow receptacle, but only another leaf of marble, in the midst of which appeared to be a key-hole : to this Middleton applied the little antique key to which we have several times alluded, and found it fit precisely. The instant it was turned, the whole mimic floor of the hall rose, by the action of a secret spring, and discovered a shallow recess beneath. Middleton looked eagerly in, and saw that it contained documents, with antique seals of wax appended ; he took but one glance at them, and closed the receptacle as it was before.

Why did he do so ? He felt that there would be a meanness and wrong in inspecting these family papers, coming to the knowledge of them, as he had, through the opportunities offered by the hospitality of the owner of the estate ; nor, on the other hand, did he feel such confidence in his host, as to make him willing to trust these papers in his hands, with any certainty that they would be put to an honorable use. The case was one demanding consideration, and he put a strong curb upon his impatient curiosity, conscious that, at all events, his first impulsive feeling was that he ought not to examine these papers without the presence of his host or some other authorized witness. Had he exercised any casuistry about the point, however, he might have argued that these papers, according to all appearance, dated from a period to which his own hereditary claims ascended, and to circumstances in which his own rightful interest was as strong as that of Mr. Eldredge. But he had acted on his first impulse, closed the secret receptacle, and hastening his toilet descended from his room ; and, it being still too early for breakfast, resolved to ramble about the immediate vicinity of the house. As he passed the little chapel, he heard within the voice of the priest performing mass, and felt how strange was this sign of mediæval religion and foreign manners in homely England.

As the story looks now : Eldredge, bred, and perhaps born, in Italy, and a Catholic, with views to the church before he inherited the estate, has not the English moral sense and simple honor ; can scarcely be called an Englishman at all. Dark suspicions of past crime, and of the possibility of future crime, may be thrown around him ; an atmosphere of doubt shall envelop him, though, as regards manners, he may be highly refined. Middleton shall find in the house a priest ; and at his first visit he shall have seen a small chapel, adorned with the richness, as to marbles, pictures, and frescoes, of those that we see in the churches at Rome ; and here the Catholic forms of worship shall be kept up. Eldredge shall have had an Italian mother, and shall have the personal characteristics of an Italian. There shall be something sinister about him, the more apparent when Middleton's visit draws to a conclusion ; and the latter shall feel convinced that they part in enmity, so far as Eldredge is concerned. He shall not speak of his discovery in the cabinet.

May 17*th, Monday.* — Unquestionably, the appointment of Middleton as minister to one of the minor Continental courts must take place in the interval between Eldredge's meeting him in the park, and his inviting him to his house. After Middleton's appointment, the two encounter each other at the Mayor's dinner in St. Mary's Hall, and Eldredge, startled at meeting the vagrant, as he deemed him, under such a character, remembers the hints of some secret knowledge of the family history, which Middleton had thrown out. He endeavors, both in person and by the priest, to make out what Middleton really is, and what he knows, and what he intends ; but Middleton is on his guard, yet cannot help arousing Eldredge's suspicions that he has views upon the estate and title. It is possible, too, that Middleton may have come to the knowledge — may have had some knowledge — of some shameful or criminal fact connected with Mr. Eldredge's life on the Continent; the old Hospitaller, possibly, may have told him this, from some secret malignity hereafter to be accounted for. Supposing Eldredge to attempt his murder, by poison for instance, bringing back into modern life his old hereditary Italian plots ; and into English life a sort of crime which does not belong to it, — which did not, at least, although at this very period there have been fresh and numerous instances of it. There might be a scene in which Middleton and Eldredge come to a fierce and bitter explanation ; for in Eldredge's character there must be the English surly boldness as well as the Italian subtlety ; and here, Middleton shall tell him what he knows of his past character and life, and also what he knows of his own hereditary claims. Eldredge might have committed a murder in Italy ; might have been a patriot, and betrayed his friends to death for a bribe, bearing another name than his own in Italy ; indeed, he might have joined them only as an informer. All this he had tried to sink, when he came to England in the character of a gentleman of ancient name and large estate. But this infamy of his previous character must be foreboded from the first by the manner in which Eldredge is introduced ; and it must make his evil designs on Middleton appear natural and probable. It may be, that Middleton has learned Eldredge's previous character, through some Italian patriot who had taken refuge in America, and there become intimate with him ; and it should be a piece of secret history, not known to the world in general, so that Middleton might seem to Eldredge the sole depositary of the secret then in England. He feels a necessity of getting rid of him ; and thenceforth Middleton's path lies always among pitfalls ; indeed, the first attempt should follow promptly and imme diately on his rupture with Eldredge. The utmost pains must be taken with this incident to give it an air of reality ; or else it must be quite removed out of the sphere of reality by an intensified atmosphere of romance. I think the old Hospitaller must interfere to prevent the success of this attempt, perhaps through the means of Alice.

The result of Eldredge's criminal and treacherous designs is, somehow or other, that he comes to his death ; and Middleton and Alice are left to administer on the remains of the story ; perhaps, the Mayor being his friend, he may be brought into play here. The foreign ecclesiastic shall likewise come forward, and he shall prove to be a man of subtile policy perhaps, yet a man of religion and honor ; with a Jesuit's principles, but a Jesuit's devotion and self-sacrifice. The old Hospitaller must die in his bed, or some other how ; or perhaps not — we shall see. He may just as well be left in the Hospital. Eldredge's attempt on Middleton must be in some way peculiar to Italy, and which he shall have learned there ; and, by the way, at his dinner-table there shall be a Venice glass, one of the kind that were supposed to be shattered when poison was put into them. When Eldredge produces his rare wine, he shall pour it into this, with a jesting allusion to the legend. Perhaps the mode of Eldredge's attempt on Middleton's life. shall be a reproduction of the attempt made two hundred years before ; and Middleton's knowledge of that incident shall be the means of his salvation. That would be a good idea ; in fact, I think it must be done so and no otherwise. It is not to be forgotten that there is a taint of insanity in Eldredge's blood, accounting for much that is wild and absurd. at the same time that it must be subtile, in his conduct ; one of those perplexing mad people, whose lunacy you are continually mistaking for wickedness or *vice versa.* This shall be the priest's explanation and apology for him, after his death. I wish I could get hold of the Newgate Calendar, the older volumes, or any other book of murders — the

Causes Célébrès, for instance. The legendary murder, or
attempt at it, will bring its own imaginative probability with
it, when repeated by Eldredge; and at the same time it will
have a dreamlike effect; so that Middleton shall hardly
know whether he is awake or not. This incident is very
essential towards bringing together the past time and the
present, and the two ends of the story.

May 18*th, Tuesday.* — All down through the ages since
Edward had disappeared from home, leaving that bloody
footstep on the threshold, there had been legends and
strange stories of the murder and the manner of it. These
legends differed very much among themselves. According
to some, his brother had awaited him there, and stabbed
him on the threshold. According to others, he had been
murdered in his chamber, and dragged out. A third story
told, that he was escaping with his lady love, when they
were overtaken on the threshold, and the young man slain.
It was impossible at this distance of time to ascertain which
of these legends was the true one, or whether either of them
had any portion of truth, further than that the young man
had actually disappeared from that night, and that it never
was certainly known to the public that any intelligence had
ever afterwards been received from him. Now, Middleton
may have communicated to Eldredge the truth in regard to
the matter; as, for instance, that he had stabbed him with
a certain dagger that was still kept among the curiosities of
the manor-house. Of course, that will not do. It must be
some very ingenious and artificially natural thing, an artistic
affair in its way, that should strike the fancy of such a man
as Eldredge, and appear to him altogether fit, mutatis mu-
tandis, to be applied to his own requirements and purposes.
I do not at present see in the least how this is to be wrought
out. There shall be everything to make Eldredge look with
the utmost horror and alarm at any chance that he may be
superseded and ousted from his possession of the estate;
for he shall only recently have established his claim to it,

tracing out his pedigree, when the family was supposed to be extinct. And he is come to these comfortable quarters after a life of poverty, uncertainty, difficulty, hanging loose on society; and therefore he shall be willing to risk soul and body both, rather than return to his former state. Perhaps his daughter shall be introduced as a young Italian girl, to whom Middleton shall decide to leave the estate.

On the failure of his design, Eldredge may commit suicide, and be found dead in the wood; at any rate, some suitable end shall be contrived, adapted to his wants. This character must not be so represented as to shut him out completely from the reader's sympathies; he shall have taste, sentiment, even a capacity for affection, nor, I think, ought he to have any hatred or bitter feeling against the man whom he resolves to murder. In the closing scenes, when he thinks the fate of Middleton approaching, there might even be a certain tenderness towards him, a desire to make the last drops of life delightful; if well done, this would produce a certain sort of horror, that I do not remember to have seen effected in literature. Possibly the ancient emigrant might be supposed to have fallen into an ancient mine, down a precipice, into some pitfall; no, not so. Into a river; into a moat. As Middleton's pretensions to birth are not publicly known, there will be no reason why, at his sudden death, suspicion should fix on Eldredge as the murderer; and it shall be his object so to contrive his death as that it shall appear the result of accident. Having failed in effecting Middleton's death by this excellent way, he shall perhaps think that he cannot do better than to make his own exit in precisely the same manner. It might be easy, and as delightful as any death could be; no ugliness in it, no blood; for the Bloody Footstep of old times might be the result of the failure of the old plot, not of its success. Poison seems to be the only elegant method; but poison is vulgar, and in many respects unfit for my purpose. It won't do. Whatever it may be, it must not come upon the reader as a sudden and new thing, but as one that might have been foreseen from afar, though he shall not actually have foreseen it until it is about to happen. It must be prevented through the agency of Alice. Alice may have been an artist in Rome, and there have known Eldredge and his daughter, and thus she may have become their guest in England ; or he may be patronizing her now — at all events she shall be the friend of the daughter, and shall have a just appreciation of the father's character. It shall be partly due to her high counsel that Middleton foregoes his claim to the estate, and prefers the life of an American, with its lofty possibilities for himself and his race, to the position of an Englishman of property and title ; and she, for her part, shall choose the condition and prospects of woman in America, to the emptiness of the life of a woman of rank in England. So they shall depart, lofty and poor, out of the home which might be their own, if they would stoop to make it so. Possibly the daughter of Eldredge may be a girl not yet in her teens, for whom Alice has the affection of an elder sister.

It should be a very carefully and highly wrought scene, occurring just before Eldredge's actual attempt on Middleton's life, in which all the brilliancy of his character — which shall before have gleamed upon the reader — shall come out, with pathos, with wit, with insight, with knowledge of life. Middleton shall be inspired by this, and shall vie with him in exhilaration of spirits ; but the ecclesiastic shall look on with singular attention, and some appearance of alarm ; and the suspicion of Alice shall likewise be aroused. The old Hospitaller may have gained his situation partly by proving himself a man of the neighborhood, by right of descent ; so that he, too, shall have a hereditary claim to be in the Romance.

Eldredge's own position as a foreigner in the midst of English home life, insulated and dreary, shall represent to Middleton, in some degree, what his own would be, were he to accept the estate. But Middleton shall not come to the decision to resign it, without having to repress a deep yearning for that sense of long, long rest in an age-consecrated home, which he had felt so deeply to be the happy lot of Englishmen. But this ought to be rejected, as not belonging to his country, nor to the age, nor any longer possible.

May 19th, Wednesday. — The connection of the old Hospitaller with the story is not at all clear. He is an American by birth, but deriving his English origin from the neighborhood of the Hospital, where he has finally established himself. Some one of his ancestors may have been somehow connected with the ancient portion of the story. He has been a friend of Middleton's father, who reposed entire confidence in him, trusting him with all his fortune, which the Hospitaller risked in his enormous speculations, and lost it all. His fame had been great in the financial world. There were circumstances that made it dangerous for his whereabouts to be known, and so he had come hither and found refuge in this institution, where Middleton finds him, but does not know who he is. In the vacancy of a mind formerly so active, he has taken to the study of local antiquities; and from his former intimacy with Middleton's father, he has a knowledge of the American part of the story, which he connects with the English portion, disclosed by his researches here ; so that he is quite aware that Middleton has claims to the estate, which might be urged successfully against the present possessor. He is kindly disposed towards the son of his friend, whom he had so greatly injured ; but he is now very old, and ——. Middleton has been directed to this old man by a friend in America, as one likely to afford him all possible assistance in his researches ; and so he seeks him out and forms an acquaintance with him, which the old man encourages to a certain extent, taking an evident interest in him, but does not disclose himself ; nor does Middleton suspect him to be an American. The characteristic life of the Hospital is brought out, and the individual character of this old man, vegetating here after an active career, melancholy and miserable ; sometimes torpid with the slow approach of utmost age ; sometimes feeble, peevish, wavering; sometimes shining out with a wisdom resulting from originally bright faculties, ripened by experience. The character must not be allowed to get vague, but, with gleams of romance, must yet be kept homely and natural by little touches of his daily life.

As for Alice, I see no necessity for her being anywise related to or connected with the old Hospitaller. As originally conceived, I think she may be an artist — a sculptress — whom Eldredge had known in Rome. No ; she might be a granddaughter of the old Hospitaller, born and bred in America, but who had resided two or three years in Rome in the study of her art, and have there acquired a knowledge of the Eldredges and have become fond of the little Italian girl his daughter. She has lodgings in the village, and of course is often at the Hospital, and often at the Hall ; she makes busts and little statues, and is free, wild, tender, proud, domestic, strange, natural, artistic ; and has at bottom the characteristics of the American woman, with the principles of the strong-minded sect ; and Middleton shall be continually puzzled at meeting such a phenomenon in England. By and by, the internal influence [evidence ?] of her sentiments (though there shall be nothing to confirm it in her manner) shall lead him to charge her with being an American.

Now, as to the arrangement of the Romance ; — it begins as an integral and essential part, with my introduction, giving a pleasant and familiar summary of my life in the Consulate at Liverpool ; the strange species of Americans, with strange purposes, in England, whom I used to meet there ; and, especially, how my countrymen used to be put out of their senses by the idea of inheritances of English property. Then I shall particularly instance one gentleman who called on me on first coming over ; a description of him must be given, with touches that shall puzzle the reader to decide whether it is not an actual portrait. And then this Romance shall be offered, half seriously, as the account of the fortunes that he met with in his search for his hereditary home. Enough of his ancestral story may be given to explain what is to follow in the Romance; or perhaps this may be left to the scenes of his intercourse with the old Hospitaller.

The Romance proper opens with Middleton's arrival at what he has reason to think is the neighborhood of his ancestral home, and here he makes application to the old Hospitaller. Middleton shall be described as approaching the Hospital, which shall be pretty literally copied after Leicester's, although the surrounding village must be on a much smaller scale of course. Much elaborateness may be given to this portion of the book. Middleton shall have assumed a plain dress, and shall seek to make no acquaintances except that of the old Hospitaller; the acquaintance of Alice naturally following. The old Hospitaller and he go together to the old Hall, where, as they pass through the rooms, they find that the proprietor is flitting like a ghost before them from chamber to chamber; they catch his reflection in a glass, &c., &c. When these have been wrought up sufficiently, shall come the scene in the wood, where Eldredge is seen yielding to the superstition that he has inherited, respecting the old secret of the family, on the discovery of which depends the enforcement of his claim to a title. All this while, Middleton has appeared in the character of a man of no note; and now, through some political change, not necessarily told, he receives a packet addressed to him as an ambassador, and containing a notice of his appointment to that dignity. A paragraph in the " Times " confirms the fact, and makes it known in the neighborhood. Middleton immediately becomes an object of attention; the gentry call upon him; the Mayor of the neighboring county-town invites him to dinner, which shall be described with all its antique formalities. Here he meets Eldredge, who is surprised, remembering the encounter in the wood ; but passes it all off, like a man of the world, makes his acquaintance, and invites him to the Hall. Perhaps he may make a visit of some time here, and become intimate, to a certain degree, with all parties; and here things shall ripen themselves for Eldredge's attempt upon his life.